I0663044

Alfedora and the Drakebureau

Because Might Doesn't Always Make Right, Even if You're a Dragon

Paul G. Krueger

Book One in the Alfedora series

for S. Paul, M. Grace, and A. Miranda

"The truth is, of course, that what one regards as interruptions are precisely one's life."

– C. S. Lewis

ISBN 978-1-7328227-9-5

Cover design by Gabriel Akinrinmade, www.boxofwolves.com

Table of Contents

1. The Burning End

Deep-fried squid. I'd never had any, but the smell was. A. Mazing. Mum and I were at the concessions stand at the Burning End Games, or B.E.G., which is what everyone called it. We were in line behind a huge, black-headed malwrack, an arsnatcher, and a drambat. Drambats were as weird to me back then as they are now. They smell like stink gas, and even though adults weren't any taller than me, they got big webbed feet. Not as big as mine, but twice as ugly. And *no scales!* How can they even call themselves dragons when they got no scales?

It seemed like we were in line for hours. One after another, the others walked away, clutching pink sacks in their teeth while we just stood there and waited. And waited. And waited some more. My nose twitched at the smells. My stomach growled. I licked my chops. The aroma made me wonder. Would I die and go to the Phoberon if I ever got any? I looked up at Mum and thrashed my tail back and forth. A string of saliva noodled its way to the ground.

"Alfedora," she muttered with one of her sideways glances. "Pay attention. You're drooling! Like a hatchling!"

I bobbed my head without taking my eyes off her. "Hatchling?" I asked. "Yeah, right." I just completed my fourth hibernation cycle. I was thirteen now – way older than any hatchling.

"Do you think they'll have any squid left?"

"I hope so."

"What if they don't?"

"We'll have to come back later – after they make more."

"When will that be?"

Mum looked away. The ground shook from the malwrack's heavy feet as he turned away from the stone counter, nearly knocking the arsnatcher into the drambat.

"Hey, watch it!" groused the arsnatcher.

"Beat it," snarled the malwrack.

"Don't make me report you to the authorities," said the arsnatcher.

The malwrack gave the arsnatcher a fierce look. "You'll be dead – or maybe you'll just *wish* you were dead."

The malwrack's head and teeth were twice as big as the arsnatcher's, but the arsnatcher didn't back down. He bobbed his orange-and-black striped head. "You've got your squid – how about you quit bothering everyone and head back to the B.E.G."

"Alfedora, get back!" exclaimed Urraca in a hushed tone. I got behind Mum and peered around her leg.

The malwrack spun around with amazing dexterity for a beast nearly one-and-a-half times the size of Mum. He lowered his big black head and got up in the arsnatcher's grille. "Who's gonna make me?"

We backed up some more while the arsnatcher held his ground. "The guards at the Viper Vault might," he said in a matter-of-fact tone.

The malwrack flicked his tongue in the arsnatcher's face, cracked his jaws, and expanded his chest.

"Don't even think about it, malwrack," sneered the skinny drambat.

I noticed he had a crooked snout and a broken fang. I grinned and looked up at Mum. "As if a drambat could tell a malwrack what to do."

The malwrack glanced at the drambat, then looked at me and chuckled.

The drambat glared at me with a sneer.

The malwrack scrunched his nose and turned to the drambat. "What's the matter, drambat, tooth botherin' ya? Would you like me to break the other one and give you a matching set?"

The drambat reached for his right front leg with a claw on his left front paw – as if he were going to scratch it, then looked away. "What do I care," he muttered, as if talking to himself. "Go ahead and roast him, but I'm afraid that might not sit too well with the Drakebureau, and especially with Gailryder."

The malwrack raised his big black head, then looked away. "You know Gailryder?"

2

"Yeah, we serve with him on the Drakebureau," said the drambat with a blank stare.

"Oh, I see," muttered the malwrack as he flicked his tongue in the arsnatcher's face. "Pardon me, your Drakenesses," he said as he picked up his sack and spun back the other way.

Mum and I ducked as the malwrack's tail swung over our heads.

"You see, Alfedora – might doesn't always make right," she whispered.

"Even if you're a malwrack?" I asked.

"Even if you're a malwrack."

I nodded, craned my neck, and let my jaw drop as a huge pink sack floated by. It dangled from the malwrack's black, bumpy snout – about as high as Mum's head. I closed my eyes and inhaled as much of the aroma as I could. Deep fried squid! But there was something else. A smell I was way too familiar with. The pink sack was made of whale gizzards. I scrunched my nose and turned away. Besides, Mum and I were nearly at the counter. I bobbed my head and looked up at Mum. "Was that a mean malwrack?"

"Some malwracks think they can bully smaller drakes," Mum said in a voice just above a whisper. "Drambats may be the smallest, but that one is better known than most. He's been a member of the Drakebureau for nearly a century."

The arsnatcher was next. Thankfully his sack was smaller – and at eye level. I sniffed the air as the sack floated by. I could tell the batter consisted of coconut and some sort of bird's egg. And even though it was deep-fried in whale blubber, I licked my chops. Twice. My mouth watered. I flicked my tongue. Another string of saliva roped its way to the ground.

The drambat was the last one between us and the spewler taking orders. I studied the two drakes standing under Mum's shadow. The drambat's pasty-gray, leathery skin contrasted with the brown-and-blue striped head and yellow underbelly of the spewler. I couldn't believe drambats – no scales! And the sparse gray hair and sagging skin under their necks – well that was just gross.

"Drakeberry deep-fried leeches!" the drambat exclaimed.

I flicked my tongue. "Yuuucckk. Who orders leeches?" I muttered. The drambat plunked down a paw full of silver coins. He was handed a sack, took a sniff, and scurried off with a pasty grin on his crooked snout.

As he passed the line of drakes, Ilgregious turned and gave the nickelnecks a sideways glance. He took a greedy look inside his bag of deep-fried leeches and slurped one up with his long, skinny tongue.

That young nickelneck had laughed – because malwracks and nickelnecks are bigger than drambats? She hadn't just insulted him – she had insulted an entire species.

"Nickelnecks! Nearly as bad as blue apes," he muttered. He headed toward the stands and said, "One day she'll pay for her insolence!"

Mum and I stepped up to a pair of stone pillars which framed a short stone slab. The spewler stood behind – ready to take our order.

Mum leaned over the pillars. "Two orders of Drakeberry deep-fried squid."

"Sorry, we're down to the last one," said the spewler.

"Give us what you've got, then." Mum plunked down a gold coin, glanced at Alfedora, then grabbed the pink sack. "We'll have to share," she said.

Too bad. I had been hoping for my very own sack of the deep-fried delectables. Mum carried the sack as we headed back. The Games hadn't started – still plenty of time to find a stall in the stands. We claimed one as close to the front as we could. It was a bit tight for the both of us even though I was no bigger than a moose.

I glanced around at the others. This was my first trip outside Brangboor and the first I'd seen of other species. A few years older than a hatchling, I was a nickelneck. Our species was second only to the malwrack in size. Arsnatchers were the next biggest, then snartches, spewlers, and drambats. It was hard to believe drambats were even

4

considered dragons. Spewlers weren't much bigger, but at least they had scales.

I looked at the sack in Mum's paw. "May I have some squid, please?"

"Not yet. Let's save them for the match."

It was best not to press things with Urraca. But it was hard not to when all I could think about was that smell – it made my gizzard go sideways. My eyes narrowed as I studied the sack dangling from Mum's paw. I forced myself to turn away and glanced around at the crowd.

Our stall was three rows back from the front and was one of hundreds which had been carved out of a hillside overlooking a large meadow between us and the mountain. I beamed at how many drakes there were. Were they here because Pa was the first nickelneck to make it to the finals? Or maybe because he was up against a malwrack? And it wasn't just any malwrack. It was the defending champion!

I glanced across the meadow and gazed up at Mt. Flargellion. A pair of craggy peaks towered overhead. At its base was a large opening which was gated and guarded by another black-headed malwrack. Likely it led to the great cavern where the Drakebureau met. I'd been told by Pa it was where they sorted things out and created rules and regulations designed to keep peace between the various species.

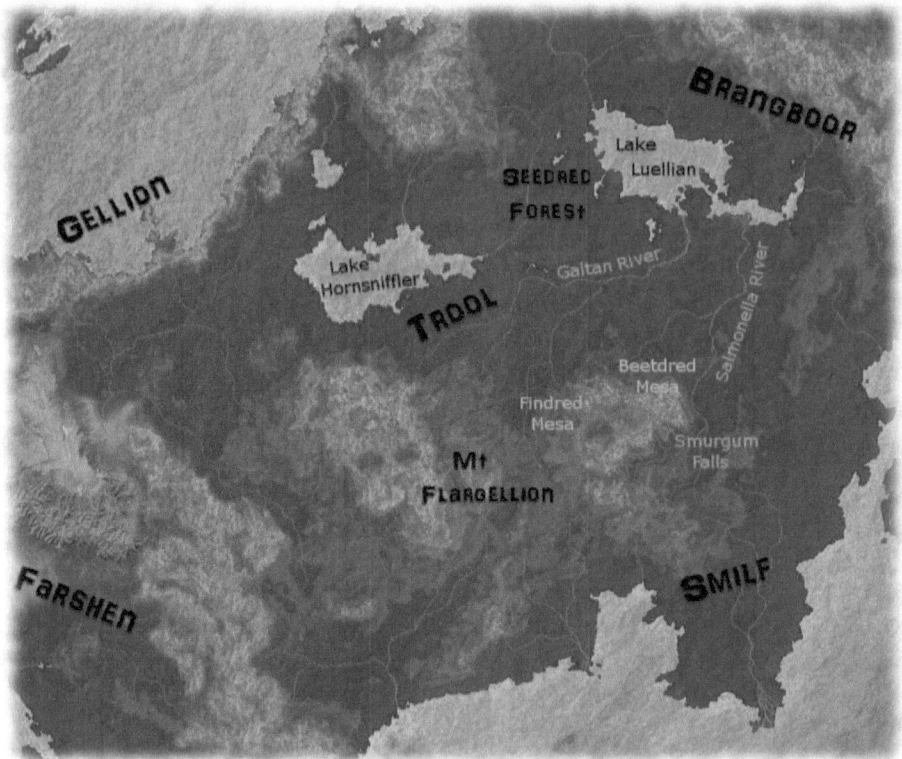

Figure 1 Northern Gaia: Lands Ruled by Flargellion

Everything about the Drakebureau fascinated me – almost as much as the smell of deep-fried squid. Pa once told me that it was the Drakebureau which sponsored and organized the B. E. G. every few years. Matches were always between two, and only two, dragons. Whichever one shot or chopped the tail off its opponent won the match and advanced to the next round. Drakes from any species could enter, but of course the malwracks usually won. Which is why we had good reason to be proud of Pa.

He had defeated an arsnatcher, a snartch, and even another malwrack. And now he was in the finals. He once said that the Games were a reminder of how we stand between chaos and order (whatever that means) and that there are things worth fighting for. He also said something about society and honor and playing by the rules. I wasn't sure what any of that meant. I just knew it was fun to watch a pair of dragons try to chop, burn, or bite each other's tail off.

I flicked my tongue and glanced around at the crowd. There were quite a few malwracks and nickelnecks of course, and more than a few spewlers and drambats. Not as many arsnatchers and snartches, but the ones that were there stood out. The orange-and-black striped heads of arsnatchers contrasted with the yellow, green, and black stripes on the heads of snartches. Yet none were as colorful as the red-and-blue striped heads of spewlers with their yellow bellies.

The other three were not so colorful – small gray-headed drambats, big black-headed malwracks, and us brown-headed nickelnecks. Two odd-looking spewlers settled into a stall above and behind us. One was tall and skinny while the other was short and squatty.

"Welcome my good spewlers, drambats, arsnatchers, nickelnecks, snartches, and malwracks!" bellowed a tall, spindly old spewler.

I raised a paw to my ear. How could such a small dragon be so loud? I wished we weren't so close – the announcer's stand was just a few rows up from ours.

"We hope you're as excited as we are for our final match of the one hundred and sixth Triennial B – E – G!" exclaimed the spewler. "This year's final features our defending champion… Gailryder! And he'll be pitted against the upstart Rotbald! The first nickelneck in twelve decades to make it to the finals! This should be an exciting match – possibly of historic proportions! Can Rotbald pull off an upset? What do you think, Siclefrid? Does the upstart have a chance against our defending champion!?"

The short, squatty spewler bobbed his abnormally smooth head. "Good question, Conbert and glad you asked! This could be one of the great matches of the century if Rotbald can use his agility and speed like he did in the earlier rounds. He eked out a win against a malwrack in the quarterfinals, but he's never faced an opponent like… Gailryder!"

The announcer paused while the malwracks and quite a few others in the stands snorted, howled, and bonked heads at the mention of Gailryder's name. "Sounds like a partisan crowd, and if the nickelneck's not on his game, I'm guessing they'll be happy when it's over."

"Yeah," replied the spindly one. "I'm guessing they'll be cauterizing Rotbald's tail before you can down a Slynkberry ale or three!"

7

I looked around. The snorts, howls and head-bonks continued. A few drakes shot flames in the air. "Mum, what's a Slynkberry ale?"

"It's a drink. You wouldn't like it."

I flicked my tongue and looked up at her. "Why not?"

"Go-oh Rotbald!" yelled Urraca. There was fire in her eyes as she glanced around at other drakes in the stands. "Nickelnecks ru-ule, malwracks da-rool!" she yelled. She turned and looked at me. "It's a drink for grown-ups. Grown-ups who aren't happy with their lives."

I thrashed my tail back and forth. "Why aren't they happy?"

"I don't know. Maybe they had a friend who lost a tail in the B.E.G."

"Is Pa going to win?"

Mum gave me a hard look. "I certainly hope so." She looked away for a second, flicked her tongue and turned back to me. "Of course, he'll win."

"That's good: I don't want him to have to drink that stink-berry stuff."

One of Pa's previous matches was against a snartch who was about half his size. I cringed as I remembered how the snartch dodged one of Pa's fireballs, then spun around and bit off a chunk of Pa's tail. Mum said that snartch was as quick as any contestant that year. But Pa was quick too and countered with a fireball that severed the snartch's tail about halfway to her butt. That ended the match and made Mum *really* happy.

And there was this old malwrack who had a patch over his left eye. He was some sort of official and tended to the bite-wound on Pa's tail. But he spent more time on the snartch, making sure the wound where her tail had been stopped bleeding. The term the announcers used was 'properly cougherized'. Weird that a severed tail could cause a snartch to catch a cough. And even weirder that they would use elk leather and fire to keep it from bleeding.

A while later I asked Pa how fireballs could sever a tail like that. He explained that they contain a significant amount of fat which makes the flaming goo massive enough to cut through most dragon's tails. It wouldn't cut through the thick part of a malwrack's tail — not all at once anyway. And malwrack firebolts were the worst: in addition to fat, they contain bits of bone fragments. They. Can. Tear. You. Up. But everybody knows that a dragon's tail would grow back in a couple years —

so if you're up against a malwrack, you just have to hope his aim is pretty good. No one's died in over three centuries – at least that's what Pa said.

The tall, spindly announcer bobbed his head and snarled, "Right you are, my friend. An ale sounds pretty good right now! And you still have time to get one or two before this match between our defending champion and the upstart nickelneck gets going."

"That does sound good," agreed the short, squatty spewler. "And take it from me, there ain't nothing better than a Slynkberry Ale after downing a few Drakeberry deep-fried leeches! Hottest this side of the Salmonella River! And get this your drakes and Drakenesses. Right now I hear they're on special! Two ales and a bag of leeches for only three staters! Well, here we go, Conbert. The referee's lining up the contestants and he's about to strike that gong! Hold onto your leeches, this should be a real lava looser!"

My eyes were glued to the malwrack's big, black, head. Its green eyes glowed like lightning bugs underneath a black, bumpy forehead. The contestants bonked heads and took their stations in opposite corners of a rectangular pit in the middle of the meadow. "Mum, why do they bonk heads?"

"It's how they show respect before the match begins," she said without looking at me.

"Why don't they just bob their heads?"

Mum didn't answer, but I was used to that. It was important to get my questions in early – before she grew tired and quit answering. I turned away and studied the pit. It was about twenty adult nickelnecks long and about half as wide. About as deep as the top of the malwrack's head.

A loud noise echoed through the stadium as the referee with the eye patch struck the gong with what looked like a leg-bone from an elk or a moose. The match was underway, and Gailryder looked really scary as he came out of his corner and launched a firebolt. But Pa was quick and dodged left as it darted past his right front leg. He let go a fireball which just missed the top of the malwrack's tail.

"Wow, what an amazing exchange!" exclaimed the tall, spindly announcer. "That shot by Rotbald might have singed Gailryder's tail. I think I see smoke!"

"Yes indeed, Conbert," said the short, squatty spewler. "Notice how much faster and larger the malwrack's firebolt is than the nickelneck's

9

fireball. But the nickelneck's agility is impressive. I think Gailryder's got his claws full!"

And just as the announcer finished, Pa fired off a second shot which nearly severed the malwrack's tail just above the bony blade at the end. My eyes grew wide. I jerked my head up at Mum, who had a slight grin, but whose gaze remained fixed on the match. "Did Pa win?"

"Not yet, but he's off to a good start."

"May I have a squid now?"

"Yes. You may have two."

I glanced at Mum, who held the sack out, and then back at the match as the malwrack spun around and climbed out of the pit. "Are they allowed to do that?" I asked.

There was no response from Mum and I noticed the malwrack's tail was smoking and that it dangled awkwardly. It snarled at Pa. I couldn't take my eyes off its huge white fangs which seemed to glare at me out of its cavernous mouth.

I reached for the sack without looking: my eyes still glued to the malwrack. The sack slipped out of my claws. I looked down. Golden morsels of squid in the middle of a pile of dragon dung. I was scared and excited and upset all at once and let out a screech. But it wasn't a little screech. It was loud, and it was long. And then I realized that might not have been the best thing during Pa's match. I glanced up. Urraca's eyes remained fixed on the match. My eyes followed hers. I was surprised to see Rotbald staring back. At me. Our eyes met just as the malwrack launched two quick firebolts. My jaw dropped when the second one severed Pa's tail clean off. The first firebolt caught Pa's tail at the skinny part near the end, but the second one hit higher up where the tail was thick, and the flaming mass of fat and bone cut through Pa's tail as if it were whale blubber.

And suddenly it felt as if every drake in the whole world was staring. At *me*. Urraca gave me a piercing look and flicked her tongue in my face. Instead of responding I stared at Pa.

The old malwrack with the eye patch struck the gong. Again.

"Wow, Conbert, those were some quick shots by Gailryder!" exclaimed the short squatty spewler. "This match is oh-ver!"

The other spewler waited while an assortment of snorts, howls, and head bonks in the crowd eventually eased up. "Yep. That's as quick as it gets!" shouted the other spewler over the din in the stands. "Looks like the nickelneck lost his focus for a second, and that's all our defending champ needed."

I looked at the ground and wiped the slime from Urraca's tongue off my face. "Pa lost, didn't he?" I asked without looking up.

"Yes, Alfedora. Pa lost."

2. Rotbald's Respite

I forced myself to look up at Urraca. "Did Pa get distracted?" I asked as she glared at me.

"He certainly did."

I turned away and something caught my eye – something red and bright behind us. It was the drambat and that arsnatcher from the concessions stand. They were two rows back and the drambat's eyes weren't just red, they were *glowing*. I had no idea that drambats, or any other species for that matter, could make their eyes glow like that.

"Mum, why are the drambat's eyes glowing?"

"Don't be ridiculous, Alfedora. Why are you worrying about a slimy little scale-challenged drambat when your Pa just lost his tail? Not to mention the match."

We watched the referee and a couple others tend to Rotbald's wound. Shiny, crimson wet stuff covered most of the brownish-green scales on what was left of Pa's tail. And there was a *lot* of it.

"Is that blood?" I asked.

Urraca didn't answer. She continued glaring at me – with that look that let me know I was in trouble.

"This one's lucky," said the referee. "Any higher and he might have lost a leg, or worse."

"That's as big a wound as we've seen in quite a while," an assistant said.

"Shaddup and patch me up!" bellowed Pa.

"Is Pa angry?" I asked.

"More disappointed than angry. Let's go hunt up something to eat while they fix up what's left of your Pa's tail."

"We're not going to wait for Pa?"

"Oh, don't worry. The B.E.G. officials will fix him up, and we'll surprise him with a nice meal when he gets home."

I followed Mum into the meadow. It seemed kinda weird that she didn't want to wait for Pa. There were no words between us as we took off toward Brangboor. Mum arched her back and blasted into the sky. I tried to follow but struggled to keep up while fighting the wind from her huge wings. It got easier once Mum made a bit of altitude, but I was already behind. I flapped my wings furiously – trying to catch up.

We flew along a meandering, clear river which had sandy banks and lots of rounded stones on the bottom. But Mum was moving a lot faster than when we had come to Flargellion a few days ago. It wasn't long before my chest muscles were burning.

"Mum, can we glide for a while? My wings are slowing down!" But Mum didn't answer. "Mum!" I shouted. Still no answer. I flapped as hard as I could but had to ease up after a bit. Mum drew farther away. I gazed at the river below – relaxing into a glide and giving my chest muscles a rest.

Urraca disappeared over some rolling hills. I drifted lower. The river came up to meet me. I was alone now and realized I was tired, thirsty, and a little scared. Why would Mum leave me like that? Maybe she's in a hurry to hunt up an elk or two for Pa.

"And besides," I told myself, "I'm a nickelneck! Even if I am just a few years past a hatchling."

A sandy riverbank came up to meet me – plenty wide to land on. I studied a patch of sky where I last saw Mum dip behind some evergreen trees. My left-front leg slammed into something hard. It must have been a boulder – something really hard. I went tumbling across sand and rocks and sand and water, and with a roll and a splash, I ended up in a shallow part of the river.

I thrashed around a bit – the current was strong – before getting my feet under me. My left front leg was sore but I could put some weight on it. The cold water on my feet reminded me how thirsty I was. I drank furiously, then glanced around at the river and wooded hills on either side.

I was confident Mum would be back soon. It would be easier to spot her if I took to the air again. But my chest muscles still ached. The sun was high and felt good on my back as I inhaled deeply and spread my wings. Except my right wing failed to extend all the way – it even looked a bit crooked. A practice flap was intensely painful. I screeched and folded my wings back in place.

Something dark flashed across the water's surface. There, to my left. Was it a shadow? There it was again. A shadow zipped by from left to right. I looked up and squinted, hoping Mum had returned. But instead of Mum, a pair of winged silhouettes approached. They weren't nearly as big as Mum but blocked the sun. They landed in the water and faced me. I took a step back, then froze when a third landed on the riverbank behind me.

"My, my, what do we have here?" sneered a drambat on the riverbank.

I snarled, spun around, and faced a skinny drambat with big, webbed feet – nearly twice the size of my own. It was an adult, but no taller than I was. I bobbed my head, scrunched my nose, exposing my fangs.

"Mum will be back," I snarled.

They were just like the one at the concessions stand – no scales and saggy, leathery, wrinkly-gray skin. Were they members of the Drakebureau too? At least their eyes weren't glowing red like that other one.

"Your mum's long gone, dearie," said the skinny drambat. "And oooh, look at those fangs! They've got a ways to go yet, haven't they?"

I thrashed my tail back and forth, then felt something weird building up inside my chest.

"Let's roast it!" snarled the shortest and fattest of the three. It was slightly shorter than I was, and nearly twice as wide.

"No. We mustn't roast this fine, young nickelneck," groused the skinny, big-footed one. "Not here, anyway. How much do you think the Leader would give us for a fine catch like this?"

My cheeks swelled up. My eyes bugged out like a bullfrog's.

"She's too big to carry back to Lake Hornsniffler," objected the short, fat one.

"I could do it," snarled the tallest of the three. "But we'll need to clip her wings first."

14

"Yeah, let's clip her wings!" snarled the fat drambat as I spun around in time to see the two in the river take a step closer, their eyes narrowing. "Don't even think of shooting a fireball, little missy."

The drambat's words fell on deaf ears. All I could think of was spewing whatever it was inside my chest. I spun around, faced the one on the riverbank, closed my eyes, and let it rip. A foul cloud of green gas enveloped the skinny drambat. He hacked and coughed, grabbed his neck with one of his paws, and fell over.

"She's killed Tarnburp!" yelled one of the drambats behind me.

"No!" yelled the other with a hack and a cough. "It's just stink gas. After her!"

Oh crap – flying was no longer an option. I gulped a breath of air, plowed through the green cloud, and took off running. I was headed downstream and glanced back. They'd be flying while all I could do was run. I scanned the riverbank for cover. There were no trees on my side of the river. I glanced to my left – a much larger shadow zipped across the water's surface.

How big do these guys get?

"Nickelneck!" yelled one of the drambats.

I looked back as the drambats scattered and the shadow approached. The sun nearly blinded me before a huge silhouette eclipsed it. I squinted as big brown paws deftly lifted me off the riverbank and carried me away. They enveloped me completely. I struggled at first, but the feet weren't webbed. Looking up, I recognized the brown and gray scales of Pa's breast plates.

I exhaled, relaxed, and said, "Thanks, Pa.". Who knew drambats could be such creepers? I don't remember much after that. I must have drifted off to sleep.

Rotbald was lying on the floor of the cave when he picked up his head and gave Urraca a hard look. "How could you leave her behind like that?"

He didn't like being mad at *her*. She was tall, well-proportioned, and fierce when she needed to be – everything he could hope for in a mate.

The light from outside gave Urraca a silhouette as she stood between him and the entrance to their lair.

She bobbed her head. "I thought she was right behind me. Do you honestly think I'd leave Alfedora in Trool on purpose? Besides, you were the one who wanted me to bring her to the B.E.G."

Rotbald looked past Urraca, out into the meadow. Shadows grew long and the sky waxed orange. "Those drambats were after her. It looked like they were about to eat her or something."

Urraca scrunched her nose, exposing her long, sharp fangs. "Don't be silly. Drambats aren't cannibals. But don't get me wrong, I find those scale-less, slimy little slug-slurpers absolutely disgusting. Yet even drambats aren't stupid – they are *dragons* after all. Even *they* know there would be consequences for attacking a nickelneck. Especially a young nickelneck who's little more than a hatchling."

Rotbald gasped for air and tried to flick his tongue, but it was sticky and stuck to the roof of his mouth. "I guess you're right, dear," he muttered. He labored to suck in some air. "But why were they chasing her like that? I wish you could have seen her. Was she ever moving! But she looked scared – way too scared."

"Maybe they wanted to get a look at her injury. They were probably just trying to help. You know how she freaks out – like when we try to help her."

Rotbald nodded and laid his head on the cold floor of the cave. "Maybe so – I just hope her wing gets better." The air grew thicker and heavier. He wheezed between each breath.

Alfedora stepped out from behind Urraca. "They were going to clip my wings! And they said Mum was *never* coming back... and. And I'm way bigger than a hatchling!"

Urraca flicked her tongue. "That's just nonsense, Alfedora. Why would they clip your wings?"

"They wanted to carry me away but said they'd have to clip my wings first."

"Carry you where?" asked Rotbald. "Drambats. Where would they carry you off to?"

"I don't know," said Alfedora. "That's just what they said."

Urraca gave Alfedora a cold stare. "Carry you away? Who'd want to carry *you* away?"

Rotbald glanced at Urraca, then turned to Alfedora. "I would," he said with a smile.

Alfedora smiled. "Thanks, Pa."

Rotbald closed his eyes and sucked some air. "Your wing will get better soon, but you must let it heal. You're still young – your bones aren't old and brittle like ours. Besides, Melohim will take care of you."

The lair began spinning inside his head. He opened his mouth slightly at the dryness inside.

"If you say so," Urraca answered. "Oh, and one more thing. How could you be so weak as to let her distract you like that?"

Her voice echoed as if it were far away. Suddenly he felt weak: too weak to answer, too weak to even listen. He licked the stalagmite next to his head, but it was dry. Water. If only there were some water.

"I don't know, hon'," he rasped. Saliva clung to his tongue and made it difficult to talk. "There was something dark... something dark inside my head. And I guess..." He paused to suck a breath. "My ears. Are tuned. To that screech she makes. I couldn't help..."

His voice trailed off. There had been a pair of red eyes. They snatched his attention away from everything – the match, the malwrack, and even Alfedora. He dropped his head and closed his eyes again. But even that wasn't easy – as if his lids were stuck to his eyeballs. A sphere of blue light appeared in his mind's eye. Foreign. Like it didn't belong, pulsing and oscillating unlike anything he'd ever seen. He studied it for a moment, then watched it disappear as he drifted off to sleep.

Pa hadn't moved for two days while Mum grew increasingly agitated. She paced back and forth and flicked her tongue and even thrashed her tail. It had *never* been okay to thrash your tail inside the lair!

Everything was a mess – a *huge* mess. Bedding was strewn about, and even the stack of gold coins had been knocked over. It wasn't like Mum to ignore *those*. Mum hadn't been this upset since I got in trouble with uncle Eam a few years back for stealing a gold coin and tying his tail to a stalagmite while he slept. But this was worse – way worse.

Mum and I stood next to one another and studied Rotbald. His breathing was uneven. What I could see of his tail under the bandages was red and swollen. His nose looked dry as a bone. The air was thick and stale. He wheezed and gasped even worse than before. The stench had grown worse. I waved a paw.

Urraca turned to me and stammered, "Pa's sick. I need you to go outside. Now."

I looked around and bobbed my head. "No. I want to stay with you and Pa!"

Urraca slid between me and Rotbald and began shoving me out toward the meadow. I took two steps back then darted to my right. Urraca snarled and bowled me over first with a paw and then with her broad brown head. After a few tumbles across the dirt floor of the cave, and then grass, I stumbled to my feet and looked around. I was outside in the meadow. My wing ached. It was sorer than it had been. I glared back at the lair. Urraca filled the entrance, big and strong and powerful – everything I was not.

"Pa's sick. I need you to play outside, Alfedora."

"Muummm…"

"Do as you're told!"

Mum stood there huge and unyielding.

"How long?" I asked.

"A few days – until Pa gets better."

I looked out over Lake Luellian and bobbed my head. The lake was calm – unlike my family. I thrashed my tail back and forth and glanced back. Urraca had gone inside and rolled the stone back in place.

I looked up at the sky. It would be dark soon. A chill ran up and down my spine. What if them drambats came back? Would their eyes glow red? Could they see me in the dark?

There were caves at the other end of Luellian – or so I'd been told. But my wing wasn't healed – there'd be no flying there. I'd have to swim. I glanced back, grimaced, and started down the path. Eventually I reached the shore at the northern end.

I slid into the water and glanced to my right. The sun was low and reflected off the water's surface. The sky glowed orange and red and purple against a backdrop of dark trees and hills to the west. I inhaled as my head slipped into the cool, clear water and I began to swim – snaking along using mostly my body and tail.

An image of Pa stood tall in my mind's eye as I knifed through the water. Lying still as a stalagmite – motionless, eyes closed. Wheezing with every breath. A startled catfish darted to my right. I ignored it as I worked to push the image of Pa out of my mind. Surely he'd recover, but his labored breathing was scary. It wasn't easy to push *that* out of my mind. Not nearly as easy as Mum had found it to kick me out of the lair.

Mum took Pa's place in my mind. I quit swimming and floated silently. Eventually I lifted my head, flicked my tongue, and glared at the southern shore. If this is how Urraca wanted it, this is how it would be.

My head slipped beneath the surface and I forged ahead with determined strokes. Time slipped away and it seemed only an instant before I reached the other end of the lake and clambered out. I was shaking the water off when I noticed a light – something glowing to my left.

I blinked, shook my head, then stared at a blue aura surrounding a black bulbous orb. A pale blue light pulsed against the dark forest behind it. The orb was mostly transparent as it hovered over a path. It bobbed slightly left, then right, then up and down. And as I crept closer, it moved up the path, illuminating a stand of trees with a cool-blue light.

It felt like I had no choice but to follow. It paused next to an outcrop in a hillside, then disappeared inside an opening. Blue light spilled from inside a cave. What was it doing in there?

Dare I get closer?

I peered around a corner of the entrance. The cave had a smaller entrance than the one I had grown up in, but inside it was nearly just as big. I studied the hovering orb with the blue aura and as I did it disappeared.

How weird was that?

The cave went dark – really dark. I realized I actually missed the mysterious orb – I was alone again. I glanced around, crept to the back of the cave, and lay down – a little wet, a little cold, and not a little hungry. I put my head down and closed my eyes, thankful that I'd found, or been led to – a little bit of shelter. And especially that there weren't any drambats in it.

My thoughts turned to Pa. Surely he'd get well soon, and then I could go home and we'd be a family again. Mum blamed *me* for him losing his match. Maybe Urraca was right – maybe I am a bad dragon. All I wanted was for Pa to win. What's so bad about wanting a little deep-fried squid?

Tomorrow I'd hunt up some catfish or something. But what would I do if those drambats came back? Or even worse – what if I couldn't hunt up enough stuff to eat? It was Pa who taught me to hunt – I couldn't wait for *him* to get better. I bobbed my head before resting it on a paw and closing my eyes. I yawned as my eyes grew heavy and it wasn't long before I fell asleep. Or dreamt that I was falling. Or both.

3. BReaKFaSt

The soft, early-morning light snuck around the boulder blocking the entrance to my cave. I pushed the boulder aside, ventured out of my lair, and studied a tree blocking my path to the lake. A tree that hadn't been there before.

Still just a sapling, it was fifteen-feet tall and full of new growth. How long had I been hibernating? I looked left, then right, then behind. Was there another path? No – this was the path. My throat and mouth were dry. Something inside my gut wanted out. I stared at the tree, then disgorged a cloud of finely dispersed burning particles of fat.

The tree disintegrated – and as I watched it felt as if any moisture that had ever existed inside my mouth evaporated with it. Waving smoke away with my right front paw, I coughed and stepped over the smoldering stump, careful not to burn a paw. I tried to flick my tongue, but it stuck to dry, cracked lips.

It didn't take long to reach the lake. I scrambled to the water's edge, lowered my head, and drank furiously. Time stood still. There was nothing but me and the water for a minute or two. I raised my head, gasped for air, and attacked the water again. I shook my jowls, looked around, and flicked my tongue – this time as if I were a frog in a mayfly hatch.

Lake Luellian was calm, and the morning sun lit the trees covering almost all the hills west of the lake. Quite a few were yellow and orange – it was that time of year when the leaves were their brightest. Across the lake were mostly evergreens interrupted by a few meadows which were no longer as green as they might have been a few weeks earlier.

I could barely make out the meadow I'd grown up in but studied it across the lake. It had been four or five decades since Mum and I'd spoken. My life had been happy up there. But then Pa died after a contest with a malwrack, and Mum took it hard. Really hard. She blamed me, kicked me out of the lair, and I was left to fend for myself. I was scared at first – worried about drambats of all things! But Pa had taught me to hunt, and now I was nearly full-grown.

My wings were always stiff after a hibernation, but this time it bordered on pain as I stretched out first my left, then my right. There was a bit of a crook in my right wing – seems like it had always been a bit testy after hibernating. I flapped slowly at first and pushed through a bit of stiffness in the joints. Eventually it felt like the ligaments and muscles were loosening up. I folded my wings and stood on the shore as small waves fanned out and faded into semi-circular ripples.

I noticed my reflection in the water below. A broad head and round snout resembled Pa more than Mum. Vertical slits in orange eyes glistened from a brown head and stared back at me. A turn to the right revealed a row of dark brown plates along my spine, which ended in a small ridge on the back of my head. I raised up to get a look at the gray band of plates on my neck and the brown plates covering my chest. Aside from the crook in my right wing, I had grown into a handsome – one might even say attractive young nickelneck. No thanks to Mum.

I slid into the water and snaked along at a leisurely pace using gentle back and forth motions of my body and tail. It was time to hunt up something to eat. There was a cove on the western shore where the water was deep enough to conceal my frame. Close to shore there was a shallow shelf of bedrock which sloped toward the center of the lake and provided access for various sorts of tasty, animated treats.

Pa and I had hunted there nearly seven decades ago. Just a couple years past a hatchling and still smaller than a moose, I hid in the trees while Pa lay in the murky water – his roughly-scaled brown snout resembling a half-submerged log. His orange eyes were narrow and focused, and it seemed as if there was ice in his veins as he lay motionless in the cove while a few elk wandered down to the water's edge. Their eyes grew wide when he burst from the water and effortlessly dispatched a pair of them.

Today I assumed a similar pose. Everything but my snout was hidden as I floated motionless in the murky water of the cove. I sniffed the air and recognized various scents including elk, deer, moose, and even bear. Another scent caught my attention – one I had never encountered before. It was distinctively musky and yet cleaner and crisper than the others. Likely not good eating from the smell of it.

Hunger and the scent of bear scat chased away my curiosity regarding this mysterious and unknown scent. I licked my chops – it had been a while since fresh bear meat. This time of year the bears get ready for winter and would sport a substantial layer of fat.

A deer wandered out of a stand of trees about half a furlong from shore. I craned my neck slightly to get a better look which created a few ripples in the still water. The deer stopped, raised its ears, sniffed the air, and scampered back to the woods. Pa would not have approved. He had taught me to be more disciplined than that.

I went back to floating motionless in the murky, mostly green water. Eventually I was rewarded when a pair of grizzlies wandered out of the forest and headed toward the lake. I held my breath and waited motionless as they drew closer. The larger of the two paused, sniffed the air, and groused a warning at the other. They looked around – a bit nervously – but continued making their way to the water's edge.

They were a few moose lengths away when I knifed through the water with a powerful thrust of my tail, slid up the bedrock shelf, and rose out of the lake. I thrust my head down and exhaled a cloud of noxious fumes. The startled bears were engulfed in green stink gas. They turned to run but managed only a few steps before falling over in their tracks.

They lay motionless while I held my breath and fanned away the fumes with my wings before dispatching each with a swipe of my claws. Pa had taught me well – they died quickly and painlessly, or so I hoped. We were meat-eaters – but we weren't savages. I pressed my brown paw on each bear's chest to expel the fumes before dining at my leisure.

I stretched out on the sandy beach. It took a while, but eventually I felt energy return to my body. I got back on my feet and exercised my wings. An urge to test the air gave way to complaints from a nearly full stomach. An hour or two later I felt ready and took off – feeling slightly less than steady.

The first flight was always like that after a hibernation. But soon my confidence in my wings and tail returned. A few barrel rolls and the wind in my face were welcome reminders of what it meant to be a dragon. I ascended then leveled off into a high glide over the lake. Banking right, I went into a dive and let my mind wander. My thoughts turned to a young male I'd had an interest in ever since I could remember.

I pulled up just above the surface, the claws on my rear paws skimming the water as I leveled off. He was taller than most other drakes our age, was looked up to as a bit of a leader and had the shiniest scales ever! I ascended and wondered if I should pay his lair a visit. No – that'd be crazy! He might think I was a stalker. Then I remembered – Cangoar would be competing in the B.E.G. this year and I hadn't been to a match since Pa lost to the malwrack.

I bobbed my head, banked right, and headed toward Urraca's. Would she be happy to see me? Maybe a quick visit before I headed to Flargellion? It had been over six decades since she kicked me out. Did she kick me out because she didn't want me to catch Rotbald's infection? Probably not – but this time I would ask. Maybe she really did care – at least that's what I liked to think.

But Mum had never wanted to talk about stuff and never let me back in – even though I tried to make amends several times. I showed up after each of my first five hibernation cycles, but eventually gave up after being shooed away for the fifth time in a row. As if I were a pest – like an iguana or a toad or something.

Her lair was at the north end of the lake and the west end of a meadow on a small plateau overlooking Lake Luellian to the south. The boulder covering the entrance to her lair was nearly as tall as I was.

"Hey Urraca!" I yelled. "You in here?"

But there was no response. Nothing but the sound of cicadas in the meadow. I was nearly as big as Urraca now, but the boulder stood there solid and immovable. Could I move it? It was no bigger than the one at my own lair yet seemed bigger in that moment. As if I were still a hatchling.

"Urraca!" I yelled a little louder, wondering if my voice was making its way inside. "Wake up! It's me, Alfedora!" I listened for a response, my ear against a crack between the entrance and the boulder.

"Come back later..." answered a muffled voice.

"Mum is that you? It's me, Alfedora!"

The stone began rolling left. I took a step back. Urraca's familiar snout – long, narrow, and brown, poked its way around the right side of the stone.

"Alfedora," she said as she gave me a hard look. "You're all grown up! What a beautiful young drake you've turned into."

I flicked my tongue and took another step back as she made her way out. "Yeah, it's been what – four or five decades? Good to see you, too." There was a slight quiver in my voice. I hated that, but at least we were talking. "You're three and a half centuries old and still looking good as ever."

A slight grin crossed her face. "Nearly four, but who's counting? You seem to be doing well. What brings you here?"

I looked away for a second. "I was, uh… I was hoping we could patch things up. You know, maybe be Mum and daughter again – maybe go hunt up some elk together. Or whatever."

Urraca glared at me, then looked away. "You're not a hatchling anymore. What's done is done."

"Yeah. It's done, all right. Pa's gone, and all we have is each other."

"Yeah, right. You disgraced Pa and I – and now you want to pretend we're like a pair of frogs in a bog?"

I glared at her. "How did I disgrace anyone?"

"You distracted him. He lost his match because of you."

I bobbed my head. "Oh, now I get it. That's what's had your tail in a knot all these decades – your precious little pride."

"What would *you* know about pride?"

"Enough to know we shouldn't let it rule our lives."

Urraca glared back. "As if you knew toad turds about ruling anything."

I looked out at the lake. "Yeah, right. I don't know toad turds. I don't know toad turds about nothing. What I do know is I was pretty stinking young when you kicked me out. Did it ever occur to you I might starve? Or those drambats might come back?"

Urraca rolled her eyes. "Oh, puh-lease! Drambats? Yeah, right. Look at yourself! Alfedora, you're as strong as a malwrack and as big as any nickelneck your age."

"No thanks to you. It was Pa who taught me to hunt."

She gave me an incredulous stare. "You're exactly right. He did. You don't need me, and I don't need you. We're dragons. Gold, food, and a place to hibernate is all we need. It was good seeing you, Alfedora. I suggest you flip a wing."

I looked at the ground, then flicked my tongue. "Taking it out on me won't bring Pa back."

"Don't try to make this about Rotbald! You need to get a grip on reality, young lady."

"Reality? What do you know about reality?" What did Mum, or anyone for that matter, know about reality? I gazed at the lake. "It wasn't my fault an infection set in after he lost his match!" Pa. Why did *he* have to be the one to die?

I flicked my tongue, then glared at Urraca. "What if *I* entered the B.E.G.!?" I exclaimed. "If I won – maybe you'd be able to get over yourself."

"Ha! You? Win the B.E.G.? That'd be the century!"

My eyes narrowed. "I could do it. And why not? You said it yourself – I'm as strong as a malwrack."

"Suit yourself, Alfedora. It'll be your tail, not mine."

"I will," I said as I flipped a wing and took off toward my lair. A deer in the meadow bounded as fast as it could about a furlong ahead. I felt my heart pounding. You *better* run, little varmint. I let go a fireball, but the deer veered right and found refuge in a stand of trees.

The gases built up again. I had learned to control these urges over the years, but today I didn't care. There. A large, lone evergreen stood in the meadow below. The fireball hit its mark and the tree blew up in flames. I circled above until all that remained was a smoldering and needle-less, nearly branchless, black trunk.

"That tree deserved what it got," I muttered to myself.

4. Dinner, Spoiled

I banked right and headed south across Luellian. A quick check of my lair, a good night's rest, and I'd be off to the Games. But instead of going as a spectator – to watch Cangoar compete, I needed to get there in time to register myself. If they let me in, I'd be trying to burn the tails off other dragons – and not let them burn off mine.

Maybe I'd get a glimpse of some leaders from the Drakebureau – I'd heard they liked to watch from their own special set of stalls. And maybe some deep-fried squid – how good did that sound?!! I licked my chops as I landed at the entrance to my lair. The sun had started its march toward the horizon as I went in and began straightening up. Always such a mess after a hibernation cycle. It was dark by the time I finished, but I made time for a side of salted fiadhain before retiring.

Morning arrived quicker than I did, but I managed to rouse myself and check that all was well with my gold and silver. I rolled my rock over the entrance and camouflaged it as best I could with branches and leaves. It would take the better part of a day to fly to Flargellion, and the sun had already climbed halfway to its highest point in the sky. I took to the air, heading west and a little south.

Tree-covered rolling hills gave way to the southern forests of Seedred which eventually yielded to grassy plains farther west. Shadows from sparse tree stands grew long as I flew along a river in what I figured was the eastern part of Trool. I glanced to my left and noticed a small lake nestled among pine-covered hills.

My stomach had been growling for a while when I spotted a small clearing by the lake which was big enough to land in. It looked like a good place to hunt, but the water wasn't deep enough to cover my frame. I crept back to the woods where I found cover among some trees and bushes next to a game trail.

Hopefully splashing around in the shallow water hadn't just scared off every tasty critter within ten furlongs. I settled in and waited motionless for whatever fare might present itself. The sun dropped behind some hills as I lay next to the trail heading to the water's edge. A few raccoons happened by and as I watched them make their way to the lake, I noticed five shining dots – flickering in a row along the opposite shore.

Drambats, no doubt. They weren't like nickelnecks – or any other species for that matter. They liked to keep a fire in their lair, as if they were warm-blooded or something.

Who does that?

I surprised an elk who was getting ready to bed down for the night, and after dinner my thoughts turned back to the lights when I noticed what sounded like the beat of a drum. It was faint, but heavy and dark and steady. A part of me wanted to ignore it and get some sleep, but my curiosity compelled me to go check it out.

A patch of clouds obscured the light of a full moon, but there was enough to make out a trail leading to the other side. It would be easy to avoid being seen, and it seemed as if the path was inviting me. I headed toward the beating drums. The trail ended in a clearing where there were five lit-up caves in the side of a hill. The lights flickered at the meadow below. I crept closer and crouched behind a tree near the base of the hill, just left of and below the lights. There was a melody with the drumbeat and singing. A song if you could call it that. It came from the second cave to my right and wasn't a happy tune.

The words weren't easy to make out at first – something like, 'Power, puke, and green blood too, we are your servants through the slough.' The refrain continued ad nauseam but was interrupted when one of the drambats let out a screech and another a howl.

I crept closer until I was just outside the cave and craned my neck up and to the right. It was a stretch, but I twisted my body and neck until my head reached the upper-left corner of the mouth of the cave where I could watch while the rest of me remained out of sight.

The cave was five or six times the size of my lair, at least twice as tall, and there were about twenty drambats facing each other in a half-circle.

Beyond them was a glowing red and orange pit. Yellow and orange light danced and licked the ceiling and walls – a lava pit, no doubt. In the middle of the half-circle stood a tall skinny drambat who appeared to be leading them in some sort of ceremony.

They all wore very serious expressions, as if they hadn't taken a dump in over a week. A purple haze appeared in their midst and seemed to be emanating near, or from, the tall skinny one. And there was something familiar about that skinny drambat – maybe it was his crooked snout. One drambat after another closed their eyes and went into a sort of a trance. The haze grew thicker and darker. Soon the skinny drambat began to glow with a red aura and the others fell silent.

"Bring the offerings!" he shouted. "Bring them now."

How does a drambat glow like that?

Two drambats carried in a blue ape, bound with chords. It had blue fur, long arms, short, stubby legs, and was less than half the size of a drambat. I'd never seen a blue ape before but imagined they'd be bigger. The leader stood on his hind legs, bobbed his head, and waved his front paws in the air. He gestured and strutted while the other drambats snorted and howled and a few shot flames in the air. The tall skinny leader looked around, scrunched his nose, and exposed his fangs – one of which was broken. He set his front legs down and glared at the two drambats which stood holding the blue ape.

"Not this one, you fools! Where's the other one?"

They put the ape down at the leader's feet and moments later reappeared with an arsnatcher – just a hatchling, bound with chains and not more than a few weeks old.

Where'd these drambats get an arsnatcher hatchling?

The chant started up again. I looked away.

"Double trouble, slimy and green, give us your power, oh mighty Dark Queen."

The gaggle fell mostly silent after three refrains, except a few who continued humming the tune.

The arsnatcher screeched and howled, and I peered back in just as the skinny leader smacked the arsnatcher across the face. Gases began building up in my gut as the arsnatcher carried on until the leader smacked it twice more. "Silence! You filthy little vermin!" It was just a hatchling, but it was more than half his size. Eventually the hatchling fell silent – its eyes wide as a fat fiadhain's butt.

That's when I realized it was him! The drambat from the Drakebureau – the one whose eyes glowed red at Pa's match! The skinny drambat closed his eyes and lifted his snout. "We do this out of reverence for Her Darkness – and for her alone! We offer up this sacrifice – this young, innocent life to signify our loyalty and dedication to your greatness!" The leader bowed to the purple haze, paused a moment, then glared at the drambats holding the hatchling's chain. "Do it now!"

Should I intervene – or is this ceremony sanctioned by the Drakebureau?

And while I pondered whether to jump in and try to save the hatchling, the drambats threw the arsnatcher – still struggling against the chains – in the pit. It screeched and howled like nothing I'd heard before. Drambats danced and shot flames in the air while the hatchling screeched. One drambat jumped around and howled frantically – attempting to douse its leg after getting too close to a flare-up from the pit.

I bobbed my head at the surreal scene as the drambats celebrated the fiery end of an innocent hatchling. The arsnatcher fell silent, and all was quiet for a few seconds before the "Double trouble" chant started up again. I'd hesitated – largely because that skinny little slime sucker is a member of the Drakebureau. Could I have saved that little one? Was this 'ceremony' sanctioned by the other leaders? Do they even know about it? I scrunched my nose then shook my jowls. My heart pounded so hard I figured they would hear it. A part of me wished they would. Or that I could have traded places with the hatchling. I looked away – ashamed that I'd let my reverence for the Drakebureau get in the way of doing what's right.

The dirge ended and I peered back in. "What about the ape, your Drakeness?" asked the drambat with the singed leg.

"Silence, you fool. His time will come," scowled the skinny leader.

I'd seen enough – or so I thought – when the lead drambat began glowing again and getting taller. At least it seemed he was getting taller. Except his feet weren't touching the ground. He floated in mid-air – without using his wings!

The others fell silent, their eyes glued to the leader while he circled the cavern. They began to hum that slow and plodding tune – same as before. And as the skinny drambat floated above them, he shouted, "Only the Dark Queen is greater than I! Bow down to me, you worms, leeches, and vermin! Bow to me, lest I squash you like a bunch of spineless slugs!"

They bowed low and gave homage to the skinny drambat, and I felt queasier than ever. I slinked away from the cave as quietly as I had come, shocked and more creeped out than I thought possible. I shook my jowls again. Ashamed and wishing I had intervened. If I had known what they were up to – I could have saved that hatchling. I glanced back at the orange light emanating from the lair.

"Bring the ape!" the skinny drambat shouted.

I debated going back – but what did I have to do with blue apes? And before I had time to flick my tongue, there was a gizzard-wrenching howl but no screech – obviously that was the ape. I turned away and headed down the path. My gut was tied in a knot. I scrunched my nose and bobbed my head. One more time. I was out of earshot and glanced back at the lights flickering in the mouth of the cave.

The leader was a member of the Drakebureau – do the other leaders know he's doing this stuff? Surely they must. I looked down, pawed the ground, and shook my head, wondering where that purple haze came from and how that skinny drambat with the broken fang floated around with no wings. Or how his eyes glowed red.

I stumbled and retched, feeling feebler than when I woke from hibernation the day before. "Bury me under a pile of dragon dung and may I never find another gold stater!" I muttered to myself. Under cover of darkness I bobbed my head, took to the air, and headed toward Flargellion.

The next morning I woke under a grand old elm, hungry enough to eat a bull elk or two. But then the memory of that hatchling's screech and even the howl of the blue ape invaded my thoughts. If I had intervened, that skinny leader would have had me arrested. No doubts there. My appetite vanished – something I'd never felt before. I glanced around. I was in a meadow next to Mt. Flargellion – not far from a gate which looked to be an entrance to the cavern known as the Great Hall.

It was an iron gate – ornately decorated with elk, moose, and bison skulls – horns still attached. Two-and-a-half times as wide and twice as tall as I was, the gate had silver spikes on top. The malwrack tending the gate was nearly one and a half times my height and by the looks of it – three times my weight.

He seemed not to notice me as he munched on a steamy mound of what appeared to be whale gizzards. I studied them for a second or two. Normally I'd be licking my chops – even for whale gizzards – but this time I turned away.

I gathered myself, turned to the malwrack, and said, "Excuse me, sir. Do you know when and where the Burning End Games are being held? I have a friend who's competing this year."

I was too embarrassed to tell him I was going to enter myself.

"Well isn't that lovely," groused the guard. "You have a friend who's competing in the B.E.G." He went back to his gizzards.

I flicked my tongue and stood there. After waiting to see if he was going to say anything else, I said, "Excuse me, your Drakeness, but could you tell me when they start?"

"Oh, yeah, sure. When what starts?"

I gave him a hard look. "The B.E.G., your Drakeness." I wanted to say, 'your Dumbness' but didn't.

The malwrack horked down some gizzards and looked down at me. "Oh, the B.E.G. Right. I figured you were here to attend your first session of the Drakebureau."

I flicked my tongue twice. "Are we able to do that?"

"You bet. In fact, it's required for young drakes like you."

"What do you mean, 'it's required'?"

"Leapin' lizard gizzards, missy! Didn't your mum ever tell ya about the Drakebureau?"

I scrunched my nose. "Of course she did. We love the Drakebureau."

"Well of course you do, but did she tell you about the rule?"

"What rule?"

"It's a new rule – just came out last year. Every drake who's never been is required to attend at least one session of the Drakebureau during their next tongue-flicking season."

"Tongue-flicking?" I asked. "Oh yeah, right. After waking from hibernation." I flicked my tongue. "And what happens if they don't?"

"What happens if they don't flick their tongue?"

"No. What happens if they don't attend the Drakebureau?"

The malwrack's eyes brightened. "Oh, not much really. You either forfeit half your gold, or you have to attend five sessions during each of your next four tongue-flicking seasons, or sometimes both."

I scrunched my nose. "You call that not much?"

"Yeah, it's not like they'd throw you in a lava pit or the Viper Vault – nothing like that."

I gave him a blank stare. Did everyone know about this lava pit except me? "The Viper Vault – what's that?"

The malwrack bobbed his big black head. "Stewed eyeballs of eel, little missy! What do they teach hatchlings these days? The Viper Vault is where they lock up drakes who steal gold, maim their neighbors, or eat another drake's eggs. Among other things."

I thrashed my tail and scrunched my nose.

That's what they oughta do with those drambats – and their leader.

"Oh, I see," I said. "Thank you, sir, you've been most helpful, but could I bother you with two more questions?"

The malwrack's jaw dropped. Whale gizzards dangled from his huge jaws as he glared at me. "One more. That's it."

I turned away at the sight of half-chewed gizzards feeling like I was going to hurl before turning back to face him. "When do the games begin and when is the next session of the Drakebureau?"

He chewed twice and swallowed most, but not all, of what was in his mouth. "That's two questions," he snarled. "The B.E.G. starts this morning – and there's a Drakebureau session that starts this afternoon."

I turned to leave before pausing and flicking my tongue. "Thank you your Drakeness and pardon me, but one more thing. Is this the entrance to the Drakebureau?"

The guard's gaze remained fixed on his pile of gizzards as he groused, "This is the Morinair Gate. The entrance for noble drakes. Common drakes like you will use the entrance on the other side of Flargellion. That's the Daor Gate, in case ya didn't know. Remember, Morinair Gate for noble drakes, and the Daor Gate for the rest of ya."

"Why thank you, your Drakeness. You've been so kind."

Kinda gross.

I turned and walked away. "This is the Morinair Gate. The entrance for *noble* drakes. Nyeh, nyeh, nyeh. Common drakes like *you* will use the entrance on the other side – nyeh... nyeh-nyeh-nyeh... nyeh..."

I headed toward the meadow and glanced back at the guard. He glared at me, bobbed his head, then turned back to his gizzards. I flipped a wing and flew around to the east side of the mountain, where a group of dragons – mostly malwracks and nickelnecks – were gathered in a meadow just outside the gate on the other side. It was nearly twice as wide as the Morinair gate but with no decorations and no silver spikes.

I landed and immediately noticed a wonderful aroma. I inhaled deeply – a bouquet of olfactory wonders coming from the concessions stand! Deep-fried squid – as intoxicating as ever! Just like the first time when I was little more than a hatchling. But then I recalled the events from last night and they ruined my appetite – even for deep-fried squid.

Drambats. I could deal with those scale-challenged, slimy little slug-slurpers if they weren't sacrificing hatchlings. I scrunched my nose. Were they all like that, or were they bent by that tall skinny one? They seemed more like big, featherless buzzards than dragons. And how could the leader be a member of *the Drakebureau?*

5. A Tale of Two Tails

The old malwrack with the patch over his left eye was the same one that had officiated Pa's match. It had been about six decades, but he hadn't changed much. He was with some malwracks and a couple of nickelnecks near the grandstands at the east end of the meadow – not far from the Daor Gate. They were huddled around a tablet when I interrupted. "Excuse me, does anyone know where I go to sign up for the B.E.G.?"

"Our brackets are already set," answered the old malwrack. "I'd encourage you to sign up for the next one. That would give you a couple years to train. This is the B.E.G. – not a game of pitch-a-grote."

"Hold on, Rimgoad," an old nickelneck interrupted. This one had both eyes, looked nearly as old the malwrack, but had a scar on his snout. "What about the arsnatcher... what's his name?" the old nickelneck asked. "He has a bye in the first round. We could match her up with him."

"Oh, you mean Maol," said one of the others – a malwrack. "Yeah, that might work. He's a rookie and it'd be good to get a nickelneck in the bracket. We haven't had a female nickelneck in what, a few decades?"

The old malwrack glanced around with one eye. He had to tilt and swivel his head to get a look at each of us. He fixed his eye on me. "The B.E.G. is serious business, missy. You could find yourself up against a malwrack! Especially in one of the later rounds."

The lone eye in his big black and gray head was a bit cringy. It was all I could do to not stare. "I can handle myself. My Pa taught me to hunt."

"This ain't about hunting, little missy. It won't be an elk or a fat fiadhain you'll be up against."

"Yes sir, I understand." But what if the old malwrack's right? Maybe I should wait and train for a year or two. I flicked my tongue, then said, "I'm good. Sign me up, please." I glanced away before blurting out, "No, I'm more than good. I'm going to win this thing."

"That's the spirit," said the old nickelneck.

"Right," the old malwrack said with a grin. "Well okay. We like to start things off with the rookies – while the crowd's still flying in. What's your name, missy?"

"Alfedora, sir."

"Alfadoor. Got it."

"Uh, actually it's 'Alfedor-a', sir, with an 'A' at the end."

"Oh, right. Got it."

The Eye looked back at me. I did my best to not stare while paying attention to the old malwrack's words.

"Let's run over the rules right quick. The match starts when I strike the gong. No shots above the waist. First violation and I throw a red rat. Second violation and you're disqualified. And for nickelnecks there's no noxious fumes – ever. First violation and you're out. Disqualified. Once either of you loses more than an eighth of your tail, I'll strike the gong and the match is over. Oh-ver – got it?"

"Yes sir, I got it."

"Any shots after the gong will result in a disqualification from the tournament. After the match is over, one or more officials will tend to any injuries. Tails should grow back in a couple years. Oh – almost forgot. As long as you're still in the tournament, you get two free snacks per round at the concessions stand. Any questions?"

"Uh, just one," I muttered.

"What's that?"

"How many rounds to win?"

"How many rounds to *win?*" One of the malwracks laughed. "She's kidding, right?"

I gave him a square-jawed glare. "How many rounds. To win."

The old nickelneck grinned. "If looks could sever a tail, I think we'd have to crown her butt."

I stared at the tall grass on the ground between them.

"Five rounds, thirty-two dragons," said the Eye. "Be ready to go in an hour."

I bobbed my head and headed off to the concessions stand. "I'll be there!" I exclaimed. There were two snartches, an arsnatcher, and a drambat in line ahead of me when I got to the concessions stand. I studied the back of the drambat's gray head. It would be easy. All too easy...

No. Forget about drambats!

"I need to eat," I muttered to no one but myself. I studied the arsnatcher and wondered if she might be my opponent. But they said my opponent was a male. I studied her anyway.

Orange and black stripes on her head and belly made her look thinner and ganglier than she really was. Her back was covered with green scales and looked wider – more like other species. Either way they were the quickest drakes in Drakedom. Her legs were almost as long as mine, and her spiked tail was thinner and nearly half as long as the rest of her body. Her head was about as high as the gray scales in the middle of my neck.

The snartches and then the arsnatcher shuffled away with their sacks. I remembered the last time – when I was here with Mum and was determined to be polite. No drooling or sniffing other drake's sacks. I closed my eyes and sniffed the air while the drambat placed an order.

"Drakeberry deep-fried leeches. Two orders, please." At least it was polite. Leeches, though? The drambat plunked down a couple of staters, smiled, then ran off with its booty. Apparently, it was in a hurry... and for leeches!

I stepped up to the stone bench. "Two orders of Drakeberry's finest."

"Leeches or squid?" the spewler asked from behind the stone slab.

I licked my chops. "Squid. Of course."

"That'll be three staters."

"Oh, I'm sorry. I'm a contestant in the B.E.G. I just signed up."

"Well good luck to you then and enjoy Drakeberry's finest – on the house."

"Thanks. Thanks a lot." The smell was amazing – just like when I was a hatchling. A mouth-watering and succulent mixture of squid, fat, and coconut – all fried golden-brown with a crisp finish and a gooey center. It wasn't long before I was down to the last one. I gnawed on it slowly – savoring each chew as I reached the judges' slab and checked in.

I swallowed as the judge directed me to the corner of the pit in the meadow which was closest to Flargellion. There were stone steps at opposite corners, and I kept one eye on the arsnatcher as I scurried down. The Eye approached an ancient bronze gong on the west side which overlooked the pit while I backed into my corner.

I inhaled deeply – my eyes fixed on the opposite corner. The gong sounded, and the arsnatcher launched out of his stall and to my right. I moved out to meet him, but he was halfway to the center of the pit before I'd taken three steps. Gases built up inside my chest. I'd have to control the urge to let loose until I had a clear shot at his tail.

Remember, no noxious fumes.

The arsnatcher ran at me but didn't appear to be angling for a shot.

He circled around my right rear leg. I landed a kick which sent him sprawling nearly all the way back to the corner he'd started in. I closed in as the arsnatcher stumbled to his feet. Everything inside me wanted to launch a fireball. But his head and body guarded his tail. I'd have to wait for a clear shot.

I veered right, then cranked my head left and let it rip. The fireball missed his tail and hit the wall of the pit. The beast crouched low. I ignored a few jeers from the stands and watched as the arsnatcher spun to my right. Before I could line up another shot, it locked its jaws on my tail, about halfway up.

A biter? Really?

Pa and I used to play a game when I was just a hatchling. I would latch my jaws on his tail and he would flip me in the air before catching me in one of his huge paws. It was great fun. But for some reason Mum would put an end to it by thinking up something for him to do. The maddening part was that *he always obeyed her.* It was like she didn't want us to have any fun.

I channeled my anger and ignored the pain as I flipped the arsnatcher in the air. It must have surprised him – because he let go of my tail. And as he sailed across the pit, I watched as his body rotated. Time seemed to slow down as I studied the scales on his tail and launched a fireball where I figured his tail would be a split-second later. He was upside down when it hit – a perfect strike about halfway to his butt. A flaming mass of undigested fat severed his tail clean off.

The old malwrack glanced at the tail after it landed near my feet. The Eye glared at me, then struck the gong indicating the match was over. Up in the stands a few drakes bonked heads, others screeched or howled, and a few shot flames in the air.

"Looks like we have a winner from the rookie class! What a shot by Aldara!" exclaimed the spindly old spewler. The voice was familiar. It was the same announcer from Pa's match. Seemed like the more things change, the more they don't. I trundled up the cobblestone steps and headed over to the old malwrack next to the gong. He looked me in the eye and instructed the arsnatcher and I to bonk heads. The arsnatcher nearly fell over. I glanced at him as the old malwrack raised my right paw. There were more cheers from the stands, but he didn't let go of my paw until I looked him in the eye.

"I don't want to see another stunt like that in my games," said the Eye as he gave me a cold stare. "Understand, little missy?"

"Yes, your Drakeness." I flicked my tongue and looked out at the stands. I wasn't sure what had his scales all roiled. All I knew was it felt good to win. Okay – technically the shot *was* above the arsnatcher's head when he was upside-down, but from his perspective it was *below* his head and there was no denying the result. A clean victory.

"You could just as easily have taken his head off," snarled the old malwrack.

But I hadn't. He had struck the gong, and the crowd seemed to love it.

"Yes, your Drakeness," I repeated. "Sorry, your Drakeness."

It was a struggle to keep a grin from appearing. I had won fair and square and was on my way to winning this thing, even if the Eye wasn't happy about it. An official tended my bite wound while two others cauterized the stump where the arsnatcher's tail had been. His wound wasn't nearly as big as Pa's had been and I was happy for that. I went back to the concessions stand, got more squid, and headed back. There was an empty stall among some snartches and arsnatchers. A pair of arsnatchers gave me a cold stare. I flicked my tongue and winked at them as I settled in with my squid.

I slurped up half a dozen as one of the announcers bellowed, "Welcome my good drambats, spewlers, snartches, arsnatchers, nickelnecks, and malwracks! This is day One of the one-hundred and twenty-sixth Triennial Burning End Games! In a few minutes we'll be starting our next match between our reigning champion Dunsneed, and Cangoar, a promising young nickelneck!"

I glanced around at the mention of Cangoar's name. One hundred and twenty-sixth tri-what?

"This should be a great match," exclaimed the announcer in a high-pitched tone. "And once it starts, you'll want to stay glued to your seats... So *now's* the time to visit Drakeberry's Cantina and get some hotter-than-a-volcano Drakeberry deep-fried leeches!"

I scrunched my nose. Deep-fried leeches? No way. Not when there's deep-fried squid around!

"They're guaranteed to put some smoke in your ears and raise a hackle on yer spine. And while yer at it, don't forget to chase 'em down with a Slynkberry ale. Ain't no better way to enjoy your day at the B.E.G.!"

Well, maybe. I licked my chops and wondered what a spicy leech tastes like.

An announcer with a deeper voice chimed in. "Thanks for those important reminders, Conbert. That last match will be a tough act to follow. This one features our defending champion and another nickelneck! How do you see this one shaping up?"

"Well, Siclefrid, I'm glad you asked. Cangoar is one quick nickelneck! In the regional tournament he evaded fireballs, teeth, and tail whacks from his opponents. But this ain't no regional tournament! I'm guessing Dunsneed's strength and firepower will have Rimgoad tending Cangoar's tail before you can down half a Slynkberry ale!"

"Ha. Good one, Conbert! Sounds like the rookie's been good so far, but he'll need to dance like a chameleon and shoot like a frog's tongue to fend off our reigning champ!"

"You got that right! Cangoar's been better than any nickelneck we've seen in quite a while, but he hasn't faced a malwrack yet. And I'm guessing he may be feeling a bit uneasy – going up against our reigning champ. Either way this should be an exciting match between two great tail-burners! Looks like they're about to bonk heads – so hold onto your Slynkberry Ale, everybody! We'll be underway in the flick of a frog's tongue!"

I closed my eyes. I wanted Cangoar to win, but what if he wins? Would we face each other in the next round? What if I shot off his tail? "He'd be mad at me for a century or two!" I muttered.

The contestants entered the rectangular pit and moved to the center. Dunsneed and Cangoar bonked heads. They bowed to the audience and backed into their corners.

The one-eyed malwrack – the Eye – spoke with a raspy voice. "Remember: no flying. I don't want to see a single fireball or firebolt aimed above your opponent's tail. There will be no shots, bites, or tail-whacks once a tail has been severed and the gong is struck. The match is over – any violations will result in disqualifications. Oh, and no noxious fumes from the nickelneck. This will be a good clean match or else. Wait for my signal and may the best drake's tail thrash... to the bitter end!"

The referee struck the gong and the two dragons came out of their corners and approached one another slowly. Step-by-step they jockeyed for position and felt each other out. Dunsneed launched a firebolt. Cangoar dodged left as the firebolt whistled by. Dunsneed followed with a strike from the bony plate at the end of his tail.

I covered my left eye with a paw and watched with my right. This was way harder to watch than it had been to compete. Cangoar twisted right to avoid the tail shot from Dunsneed. It missed his tail but sliced off a toe on his left-rear foot. I winced.

"Dunsneed's tail shot nearly ended the match!" exclaimed the announcer with the deep voice. "The nickelneck's agility helped him keep his tail, but he's lost a bit of his foot I'm afraid. Conbert, we'll have to keep on eye on how that affects his agility!"

"You got that right," agreed the high-pitched announcer. "And I don't care what species you are. That had to hurt like a bee up yer snout!"

I'd never paid much attention to the flat and bony blade-like protrusion at the end of a malwrack's tail. It was an effective weapon which nickelnecks don't have. Didn't quite seem fair to me. "C'mon, Cangoar!" I yelled. "You can do this!" Oh, wait. "C'mon, Dunsneed!"

Why am I even watching this?

Cangoar fired a shot which sailed high and a little right.

"Cangoar looks a bit unnerved," said the deep-voiced announcer. "That counter-shot was way too high. Do you think it may have seared the horn on Dunsneed's head?"

"I couldn't say, but I'll bet that's going to cost him," said the tall spindly one.

"No red rat from Rimgoad – not yet anyway," said the short, squatty announcer. "A shot that high is clearly a violation, and I'll bet Dunsneed is really ticked off about it!" he exclaimed, now standing on his hind legs.

The malwrack climbed out of the pit, glared at Cangoar, and bobbed his big black head.

I nearly screeched, then looked away and closed my eyes. It looked a lot like Rotbald's malwrack – and now it was acting like it.

The low-pitched announcer chuckled. "Easy does it, partner. Down on all fours before you spill yer Slynkberry ale. Time will tell if Cangoar gets a red rat for that one."

Dunsneed let out a screech, but only the very start of the screech was audible before everything went silent. It must have been a powerful one, because as I looked around, the other species clutched their heads in pain. How weird is that? We never paid attention to malwrack screeches. I remembered Pa explaining that nickelnecks are the only species which have flaps in our inner ears. They shut tight to protect us from very loud noises and when diving in deep water.

I glanced around as a judge – a drambat – in a stall on a ledge above me, clutched his head. His eyes bulged like a bullfrog as he tumbled out of his stall and landed on a spewler.

I grinned and turned back to the match in time to see Cangoar let go a fireball. It was a partial hit just above the blade on the malwrack's tail. Dunsneed twisted around and brushed the flaming goo off with a paw before it burned all the way through.

The high-pitched announcer's voice slowly grew louder as my inner ear flaps relaxed. "Whoa, what a screech that was!"

"Right you are," the deep-voiced announcer exclaimed.

"It appears as if Dunsneed forgot it would have no effect on his opponent," the high-pitched announcer said. "He may be young, but you'd think our defending champion would have been coached up on nickelnecks."

"That's the first thing you learn about these drakes if you're a malwrack," added the deep-voiced spewler. "And what a shot by Cangoar! Looks like the malwrack's tail is damaged above the blade. I'm guessing Dunsneed won't be scoring any more shots with his tail. A slightly more accurate shot by Cangoar and we'd have an upset of epic proportions!"

The malwrack glared at Cangoar while backing down to the end of the meadow and behind a ridge of rocks.

"Dunsneed has retreated to the boar-backs!" exclaimed the high-pitched announcer. "Hold onto your deep-fried leeches! We'll find out in the flick of a frog's tongue whether he's injured or laying a trap for his opponent."

"Well slap me silly with a big old squid!" exclaimed the deep-voiced spewler. "The nickelneck appears to have the upper hand!"

"No doubts there," agreed the high-pitched announcer.

The short, squatty announcer lowered his tone. "They're both out of the pit – and Cangoar is circling behind some boulders among the boar-backs."

"But what's this?" asked the high-pitched announcer. "Dunsneed's caught Cangoar in a blast of wind from his wings."

A hurricane-force blast sent Cangoar tumbling down a path, along with a couple of tree limbs and what remained of a half-dead oak tree.

"Gale-force winds from Dunsneed!" exclaimed the deep-voiced announcer. "And now he's advancing! Cangoar's in trouble!"

No way. Rotbald is not going to die – not on my watch.

I jumped out of my stall and took off toward Cangoar, leaping and using my wings to glide past the referee. I crossed the meadow. A couple of glides, a deft landing, and there I was – standing in the path of the on-rushing malwrack. I dug in my claws, bobbed my head, and snarled as the malwrack slammed into me.

Trees and sky and ground spun round and round. Everything seemed to continue spinning even after I rolled to a stop. I was dazed and disoriented and shook my head. The trees were fuzzy – like little green clouds. Suddenly a bright light cut across the path. My vision cleared enough to make out the malwrack's firebolt and the nickelneck's fireball pass each other in midair.

I followed the firebolt as it lopped off the last quarter of Cangoar's tail. It wasn't up near his butt like Rotbald's had been. I exhaled and shook my jowls.

"Whoa, hit me up the side of the head and call me a slug!" exclaimed the short squatty spewler. "Can you believe what just happened? Two nickelnecks against one malwrack, and two tails on the ground!"

I glanced at the malwrack. A good chunk of his tail was on the ground too. Cangoar's shot must have been right on the money.

"Siclefrid, I believe this is a first for the B.E.G.!" exclaimed the high-pitched spewler. "What a clever maneuver by Dunsneed! And what a shot by Cangoar! But who's the other nickelneck?"

"It looks like Aldara!" exclaimed the low-pitched announcer. "Blatant! That was blatant interference! There's not a judge in Drakedom who wouldn't throw a red rat on that one!"

I glanced at the announcers' stall and saw them both standing on hind legs.

"No doubt, Siclefrid!" exclaimed the tall spindly spewler. "And there you have it, my fellow drakes. Our match between the rookie Cangoar and the defending champ Dunsneed has ended in a two-tail draw! Who'd a thunk it? What we have here is a tale of two tails!"

"Ha! Good one, Conbert," said the short squatty spewler as he waved his right paw at the contestants. "Well that's all for now! We'll be back as soon as the judges sort out the brackets and let you know how the tournament moves forward. What an unexpected turn of events! In the meantime, don't forget to visit the Drakeberry Cantina! Have a good rest of the morning my friends, and to all drakes everywhere, 'May your game be as good as gold, and may the Drakebureau be your companion for years untold!'"

I glanced at Cangoar as he glared back at me. I turned away and saw the referee heading my way – and two turds of a toad if that ancient malwrack wasn't moving as fast as an arsnatcher! I turned tail toward the forest but hadn't gotten far when the malwrack yelled, "Hold it right there, young lady!"

6. A Visitor from Out of the Black

The twin peaks of Flargellion were visible above the tree-tops, but Bannabard's goal of stating his case to the Drakebureau seemed more impossible than ever. His only plan at this point was to sneak in – hoping to find some way to raise the issue of treaty violations with the Drakebureau. Without getting eaten, roasted alive, or both. But he would keep his promise to the Elderarn. There would be no rescue attempt – not if it meant endangering Ape Town.

He hadn't slept since Gorby had been taken and found himself fighting to set aside thoughts of being incinerated, slowly roasted on a spit, or worse. The sun was past its zenith as he arrived at the edge of the forest just east of Flargellion. He hoped there wouldn't be anyone around but was disappointed to see members from every species of dragon. There were hundreds – in row after row of stalls cut in the side of a hill. Most of them watched intently as two drakes in a pit shot fireballs at each other in the meadow below. It appeared to be some sort of competition.

Blue apes weren't welcome here, but there was a gated entrance to a cave on the other side of the meadow where he guessed he might be able to sneak into the Great Hall. The gate extended nearly to the top of the mouth of the cave, but from where he stood it looked like there might be room for a blue ape to squeeze over the top. It was the only plan he had, so he'd wait until dark.

He climbed a tree at the northeast end of the meadow and watched the contest as a young malwrack dodged the spiked-tail of an arsnatcher that was half its size. Suppose he did manage to sneak in – what then? They'd arrest him or roast him as soon as look at him. His eyes were heavy. It felt like he could count every bone in his body.

45

The arsnatcher's tail stuck fast in the trunk of a tree, and the malwrack disabled it with an ear-splitting screech which stunned nearly half the audience. Bannabard held his hands over his ears and winced.

The malwrack casually burned off the tail of its opponent with a well-aimed firebolt. A third dragon struck a gong with what looked like a moose femur, apparently indicating that the match was over. It ended too quickly for many in the stands, who jeered and howled and shot flames in the air.

The quick end to the match stirred him. What was he doing? Focus. All he could think of were his mate and their three sons. What if Lais gets an infection? He rubbed the fir under his chin. He'd just have to trust Fergal to take care of her.

Focus. Focus on your mission. This is for Gorby.

The malwrack across the meadow bobbed his head. "Good game. Sorry about your tail, mate."

The arsnatcher yelled back, "HUH? WHAT'S THAT YOU SAY?"

"Wow, what a quick match that was!" the announcer exclaimed.

He tried to push the announcer's voice out of his head. Maybe there's another entrance. He started down the tree when he recognized an old familiar voice.

"Good match," said a deep voice which carried even better than the announcers'. "Dunsneed, stay focused! All it takes is one mistake and you're out."

"Gailryder!" he muttered to himself. Surely he'd remember him from the treaty negotiations. And if he remembered right, the malwrack doesn't care much for drambats. Shadows had grown long by the time he climbed down and headed into the forest. He circled behind the stalls as quietly as he could. Was he deluding himself? Even if he got close enough to talk to the big drake, the others would be on him in an instant.

He looked down on the meadow from a stand of bushes on a hill next to the stalls. Gailryder was there, talking to the winner and one of the officials. It looked like they were taking a break. The crowd was thinning, but there were still fifteen or twenty drakes between him and the malwrack.

He looked left, right, then up. This was nothing like Seedred Forest, but one of the few vines he saw was close. And even though the oak it hung from was nothing like a redwood, it might be tall enough to get him close to Gailryder. Up the tree he went, and when he had nearly reached the vine, he glanced down in time to see a spewler staring back. At him.

"Blue ape!" yelled the spewler.

"Get him!" screeched a couple of drambats.

He grabbed the vine and swung from it, flexing his body at the bottom. It felt as if every drake were watching as he swung again, gaining speed with a second and then a third swing. Several drakes plowed through the undergrowth and drew close to the tree, leaving Gailryder and the other malwrack alone in the meadow. The tree bowed under his weight and when its tension released, he catapulted over trees, drambats, spewlers, snartches, and arsnatchers.

There was a lightness in his gut just before the ground rushed up at him. His left foot hit the ground as he tucked his head and right shoulder. He rolled head over heels and landed on his feet. A single step to steady himself, and there he stood – facing Gailryder and the young malwrack next to him. A few drakes remained in the stall-stands – some hooted and snorted and a few shot flames in the air.

He turned to the big malwrack and said, "Gailryder, right?"

"Bannabard, is that you?" asked the malwrack with a grin. "Nice maneuver, but I'm not sure if that was brave or just plain stupid. These drambats and nickelnecks might not..."

"Might not let me live to see another day," interrupted Bannabard. "Yeah, I know." Bannabard's eyes narrowed. "I'm here because some drambats snatched my son out of Seedred Forest two days ago. The drambats have been violating the treaty of Flargenmoore ever since we signed it, and blue apes are on the verge of being wiped out."

The sound of plodding feet and tails dragging were hard to ignore.

Gailryder raised his head and spread his wings. "Stand down, my friends. This blue ape and I have some business to discuss."

Bannabard glanced around in time to see fifteen drakes stop dead in their tracks.

"What business does a malwrack have with a blue ape?" asked a snartch. "Let's roast his butt. Let's roast him now!"

"This is Bannabard – leader of the Elderarn," growled Gailryder. "He and I negotiated the Treaty of Flargenmoore together."

"What? The treaty of Flargenpoop?" asked a drambat.

Gailryder glared at the drambat. "What did you say – drambat?"

The drambat squealed and took off as the others backed up a few steps.

Bannabard turned and faced Gailryder. "Thanks. Any chance you could get me in to see the Drakebureau?"

"The Drakebureau? You can't be serious."

"As serious as it gets. There have been many others besides my son, and I want to discuss the treaty violations with the council."

Gailryder lowered his wings and head and looked Bannabard in the eye. "I don't think the Drakebureau would care much about that, to be honest. Other than Farl and me – the others, well, they'd just as soon roast you as flick their tongues at you."

Bannabard thumped his chest with his fist. "I'm willing to take that chance."

Gailryder looked away for a second. "I can see that you are. But there's no way..." He leaned in close, lowering his voice. "There's no way those fools would help blue apes – Treaty of Flargenmoore, or not."

Bannabard hardened his gaze and said, "You're no fool."

Gailryder, still whispering, reminded him, "It'd be your word against the drambats. And although I have little patience for drambats, there's no way the others would believe a blue ape's word against a dragon's."

"I can't let go of this, Gailryder. We have lost many apes in the last few years. And now they have my *son*."

Chants of "roasted ape" rose among the on-lookers. Gailryder picked up his head and glared at them, but they continued drawing closer until the other malwrack turned and glared too.

"You hear their chants, Bannabard. Perhaps you apes have stronger family bonds than we dragons, but I refuse to watch you sacrifice yourself in a hopeless endeavor such as this." Gailryder lowered his head and voice and covered Bannabard with a wing. "Beware, Bannabard. You've been seen outside of Seedred. Do what you must but remember – drambats won't be the only ones hunting you down. Come with me. Let's get you back to the forest."

Gailryder took him under his wing and ushered him to a stand of trees. Afternoon shadows disappeared with the sun as they arrived at the edge of the forest. He thanked Gailryder and headed into a thick stand of trees.

"Where's the blue ape?" yelled a drambat.

"This is Drakebureau business. Anyone who wants the ape will have to go through me," said Gailryder – in a voice almost like thunder.

Bannabard bounded down a game trail and glanced back every few strides. He hadn't gone far before he stumbled across a small cave. It was dark inside, and after verifying there were no drakes or other pests, he gathered some wood, built a fire near the entrance, and lay down, warming himself.

He'd gotten to see Gailryder but getting in to see the Drakebureau seemed more hopeless now than ever. Even Gailryder said so. Still, he wouldn't let Gailryder's words be the end of it.

He was just beginning to doze when he sat up with a start. A subdued, blue light illuminated the trees outside. He bounded to the back of the cave. Were dragons hunting for him? His jaw dropped as he watched a translucent bulbous black orb surrounded by a blue aura float slowly past the entrance.

And then it floated toward him. Right through the wall of the cave. The rock wall had somehow gone transparent.

Whatever it was moved through solid rock like it was air – and made the rock transparent like glass.

He rubbed his eyes. He could see trees behind the orb – and through the wall of the cave. The aura of blue light grew more intense as it floated to the middle of the cave. He glanced left. The rock wall was opaque again. He took a step back and plastered himself against the wall. That was when it spoke.

"Bannabard," it said.

He glanced around. It was muted, yet serene, and sounded like it came from nowhere and everywhere.

No. Don't answer.

"Bannabard."

This time the voice was louder. He glanced around. Were there others? How did it know his name? He glanced at the orb and then at the entrance of the cave. His eyes narrowed. It had moved between him and the entrance. Maybe keep it talking? "Yeah, that's me," he said, his voice trembling a bit.

Would it make him transparent if it touched him? What would happen if it did? He crept along the wall feeling like a cockroach as he inched toward the entrance. If only he were as quick as a cockroach.

"What are you and how do you know my name?" he asked as he glanced at the entrance and continued inching along the wall. "Maybe that tumble messed with my head," he muttered to himself.

"It wasn't the tumble – your head's fine. There's no need to be afraid. I come from what you call the Numinous, and I come in peace. I was sent here by the One. The One who has seen the suffering of your species."

The orb pulsated and its voice echoed.

"You come from where? How do you know my name?"

The orb spoke slowly and deliberately. "Melohim has seen the plight of the blue apes. He has sent me here to help. To help your species."

"Melohim?"

Really? The Numinous had always been a superstition among him and his kin. Nothing but a myth. Bannabard shook his head and looked away. "Melohim?" he asked more to himself than the orb, which was still there when he looked back. "You mean he exists?" He didn't wait for an answer. "Who are you and *what* are you?" The bulbous black orb pulsed and hovered and held its position as he continued to creep to his right. This can't be real. He forced his eyes shut, then opened them slowly, hoping it would be gone.

"I'm as real as you are. My name is Jendal and I come from the realm of dark matter and dark energy."

"Realm of what?" Bannabard asked. "What, like the north pole? I hear it's dark all day there."

"No, it's a different realm, a different dimension. I believe you apes call it the Numinous." The orb oscillated slightly as it spoke – but in a calm and steady voice. "I have been sent to help, but only for a season."

He and his friends had heard about the Obelisk of Hornath when he was a youth. It was in Flargellion and full of myths about Melohim and beings from what dragons called 'the Phoberon'. The orb had that part right – apes referred to it as 'the Numinous', but he had never given those stories any credence.

He rubbed his eyes and thumped his chest in disbelief as the orb transformed into a female blue ape. He turned away, shook his head, and stared at the ground.

This can't be real. Am I hallucinating, or is it a dream?

He dared to look at her.

The female ape smiled gracefully and asked, "Do you find my appearance disagreeable?"

"Oh, no. Not at all. Much nicer than a floating black orb. That was creeping me out. A *lot*." He inhaled and shook his head. "Seriously, though? Melohim sent you here to help? To help us?"

"Yes, Melohim sent me. More than a few apes have asked for his help, having suffered at the claws of drambats."

He pulled the fir on his cheek – and felt it. It was hard to argue – this didn't feel like a dream. But how did she know about drambats? And now she even looked like a blue ape. Bannabard exhaled, reminded himself to breathe, and stepped away from the wall of the cave. "What exactly, are dark matter and dark energy?"

"They are phases of matter and energy which are invisible and untouchable in this realm."

Her eyes flashed, and as she spoke her voice shook the walls of the cave. His legs felt mushy, like over-ripe bananas.

"Fundamental elements of the realm you call 'the Numinous'. And it is inhabited by beings like me. We consist of dark matter and dark energy – like all other things in our realm. But do not fear. I am here to offer hope for your species – if you are willing to accept it." Jendal stared at him for a second and then asked, "Will you?"

"Will I what?"

It was a struggle to wrap his head around the notion that the Numinous or a being like her even existed.

Jendal smiled slightly. "Accept my help, of course. Accept help from the One."

Bannabard gazed outside, then gave her a cold look. "Hold on a second. Our species has always been able to take care of itself, thank you very much. I'm not sure Melohim exists or can even be trusted if he does. If he's real, why hasn't he shown himself?"

Jendal's eyes flashed. "If he were to appear in this realm, the radiance of his countenance would burn your eyes as if you stared directly at a hundred suns. And if he took a step, the sound of it would be louder than a thousand malwrack screeches."

"What if I looked away and stuffed moss in my ears?"

"You would never survive – and your soul would transition to our realm. He has given you the Obelisk and has sent me here. That should be enough. Or are you going to let your love for the things of this realm stand in the way of the survival of your species?"

Bannabard looked away. Why was it so hard to accept her help?

Be strong: do it for Gorby.

He studied the dirt floor, then looked up. "I guess you're right. We need your uh… We, uh…"

It was hard to get the words out – hard to admit that this being from the Numinous was someone he could trust. Maybe he was delusional – from lack of sleep. Was the Numinous even real? His time as leader of the Elderarn had taught him that sometimes he had no choice but to trust others. And sometimes even other species – but never had he been asked to trust a being from another realm.

He thumped his chest and looked her in the eye. "We need… We need your help." It wasn't easy, but he finally said it. "Drambats," he said with a bit of a snarl. "They've been hunting and killing apes in violation of our treaty with the Drakebureau."

"And so I've seen," said Jendal. "Your numbers have dwindled."

"Yes they have. The other day they took my son. And although drambats are the smallest and weakest of dragons, our leaders fear Flargellion would retaliate if we fight back. The larger species could wipe us out in a heartbeat."

Jendal gave him a look that seemed to penetrate the core of his being. "Very well. You have chosen wisely. You shall have my help. But I am curious – how much of the Obelisk have you read?"

He looked away for a moment. What an odd question.

"I've read parts of it. But that was before the war – when there were a few tablets floating around. But what does that have to do with blue apes and drambats?"

"What did you think of it?"

Bannabard folded his arms across his chest. "Actually, I don't remember much. I was young and always thought of myself as a fairly regular shade of blue. I was never the studious type, but some of it made sense. At least in my mind..." He looked at the ground.

Jendal put a hand on his shoulder. "How much do you remember?"

A sensation that was somehow both cool and warm penetrated his shoulder and seemed to dance up and down his spine. He looked up and his gaze met hers. What a weird feeling *that* was.

"Not much... maybe a little, I guess. I remember it described how Melohim gave creatures the ability to make choices as they live out their lives. Some stuff about love and faith and hope. But it seems like he could have kept a little more control over things – if he really is *good*, that is. Maybe then we wouldn't be talking about my kidnapped son, or the survival of our species."

Jendal grinned slightly. "Indeed. And when you're in charge of the universe we'll see how things should *really* be run! But for now, and if you'll allow it, I've been instructed to accompany you to the Great Hall. Today you risked your life and made your concerns known to Gailryder. Tomorrow, you shall address the Drakebureau."

"The Drakebureau?"

Yeah, right.

He looked away and rolled his eyes slightly. "How's *that* gonna happen?"

"Leave that to me," she said with a slight grin.

"Well okay – but what's the catch? Why do you or Melohim, or anyone else for that matter, give a swamp-rat's butt about what happens between drambats and blue apes?"

"Melohim has sent me here because he cares about all beings – in this realm and in ours. We are like him in more ways than we know. We all feel things, share experiences, communicate with one another, and even with him as we choose. We experience pain, loss, and suffering. But there is also love, joy, hope, and kindness. Even the weakest among us can accomplish great things with his help. It may surprise you to know that although the strength of beings who inhabit this realm are like a gnat compared to ours, he does not think any less of them."

He was still trying to wrap his head around her words when she transformed into the black orb, disappeared into the rock wall, and was gone. Suddenly he felt more alone than he could remember. He hadn't felt like this since losing his parents in the war.

His thoughts turned to Lais and their sons. Hopefully she was recovering. Hopefully Hotch and Reebus would be able to forget. No, never forget. But learn to deal with that day their brother was snatched. He sat in front of the fire and stared at the bouncing flames and thought about Gorby.

Maybe he'd been awake too long. He wondered if Jendal hadn't been a hallucination. He shook his head and nearly laughed out loud at the thought of stating his case before the Drakebureau. Perhaps it was exhaustion. Or maybe his emotions had gotten the best of him. Either way, he'd have to figure something out tomorrow. For Gorby. But now it was time to sleep.

7. THE GREAT HALL

He woke the next morning to the sound of a malwrack's caterwaul.

"Whoa. Beauty, that is. Just beauty," he muttered. He shook his head, stretched, and headed out the small cave in the general direction of Flargellion. It was the first time he had slept since Gorby got snatched. Somehow that dream or hallucination or whatever it was – had allowed him to think more clearly. He'd be no good for Gorby or anyone else if he expired from exhaustion.

A path through the woods led to a clearing near the meadow where the dragons were holding their competition. He climbed up a tree next to a fork in the trail with some breakfast items he had caught or gathered along the way. A lizard, a snake, a couple of turnips, and some blackberries. It wasn't long before a couple of dragons came trundling down the wider of the two forks, and he listened as a spewler and an arsnatcher passed under the tree.

The spewler waved a paw and bobbed his head. "The first session is scheduled for later this morning. It will be dedicated to introductions, and whatever important business the day brings."

The arsnatcher stumbled over a root in the path. "What kind of business?"

"Mostly territorial disputes, but if we're lucky there'll be a trial," said the spewler. "But I like it best when they debate stuff."

"Ooh, a debate, I love debates!" exclaimed the arsnatcher. "But I'm surprised they do that in the Drakebureau. What stuff do they have debates about?"

"You know. Like how some drakes are more gold-challenged than others and how to fix that. Sometimes they debate the need to educate young dragons in the ways of Flargellion or how to grow the stash of gold in the treasury. Or whether or not a snartch really did eat a nickelneck's clutch of eggs. You know – stuff like that." The spewler sat down in the path, scratched his belly with one of his rear legs, and then got back up. "Last time I was here, old Pinhammer had quite a time talking about how important it was for the Drakebureau to increase the community's stash of gold. He said it would help them serve the greater good – the greater good of Drakedom no less."

The arsnatcher bobbed his head. "Greater good, my butt! The greater good of their own stashes! No way I'm giving those gold-grubbing ganders any of my stash!"

The spewler grinned and bobbed his head. "You might not have a choice. There was even talk of instituting a stash tax."

"A stash tax? They wouldn't dare!" exclaimed the spewler. "Don't they get enough from all those fines they dole out?"

"Apparently not."

That sounded all too familiar, and it was good to know dragons had their disagreements too. Bannabard finished breakfast, happy to know the Drakebureau's schedule, and listened a little as an announcer moderated the end of a match between two dragons.

"Yecchh," he muttered to himself. "I'm no drake, but what self-respecting dragon wants the Drakebureau to be their companion – for years untold?"

He climbed down the tree and bounded into the forest behind the stands, his mind preoccupied with how to get Gorby back. He found a trail and decided he'd skirt the mountain while the drakes were busy with their games. He'd heard there was an entrance on the other side and figured this was his best chance of sneaking into the Great Hall. A small lake appeared on the right side of the trail, and he realized how thirsty he was. But as he turned toward it, somehow his left fist missed the ground, then his right fist, and before he knew it both feet no longer had solid ground beneath them.

"Whoa!" he yelled, looking down as he fell *through* the path which had somehow evaporated beneath him.

A dark, rocky floor came up at him – quickly. He was falling. Face first. It was all he could do to flip his legs under before he hit the wet, hard surface. Except he didn't land square. Whumpf! He landed on his hind end and sat there looking around. It took a second for his eyes to adjust to the dim light. He was on the floor of a cavern surrounded by a few stalagmites.

He got up, rubbed his tailbone and lower back. Musta. Been. A sinkhole. He looked up, but instead of sky, there was nothing but a few silhouettes of stalactites overhead. What the...?

Diffused light from a corridor in another part of the cave drew his gaze left. Distant voices emanated from that direction. He recognized dragon voices and got up and headed the other way. But the cavern ended before he could take ten steps.

He sat down in what turned out to be a puddle, and as he sat there and pondered his predicament, a blue light caught his eye. It appeared to be reflecting off the rock wall to his left. But when he looked directly at it, the light was coming from *inside* the rock wall. As he studied it a black, translucent orb with a blue aura floated out of the wall and transformed into the female blue ape from the night before. Jendal. Was. Back.

He stared as she stood there, then looked away and said, "Well. It appears you're really not just a hallucination – from those mushrooms I ate."

Jendal grinned slightly. "No, I have nothing to do with mushrooms, indigestion, or hallucinations."

Bannabard's gaze met hers. "And do I have you to thank for ending up in this dragon-infested dungeon with a sore tail bone?"

Jendal smirked a little. "Yes. And you are most welcome. Sorry about your bruised caboose, but good job not landing on your face. It can be a bit of a fixer-upper when that happens. But this is no dungeon. It's a passage into the Great Hall."

Bannabard looked past Jendal to where the light was coming from. "The Great Hall? We're inside?"

"Yeah, it's not far at all, just down that passageway. You didn't think I'd appear to you from the Numinous, promise you an audience with the Drakebureau, and then just forget about it, did you?"

Bannabard smiled and looked away. His thoughts weren't nearly as silly as she made them sound.

"This leads to the cavern where the Drakebureau is in session," said Jendal, starting down the passage. A step or two later she spun around while walking backwards and said, "Are you coming, or would you prefer to sit in that puddle all day?"

Bannabard leaned on a stalagmite and pulled himself up. He brushed off his backside, knuckled up, and caught up with her.

"Hold on a second. I wouldn't know what to say to the Drakebureau, even if they did let me in."

Jendal was still walking backward, facing him. "The drambats have taken more than just a few blue apes, and now they've taken your son. They've been breaking the Treaty of Flargenmoore for the last seven years, right?"

"Yeah, that's right."

"And you have some numbers to back that up, don't you?"

He glanced at her, then looked at the ground. "Yes, I do."

"How many others?"

"Yeah, well, over three-hundred dead or missing in the last year, and nearly four thousand in the last six. Our species will be wiped out in a few years at this rate."

Jendal turned and faced forward again. "Fine. Stick to that. That should be enough. I'll take care of the rest."

He followed her as they emerged from the corridor into what appeared to be a huge, dimly lit cavern. They were behind many rows of raised stalls, and the silhouettes of a few dragons at the back were visible as dragon voices rumbled over a din of gurgling stomachs, thumping tails, and noises from other bodily functions he preferred not to think about.

"These stall stands are where common drakes watch the proceedings," Jendal said in a hushed tone.

They found an aisle where they could see rows of stalls sloping down to the floor of the Great Hall where great torches flickered and where he presumed the Drakebureau conducted its business. It was an underground amphitheater, and from what he could tell the audience consisted mostly of drambats, spewlers, snartches, and arsnatchers along with a few malwracks and nickelnecks. He turned away and waved a hand in front of his face. The stench. Was. Amazing.

"What do we do now?" he whispered.

"Relax, keep still, and stay out of sight. We'll know when it's time. Don't let the guards see you."

A second later, and she was gone. He looked around. It was too dark to see much, but the sound of the proceedings grabbed his attention. Six different species of dragon were gathered to work out their differences. Pretty impressive, he thought to himself. The Elderarn had plenty of challenges dealing with just one species.

He moved along the back of the stalls and found a spot at the end of an aisle which had a view of the floor of the Great Hall. There were malwracks stationed about halfway down the aisles – apparently guards – and in the torchlight he could see ten drakes gathered round an oblong table. Those must be the leaders.

He shrank back as he realized the light from the torches could reach him and squeezed into a space among the shadows. It was between posts and cross-members and under the stall stands, but he could see the leaders at the table. A strong, fishy smell, maybe like week-old fish gizzards, drifted his way. It was all he could do to keep from retching.

The oblong table was big enough to accommodate more than the ten dragons stationed around it and appeared to have been fashioned from a piece of slate. It was massive and there was a peculiar sheen about it, as iron, bronze, and copper colors danced on it while the torches flickered.

Each of the six species had at least one representative. He recognized Gailryder as the lone malwrack, along with a male nickelneck, two male drambats (one of which was quite skinny), a male and female snartch, one arsnatcher, a male and female spewler, and another male spewler stationed at the head of the table. The spewler appeared to be overseeing the proceedings.

"If we should *fail*..." The spewler paused, apparently waiting for the others to focus their attention on his words. "If we should *fail* to levy a gold tax of sufficient magnitude, there are dragons everywhere who will suffer emotional trauma. They might develop a deep sense of... how shall I say it? They could develop a sense of, pardon the word, a sense of... *inadequacy*."

He waved a paw, paused again, and looked out into the gallery as most of the drambats and spewlers, a few snartches, and one or two arsnatchers gasped in disbelief.

"Inadequacy. Yes, that is the word. Because their stash of gold isn't as big as their neighbor's, or maybe doesn't contain *any gold at all.*"

Even more incredulous gasps were heard from the spewlers and drambats around the table, along with quite a few others in the gallery.

Gailryder bobbed his big black head. "Inadequacy? Inadequacy, my butt! Every dragon's stash of gold is his own concern, and not something the Drakebureau needs to stick its nose or stater-grubbing claws into. Next thing you know, he'll want to levy a dragon-egg tax, so we can distribute eggs to families who haven't been laying their own. How much, your Drakeness? Five percent? Would that do ya proud? Or would ten percent be better?"

There were some head butts and a few howls in the audience, especially among the larger species. The spewler at the head of the table bobbed his head vigorously and gave the malwrack a fierce look as the din in the gallery continued. "Order! Order! I will have ORD-DER!" he yelled. "Gailryder! That's quite enough, or I'll have you held in repugnance!"

Gailryder grinned at the spewler. "Oh no. Not that. Not *repugnance.*"

The spewler bobbed his head, looked around the table, and glared at the malwrack. "Don't test me, Gailryder!"

The nickelneck next to Gailryder smirked as Gailryder continued. "Yes, your Drakeness. Maybe I crossed a river with the dragon egg thing, but I was just making a point. Since when did it become the Drakebureau's business to be sticking its snout into every drake's private stash of valuables? We need to remain focused on why we're here."

The nickelneck next to him flicked his tongue. "Good point, my friend. And why *are* we here?"

Gailryder waved a paw and said, "Well, Farl, I'm glad you asked. The Drakebureau's charter is based on the belief that all drakes are endowed by their creator with certain unalienable rights. That among these are life, liberty, and the pursuit of game, hibernation shelters, shiny objects, and the raising of hatchlings, so long as they're not harming others."

The malwrack paused to bob his big black head and glanced around the table. The spewler at the head of the table looked up at the ceiling as if to say, 'Enough already.'

Gailryder continued, "We're also here to protect hunting grounds and resolve territorial disputes among peaceful dragons. And to dole out consequences for those who infringe on other dragons' hunting territories, or otherwise injure, maim, or incinerate their neighbors. I'm convinced we've been so successful in recent centuries that many drakes are beginning to think the Drakebureau ought to delve into matters beyond its charter."

The drambats were tiny compared to Gailryder, and the one seated next to the tall, skinny one bobbed his head and glared at him. "And what would be the harm in that? You malwracks and nickelnecks are all alike – always trying to stop progress. Our great society of drakes must look beyond individual desires and work together to help the less fortunate in our midst!" The drambat grinned widely as quite a few drambats and spewlers in the gallery snorted and bonked heads.

Gailryder gazed at the drambat, then at the others. "Yes indeed, Qualmsneed, we have a great society, no doubts there. But my fellow drakes, I urge you. Do not be deceived by those who wish to use the force of malwrack and nickelneck gaggles to interfere in areas of the lives of our constituents that ought not to be meddled with." Gailryder leaned in close to the drambat, towering over him with a hint of a sneer. "Once we trade basic freedoms for a few securities and niceties promised by this body, we'll find ourselves with neither."

More than a few drakes in the gallery shot flames in the air and howled raucously – mostly malwracks, nickelnecks, and arsnatchers. The lead spewler bobbed his head, this time more vigorously.

"Order, order!" he exclaimed as he glared at Gailryder and waited for the gallery to quiet down. "Thank you for those illuminating remarks, Qualmsneed! And yours too, Gailryder. Let us table this discussion of protecting, nay enhancing, the lives and dignity of dragons everywhere by helping the less fortunate among us, until a more benevolent mood exists among *all* our members!"

He glared again at the malwrack, who allowed a bit of a grin to expose itself.

"Let us proceed with our agenda for today, shall we? And the first item on the docket is a territorial dispute between Snule and Ferndim. As you may recall, the southern snartches were awarded the hunting grounds east of…"

Bannabard was starting to doze when someone nudged him on his left shoulder.

61

"Wake up. It's time!" exclaimed a disembodied voice in a hushed tone.

Bannabard shook his head, then sat bolt upright. "Oh yeah. Time. Time for what?"

"Time for you to address the Drakebureau. Are you ready?"

Bannabard looked where the voice was coming from, but saw no one, not even the black orb with the blue aura. "Yeah. Let's do this," he whispered.

A blue dot appeared at his feet. Was it Jendal? It was all he could do to keep from howling as first his feet then the rest of him began to sink into the bedrock. The ground in his immediate vicinity went transparent as his body sank and he began moving *through bedrock* toward the oblong table where the leaders were gathered. He was gliding *under* the stall-stands. He looked up at the dragons in the gallery as he floated beneath them.

Could they see him?

His journey through bedrock ended directly beneath the center of the oblong stone table.

Oh, crap. Here we go. Again.

He wasn't sure how, but his body twisted around, and a moment later he found himself ascending head-first through the middle of the stone table. He landed on his feet and glanced around as he tapped a foot on the table to make sure it was solid.

There he stood. A lone blue ape in the middle of the leaders of the Drakebureau. He was surrounded by an arsnatcher, a nickelneck, Gailryder, two drambats, three spewlers, and two snartches. They stared at him as light from the torches danced off their snouts. He glanced around as the drambats and spewlers looked up at him, while the larger species looked down – some with huge gaping jaws.

8. A Malwrack's Shackle

There was a gasp, a couple shrieks, and then, as he stood there, a celebration broke out among the drakes in the gallery. Perhaps they thought it was some sort of an act or play or something. He glanced at the host of dragons in the gallery, somewhat relieved that he hadn't fallen on his butt.

More than a few bonked heads, howled, and shot flames in the air. The spewler at the head of the table, along with the skinny drambat and another spewler, got up from under the stone slab where they had ducked for cover.

Soon a chant rose from the gallery, "Roasted ape! Roasted ape! Roasted Ape!"

A chill ran up and down his spine.

"Silence!" shouted the lead spewler, as he wrapped his right paw on the table and bobbed his head vigorously.

But the racket continued.

"Silence!" he yelled again. But when the gallery continued, he squeezed the fat fiadhain chained up next to him. It squealed, and the hall went silent as nearly every dragon flicked their tongues and licked their chops.

The spewler glared at Bannabard. "Who are *you*, and just what *is* the meaning of this? Why is a blue ape interrupting *my* proceedings... err, *our* proceedings?"

Gailryder leaned closer and grinned. "Bannabard, is that you, or are you his sister? I can never tell." His grin widened as he glanced around at the others. "And where'd you learn a trick like *that*? That was freakin' frog-tastic!"

"Frog-tastic? Really!?" exclaimed the nickelneck next to Gailryder. "I'd wager he learned it from Ilgregious," he said while giving the skinny drambat a hard look.

The skinny drambat bobbed his head and sneered. "He didn't learn it from me. I say we roast him and serve him up to the commoners."

Bannabard looked at the gallery as chants of 'Roasted ape!' started up again.

"Silence!" shouted the spewler as he stood up, bobbed his head, and even flapped his wings a few times. "Just what *is* the meaning of this? Gailryder! Do you *know* the blue ape?"

Gailryder grinned. "Yeah, I know the ape. He's the head of the Elderarn. He and I negotiated the treaty of Flargenmoore."

"Well, how did he get *here*? How's a blue ape standing in the middle of *my* Stone Ingot?"

"How would I know? But I'll be glad to help you get him out," answered Gailryder with a grin.

Bannabard didn't appreciate that as much as the gallery did. Snorts, howls, a few head bonks, and chants of 'Roasted ape!' started up again.

The spewler squeezed the fiadhain and when it squealed, the room fell silent once more. "What's your name, and how did you get here?"

Bannabard looked down for a second. "My name is Bannabard. I'm a blue ape from the Great Seedred Forest."

The spewler glared at him, then at Gailryder. "Thank you, Bannabard. I can see you are a blue ape – and of course you're from Seedred. But how did you get into our Great Hall, and onto the Stone Ingot?"

"I'm not quite sure, your Drakeness... I had help from a friend. Jendal?" His voice trailed off as he glanced around the Great Hall. It was weird the spewler was in charge – as Gailryder towered over everyone except the nickelneck. "Sorry, your Drakeness, but I don't see my friend anywhere... your Drakeness."

The leader leaned in close and glared at him as chants of 'Roasted Ape' started up again. The spewler yelled over the din of the gallery, "Answer the question – before I give the gallery what it wants!"

Bannabard wiped beads of sweat off his forehead and looked around. Jendal was nowhere to be seen.

The leader backed away and turned to the stands. "How do you prefer your ape? Rare, or extra crispy?"

The gallery chanted, "Roasted ape, either way! Roasted ape, any day!"

The leader turned to the drakes gathered around the Stone Ingot and shouted, "On the count of three. One, two…"

Bannabard had to yell to be heard. "Uh, I'm not sure how I got here, your Drakeness!" He looked up at the ceiling, wondering if this would be the end – and if Jendal had abandoned him.

A disembodied voice whispered, "Don't be afraid, I'm with you. Tell them you have powers they don't understand – but don't mention me."

Bannabard looked at the leader and stammered, "My friend says, um, I um…"

"Speak up, little ape! Our patience is wearing thin!"

The chants in the stands died down a bit, and he looked up at the ceiling again, then back at the spewler. "I have pa-powers you don't understand – your Da-Drakenesses." He glanced at the table, hating that he stuttered.

The leader leaned forward and got up in his grille. "Powers we don't understand!?" He bobbed his head and flicked his tongue in Bannabard's face. "Let's see if you understand this. Let him have it, boys!"

Bannabard glanced at the gallery as a few drakes shot flames in the air, then watched the spewler back away. He knew what was coming as he wiped spewler goo off his face. But instead of cowering and trying to shield himself, he stood tall. A sense of confidence took hold of him. "This is it, I guess," he muttered to himself. His thoughts turned to Lais and their sons. He wished he had another chance to say goodbye and tell them how much he loved them. He gazed at the drambats and another spewler who, along with most of the others, unleashed their fireballs.

Instinctively he shielded his face with his arm, but instead of searing heat and burning fur, each fireball splattered against an invisible shield – somehow unable to reach his body. He looked left, then right, and then behind as flames danced around and licked the table at his feet. They danced around a translucent, purplish dome which surrounded and protected him.

He dropped his arm and tried not to grin as fireballs slid to the table. He watched as a few of the drakes caught their breath – having expended considerable effort in their attack. The tall, skinny drambat coughed and hacked. Gailryder and the nickelneck had curious looks on their faces. They had abstained – apparently uninterested in joining the 'fun'.

"Thanks. I thought I was done for," he whispered.

"No worries, I'm here for ya," whispered Jendal.

A few members of the Drakebureau bobbed their heads, while drakes in the stands roared, shrieked, bonked heads, and shot flames in the air.

"Silence!" yelled the leader, as he stood and addressed the gallery.

The leader squeezed the boar, but the squeal could barely be heard over the din of the drakes in the stands. "Everyone out!" he bellowed. The leader bobbed his head, pounded the Ingot, and shot flames in the air. "I need everyone out! Everyone! Out... Now!"

A few drambats and spewlers in the gallery hissed their disapproval as the celebrations abated. The gallery slowly grew quiet as dragons began clearing out of the stall stands. Malwrack guards made sure the leader's orders were followed. Drakes of every size and species began filing out of the Great Hall, murmuring as they went. Quite a few eyed the fat fiadhain and licked their chops on their way out.

The crowd was still filing out when the leader turned and glared at him. "Banana-beard! That was quite a show! But I must ask. What brings you here and why have you interrupted my – uh, our proceedings!?"

Bannabard's gaze met the spewler's. "If you please, your Drakeness, the name's Bannabard. I'm here because our species is under attack."

"That's nonsense," snarled the skinny drambat.

"If you please, your Drakeness. It's been going on for seven years – ever since we signed the Treaty of Flargenmoore. My youngest son was carried off by a dragon just the other day. These are clear violations of the Treaty, which, as you may recall, your Drakeness – was signed and agreed to by members of *this* body."

The leader nodded. "Hrrmm. Yes, I do recall the treaty. It was the end of a difficult era between our species. An era that ended badly for yours, I'm afraid."

Bannabard's gaze hardened. "Indeed it was, your Drakeness. And although we have obeyed the Treaty, our casualties haven't stopped. Over three hundred of my kin have died in the last year alone, and nearly four thousand in the last six. We'll be wiped out in the next few years if it continues."

He tried not to think of Gorby and how he had been a captive now for more than two days. He needed to stay focused – for Lais, their sons

Hotch and Reebus, and the Elderarn. But most of all for Gorby – if there was still hope. He looked up and wrapped a fist on his chest.

"I'm sorry to hear about your son, but you signed the treaty. How is it a concern of the Drakebureau's if blue apes are dying of sickness or starving to death?" The leader glanced at the other members of the Drakebureau while the female snartch, the drambats, and a few others around the table nodded in agreement.

Bannabard stood tall and replied, "That's just it, your Drakeness. We haven't been dying from sickness, disease, or starvation. Our species is under attack."

"Attack? What kind of attack?"

Bannabard stared into the leader's face and paused to make sure he had the spewler's attention. "Dragon attacks. Your Drakeness."

The tall skinny drambat with a crooked snout bobbed his gray head and yelled, "Nonsense!" He looked around the table and gave the others an incredulous look, ignoring Bannabard as if he weren't there. "Does this ape expect us to believe there is some rogue band of drakes running around attacking the few blue apes left in this world? What interest would dragons, and especially drambats, have in attacking *blue apes?*"

The other drambat and the female snartch bonked heads. The skinny drambat snarled, "They have no gold, they stink to high heaven, and they taste… terrible! No one wants to eat *them.*"

Gailryder scrunched his nose, leaned toward the drambat, and bobbed his big black head. "He didn't say anything about drambats, Ilgregious. Is there something you aren't telling us?" The malwrack's fangs were up in the drambat's face and nearly as tall as his head.

The skinny drambat sneered and looked away. "He didn't have to say 'drambats', you snail brain. Everyone knows blue apes have been accusing drambats – for decades."

"Ilgregious, you better not be hiding something," snarled Gailryder.

Ilgregious ignored the malwrack and leaned over to the other drambat and whispered something. It sounded as if he said, "This ape might be useful. I hope he survives."

Gailryder and Ilgregious exchanged a few more barbs while Bannabard watched the two lines of drakes make their way out of the hall, each in single file. They ambled past either side of the Stone Ingot on their way out. Among them was a female nickelneck who looked somewhat familiar. She was near the end of the line on the left side, behind some arsnatchers.

Just when the proceedings were starting to get dull, the ending was way more entertaining than I could have imagined. That blue ape's a lot bigger than the one I'd seen in the drambat's lair, and he did some amazing tricks! Who knew the Drakebureau could be so much fun?! But now they wanted us all out. "Everyone out! Everyone out now!" said the leader.

I'd probably have to come back later and clean up. Not only did the B.E.G. officials sentence me to attend ten sessions of the Drakebureau – I also had to clean stall-stands in the Great Hall after each session! But worst of all, they disqualified me from *the Games*. They said I interfered with Cangoar's little match. Maybe I did – maybe I deserved to be punished, but no one seemed to get it. *Cangoar could have died!*

I looked around. Other drakes chatted and carried on while we moved slowly toward an exit at the front of the hall. I couldn't help overhearing the musings of two arsnatchers as I followed them toward the Stone Ingot.

"But if it was a show, why are they clearing the hall?" asked the shorter of the two.

"Apparently it wasn't," the other answered. "I wonder what's going on – and why is that blue ape here and not in Seedred?"

"Yeah, what's he doing? But really – I was hopin' for a roastin'!"

"Me too! And just last night there were rumors of a blue ape sighting at the B.E.G.!" exclaimed the other. "Is this the same one or are there others?!"

We were filing past the Stone Ingot when I looked up and recognized the skinny drambat from the night before. I scrunched my nose and sneered at him.

The drambat bobbed his head. "I've got nothing to hide, Gailryder," said the drambat with a sneer, while looking at me. "Perhaps you should work a little harder at hiding your derision and hatred of the smaller species."

Seeing him here at the Stone Ingot with the other leaders was just wrong. It was beyond wrong after what they did to that hatchling. "Don't listen to that drambat, he can't be trusted!" I exclaimed as I gave the drambat a piercing look. "I saw you and your toadies throw a young arsnatcher into a lava pit! Just last night... just an innocent hatchling!"

The two arsnatchers turned around and looked up at me with gaping jaws and wide eyes.

I gave them a glance and glared at the drambat. "It was some sort of ceremony. After they threw an innocent hatchling into the lava pit – I can still hear it screeching – this drambat floated around, ranting about how great he is, and yelled at the others to bow down to him. All the while the poor little hatchling burned and screeched. And your toady little friends chanted a dirge about some dark queen. It was the most disgustingest thing I've ever seen... in my *whole* life!"

The tall skinny drambat looked around at the others and bobbed his gray head. He scrunched his nose and responded without looking at me. "Nonsense. Clearly this nickelneck is delusional." He calmly looked around at the other leaders, apparently unfazed by my accusations. "Everyone knows drambats can fly. But you said 'floating' if I heard you correctly. Was I *floating* or *flying?*"

I flicked my tongue, then glared at him. "You were floating. It was creepy – double-triple-extra creepy. He wasn't even using his wings. But what difference does *that* make? What matters is he threw a live hatchling into a lava pit!"

"Floating about without using my wings? Really?" The drambat grinned widely, exposing a broken fang. "Isn't it obvious to all? Is this nickelneck delusional or is she conjuring up lies to smear my good name – and therefore the good name of the Drakebureau itself?!" His grin turned into a bit of a sneer as he looked up at the leader.

The nickelneck next to Gailryder bobbed his head. "Why? Why would she do that, Ilgregious?"

"Because I'm a drambat, Farl!" he exclaimed, refusing to look at the nickelneck. "Everyone knows nickelnecks have had it in for drambats ever since... well, since before any of *us* were born. Everyone knows that nickelnecks are always looking to take advantage of weaker, less fortunate species than themselves. Pinhammer, I want this blue ape and this nickelneck friend of his arrested!"

Pinhammer bobbed his head and gave the drambat a hard look. "Hold on, Ilgregious. Arrest this fine young nickelneck? On what charges? I see no point in arresting one of our own." He paused, turned to me, and softened his tone. "And what, might I ask, is your name, miss?"

I looked down at the leader and smiled slightly. "My name is Alfedora, your Drakeness."

Pinhammer bowed his head. "Pleased to make your acquaintance, Alfedora."

He certainly has nice manners – for a spewler, that is. My smile broadened, and I bowed my head slightly. "Likewise, your Drakeness."

The hall went quiet for a moment before Ilgregious bobbed his head and yelled, "Subversion! The charges are subversion! Clearly the blue ape and this nickelneck friend of his are attempting to subvert the Drakebureau's ability to deal with draconian issues by getting us to focus on matters of lesser import!"

I glared at the drambat. "And you would know all about lesser import, wouldn't you, Ilgregious? Whether he floated or flew is more important than whether he burned an innocent hatchling in a lava pit!"

Gailryder looked around. "Subversion my tail! I'm sure Alfedora and Bannabard have been planning their little subversive maneuver for months. Everyone knows blue apes and nickelnecks plan together and get along like staters and drachmas!" He glared at Ilgregious. "And that's why my little friend Bananabeard couldn't explain how he got onto the Stone Ingot. He didn't want to rat out his nickelneck friend. Isn't that right, Banana?"

The blue ape looked up at the malwrack and said, "Uh no, not really. I had help from a friend, but it wasn't a dragon, and certainly not a nickelneck."

Pinhammer glanced around at the others. "Are there other apes besides you in Flargellion?" His gaze turned cold toward the blue ape. "Where is this friend of yours, and is he or she from Seedred also?"

The blue ape looked down, then turned to the leader and said, "I'm not sure where she is, your Drakeness. She's not really from around these parts."

Pinhammer stared at the blue ape. "Are there blue apes living outside of Seedred?"

"Well, no. You see the first time I met her – she was kind of like this dis-embodied black orb with a kind of a blue aura. But then she transformed into a female blue ape and…" He cut his sentence short as the spewler gave him an incredulous stare. He glanced at the drambat, then at the ground.

Ilgregious grinned widely and leaned toward the blue ape. "Oh really? She just transformed from a black orb into a blue ape?" He flicked his tongue and looked around at the others. "Is it not obvious that this ape is either delusional or playing us all for fools? Maybe we can't roast him, but let's see how his tricks work against dragon claws. Give me the word and I'll pluck out his gizzard!"

Gailryder glared at the drambat. "You'll be going through me first, you sleaze-a-saurus."

Ilgregious smirked. "Oh, so you care about the ape? Is he your pet? You know they'll be extinct in a few years!" He scrunched his nose, baring his crooked teeth and broken fang. "And why do you want to save these little blue fur-balls? Is it because you miss the glory years? Maybe you want to restore their numbers and re-kindle the Great Ape Wars!"

Pinhammer waved off Ilgregious and Gailryder – who had scrunched his nose and was leaning in toward the drambat. He pounded the Ingot and bobbed his head three times. "Silence!" he yelled. "I've had enough of these interruptions and distractions. Guards! I want chords on the ape and a shackle on the nickelneck!"

I watched as a malwrack slapped chords around the blue ape and dragged him off the table. A heavy paw pressed against the back of my head and before I could react – wham! A metal shackle clamped down on my snout. The chain went taught as I struggled against it. On the other end of it a malwrack grinned back at me. His eyes narrowed. I relented and as the chain went limp, I stared at the leader – still at the head of the Stone Ingot.

Pinhammer bobbed his head. "Take them to the Viper Vault! We'll have a closed-door meeting first thing tomorrow. Meeting adjourned!"

The fat fiadhain squealed twice as the guard dragged me out of the hall. "Maybe I deserve this," I muttered to myself.

A female snartch stood outside the hall and stared as we approached. She bobbed her head and thrashed her tail. "This nickelneck deserves more than the Viper Vault!" she exclaimed. "Soon, she'll be off to the Red Lair! And thrown in the lava pit, she will!"

9. LOCKED UP

T he cell was secured with steel bars and a lock on the door. And no surprise, nothing to eat. Not even whale gizzards. On the way in it looked like the Viper Vault had about half a dozen rows of ten cells each. This one was barely big enough for me, but they had thrown the blue ape in with me. He was close enough I could smell his breath. And it wasn't like there weren't enough cells. My snout shackle was secured with a chain to a heavy metal ring in the floor. The chain was rather short – I couldn't move my head very far. My tail and legs had shackles and were chained to heavy metal rings – also in the floor.

My stomach growled. I wondered what blue ape tasted like. Not that my stomach was back to normal. I had briefly forgotten about the events at the lava pit during the excitement of the match and deep-fried squid at the concessions stand. But now there was time. Time to ponder why those nasty drambats were throwing hatchlings into lava pits – and why *I* was the one arrested! Suddenly I recognized that smell. I licked my chops and raised my head as far as the shackle allowed. So that's what that smell was down by the lake – it was this blue ape!

I'd heard they were omnivores. Probably not as sweet or juicy as bear, but probably not as dry and gamy as grass-munchers either. Still, he smelled too clean for my discriminating pallet. And here we were, face-to-face. I snorted and tried to turn my head, but the chain was too short. How long would I be locked up in here?

The blue ape's hands and feet were bound with chords and there was a shackle around his neck which was chained to the wall. His head pivoted away after I snorted again. Oh sure – he could move his head!

73

He coughed, then turned to me. "Excuse me, your Drakeness. Aladoor was it?"

Great. Just great. Locked up with the only ape in Seedred who wants to get chatty with a nickelneck. Doesn't he know nickelnecks and blue apes don't get along? I closed my eyes and snorted again – hoping he would get the hint.

"Excuse me, Aladoor?"

He wasn't giving up. I opened one eye and snorted yet again – right in his face. He turned away, then turned back to face me with questioning eyes.

"The name's Alfedora. What's it to you?" I snarled. The snout shackle made it hard as fiadhain bones to talk.

"Yes, yes. Of course. Alfedora. My apologies."

I opened my other eye halfway as the blue ape smiled and nodded graciously.

"My name's Bannabard, and if you will please excuse my curiosity, but was it you I saw at Lake Luellian on the eastern edge of the Great Seedred Forest? I believe you caught a pair of bears just a few days ago."

I opened my eyes fully and glared at him. "What? You were spying on me?" I struggled against the chains for a moment. "Why's a creepy little ape like you – spying on a young, beautiful nickelneck like me? You're lucky there's a shackle on my snout."

"Oh, yes. Very lucky indeed, your Drakeness." He smiled and tried to bow, but the chords wouldn't allow it. "With all due respect, I wasn't exactly spying or creeping. I hadn't seen a nickelneck in years and was a bit curious. I had forgotten how magnificent your species is."

Well, he did have nice manners – for an ape, that is. I flicked my tongue. It took a couple tries to make it through the shackle. Another inch or two and it would have reached his nose.

"And I beg your pardon, your Drakeness, but if you will bear with me, I am fascinated by what you told the leader about the skinny drambat. I believe you said something about drambats? They threw an arsnatcher into a lava pit?"

I was in no mood for talking about *that*. "Why would I tell the likes of you?"

"I think we both have an interest in finding out what the drambats are up to."

"Maybe so, but why would I talk to a blue ape about it?" This conversation needed to be oh-ver. Like now. He was right about one thing, though. What were those drambats up to?

The blue ape shrugged. "It can't hurt to talk, can it?"

I picked my head up. "Okay, but you have to tell me about yourself first."

The blue ape nodded. "Sure, anything. What would you like to know?"

I flicked my tongue and gave him a cold stare. "I have three questions. How did you get into the Great Hall, how did you get onto the Stone Ingot, and how did you survive those fireballs?"

The blue ape smiled slightly, glanced at the door, then looked me in the eye. "To be honest I had help from a friend who claims to be from another dimension. She says…"

"Wait," I interrupted. "Did you say, 'another dimension'?" I tried to bob my head, but the chain was too short.

"Yeah, she said the Obelisk describes it as 'the Phoberon', but we apes call it 'the Numinous'. That's what she called it when she appeared to me yesterday in a cave. The Numinous. Another dimension – another realm."

"What do you mean – she appeared?"

"I was settling into a small cave the other night when one of the walls went transparent and a black bulbous orb with a blue aura floated right through the wall," he said with a bit of urgency in his voice. "It came through solid rock as if it were traveling through thin air. Things got even crazier when the orb transformed into a blue ape – a female blue ape. And then she told me I was going to make a case for what drambats have been doing to apes, in front of the Drakebureau, no less. Well naturally I didn't believe her, but I guess I should have, and…"

"Wait," I interrupted. "Stop right there."

No wonder he's chattin' up a blue streak – he's delusional.

I flicked my tongue a couple times. "A black orb floated through solid rock like it was air? Seriously. You been bit by a drambat or something? Maybe a snartch? Either way there's got to be an infection. You should get some help. But maybe it's too late – it sounds like the infection's already reached your brain."

"No. I haven't been bit and I don't have an infection," he answered. "I get it. This all sounds crazy. But she was the one who got me into the Great Hall and put me in the middle of the Stone Ingot. She was the one who protected me from the fire balls. I don't know how she does that stuff, but if she claims to have been sent from the Numinous... Well, either *she's* delusional, or she knows what she's talking about."

I glared at the ape and struggled against my chains. For a moment it felt like they might break. The blue ape tried to shield himself, but the chains held, and I slumped to the floor. I put my head down and flicked my tongue. "The Phoberon is nothing but a myth – everyone knows that. Everyone's who's not delusional, that is."

"I'm not delusional. I know what I saw. You saw it too."

Yeah – pretty impressive trick all right.

"What's your friend's name?" I asked.

"Her name's Jendal. She was sent here by Melohim to help our species. I think the Big Guy doesn't want blue apes to be wiped out. What do you think?"

I scrunched my nose: I'd heard myths about the Phoberon and Melohim. He was supposed to be some sort of benevolent, all-powerful creator.

Yeah, right. A benevolent, all-powerful being who lets innocent hatchlings get thrown into lava pits.

"I think you did get bit by a drambat. Or was it a snartch?"

Bannabard smiled. "I didn't get bit by a drambat or a snartch, and I'm not delusional. She has an ability to manipulate matter in this realm – it looks like magic when she does it. Says it's dark energy or something. How else could I survive those fireballs?"

The ape had a point – how did he survive? "And this friend of yours – says she's from the Phoberon?"

"Yeah. Said she came from the Phoberon, and that beings from her realm are powerful. More powerful than nickelnecks or malwracks even."

Ah, that's better. I found a way to talk through the shackle – by limiting my jaw movements. "Hold on a second. You don't actually believe the Phoberon is real, do you? Or that I should believe it because some blue ape believes it."

"To be honest, I don't pretend to know what you should or shouldn't believe. But when a black orb floats through solid rock, I can't explain that. And when it transforms into a blue ape, I can't explain that either. She said she was sent here because Melohim was concerned about blue apes going extinct. And that's been our experience. She knows what's going on in this realm, and well, yeah, I believe her. What you believe is up to you. But I don't know how else to describe what I saw with my eyes and heard with my ears."

I tried to bob my head again.

Stupid chain.

"Maybe you were having a weird dream. Maybe it was a nightmare. Or maybe you ate something which caused you to hallucinate. Was it mushrooms?"

"No, I didn't eat any mushrooms. Besides, none of that would explain how I survived those fireballs."

Yeah, but… if the Phoberon were real, then Melohim might exist. And if he exists but won't protect innocent hatchlings from the likes of Ilgregious, well, I couldn't believe in *that*. And why would he send help for blue apes, but not lift a finger to save an innocent hatchling from being burned alive in a lava pit? I scrunched my nose, flicked my tongue, and shook the snout shackle.

"There are things in life we can't explain," I said. "Like those stunts you pulled. Hey! Got any more? How about getting me out of these shackles?"

"Sorry, but those weren't stunts. And isn't it all in the Obelisk? Doesn't it talk about Melohim, the dosara, and the Phoberon?"

I glanced at the ceiling, then gave the ape a hard look. "Couldn't say. I never read the Obelisk, nor would I want to."

"Wow, you never read the Obelisk of Hornath? I figured dragons were down with the writings, especially since the Obelisk is right outside the Great Hall."

I gave him an icy stare. "No one believes that stuff anymore. We've got more important things to do than read ancient etchings on a stone pillar. Our wisest drakes say the Obelisk is for the simple-minded and weak-hearted."

"But what if the Obelisk is true? Wouldn't the wise ones want to know that?"

"I couldn't say, really. They say it was fabricated by religious zealots who used those myths to manipulate and control others. A few drakes got everyone to believe they were tight with some supreme being who doesn't exist now and never has existed. It's a crutch – for the weak-minded."

"Yeah, I have friends who say things like that. But Jendal isn't weak-minded. She's smart. Smart as anyone I know, and powerful too. And she wants to help."

I smirked. What if there's some truth to his story?

Ah, they'd think I'm daft. 'Your Daftness,' they'd call me.

I flicked my tongue. "If this friend of yours wants to help you so much, and if she's so powerful, why would she leave you locked up in the Viper Vault?"

"Good question. I don't have an answer for that."

"I thought so." I looked away as much as the shackle and chain allowed. "Has anyone ever seen Melohim? Has it ever been documented that he ever even helped anyone?" I waited for an answer. Then gave him a hard look. "Didn't think so. In the end all we really have is ourselves and the Drakebureau."

"Then it's good we understand one another," Bannabard said as he relaxed against the wall behind him. "Yeah, I get what you're saying. Just a few days ago I thought the same thing, but recent events…"

"Recent events?" I interrupted. "Events like your brain being invaded by weevils?" I grinned and bobbed my head slightly. "Does it hurt? Just say the word and I'll put you out of your misery. Once I get out of this shackle, that is."

Bannabard smiled slightly. "Seriously – do you actually have *faith* in the Drakebureau?"

I'd be smoking his butt right now if not for this shackle.

I glared at the blue ape. "What else is there? We should all have faith. And I don't think it's faith in the Drakebureau so much as faith in drakes being good and in the wise ones among us having the ability to sort things out for everyone else. We can't depend on farty-snartch tales to help us work through problems in the *real* world."

"Who said anything about farty-snartch tales? And besides, I've seen how things work. I was the leader of the Elderarn not too long ago. I've seen how power corrupts. Perhaps there ought to be limits on what the Drakebureau does."

"What's the Elderarn?"

"It's the ruling body of apes – kinda like the Drakebureau, except we only have one species to deal with."

"Ah yes, the ruling body of apes," I said with a bit of a smirk. "You and your fellow Elderarns must have been very courageous – especially during the Great Ape Wars. And yet everyone knows there are limits to what *they* can do. But the Drakebureau? That's different. It regulates the great society. The greatest society ever – the Great Society of Dragons."

Bannabard smiled. "Okay, yeah, I get it. The Drakebureau is the greatest ever. No need to get your scales roiled up about it."

I strained against the chains. "My scales aren't roiling," I sneered. "Besides, I'll be roiling my scales if I want to." I scrunched my snout. "The Phoberon? I don't think so. You need to face reality, my little blue friend. There's no such thing – and I'm afraid this imaginary friend of yours has abandoned you."

"Maybe you're right. But she's not imaginary. And even if she did abandon me, I'm grateful for what she did. She helped me state my case for my son and my species. There was no way that would have happened without her help."

"Yeah, that was kind of her. I guess. But if this friend of yours is so powerful, why can't she just wipe out the evil ones and be done with it?"

"I don't know. Maybe you should ask her."

"I will, if she ever shows herself." I put my head down and closed my eyes.

"Okay. I've told you all about me – what can you tell me about the drambats?"

I picked my head up and stared at the dirt floor, not wanting to talk about *that* and certainly not with a delusional ape. It might just send him over the edge. What if he hurts himself? But a promise is not to be flicked away lightly, at least that's what Pa used to say. "Okay," I said. "What would you like to know?"

"What can you tell me about the drambats and the arsnatcher?"

"Well there was a half-circle of drambats around that tall skinny one with the broken fang – his name is Ilgregious I believe. And they were chanting about some dark queen and how great she was. And then they grabbed an arsnatcher, just a hatchling, mind you. They grabbed the hatchling and threw him into the lava pit – and for no good reason that I could tell!"

"That's it?" asked the blue ape. "They threw an arsnatcher hatchling into a lava pit, and for no good reason?"

I gave him a blank stare, not wanting to admit the drambats believed in a being from the Phoberon too. "Yeah, well, I think... maybe they think the Dark Queen will give them things if they do stupid stuff like that."

"Who's this dark queen?"

"I'm not sure, exactly. There was this purple haze, like fog on a riverbank on a spring morning. Except it was purple and I don't know where it came from."

"In the Great Hall, you mentioned he floated around without his wings. How does that happen?"

I flicked my tongue and nearly reached his face with it. "Exactly! How *does* that happen?"

This conversation needed to be oh-ver.

"Do you think the dark queen had something to do with that?"

"I don't think so. Err, yeah, well... I don't know."

"But drambats don't just float about without their wings. Do you think it was the dark queen – or something else?"

This ape was nothing, if not persistent. "I don't know, and I really don't care."

"Really? That's it?"

"Yeah, really. Speaking of the dark queen, where's your friend, the one that floats through walls and stuff?"

The ape gave me a blank look. "Maybe she's not willing to show herself because you're here."

I nodded. "Yeah. She's probably scared. I'd be scared of me too."

The blue ape turned toward the vault door. "Jendal? You around? We could use some help here."

But there was no response. I grinned and said, "Save your breath, blue brain. Your imaginary friend isn't gonna show. I'm afraid there's not much to do but wait for morning and see what the Drakebureau does with us."

I put my head down on the dirt floor. Here I was, locked up in the Viper Vault with a blue ape. And on top of that, I'd been disqualified from the B.E.G. Cangoar could have died! It's not my fault no one else seems to understand that.

I'd saved Cangoar – and it didn't feel like I should be punished for it. But now I'd have to wait a few years to try to win the B.E.G. One thing was certain, though. I'd never let Urraca know I'd been disqualified. I closed my eyes hard. Maybe sleep would come quickly. And maybe when I wake up this nightmare would be oh-ver.

10. Twisted Drakes

Ilgregious led a contingent of thirteen drambats as they approached the guard hut at the Viper Vault. The guard bobbed his head twice as was the custom when greeting a member of the Drakebureau.

"I'm here by decree of Pinhammer," said Ilgregious. "We need to move the prisoners who disturbed the Great Hall to a facility in Trool where they can be de-briefed concerning tomorrow's agenda."

He showed the largest guard a stone tablet with the letters "D-Q-R-F" scrawled at the top along with the signature, "Yours Truly, Pin-ham-butt-brain", at the bottom.

The malwrack towered over the drambats. He gave Ilgregious a look that caused some of the others to take a step back. He looked at the tablet, then at Ilgregious, then scrunched his nose. "That's not Pinhammer's signature! And what is D-Q-R-F? What are you drambats up to – do you think I'm stupid?"

Ilgregious held his ground, his nose not more than a foot from the malwrack's. He raised up on his hind legs and scratched his right front leg until it bled. "Not as stupid as you *will* be," he muttered. "And D-Q-R-F stands for the Dark Queen Rules Forever."

The malwrack's lower jaw dropped as Ilgregious' eyes began to glow red. A second later he was inside the malwrack's head and riding the Queen's dark energy, bouncing from one memory to another.

Most of the malwrack's memories were happy – way too happy. He searched for a dark one and saw that the malwrack's name was Laudus and that his pa had been a commander in the Ape Wars.

Ah, there's something. During the Great Ape Wars Laudus followed his pa in a gaggle as they flew along the Galtan River in Seedred Forest. They were attacked by apes slinging rocks from the trees below. One broke the leading-edge of Pa's right wing. Ilgregious used dark energy from the Dark Queen to focus on the memory and forced it to repeat inside Laudus' head. The malwrack's eyes grew wide as Pa tumbled through the air more vividly than he had remembered.

Another six or seven apes jumped out of a tree onto Pa's back just before the big malwrack hit the river. Laudus swooped in hoping to light up the apes but took a stone to his left wing and crashed into the river upstream from where Pa had gone down. Three apes were on him as he thrashed in the water. Two had a lock on his snout while a third climbed up and attempted to gouge out his eyes. He flipped it off by thrashing his head back and forth but the other two held fast.

He plunged his head under water. No ape could hold their breath as long as he could. Eventually one let go and then the other, and he ended them before they reached the surface with his powerful jaws.

He surfaced and glanced around, scanning for the third ape. It was headed for shore. He was on it in a few seconds and put an end to it and then glanced around to see how Pa was doing. Three apes held Pa's snout closed while three others wrestled furiously to keep his head under water. There were too many – even for Pa.

Laudus dove into the current, but before he caught up to the struggle, he picked his head up. He watched Pa's big frame go limp. His anger burned as he caught up and dispatched three apes. The rest escaped while he went for Pa's body before it floated away.

Ilgregious felt a surge of dark energy as it forced the memory to play itself inside the beast's head. He licked his chops as they manipulated and twisted the memory. The malwrack's pride was his weakness, and together he and the Dark Queen told him, "It's your fault Pa died. He died because you were weak – too slow and stupid to save him."

The words dove deep into the malwrack's heart and mind, and a greedy grin appeared on Ilgregious' face as the malwrack went limp and fell over on his side.

When had a drambat ever gained the upper paw on a malwrack?

He barely managed to contain his euphoria as he looked up, thanked Her Darkness, then noticed two more guards. Another malwrack and a nickelneck – arriving at the guard hut.

The malwrack saw his buddy out cold, glanced at Ilgregious, and made a move toward his buddy. He didn't take two steps before Ilgregious focused on the malwrack's left ear. The malwrack's screech was cut short as dark energy penetrated his mind and took control of his body.

The nickelneck met a similar fate, and Ilgregious' grin grew wide as dark energy flowed through him and his victims. He scrunched his nose and bobbed his head at the sight of three huge guards, lying on the ground and helpless as hermit crabs in a snowstorm.

He glared at the other drambats. "Gut the malwracks and put a shackle on the nickelneck!"

The drambats glanced around as they struggled to get through the thickly scaled bellies of the malwracks using their claws and teeth.

"They can't fight back, you idiots, get on with it!"

Eventually the malwracks stopped breathing and they led the captive nickelneck away from a bloody mess at the guard hut. The nickelneck wore a dazed look and as they headed to cell eleven twenty-seven, he put up no resistance even though only two drambats held his chain. Ilgregious' thoughts wandered back to the night the Dark Queen had given him the ability to wield dark energy against his enemies.

The drambat and his minions had called for her that night, and Krimeny was more than happy to oblige. The first thing would be to see what made this stinky little drambat tick. She invaded its mind with a wave of dark energy and incapacitated the weak little beast, then began evaluating episodic memories in its neocortex. She nearly looked away, feeling somewhat conflicted. There was the usual exhilaration of invading another being's mind. But channeling dark energy into such a weak and putrid little creature – that just seemed, well, beneath her. It would be beneath any arsnarm, but she would endure whatever was necessary – for Korgarag and the Cause.

She pushed ahead and found a set of seemingly disconnected memories which shared a common theme. A slight grin appeared as she peered into a memory where he lost his parents when he was just a hatchling. Too young to understand why they were gone, he had gone to live with uncle Loadstifle and aunt Farth. A few years later they told him his parents fell into a lava pit while attempting to escape after robbing an arsnatcher's lair. Whether it was true or not didn't matter. It was what the little maggot-sack believed.

And if that wasn't delightful enough, a few years later they forced him to use his long and skinny frame as a bridge over a narrow canyon while younger drakes walked over his back on their way to ancient obelisks class. The canyon was fifteen-hundred feet deep and the young drambats weren't old enough to fly or legs strong enough to leap over. Day after day the little maggot-sack feared he would plunge to his death as he lunged for the root of a tree on the other side while holding onto a rock with his tail.

It was especially tenuous when Flimfluffer crossed. The drambat was a year younger but heavy-set and nearly twice Ilgregious' weight. And how delicious! The putrid little pestilence had nightmares about falling to his death – a hundred and seventy-five years later!

As if that weren't enough, there were days away from school when Loadstifle would hit rocks off his head with a steel striker tied to a hickory stick – like a big hammer. They called it an 'arbalink'. The maggot-sack's uncle used it to practice a game they called 'glour'.

It required a prairie dog village, an arbalink, and a big rock or boulder. The goal was to hit a boulder with the arbalink and try to get rock fragments in the prairie dog holes. Whoever got the most rocks in from a single strike won the round. There were usually five rounds – or until the holes were filled. Lots of practice was needed – and Loadstifle liked having company when he practiced. Ilgregious was forced to lay on the ground while his uncle hit rocks off the young drambat's head. The little pest hated that, but his uncle threatened to throw him in a lava pit if he didn't obey.

He heard other young drakes playing catch-a-newt around the neighborhood while he stayed as still as possible – hoping his uncle didn't miss. Occasionally a fragment flew off on a trajectory which damaged his snout. His top-right fang was broken, and the faculty of smell eludes him to this day.

Krimeny's grin widened – his uncle's obsession with such a silly little game caused so much pain in a young drambat's world. And having seen all these things in his past, it became clear that this putrid little pest could be controlled through the darkness of those experiences and through a dearth of healthy relationships. Not just in his younger days, but throughout his life.

This disgusting little drambat presented himself to her as a willing vehicle through which she would carry out the business of wreaking havoc in his realm. He had even proven his allegiance by sacrificing an innocent hatchling! How exquisite is that? Korgarag himself would be impressed. And so she bestowed on him the ability to wield dark energy against the minds of his enemies and to replace any faith, hope, or love he might find in their hearts and minds with fear, despair, and even malice.

But Krimeny had to pay a price to interact with this realm and would require this stupid little drambat to do the same. He must be willing to experience pain to activate her gift – he would be required to scratch himself until he bled. She had to suffer the waters of Livenmoore to engage these putrid little pests in this stupid realm of theirs, and she would make them pay a price for her power.

11. WHO DAT?

I partially opened my left eye. Was I still half asleep or did a blue aura surround the blue ape and illuminate our cell? I opened the other eye. The aura faded, and I wondered if I'd been dreaming. But when the blue ape's chords fell to the ground and the shackle fell off his neck, I opened both eyes. Wide. A second ape appeared where the aura had been. "Holy drambat dung, now there's two!" I exclaimed.

Bannabard glanced at the chords on the ground and smiled. "Thanks. I was beginning to wonder whether you were coming back."

"Where did you come from?" I asked.

"Sorry about that. I had some things to tend to," said the other ape as it fluffed his fur where the chords had matted it down.

I strained against the shackles. "Are you two deaf or deliberately ignoring me?"

The other ape glanced at me. "We're both deaf. Don't mind us."

"I can't tell you how good it is to see you, Jendal," said Bannabard. "I have to say it looks like our plan failed. Where do we go from here?"

"What happens next is up to you and your reptilian friend," the other ape said as it turned and faced me.

I glared back. "I'm not reptilian, you blue monkey. I'm a nickelneck!"

"And so you are," answered the blue ape with a cordial smile.

Bannabard gave the other ape a hard look. "What do we need the dragon for?"

"She's a witness to what the drambats are up to. If she's willing, that is."

I flicked my tongue. "Me willing? Of course not! Willing to do what?"

The other ape looked me in the eye, but it wasn't a cold or intimidating stare. "Why testify, of course – about the conjuring ceremony. You saw some dragons throw a hatchling into a lava pit. Am I right?"

I nodded. "Yeah, but how'd you know that? There was only one ape at the Stone Ingot."

"Oh yes, pardon me. Bannabard was the only one who knew I was there. My name is Jendal and I've been sent by Melohim to help the blue apes avoid extinction."

"What?" I flicked my tongue and bobbed my head slightly. "Melohim? Do you really expect me to believe you were sent by Melohim?" Perhaps they were just messing with me.

They know as well as I that Melohim is just a myth.

Jendal laughed. "I don't see why not. But you are free to believe what you like."

"Really? Believe – what she likes?" muttered Bannabard.

Jendal didn't answer him.

"Well that's mighty big of you," I said with a bit of a sneer.

Jendal faced me and bowed. "Isn't that right, Bannabard?"

"Oh, right," said Bannabard. He glanced at Jendal before bowing.

My sneer widened into a bit of a grin. "Now we're getting somewhere. My name is Alfedora and am pleased to meet you. It sounds like you know a little bit about nickelnecks."

The two blue apes straightened up. "What makes you say that?" asked Bannabard.

I scrunched my nose beneath the shackle. "Because your friend bowed."

"Yes, I know quite a bit about nickelnecks," said Jendal. "So will you?"

"Will I what?"

"Will you testify about the sacrifice – the hatchling?"

"I don't see what a nickelneck like me has to do with Ilgregious and his drambats."

"This isn't about what you have to do with drambats, but I think you know that," answered Jendal.

I arched against the chains, but they held fast. I slumped to the floor again. "I most certainly do not," I said with a cold stare. "I'd suggest you take this whole thing up with Farl — someone who might be able to do something about it. There's nothing I can do about a squabble between blue apes and drambats."

"Who's Farl?" asked Bannabard.

"He represents the nickelnecks on the Drakebureau," I answered.

"Oh, yeah. The one next to Gailryder."

"Yeah, you got it."

"Your concern for the hatchling is admirable," said Jendal. "But there was another besides the arsnatcher, wasn't there?"

I glanced at Bannabard, then back at Jendal. "Yeah."

"What was it?" asked Jendal.

I flicked my tongue. Twice. "I'd rather not say."

"He deserves to know," said Jendal. "If you won't tell him, I will."

I scrunched my nose. "It was a young blue ape."

Bannabard's eyes narrowed. "That was Gorby, wasn't it?"

Jendal put a hand on his shoulder. "Yes, it was. I'm so sorry."

"Is he alive?" Bannabard asked through clenched teeth.

"I'm afraid not," I answered. "But he was braver than the arsnatcher."

Bannabard's short legs buckled. His butt hit the floor and he pounded the ground with clenched fists. He looked up and glared at me.

"If it weren't for you dragons, my son would be alive!" he shouted.

He stood up, thumped his chest, and leapt at me, pounding my head with his fist. I swung my head as far as the chain allowed, trying to shake him off. But the ape clung to my neck with one hand while pounding my head and the shackle on my snout with the other.

The ape bloodied his fist as he pounded the steel shackle on my snout. I jerked my head left and right and tried to shake him off. Eventually the chain broke. I swung my head left and then swiftly back to the right. The ape went flying and crashed against the steel bars on the door of the cell. He slumped to the floor.

"Do that again, and I'll roast ya," I snarled.

Jendal held an open hand toward me. "Easy. He just found out his son is dead." She knuckle-walked over to him. "Bannabard, you okay?"

"I think a rib or two might be... It hurts to breathe."

"You're lucky that's all that hurts," I groused. Even if he did just lose his son.

Jendal gave me a hard look, then turned to Bannabard and put a hand on his side.

"Ouch!" The blue ape winced, then closed his eyes. "Ooh, that's nice." He rolled over on his back and inhaled deeply. "Thanks. I can breathe again."

Jendal steadied him as he got back on his feet. "Are you two going to be okay?"

I didn't respond.

Bannabard rubbed his side and glared at me. "Those drambats killed my son. They had no right. They had no reason." He got up in Jendal's face. "He was young – too young. Way too young..."

"I know," Jendal answered. "But attacking Alfedora – is that an appropriate response?"

"She's a dragon."

Jendal and Bannabard were nearly nose-to-nose. "Alfedora had nothing to do with Gorby's death," said Jendal. "But now we know it was Ilgregious. And if she hadn't spoken up, Ilgregious' secret sacrifices would have remained hidden."

"Yeah, and I wouldn't be locked up in these shackles," I said with a snarl.

Bannabard looked down for a second, then looked up at Jendal. "I guess..." He looked out through the cell door then turned and faced me. "I guess I owe you an apology, Alfedora. Sorry about that. Jendal's right, you're not like those drambats. How's your head?"

I nodded and looked away as gases built up and the urge to fling a fireball flooded my mind. The bent shackle was tighter around my snout than it had been – a fireball would never make it out of there. My eyes grew big. I turned to the cell door, my mouth clamped shut, my cheeks bulging.

Maybe if I don't click my teeth.

I let go a cloud of gas and a gooey mass. Somehow I managed to avoid igniting either one. Some of the fat and saliva made it through the shackle and clung to the bars of the cell door, but the bulk of it covered my snout and dangled from the shackle. A few strings of pale pink goo nearly reached the ground.

I jerked my head back and forth and flung the goo on the ceiling where it stuck and began to sag, almost like a shiny new stalactite. After coughing and sputtering a few times, I shook my head, then stared at the blue apes with wide eyes and a blank look.

"Sorry about that," I said. I turned to Bannabard. "My head? It'd take more than a few punches from a blue ape to hurt me." I flicked my tongue. "And sorry about your son, Bannabard. Why would drambats do such a thing?" My eyes grew moist.

Jendal turned to me. "Ilgregious loves neither his creator nor his fellow beings. He loves only power – and in a sense he's addicted to it. Once someone's addicted, they'd kill their own mum to feed the need."

"I know he's a leader of the Drakebureau, but what power can a drambat hope to wield?" I asked.

"*Do not* underestimate the Dark Queen," Jendal said. "She's nearly as powerful as me and hates all that we consider good in this realm."

"As powerful as you?" I asked with a grin. I didn't say it, but I was thinking, 'You're just an ape.'

"Yeah. As powerful as me." Her gaze bounced between Bannabard and me. "Can I trust you two to bury the maul?"

I flicked my tongue. "What maul? I don't have a maul."

Bannabard looked up and rolled his eyes slightly. "It's a metaphor. A maul is a weapon. You know, 'Bury the maul' – make peace?"

"Peace?" I snorted. "I guess I'm good if he's good."

Bannabard nodded. "Consider the maul buried."

I looked away – what a stupid phrase, 'bury the maul.' It's not like I could bury my claws or my fangs or the stuff inside me where fireballs come from.

Jendal smiled and touched the shackle on my snout. It fell to the ground.

I stretched my jaws and shook my head. "Thanks, but how in the name of a fat fiadhain did you do that?"

"You're quite welcome, but I have something to ask in return," said Jendal with a nod.

"What's that?"

"I hate to repeat myself, but will you testify about what you saw Ilgregious and the drambats do? The Drakebureau needs to hear about it."

I looked out through the bars in the cell door. As much as I wanted to put an end to any more talk about the Phoberon and Melohim and

Ilgregious and his Dark Queen, it wouldn't be right to roast Bannabard and his friend. After all, she did just get me out of that shackle.

Instead I turned to Jendal. "Ilgregious will convince the other leaders they can't trust me before I ever get the chance. I'm just a young nickelneck from Brangboor while he's been a leader on the Drakebureau for decades. Why would they listen to me? Besides, I already testified, and that's what got me thrown in *here*."

Jendal gave me a blank stare. "Well, for one thing, they'd listen because you're a dragon and not a blue ape. And second, you can leave getting the Drakebureau's attention up to me."

I bobbed my head. "Do we really need to stir up the Drakebureau when that stuff will probably never happen again?"

Jendal glanced at Bannabard, then fixed her gaze on me. "What Ilgregious and his minions did at the lava pit is like the first smoke from a volcano that's about to erupt. Many more will suffer and die if the Drakebureau doesn't put a stop to it."

My eyes lit up. "Volcano? I love volcanos! There's nothing quite like the smell of fresh ash and lava on a hillside. Or the sound of sizzling dew first thing in the morning."

"It's another metaphor," said Bannabard. "There's no volcano."

"Rats. I love volcanos."

Jendal glanced at Bannabard and then stared at me. "More hatchlings will die if we do nothing. Are you willing to testify before the Drakebureau?"

My gaze turned back to the bars in the cell door. There would be consequences if I testified against a leader of the Drakebureau. And I had always been taught to respect the Drakebureau above all other things (except perhaps my stash of gold). In any case, I didn't want to give up what little chance I had to lead a normal life – the life of a young, attractive, gold-snatching, bear-eating nickelneck in her prime. "Why would I do that?" I muttered.

Bannabard gave me a fierce look. "Maybe because other dragons and apes will die if you don't."

The sound of the drambat dirge and the image of a hatchling being thrown into a lava pit played in my mind. I looked at the ground, then at the blue apes. "Well, maybe you guys are right. I'll give it a shot. But I'm doing this for the hatchlings – and only the hatchlings. And I have one condition – don't ask me to appear in the middle of that Stone Ingot. I don't want anything to do with dark energy, or anything weird from other realms."

12.   FREEDOM FEIGNED

"I 'll take that as a yes," said Jendal. "And if Melohim grants us success in exposing Ilgregious' deeds to the Drakebureau, it will be interesting to see how Pinhammer and the others deal with the situation."

I glared at Jendal. "You're pulling my tail. You're going to leave it up to Pinhammer? What if he sides with Ilgregious?"

Jendal put a hand on my shoulder. "I get it – sometimes it feels like no one can be trusted."

She had barely finished speaking when something like a malwrack screech whistled through the corridor. It was cut short – as if swallowed by a great sack.

I bobbed my head. "Sounds like something's up at the guard hut!"

Jendal touched the ground at my feet. The leg and tail shackles fell to the ground. I shook my jowls.

How does she do that?

"Thanks!" I exclaimed. It was great to stretch my legs and thrash my tail again.

Jendal gestured for us to keep our voices down. "Follow me," she whispered. "I hadn't planned on busting you out of here, but if Ilgregious is up to something, I'm afraid we'll have no choice."

She breathed on the steel bars of the cell door, which became liquid and flowed into a puddle of silver on the floor of the cave.

"Whoa, that's weirder than a fat fiadhain falling in love with a toad," I whispered to Bannabard. I licked my chops. "Did you see that?" I asked.

Bannabard took a step back. "Yeah, that's weird all right."

"Quiet," whispered Jendal. "We don't want the drambats to hear us."

"Why not?" I whispered as I bobbed my head. "Between Bannabard, me, and your magic tricks, they wouldn't stand a chance."

"Shhh!" Jendal gestured with a finger to her lips. "Melohim has not sent me here to fight drambats," she whispered emphatically. "I am here to help those who cannot help themselves, and I won't be able to do that if we don't follow certain rules."

"Well that's no fun," I whispered to no one in particular.

Jendal led us away from the cell and into a corridor down a different row of vaults. In a direction away from the guard hut.

"Isn't the guard hut that way?" I whispered, pointing behind.

"Yes," whispered Jendal. "We need to go around. There are drambats coming down those halls."

"Look at that," I whispered, pointing ahead with the first claw on my right-front paw.

A solitary young drambat was headed our way. Apparently it had wandered away from the others and hadn't noticed us in the dimly-lit corridor. Oblivious to our presence, it was engrossed in a variant of the dirge I had heard a few nights before.

"Yay-oh. Yay-oh – ooh, we gutted them guards and we'll gut her too! Yay-oh. Yay-oh – ooh. Together they'll make a smelly old stew. Yay-oh. Yay-oh. Yah-oh – ooh."

The drambat was doing a dance as it sauntered along, and it was hard not to laugh at what was sort of a two-step boogie with a stiff, mechanical move every fourth step or so. I suppressed a grin and remembered the hatchling and Bannabard's son. "Give me one second with that slithering little worm-eater," I muttered through clenched teeth.

Jendal got all up in my snout. "No. Now's not the time. There'll be a time and a place for that later. But right now, I need both of you to follow me." She slid up against the left side of the corridor and motioned for Bannabard and me to do the same.

I scrunched against the wall as the drambat drew closer – barely breathing as I waited for him to pass by. The corridor was wide enough for two malwracks – plenty of room to stay out of the drambat's path. Bummer, that.

It continued dancing as it sang, "Yay-oh. Yay-oh – ooh. We gutted them guards and we'll gut her too! Yay-oh. Yay-oh – ooh. Malwracks and nickelnecks thinking they're so cool! Yay-oh. Yay-oh. Yay-oh – ooh."

Was this fool singing about me? Bring it on, you sorry little slug-sucker!

As the drambat passed by – one swipe of my claws could have ended it but I restrained myself. I hoped it would notice a few strings of saliva hanging off my bared fangs, but it didn't. I kept silent while the drambat continued its dirge and dance. And with no apparent urgency, it turned left and headed toward the cell we just came from.

Jendal seemed to know where she was going – I followed her and Bannabard as we approached the guard hut. I nearly retched when we encountered the remains of two malwracks – guards who were barely recognizable. I turned to Bannabard and whispered, "It would take four or five drambat gaggles to bring down a single malwrack! And there were *two* malwracks here."

I gawked at the bodies, then turned away and shook my jowls. How could drambats do that to another drake – even if they were malwracks? Couldn't the Drakebureau do something to prevent this sort of thing? Oh, wait. Ilgregious *is* the Drakebureau.

"What's a gaggle?" whispered Bannabard.

"Weren't you in the Ape Wars?" I asked.

Bannabard shrugged and whispered, "Oh, yeah, it's what, about five to seven drakes trained to fight together?"

I gave him a nod.

Jendal turned to me and whispered, "You are right to wonder how drambats defeated these malwracks. They had help. I'll tell you about it later. Let's keep moving."

She pointed to her right and headed toward the commoner's exit. The Daor Gate was to our right as we left the Viper Vault and was unguarded. Bannabard pushed against the gate, but it didn't budge.

"What do we do now?" he whispered.

"Shouldn't be a problem," said Jendal as she pressed down on the latch and opened the gate. She pointed to her head as she passed by.

I closed the gate behind us using my tail. "We made it," I announced in a muffled, but excited tone. "Where to next?"

The sky was clear, and the moon was full as we followed Jendal across the meadow to the trees on the edge of the forest.

Jendal turned and faced us both. "Ilgregious will be hot on your tails once they find your cell empty. But it won't be just him and his drambats – he'll have the forces of Flargellion after you. Alfedora, can you fly while carrying Bannabard? And can I trust you not to eat him along the way?"

Bannabard's eyes narrowed. "Did you just say, 'eat him along the way'?"

"Yeah. Alfedora, can I trust you not to make a snack out of our friend?"

I gave Jendal a quizzical glance — why was that even a question? Blue apes don't even *smell good.* "Oh yeah. Shouldn't be a problem. As long as there's game around, he'll be fine." Which reminded me, I *was* hungry.

"Okay, good," said Jendal. "I need you two to look out for each other and head to the canyons in Farshen."

I gave Jendal a blank stare and flicked my tongue. "The canyons of Farshen. Really? Farshen's a desert — there'll be naught but catfish and lizards out there."

"Flargellion will be after you — with malwrack gaggles. You need to lay low for a while."

I bobbed my head. "We should have killed Ilgregious and his drambats when we had the chance."

"He would have done to you what he did to those malwracks," said Jendal.

I bobbed my head and glared at the Daor Gate. "I'd like to see him try."

"He doesn't fight fair," said Jendal. "Krimeny — uh, the Dark Queen — gives him power to invade minds. They disable their opponents so they can't fight back."

"But you could stop him from invading my mind, right?"

"It would devolve into a battle between myself and the Dark Queen," said Jendal. "One which would kill Ilgregious — and likely others. Including you and Bannabard."

I glared at Jendal. "That's a risk I'd be willing to take — if it would save a few hatchlings."

"Your concern for the hatchlings is a credit to you," said Jendal. "But I will not risk the lives of other beings in your realm."

I bobbed my head and glared at Jendal. "Then you are the one who is weak."

"It is not weak to control your passions when you have the power to do otherwise. There is no honor in a dosara engaging in violence which might cause weaker beings to be hurt. Melohim would not be pleased."

I gave Jendal a blank stare. "Melohim, schmellohim!" I exclaimed. "How can I believe in someone who never shows himself, claims to be all-powerful, and won't lift a finger to save innocent hatchlings?"

"The hatchling is with him now," answered Jendal.

I glared at her. "As if. As if you expect me to believe. All I know is an innocent hatchling suffered and is gone."

"There are times when you have to trust things you can't see or don't understand."

"No surprise you'd say *that*," I said as I bobbed my head. "You want me to trust things I don't understand, but if you're not willing to use your powers while the Dark Queen uses hers – where does that leave *us?*"

"Power corrupts," answered Jendal.

"So if Melohim is all-powerful, then *he* must be corrupt," I said with a wry smile.

"No," said Jendal as her eyes narrowed. "He is all-powerful, but never forces others – even the beings he created – to do anything against their will. He values the free-moral agency of all creatures – more than you can imagine."

I bobbed my head again. "So he's all-powerful. Yet he does nothing while Ilgregious throws innocent hatchlings into a lava pit?"

"Yeah, I think you're starting to get it."

"Who's the Dark Queen?" asked Bannabard.

"She exists in the Numinous – what the drakes call the Phoberon. She used to be a dosara like me. At one time her name was Stella and was more powerful than I. Sad to say, but she's become a shadow of her former self."

"Why would she do that?" I asked. Wait. Why was I talking as if this stuff were real? This talk of Melohim and the Phoberon – I'd been told these were nothing but farty-snartch tales.

"Together she and Korgarag have led many dosara astray," said Jendal. "We call them 'arsnarms'. Korgarag is their leader and they hate Melohim and everything and everyone he has ever created."

I thought of the hatchling and the young blue ape. "That makes no sense. How can anyone hate everything and everybody?"

Jendal's eyes flashed. "And the one Ilgregious calls 'the Dark Queen' has given up the name 'Stella' in our realm. Now she is known as 'Krimeny'. She has grown twisted and weaker than she once was – loving power above all other things. So much so that they are willing to consume one another in their struggle for personal power."

"A bunch of farty-snartch tales," I muttered – mostly to myself.

Jendal gave me a hard look. "It's as real as the Drakebureau and Flargellion."

"I understand power corrupts – but why consume one another?" asked Bannabard.

"Their love for power has made them enemies of Melohim, and he has given them what they have chosen – an existence apart from him. They hate all who haven't joined their rebellion and label them as haters – haters of their view that might makes right and haters of the power they believe they are entitled to. They cannot comprehend how Melohim could love creatures that are weaker and more fragile than themselves. Unable to create, they corrupt whoever and whatever they meet. In a certain sense – we should feel pity for Ilgregious."

I licked my chops. "Okay, I think I'm starting to get it. The Dark Queen is free to use her power however she wishes, but you are not."

"Yes... and no," answered Jendal. "We exist in the realm of dark matter and dark energy – what you call the Phoberon and blue apes call the Numinous. We are more powerful than any creature in this realm, yet none can interact with your realm unless we first drink from the river Livenmoore. And even then we can intervene only when a creature in this realm asks us to."

"Yeah, right," I said scrunching my nose. "The society of drakes would think me daft if I bought into these farty-snartch tales about arsnarms and dosara and the Phoberon."

The river Livenmoore – really?

Jendal gave me a hard look. "For the dosara, the waters of Livenmoore are sweet, but for arsnarms, they are bitter. There are few left who can endure it. Korgarag himself cannot, and while Krimeny can still do it, even after having drunk the water, she cannot interact with this realm unless someone opens a window or a crack through which she can work."

I scrunched my nose and looked away.

"In other words, the Dark Queen needs someone like Ilgregious to get her foot in the door," said Bannabard.

"Exactly," said Jendal. "Without someone like him, her hands are tied. But enough about arsnarms. You two need to get moving. I'll meet you in Farshen – in a couple days."

The blue ape morphed into a black orb and disappeared. My jaw dropped. I shook my head and flicked my tongue. Dare I believe? But I just saw it. "Enough about arsnarms, indeed. And the Phoberon too," I muttered. "The Drakebureau is what's real. It's what really matters – where the future will be forged."

"What?" asked Bannabard.

"Oh nothing," I said. Now wasn't the time to get into a discussion about realms and societies and solving the world's problems. "Let's do this," I said as I bent my right front leg and motioned Bannabard to climb up. His arms locked around my neck. I hoped he wouldn't fall off as I arched my back and leapt into the air – toward the canyons of Farshen.

13. CELL ELEVEN TWENTY-SEVEN

lgregious and his drambats reached cell eleven twenty-seven and found it empty. Even the bars on the door were gone. He scrunched his nose at the thought of not being able to do the nickelneck who had tried to ruin him. How could she have escaped? Tonight should have been the end of her and that insolent little ape. He bobbed his head and thrashed his tail – twice. "I knew I couldn't trust those guards. I'd have their heads if we hadn't already gutted them!"

He glared at his prisoner and stretched to get up in the nickelneck's snout. "Cangoar," he snarled. "Tell me what you know, or you'll end up like your malwrack friends. How did the female and that blue ape get free?"

The prisoner straightened up a bit and towered over him. "I don't know, your Drakeness. The vault was locked and the prisoners secured when Lutjen and I left them an hour ago."

"Nonsense!" shouted Ilgregious. "You're lying. You expect me to believe they escaped without any help?"

Some of the drambats snorted and a few chanted, "Yay-oh. Yay-oh – ooh. We gutted his friends, we'll gut him too."

"Silence!" shouted Ilgregious. "Let's see if this nickelneck has the foresight and the courage – to tell the truth."

The prisoner flicked his tongue and said, "I'm sorry your Drakeness. That's as much as I know."

Ilgregious glared at Cangoar and stretched out his arm. "Then this will be the last thing you know."

The prisoner looked up, looked down, closed his eyes, and muttered, "I don't know if you're there, or if you can hear me, but I could use your help... and thanks, Melo—"

"Silence!" interrupted Ilgregious. "Forget about that myth. You will soon know the power of Her Darkness. Up close and personal." He scratched his left arm and chanted in a sing-song voice, "Oh great and mighty Queen, grant your precious powers to thy servant once more! Together, let us bring down this beast which is greater than I and may the fear of your Darkness rise among all creatures, great and small!"

His red eyes focused on Cangoar's right ear, but something wasn't right. He couldn't penetrate the nickelneck's head. Instead, thoughts of young dragons falling to their deaths in a canyon and being disfigured by adult drambats practicing glour invaded *his* mind. Ilgregious screeched and fell to the ground. Fear and the pain of his hatchling days gripped his mind. He writhed with front paws clamped to his head. His legs moved frantically as if he were running. Running from Loadstifle. Faster and faster he ran. Why couldn't he fly? His left wing was stuck.

It couldn't have been more than a minute or two, but it seemed like an hour later when the images finally abated. He stumbled to his feet, shook his head, and began to gather himself. "How did *that* happen?" he muttered.

He looked up as three drambats came at him with bared teeth and shining claws still red with malwrack blood. He bobbed his head, clenched his teeth, and tried again. They wanted *his* power, and that is what he would give them. A taste of dark energy! He entreated the Dark Queen and felt her power flowing through him. Again. And this time it didn't turn against him. Dark energy entered their minds and they fell over. Ilgregious ended the helpless drakes with his claws.

Unfortunate they were drambats — but an example the others needed to see. How stupid could they have been? They know nothing of the Dark Queen's power. He bobbed his head, flapped his wings, and glared at the others. "Anyone else?" he snarled.

The largest of the remaining drambats glanced around, then bowed low. "No, my lord, we are your loyal and humble servants — to the end."

Ilgregious scrunched his nose, exposing sharp, needle-like teeth and a broken fang. It was a shame those fools had to die, simply because they failed to understand that the Dark Queen had chosen him and him alone.

"Garsniffle, your loyalty will not go un-rewarded," he said as he glared at the others. "Now, can someone please explain how our prisoner got away?"

Garsniffle glanced around, then turned to Ilgregious with a sheepish look. "When you were incapacitated, your Drakeness, the nickelneck overpowered us and flew off." His tone went slightly higher at the end, as if it were more of a question than a statement. "Your Drakeness," he added – as if he were convincing himself.

Ilgregious bobbed his head and looked away. "You had him by a shackle! How could you let that newt-tongued nickelneck escape?"

"We're not sure, your Drakeness," stammered one of the other drambats before stepping back, lowering her head, and staring at her feet.

Ilgregious glared at her. At least she was smart enough to fear his power.

"We couldn't hold him without your power, your Drakeness. He broke loose and took off that way," said Garsniffle, pointing toward a corridor leading to the guard station. "Went right past the 'No-Fly Zone' sign with wings flapping and chains flailing."

"Yes," said another. "We needed your power, your Drakeness. You are great – greater even than the malwracks – your Drakeness."

Ilgregious bobbed his head. The last thing he needed was that nickelneck to be running off at the mouth about what happened here tonight. "I fear Melohim might have interfered," he muttered.

Garsniffle shook his head. "Oh no, my lord! You yourself have said that Melohim is nothing but a myth, a fairy tale. A legend at best."

Ilgregious turned away and licked the wound on his left forearm.

A myth indeed. It was a mistake to mention the enemy, but how dare this turd of a toad question me!?

"Ah, yes, you're right, my gray-headed friend," he muttered.

A few members of the group bobbed their heads and snorted.

"Silence!" he shouted. "You are quite right, Garsniffle. Melohim is nothing. Nothing but a myth. That nickelneck had a weapon, and I suspect it was developed by arsnatchers. I caught a glimpse of it just before I became incapacitated. It affected me more than I could have imagined. Tiny metal plates wedged under the scales on his head. Only the slimiest of species could think of such a thing. And that is why we must stick together. That is why we must fight the evil that is arrayed against us at every turn. Because if we fail to stand against those who oppress us, they will take our treasure, our offspring, our hunting grounds, and make us their slaves."

Garsniffle bobbed his head. "Yes, we shall fight for our freedom! All hail your Drakeness, all hail! Your Drakeness!"

A few of the drambats shot flames in the air while others bonked heads.

Ilgregious raised his snout with a sneer and flicked his tongue. "I do not say these things for myself. Sometimes what needs to be done is for the greater good of all drakes everywhere. If we don't fight for our rights, Drakedom will devolve into one giant gaggle of greedy, bigoted, stater-grubbing beasts. And our fair species... the only species which has evolved beyond all others – beyond those which have scales – will be at the mercy of them all."

"No!" gasped Garsniffle and a few others.

"Yes!" sneered Illgregious. "And we will continue to be oppressed by bigger, stronger, and faster species than ourselves. It is because of this that I'm afraid our great society – the greatest society ever – may be on the verge of collapse! And why we must fight for justice... real justice – for the weak, the disenfranchised, and the stater-challenged among us."

"Forgive us for doubting you, your Drakeness," said Garsniffle as he bowed low. "You are both wise and powerful, and I speak for all of us when I say we would follow you to the ends of..."

"Silence!" interrupted Ilgregious. His eyes flashed as he thrashed his tail back and forth. "Enough talk. We have work to do. There will be an investigation. And the security detail must be given every opportunity to convince themselves that Cangoar is in league with Alfedora and that he killed those two guards and set the prisoners free."

The other drambats bowed low.

"Let truth prevail!" exclaimed Garsniffle.

"Long live the Drakebureau and long live your Drakeness!" exclaimed a short squatty drambat.

"Long live your Drakeness!" bellowed the others before they began the work of making the escape of Alfedora and Bannabard and the death of the malwracks at the guard hut look like an inside job.

They incinerated the remains of the dead drambats, scrubbed the soot and blood off the floor, and replaced the door with one which had bars. After covering the metal on the floor with dirt, they left the door open and went to the guard hut where they smashed the gate to make it look like there had been a struggle between Cangoar and the malwrack guards.

Ilgregious, satisfied with their work, led them outside. The sun was about to make an appearance as they filed out the Daor Gate. Once outside, they began chattering and carrying on about how they killed not one, but two malwracks.

Ilgregious slapped a couple of them up the side of the head. "Silence, you fools! Not a word of this to anyone, or you'll end up like those malwracks. The security detail must reach its own conclusions about what happened here tonight. Split up on your way back to Trool, and if anyone sees those nickelnecks or that blue ape along the way, I want to be the first to know about it."

The drambats took off – their nearly black silhouettes against an orange sky – and headed in disparate directions. Ilgregious was the last to flip a wing. He watched as the others turned back to the north and east – toward their lairs in the hill country in eastern Trool. He glanced back at Flargellion. The Daor Gate was lit up and glowed red – lit by the morning sun and redder than he'd ever seen it. "Reminds me of the Red Lair," he muttered as he banked right and headed south.

14. Lunch, Interrupted

few days earlier, Bannabard had just returned from Lake Luellian to his hut. Ape Town was the last large settlement of apes in the middle of the Great Seedred Forest. Lais was there with their three offspring. Gorby, the youngest, knuckled up and swung into Bannabard's arms. "Pa's home!" he exclaimed.

Bannabard looked into Gorby's face. "Hey big guy, you been taking care of things while I been gone?" He gave Lais a peck on her furry blue cheek without waiting for an answer from Gorby. "Hey hon', how's it hangin'?"

Lais smiled and exhaled. "We're hangin'. And am I glad to see you! These guys need to get out and swing from some vines or something."

"Hey Pa, can we go fiadhain hunting?" asked Hotch, their oldest. "I'm hungry."

"Yeah! Can we go foodheen hunting?" parroted Gorby.

Reebus, the middle-aged one, sneered. "It's fiadhain, you blue baboon."

Bannabard managed to keep a straight face while Lais gave Reebus a stern look.

"O-kayyyyyy. Sorrrrry," muttered Reebus while looking at Lais.

"Don't tell me," she answered.

"Okayyyy," Reebus said while turning to Gorby. "I'm. Sorry. I. Called. You. A. Blue. Baboon. Yeeeesh."

"Thank you," said Lais. "I think a hunt would be a great idea. A wild boar could feed us for a week."

"C'mon' Mum, they're called FEE-AHH-DANE," said Reebus.

"Oh, right. Foodheen." Said Lais as she winked at Gorby.

106

Bannabard put a hand on Reebus' shoulder. "Great! Now that we've had our lessons... It's time... For everyone... To head out... And grab yourself... A vine!"

"Yeah!" Reebus and Gorby exclaimed, almost in unison.

"Which way we goin', Pa?" asked Hotch. "My friend Karbis says they've been rooting around the western part of the forest near the Galtan River."

Bannabard turned to Hotch. "And do you trust your friend Karbis?"

Hotch's eyes lit up. "Yeah! He and his pa caught three down there a few weeks ago."

Bannabard turned to Reebus and Gorby. "Well, upon the recommendation of Karbis and his pa, it's settled then. We're off to the Galtan!"

"Off to the Galtan River!" Reebus exclaimed.

"Off to Galtland!" exclaimed Gorby.

The others followed as Bannabard knuckled up and bounded past a few dozen huts, down a path toward the forest, and out of town. He turned and waited at the base of a redwood as Lais and the young apes bounded up behind him. "Reebus, you go first, then Gorby, then Hotch. Your mum and I will be right behind."

Up the tree they went. It was one they were familiar with – nearly a third of a furlong tall and enough vines for all. Bannabard grabbed one and launched himself. He looked back to make sure Lais and the boys followed as he swung from one tree to the next.

Gorby had just learned to swing one vine to another, and Bannabard checked back frequently to make sure everyone was keeping up.

It wasn't long after they reached the river when Lais spotted one. "Hey Bannabard! Down there!" she exclaimed in a hushed voice and pointed to the right bank a short distance ahead.

"Wow, that's a big one. Good eye, hon'!" He looked back, made sure Reebus and Gorby were close, then whispered, "Let's get that fat fiadhain! Follow me and see if you can keep up!"

They were about fifty feet above the river as Bannabard swung and let go of his vine just before the bottom of its arc. Like an eight-hundred-pound flying squirrel, he launched himself toward another vine, caught it with his right hand, swung for a moment, and landed gracefully on the sand next to the river.

Lais and Hotch were right behind, and the three of them surrounded the fiadhain. The startled boar glanced at Bannabard, spun to its right, stared at Lais, spun further right and then charged Hotch. His son deftly grabbed its tusks while Bannabard put an end to its squealing with a blade he had fashioned from a fiadhain tusk. A little later Reebus and Gorby climbed down a vine and the five of them made a circle around their catch on the sandy bank next to the river.

"What a fat foodheen!" exclaimed Gorby.

"Yeah, that's a hefty one," said Lais.

Bannabard winked at Hotch. "Yeah, we'll have to thank your friend Karbis next time we see him."

"How big do you think he is, Pa?" Reebus asked.

"I'm guessing four or five hundred pounds."

"I'm so hungry I could eat a drambat!" exclaimed Gorby.

"Ewww," Reebus said, "who'd wanna eat a drambat?"

Gorby gave Reebus an icy stare. "I would!"

Hotch pulled out a knife and began skinning the beast. He glanced up at Gorby. "That's disgusting, Gorb. Drambats are all leathery and bony and slimy."

"That's what I like about 'em."

Reebus sneered. "You would."

Lais glared at the young ones. "That's enough, you two."

"I hate it when Hotch sides with Reebus," muttered Gorby.

Bannabard looked out across the river. He turned to Lais – maybe they could come up with a way to keep the young ones entertained while they cleaned the catch.

"Wouldn't it be great if we had something to go with this?" she asked – as if she knew his thoughts.

Bannabard nodded. "Hotch, we need you and your brothers to find some firewood, so we can cook this thing. And maybe hunt up some tubers or mushrooms while you're at it."

Hotch continued working on the carcass without looking up. "Pa, I'm busy – I need to finish skinning this guy."

"Don't worry. Mum and I will finish."

Hotch looked away. "Why can't they go without me? I wanted to skin this one – by myself."

Bannabard put a hand on Hotch's shoulder. "You know Reebus isn't old enough to take care of Gorby without some help. You can skin the next one. I promise."

"Okay, but only if I get to do all of it." Hotch started to hand the knife to Bannabard, then withdrew his hand and waited for a response.

Bannabard gave Hotch's shoulder a gentle squeeze and said, "I guess you'll have to trust me."

"You know I do, Pa." Hotch handed him the knife and turned to his brothers. "Reebus. Gorby. Let's go."

Reebus jumped up and together they headed upriver.

Gorby had just started playing in the water and looked up and saw them leaving. "I get to go, too!" he protested, scrambling to catch up.

Reebus looked back. "Mum, Gorby's not gonna be able to keep up!"

Lais gave Reebus a stern look. "You can wait for him."

"But muu-uuum…"

"But nothing," interrupted Lais. "He'll help you carry some wood and maybe find some tubers or mushrooms."

Gorby caught up, grinned, and tried to get in Reebus' face but wasn't tall enough. "Yeah, maybe I'll find some tubers or rats or something."

Reebus gave Gorby a nudge. "Yeah, right."

It was gentle enough and Bannabard appreciated that Gorby didn't whine about it. He watched as the three brothers headed upriver. "Hey Hotch – try to find an easy vine to climb."

"I will, Pa. We'll throw the firewood on the riverbank."

Bannabard smiled at Lais. "Good job hon'. This is nice. Just the two of us dressing a fat foodheen."

Lais smiled. "Yeah, right. Nothing says romance like skinning a beast together. And it's fee-ah-dane."

"Oh, right. Fee-ah-dane," said Bannabard.

The sun was high in the sky by the time they had nearly finished cleaning the carcass.

"Where do you think the boys are?" asked Lais. "They should be back by now, don't you think?"

Bannabard smiled. "They're probably playing in the river – they'll be back soon – don't worry your pretty blue…"

His words were interrupted by a screech. His eyes locked on hers.

She said what they were both thinking. "That sounded like…"

"A drambat!" they exclaimed in unison.

Bannabard dropped his knife. They knuckled up, bounding upriver as fast as their long arms and short legs could carry them. They skirted a bend. Bannabard's eyes darted up and down – studying tracks in the sand while scanning the sky above.

"There!" Lais shouted, as she pointed to three drambats flying upriver, the farthest one carrying what looked like their youngest son.

They halted abruptly and stood with nostrils flaring, bodies erect, staring at the little one struggling to free himself from the grip of a dragon heading west.

Bannabard beat his chest as he scanned the sky, the trees, the ground.

"GORBEEEE!!" shrieked Lais – longer and louder than he thought was possible.

There. A rounded stone by the river. He picked it up and heaved it with everything he had. It whistled through the air and clipped the trailing drambat's right wing. The drambat banked left, screeched, and headed toward them. The second drambat followed, while the third looked back but continued flying upriver *with their son.*

Bannabard's eyes narrowed. It would do Gorby no good if they got roasted. He turned to Lais and yelled, "Get behind those boulders!" They ducked between three boulders and the wall of the canyon. "I wish I had my sling," he muttered to himself. "Brace yourself. There's gonna be some heat!"

The boulders were tall enough to provide cover without having to crouch.

"Grab some stones – the rounder the better!" he exclaimed.

Lais jumped out and heaved a stone but missed. She stood and glared at the drambat, then dodged a fireball and jumped back behind the boulder.

Bannabard glanced between Lais and the drambat. "Not yet, hon'. Wait until they pass by. Keep your head up and don't let them get a clear shot at you. Once they go by – jump out and aim for the thin bones that support the wings."

He kept one eye on Gorby and another on the two drambats. They came in fast and hot, launching fireballs that mostly crashed into the ground or the boulders. He stepped aside as one hit the wall of the

110

canyon above and behind. Gooey, flaming remnants fell where he once stood.

The drambats passed over and banked left to make another pass. They both jumped out, heaving stones at the nearest one. One hit its mark and buckled the drambat's right wing. They watched it crash into the river, its wing flailing as it fell.

The other drambat looked back at its companion struggling in the water, then took off in the other direction, leaving the wounded drake to fend for itself. Bannabard caught Lais' eye and gave her a nod. They bounded to the river and crashed into the water. The wounded drambat floundered in the current as they moved to intercept it.

Its eyes grew wide as it struggled. It shot a fireball which nearly hit Bannabard. They were on it an instant later. Bannabard locked his arms around its snout and forced its head under water. Lais locked her jaws on its left front leg and grabbed its right-front leg with her hands to keep it from clawing at them. The drake was on its back, its rear legs flailing and clawing as it struggled to free itself.

Bannabard held its head under as it thrashed back and forth. It took a while, but eventually it felt like the beast was nearly done. He pulled its head out of the water. "Tell me," he snarled. "Where are they taking my son?!"

The drambat coughed, hacked, and sucked in some air. Then it looked Bannabard in the eye and grinned defiantly.

"Tell me, drambat! Where?!"

The beast's eyes narrowed. "Never!"

"If that's how you want it," he said.

Down went its head. After a while he pulled it back up, its eyes wide as it coughed and gasped for air.

"Where are they taking my son?!" he demanded.

The drambat caught its breath and grinned again.

Lais howled. He glanced over. Her back was bloody. The beast's rear feet and claws.

Crap, that looks bad.

Down went the drambat's head, this time with a wrenching of its neck. He wouldn't risk further injury to Lais. The drake thrashed about for a moment and went limp.

Bannabard and Lais let go and watched the carcass float away, belly-side up. They inhaled, glanced at one another, then glanced upriver in time to see the other two drambats disappear over the tree-lined horizon.

He pivoted back to Lais. There were gaping wounds on her back. Her breathing was heavy and labored.

"Gorby. Got to get Gorby. Back..." she said just before fainting.

He cradled her as she fell over, careful not to touch her wounds. His head swiveled up and down the riverbank. There. A vine. He hiked Lais over his shoulder as gingerly as he could and headed for it, wondering if he had the strength to get them to the top. He glanced up and down the river – wondering about Hotch and Reebus. Were they safe?

He grabbed the vine with his left hand while holding her on his shoulder with the right. He hiked up on the vine and managed to wrap his feet around it. His feet bore most of their weight but slipped a bit each time he slid his left hand up the vine – between one-armed pull-ups.

Eventually they made it to the top. He shook out his nearly limp left arm. His eyes scanned the ground for a path as he carried her through bushes and tall grass. There – a path.

He laid Lais gently on her side, making sure her wounds stayed off the dirt. He needed to get her back to Ape Town but wanted to give providence a chance before he left.

"HOTCH!" he yelled. "REEBUS!"

The words echoed – as if to mock him. As if to mock his family. "So much for providence," he muttered.

He looked up the path and yelled there too but didn't get a response. No telling where they might be. He'd have to trust Hotch to take care of Reebus while he took care of Lais.

He picked her up and cradled her over his shoulder. She was unconscious – but breathing. He tried not to touch her wounds and headed toward Ape Town. Fergal would know how to dress her wounds. After what seemed like hours of one-handed knuckle-walking, he finally caught a glimpse of huts poking through treetops as the path crested a hill.

They emerged from the forest on the west end of town. It wasn't long before other apes joined them. Young and old followed, chattering and murmuring as they headed to the community hut.

"What happened to Lais?" they asked, mostly to one another.

112

He felt the eyes of some of the younger ones as they gawked at her gaping wounds.

"Looks like she fell off a cliff," said one young ape.

Bannabard kept silent, wondering if she'd be all right. But they persisted. Eventually he snarled, "Drambats."

A couple of them howled. A few young males beat their chests and pounded the ground with their fists. Two spun around, howled, and tossed dirt in the air.

"Not surprised. Not surprised at all," muttered an older ape. "I remember a time when apes and dragons respected one another and run-ins were rare. These days, well, not so much. Them drambats been a plague ever since the war ended."

They were nearly at the community hut when Bannabard turned to the others. "Find Fergal!" he commanded.

"Sure thing," answered a young male as he knuckled up and bounded off.

Bannabard arrived at the community hut and laid Lais on a bench as gently as he could. The young male returned with Fergal. Bannabard looked up at Fergal, flared his nostrils, and muttered, "Drambat."

Fergal examined her wounds. "She's lost a lot of blood. I'm afraid there's a good chance of infection with drambat wounds."

Bannabard looked up and closed his eyes. He was torn between staying with Lais or going back to find Hotch and Reebus. As Fergal started cleaning the wounds, he muttered, "Our sons are missing."

The adrenaline began to wear off and reality started to sink in.

Gorby.

His legs buckled. His knees hit the floor. He held his head in his hands as if shielding his mind. He didn't want the others to see what he'd seen. There was a hand on his shoulder. He straightened up, shook his head, and got back on his feet. Fergal would take care of Lais. There was nothing he could do here.

Hotch. Reebus.

"I've got to find my sons," he muttered, mostly to himself. His gaze turned to a few young males who had gathered around. "We need help. Two of our sons are missing. Anybody?"

A young male stepped forward.

"My name is Haldor, and I'd like to help," said the young male who was half a head taller than he. "Where were they last seen?"

Bannabard nodded, then turned to the others. "Anyone else?"

Another young ape raised a hand and said, "My name is Wingalorn, sir."

He motioned and led them outside. "My name is Bannabard. We were hunting fiadhain along the Galtan River when three drambats took off with one of our sons. The older two are still out there."

Haldor shook his head. "We know who you are, sir. It'll be an honor to help."

Bannabard looked at the ground and fought to put the image of Gorby being carried off out of his head. He glanced at the tall ape. "Thanks. We're looking for Hotch and Reebus. Hotch is the oldest. He's nearly full-grown."

They knuckled up and bounded toward the forest. They climbed the nearest redwood, grabbed vines, and swung off toward the Galtan. Bannabard led them to the riverbank where the fiadhain carcass was, and as luck or providence would have it, Hotch and Reebus emerged from behind a nearby boulder.

He bounded up to them. "Pa," they said in unison as they gave him a hug.

Hotch looked into Bannabard's eyes. "There were three drambats, and one of them snatched Gorby off the vine. We didn't know what to do so we hid in some bushes. Once they were gone we came back here and couldn't find you *or* Mum."

"You did the right thing, son. I'm proud of you both. Sorry I wasn't here sooner. Your mum and I got in a fight with one of the drambats, and I had to take her back to Ape Town."

Reebus' eyes grew wide. "Is she okay?"

"Yeah. She's got some wounds, but Fergal is fixing her up."

Reebus nodded. "Did you get the drambat? The one who got Gorby?"

Bannabard looked at the ground for a second. "No. He got away. I'm just glad you two are safe. I'll tell you more later, but right now we need to get back to Ape Town and see how Mum's doing."

Reebus looked up with moist eyes. "Gorby was climbing up a vine and I was right behind him. And then there was this screech and three giant bat-lizards flew right at us. We weren't too high – Hotch and I jumped, but Gorby got snatched."

Bannabard held the back of his head with his hand. "There was nothing you could've done. It's not like you can fly or breathe fire, right? These are drambats we're talking about!"

Reebus exhaled. "I guess you're right. Thanks, Pa."

It was early evening by the time he returned with Hotch and Reebus. Bannabard thanked Haldor and Wingalorn.

"Our pleasure, sir," said Wingalorn.

"Can we go see Mum?" asked Hotch as they headed for the family hut.

"Not right now," answered Bannabard. "You guys need some rest and I need to see what can be done for your brother." They ducked inside the hut and he gave them both a hug. "I'm so glad you two are safe."

He gave them some water and made sure they were comfortable. "Try to get some sleep. I'm going to check on Mum and then go see the Elderarn about your brother."

"What's an Elderarm?" asked Reebus.

"The Elderarn is the ruling body of apes. They'll know what to do."

"Will they save Gorby?" asked Hotch.

"They'll do what they can, you can bet on that."

He headed over to the community hut and found Fergal who was putting in the last row of stitches. "How is she?"

"Nearly done stitching her up. She'll be fine as long as an infection doesn't set in."

Bannabard bent down. She was awake. He put a hand gently on her face. "How you doin', hon'?"

She smiled a little and turned her face toward his. "I've been better. Tell me you found Hotch and Reebus."

"Yeah. They're a little shook up, but they're home now. They're both fine."

Lais closed her eyes and a slight grin appeared. "Thank goodness!" She opened her eyes and gave him that look of a mother ready to fight for her kid. "What are we going to do about Gorby?"

He put a hand on her shoulder. "I'm going to go talk to Otger and see what can be done. Maybe the Elderarn will make an exception."

"They better, or…"

"Or we'll figure something out," he interrupted. He couldn't promise her anything and didn't want to get her hopes up. "It looks like you're in good hands here. Try to get some rest."

"Let me know when you guys meet," Fergal said. "I'll be finished here shortly."

Bannabard bounded down the path, thrust his head in the door of a hut and yelled, "Otger, you in here?"

"Coming," scowled a voice from a room in the back. "Who's raising a fuss at this hour? Oh, it's you. Bannabard. Come in, come in. What swings, old friend?"

"You may have heard. Three drambats attacked my sons down by the Galtan a few hours ago."

Otger raised a brow. "Oh my. That is serious. There haven't been attacks this close to Ape Town since the war."

"They took off with my youngest." It was his duty to notify the Elderarn of any conflicts with drakes, but there was a part of him which regretted – now that he'd done it.

Otger gave him a concerned look. "How are Lais and the other two?"

"We downed one of the drambats. Lais was injured in a fight with the drambat, but Fergal stitched her up. She'll be fine – if it doesn't get infected. Hotch and Reebus – my other two sons – they're both fine."

"Oh, that's good to hear," said Otger. "And how are you and Lais holding up?"

"We're hanging on, doing our best. It looks like Lais is going to recover. Our only hope for Gorby is that drambats don't like the taste of blue ape."

Otger nodded. "But what else would they want him for?"

Bannabard gazed outside, and his eyes narrowed. "That's just it. I have no idea."

Otger hit his chest with his right fist.

Bannabard did the same. They had fought together in the War. It almost felt like old times, except it wasn't. "I want to assemble the Elderarn and see what can be done for Gorby."

Otger looked away, then turned back with a hard gaze. "Repercussions – a downed drambat. There'll be repercussions from Flargellion, you can be sure of that. You were once in my shoes,

116

Bannabard. I don't expect it will be a surprise when I tell you that the Elderarn aren't likely to approve an operation that might jeopardize the community. We can't risk a response – our numbers are too few as it is."

Bannabard rolled his head back. "Lais and I need to hear that directly from the council."

"Understood. I'll call for a meeting right away." Otger nodded at a servant and gave him orders to gather the Elderarn. "Tell them to meet us here in half an hour."

The servant bounded out of the hut and was gone. Bannabard followed him outside and headed toward the community hut. Fergal had finished stitching up Lais and she was sleeping soundly. He bent down and kissed her on the forehead before heading back to Otger's with Fergal. By the time they arrived, most of the twelve Elderarn were discussing the issue.

"A shame, a terrible shame about the little one, but I'm afraid there's nothing to be done about it," said one. "We couldn't possibly… risk an intervention. If there were even a single casualty in Trool, we'd be in violation of the Treaty and Flargellion would be certain to retaliate."

"Indeed," said another. "The Drakebureau might send a gaggle or two to avenge the drambat as it is. I say we put Ape Town on high alert."

The last two leaders arrived, and Otger briefed them about why they were there.

Bannabard's eyes narrowed as he thumped his chest. "They were headed upriver, toward Trool. If we send a posse, we can be there by dawn."

Otger's eyes flashed around the room. "What do the Elderarn say? Do we dare send a rescue squad?"

"The Drakebureau would view that as an act of aggression," bellowed one of the older members.

"Yes, indeed," exclaimed another. "And what if they retaliate? What if instead of sending drambats, they send arsnatchers – or worse?"

"What if they send nickelnecks or malwracks?" asked another.

"It would be the end of Ape Town," the older ape said with a thump of his chest.

Another pounded a heavy fist on the floor. "It could be the end of our species."

Otger looked at the ground, then at Bannabard. "I'm afraid they're right. Bannabard, you used to be a member of this body. What do you say?"

Bannabard glared at the others. "My son was snatched by a drambat not far from here. If we do nothing, the drambats will grow bolder. You know there will be others."

Otger nodded. "If we send a squad, you know there'll be casualties which would incite a response. Our numbers are far too few to withstand an attack by Flargellion. But you know the score better than anyone. Ninety percent of our kind were wiped out during the war. I'm afraid drambat raids are something we'll have to put up with unless the Drakebureau decides to intervene."

Bannabard stared past Otger, out into the forest. "Given our situation, I understand the position of the Elderarn. But the treaty violations and the plight of blue apes in general will continue to be ignored unless our cause is brought before the Drakebureau. It is quite likely they'll continue to ignore these attacks, but it's the only chance we have. I'll go alone if I must."

"That would be a suicide mission," declared the older ape. "You know as well as anyone that the Treaty of Flargenmoore forbids us to leave Seedred."

Bannabard thumped his chest and looked around at the others. "We've been losing apes every year by the hundreds. And now they have my son. I'll make it clear that I'm acting alone, but this is something I have to do."

Otger's gaze met his. "And what would you say to them?"

"The truth. That drambats have been violating the Treaty since the day we signed it."

They signed the treaty a couple decades ago — just after the apes surrendered. They had nearly been wiped out, and as leader of the Elderarn, it had fallen on Bannabard to negotiate the signing with a malwrack named Gailryder. The negotiations centered on where blue apes would be allowed to live, hunt, and gather food.

He lobbied to include the grasslands west of Seedred because of abundant small game and certain types of plant tubers. But the apes had no leverage in the negotiations, and Gailryder was determined to show some strength. He restricted them to the forest, which was ridiculous in Bannabard's mind. Blue apes rarely if ever hunted the same game as dragons, other than an occasional fiadhain. In the end Gailryder embarrassed Bannabard further by restricting them to the northern half of the forest, something which cost him his seat on the Elderarn, and which his peers never forgot.

"What makes you think the Drakebureau would listen?" asked Otger.

Bannabard glanced outside, then looked slowly around the room. "Nothing. But if this body refuses to act, I will make an appeal to the Drakebureau myself. I'll do what I have to – for Ape Town and for my son."

"It'll be a suicide mission," repeated the older ape.

Bannabard glanced at the older ape and said, "Whether I burn or not, I have to do what's right. Somebody's got to take a stand." He thumped his chest and disappeared into the night.

15. Fugitives From Flargellion

It was a few days later. Gorby was gone and he now knew he hadn't been hallucinating about Jendal. He was riding on the back of a nickelneck and there was time. Time to think about how much he missed his son. Lais would take it hard. His eyes grew moist as he gazed at the night sky. Perhaps Gorby was watching from the Numinous. Jendal had seen to it that he got to state his case, and now he and Alfedora were on their way to Farshen. Fugitives from Flargellion and the ruling body of dragons.

His mission had failed, and he was a fugitive from what had been his best hope of saving his species. An urge to abandon Jendal's plan and go kill some drambats took root in his heart and mind. But getting himself killed would do no good. Certainly not for Lais, Hotch, and Reebus. Somehow Jendal gave him hope – even though his plan of getting help from the Drakebureau had gone nowhere. Ilgregious had seen to that. No, he would stick with Jendal and this nickelneck and do whatever it took to expose the drambat and his toadies for what they were.

I shuddered – hating the thin cold air. At least the blue ape was keeping my neck warm. It was a long flight to the canyons of Farshen. We had just crossed the continental divide over a pass in the southern mountains and whatever warmth the early morning sun might have provided was whisked away by a steady rush of cold mountain air.

I glanced to my left and recognized one of the small streams which fed into and formed the head of the Farnheim River. I had flown the Farnheim after my third hibernation following Rotbald's death. Alpine grasslands and tundra gave way to a subalpine forest, as the river fell into valleys and ravines while it twisted and grew wider. Farshen was where it carved canyons out of the plateau on its way to the ocean.

I craned my neck toward Bannabard while he clung to the base of it. "We'll follow this stream to the canyons," I yelled. "I'll try to find a spot where we can scare up some breakfast and warm up a bit."

"Yeah, I could use a..." shouted Bannabard.

I couldn't make out the last word. "What? You could use a steak?"

"No, I could use a..."

Again, I couldn't make out the last word. Sounded like steak. "Yeah, that would be nice! Elk, deer, buffalo – whatever!"

"No, I could use a break!" he shouted.

I swooped low, flying just above the stream which had grown wider and could almost be considered a river. The air grew warmer and our prospects for finding food improved.

"That sun feels great!" shouted Bannabard.

"Yeah, my tum is aching too!" I yelled. "I'll find somewhere to land where we can hunt up some grub."

Just ahead the river slowed and widened into a good-sized pond. It was in the middle of a forested flood plain surrounded by ridges which reached above tree line. We approached a clearing and touched down gently. A second stream flowed into the pond just above a beaver dam.

Bannabard's grip on my neck loosened as I came to a stop near some trees at the edge of the clearing. He climbed down and shook his hands and arms.

"Whew!" he exclaimed. "I was going numb up there. Thanks for taking a break."

"No worries. But shhh," I whispered. "Are you as hungry as I am?" I asked, licking my chops. I didn't wait for an answer. "Maybe you can find some food in the forest while I hunt up some game near this pond. Whatever you do, keep it quiet. We wouldn't want to scare away any tasties."

"Gotcha," he whispered.

He turned quickly and headed into the forest, while I slipped into the pond, hoping it would be deep enough to conceal my frame. Thankfully it was. I waited motionless in the still water. My patience was rewarded when five elk approached the water's edge. They were almost within reach when in my eagerness I rose a moment too soon.

The elk scattered and dashed back to the forest, but I managed to get a swipe at one elk's hind leg with my claws. I scurried after it as it limped into the trees. I stopped abruptly and snarled. Another nickelneck had been hiding next to the game trail and surprised me. He grabbed the elk and dispatched it with a stroke of his claws. But his attempt to eat was thwarted by a shackle on his snout.

I bobbed my head and glared at a young male, about my age, only a bit larger. Apparently he was too occupied with the shackle to notice me. I let out a low-pitched, rumbling growl. "That's my elk! Go get your own." I bobbed my head again and scrunched my nose. But then I recognized him through the shackle. "Cangoar, is that you? What are *you* doing here?"

He stopped clawing at the shackle, looked up and said, "Oh. Hey, Alfedora. I was about to ask you the same thing. Shouldn't you be interfering with matches at the B.E.G.? Oh, wait, I forgot. You've been too busy getting arrested."

"Listen, Cangoar. I never got a chance to apologize for that."

"Save your breath. I think you're going to need it for the Drakebureau."

I looked away, then turned and glared at him. "Fine. But you should know that my pa died fighting a malwrack in the B.E.G. I was scared for you... I was just trying to help."

"Yeah, you helped all right. You helped me get disqualified. I tied the reigning champ, but that's not what the record books will say. The record books will say, 'Cangoar: Disqualified'."

"Yes – I'm so sorry. That malwrack looked angry and I couldn't just stand there and watch him..."

"Cut my tail off?" he interrupted. "That's what the Games are about, Alfedora. That's what every other drake in the stands does. They stand there and watch while one dragon whacks another dragon's tail off. But you couldn't do that, could you?"

"Sorry. I didn't want you to end up like Pa."

"What are you talking about? What's wrong with you?"

My words suddenly sounded hollow. Cangoar was right. No one worries about drakes actually *dying* in the B.E.G. "I don't know," I muttered. Which wasn't exactly true. Truth is I wanted to spare us both a discourse about how Pa died.

"Alfedora, what's done is done," he grunted while clawing at the shackle. "I guess we could call it even if you help me get this shackle off."

"Cool." I glanced around. "Hey, Bannabard! Come here for a minute!"

Cangoar shook his head vigorously, but the shackle held fast. "Who's Bannabard?"

"He's that blue ape – the one who interrupted the session at the Drakebureau."

"Oh, right. I thought you and that blue ape were goners once Ilgregious and his drambats showed up at the Vault. I was glad you made it out when you did. That nasty little drambat and his toadies were after you."

I flicked my tongue. "How did you know I was in the Viper Vault?"

Cangoar didn't look up but continued clawing at the shackle. "I'm a guard there. Or at least I was until last night."

"I didn't know you worked at the Viper Vault. Sorry about your…"

I was about to say 'friends' before my voice trailed off.

What if he needed to do his duty?

Maybe I deserved to be punished, but I'd seen what Ilgregious had done, and there was no way I was going back to the Viper Vault. Not even if Cangoar was the one who hauled me in. I looked to my right and studied a gap between the trees. There was a clear lane for a takeoff – big enough for my wings.

"Uh, Cangoar, I hope you don't mind my asking, but why is there a shackle on your snout?"

He looked across the pond and flicked his tongue. "Oh, yeah. Uh, well… Ilgregious put that there. I was his prisoner, before I busted out, that is. You shoulda been there. Twelve drambats sprawling and tumbling in all different directions and I flew outta there faster than a bat out of a volcano. And then…"

"Wait," I interrupted. "You were Ilgregious' prisoner?"

"Yeah, but don't ask how that happened." Cangoar glanced across the pond. "I think they killed those two malwracks. But I can barely remember. It's all kind of fuzzy, actually." He gave me a blank stare as he clawed at the shackle. "Any chance you could help me out of this thing?"

I circled to my right. "Tell me why you're out here in the middle of nowhere with a shackle on your snout. Then maybe we'll help you get it off."

"Yeah, right. I guess I'm here by the grace of Melohim. Ilgregious was about to kill me too, but I guess the Great Drake in the sky had something else in mind."

I took a deep breath and bobbed my head. "So you aren't out here tracking me down, and you aren't going to arrest me?"

"Uh, no. I hadn't really planned on it. But I can if you want me to," he said with a grin.

"Here we are running for our lives, out in the middle of nowhere. You've got a shackle on your snout – and making jokes." I glanced to my left and caught a glimpse of Bannabard knuckle-walking up the deer trail. We both looked his way.

He gawked at Cangoar and slid sideways behind a huge old fir tree. "Hey Alfedora! Who's your friend?"

"Wait a second. Who says I'm running for my life?" asked Cangoar. "Speak for yourself!" He picked at the shackle with a claw. "Any chance your pet ape can help with this thing?"

I turned to Bannabard. "This is Cangoar. He was the other guard at the Viper Vault. He's a friend. At least I think he is." I glanced his way with a slight grin. "Do you think you can help him get that shackle off?"

Bannabard emerged slowly from the tree, staring at Cangoar. "I'm nobody's pet!" he said with a thump of his chest. "The name's Bannabard. I represented the blue apes when we negotiated the treaty of Flargenmoore."

"Yes, of course," said Cangoar. "The treaty of Flarber-wuh?" But before Bannabard could answer, Cangoar's face lit up. "Hey, you're the one who was doing tricks at the Stone Ingot! It's a pleasure to meet you, your Apeness! Sure as I'll be shooting fireballs!"

Bannabard glanced at the path back to the forest. "Likewise, I'm sure."

Cangoar took a step closer. "Can you do any more?"

"Any more what?"

"You know, tricks. Like appearing out of nowhere and standing in the middle of an inferno without so much as singing a single hair."

Bannabard shook his head. "Uh, no, not really. And I wasn't exactly doing tricks. My son was snatched by a band of drambats. I came to Flargellion to get help."

Cangoar waved a paw. "Sorry to hear that. Alfedora, we should help him get his son back."

"Too late," I said with a slight sniffle. "I'm afraid his son didn't make it."

"Losing a son – that must be tough," said Cangoar.

Bannabard looked away. "Words can't describe it. But I'm not alone. Drambats have taken quite a few friends and family – and many others I never knew."

"I can't imagine," said Cangoar, scrunching his nose. "Never cared much for drambats. Overgrown buzzards if you ask me. I'm just glad you two made it out when you did – Ilgregious and his toadies were coming for you."

I bobbed my head. "Yeah, we saw what they did to those guards. I'm just glad he didn't get you."

Cangoar glanced at the ground.

"Were they your friends?" I asked.

"I hadn't been working there long, but yeah, we were friends."

I looked him in the eye. "I'm so sorry."

"Me too," added Bannabard.

"Thanks," said Cangoar.

"Glad you got away. But what are you doing out here in the middle of nowhere?" I asked.

"Before I escaped, Ilgregious did a trick on my mind… It doesn't feel like I've recovered yet." He looked up at the sky. "I needed some time away from the Viper Vault to get my wits about me."

I thrashed my tail. "What kind of trick?"

Cangoar's eyes grew a bit wider. "It was weird and scary. Really weird… and really scary. First, he scratched his left front leg until it bled. Then he started talking about some dark queen in a sort of sing-song voice – like a prayer or something. And after he asked her to grant him

125

power – his eyes glowed red! It's all a bit fuzzy, but when those red eyes get inside your head, all you ever knew in life becomes dark and twisted. Everything went black. Meaningless malevolence and despair took over my mind. And I. Could. Not. Fight back. I'd fought a malwrack in the B.E.G., but against that skinny little drambat I was helpless as a newt's hatchling."

I looked away. "That sounds terrible. Terribly ridiculous, that is." I glanced at him and said, "Is this how you impress the females?"

Cangoar looked at the ground, then bobbed his head and gave me a hard look. "I'm not making this up. And no, this is *not* how I impress females. I'm a guard! At the Viper Vault!"

I grinned slightly – still confident he was trying to impress me. "Oh, because you're a guard? That's why I should believe you?"

Bannabard had taken a seat but stood up. "That would explain how those drambats were able to kill two malwracks."

Cangoar's eyes brightened. "Yeah, I'm starting to remember now. That's how they killed Lutjen and Laudus, and that's how they took me prisoner! Mind tricks! And he was gonna kill me too – that slug-slurping slime-fest!"

I bobbed my head. "Let me get this straight. Ilgregious got inside their heads, and the malwracks just gave up while the drambats split their guts open?"

Cangoar nodded as if he were a hatchling. "Yeah, and he was quick about it. That's when they took me hostage and killed the other two. Once those red eyes get inside your head, you're helpless. You might as well be trying to swim out of a tar pit."

"Green gizzards of a gecko!" I exclaimed. Maybe he wasn't just trying to impress me. I flicked my tongue. "That sounds terrible, but why didn't they kill you too?"

"At first, he wanted me for a hostage. But when he found the vault empty, he figured I helped you two escape. He got *really* mad when I couldn't explain how you got away."

Bannabard took a step closer. "Whoa, and then what happened?"

"He was gonna kill me too, and I figured I was done for. I didn't know what to do so I asked for help – from Melohim. Ilgregious' mind trick musta backfired or something. Next thing I knew, he fell to the ground and I flew outa there like a bat out of a volcano. And now he knows that I know that they murdered those guards."

"Whoa, and since Ilgregious is on the Drakebureau, you're a fugitive too," said Bannabard.

"Yeah. I guess so."

I flicked my tongue and bobbed my head. "Can't you just tell the Drakebureau what happened? They'd believe a guard at the Viper Vault, right?"

Cangoar glanced at the ground. "Maybe. But since there's no witnesses, it would be my word against his. Who'd believe an apprentice like me over a leader of the Drakebureau?"

I looked at the blue ape and smiled. "Hey, I know! Bannabard and I could be your witnesses! We heard one of the drambats brag about how they gutted the guards and wanted to gut us too."

Cangoar scrunched his nose. "I was a guard, you were my prisoners, and Bannabard crashed their meeting in the Great Hall. I don't think they would believe our stories over one of their leaders."

I glanced at Bannabard, then back at Cangoar. "Okay. Good point. Maybe you're right. So what do we do now? We can't just let Ill-greega-butt get away with murder and turn us into fugitives, right? We'll be fugitives forever."

Cangoar bobbed his head. "We've got to clear our names and expose him for what he is."

I scrunched my nose. "Right. But how we gonna do that?"

Cangoar clawed at the shackle. "We could start by getting this shackle off my snout."

I turned to Bannabard. "Could you help Cangoar, please? His snout is stuck."

Bannabard approached Cangoar slowly and studied the shackle. "Shouldn't be a problem."

He pulled a pair of pins, undid a latch, and slid the shackle off.

"Thanks, I owe you one," said Cangoar as he stretched his jaws.

Bannabard stared at Cangoar's teeth. "Don't mention it," he said, backing away slowly.

Cangoar started in on the elk.

"Cangoar, I'm sorry you got caught up in this. Ever since I saw Ilgregious make that sacrifice, it's like a dark cloud has been following me around."

"What sacrifice?" Cangoar asked.

Bannabard turned and headed toward the lake.

I glanced at the ground. "It's kind of gross, really. Better to save it for after you've eaten."

Cangoar gulped down a hunk of elk flank. "Oh, I'm good. Do tell, please."

"It's your stomach." I watched Bannabard instead of Cangoar eating. "It was a couple of days ago – I was on my way to Flargellion and stopped at a lake in Trool. I was hunting up some grub when I saw a light across the lake and went to check it out."

"On your way to the B.E.G.?"

"Yeah. There were drums and singing from inside a cave, and I was curious, so I crept closer. When I peered in, Ilgregious and a band of drambats were doing some kind of creepy ceremony. They were singing a dirge, and there was this weird purple haze. Next thing I knew they threw an arsnatcher – just a hatchling mind you – they threw a hatchling into a lava pit! They burned him alive!"

The nausea from a few nights ago reared its ugly head. Again.

"No way!" exclaimed Cangoar as he bobbed his head and took another bite.

"Way! Just a hatchling!"

Bannabard beat his chest and howled.

"He doesn't sound too happy," said Cangoar.

"You got that right," I whispered. "They had his son. He was next."

"Oh no, that's terrible! Who does that?" mumbled Cangoar as he gulped down some more.

I gave him a blank stare. "I know, right? Then they began to celebrate. Can you imagine? And get this – the next thing I knew Ilgreega butt was floating around the cavern in mid-air without using his wings!"

"No way," said Cangoar. "I'd like to see that!"

"Yeah, and then he claimed to be all powerful, second only to some dark queen. He ordered the others to bow to him, and that's when I left. I was so creeped out I couldn't even eat."

Cangoar bobbed his head. "Wow, that's some deep, dark, drambat dung!"

I gazed at the half-eaten elk. "Yes, it is. Apparently Ilgregious is in league with someone he calls the Dark Queen. She gives him power to get inside other drake's heads. But I guess you already knew that."

"Yep. I know what that's like."

"How do we fight *that*?" I asked as I bobbed my head and watched Bannabard knuckle up and join us.

"We don't," said Bannabard. "Not by ourselves, anyway. We need to do as Jendal suggested. We need to wait for her in the canyons of Farshen."

Cangoar glanced at the elk carcass, then at me. "You can have the rest if you like."

I stared at it for a moment. "Uh, no thanks. I'm good."

"Who is Jendal?" asked Cangoar. "And what's in Farshen?"

"Jendal is one of the dosara," answered Bannabard. "She's been sent here to help our species."

"What's a dosara?"

Bannabard turned to Cangoar and lowered his voice. "She's a powerful being from what she calls 'the realm of dark matter and dark energy'. We call it 'the Numinous'."

I stared at Cangoar. "It's cool," I whispered. "I don't believe it either."

Cangoar's eyes lit up. "Wow! Now that you mention it, I remember reading about those. You've actually met a dosara?"

"Yeah. We've nearly been wiped out by drambats over the last few years, and she said Melohim sent her here to help. She's the one who got me into the Great Hall and shielded me from the flames."

"Whoa, how cool is that? Alfedora, can you believe it – a dosara!? That must mean the Phoberon is real!?"

I gave Cangoar a blank look. "Yeah. Pretty amazing!" I flicked my tongue and looked away. "Seriously? You're like a hatchling. Both of you. Gullible as hatchlings. Of course the Phoberon's not real."

"How many realms are there?" Cangoar asked as he turned to Bannabard.

"I don't know," answered the blue ape. "But there's at least two – ours and theirs."

I rolled my eyes.

"And who's this 'dark queen'?" asked Cangoar.

"Jendal calls her Krimeny," said Bannabard. "She used to be a dosara, but she turned, along with a bunch of others. Jendal calls them the arsnarms."

Cangoar bobbed his head. "Wow, an arsnarm! She's the one who gives Ilgregious his power? Did you hear that, Alfedora?"

"Yeah, I heard it. An arsnarm."

Bannabard took a step closer and lowered his voice. "Yeah. Jendal says she hates everything and everybody in this realm. But Jendal isn't like that."

"You like her, don't you?" I said with a slight grin.

Anything to change the subject.

Bannabard glared at me and pounded his chest with his right fist. "Absolutely not! I already have a mate! And Jendal is different. Way different. Like I said, she's powerful, but she doesn't flaunt it or use her power to take advantage of others."

I bobbed my head. "Okay. But if she's so powerful why does Jendal let Ilgregious throw hatchlings into a lava pit?"

"I don't know," answered the blue ape.

I flicked my tongue. Twice. "And why would Melohim, if he even exists – why would he allow this Dark Queen to help Ill-greega-butt do stuff like that – in our realm?"

Bannabard shrugged.

Cangoar's gaze bounced from me to the blue ape. "Yeah, and why doesn't Melohim just wipe out all those nasty old arsnarms?"

"Good question," replied Bannabard. "Perhaps Jendal can shed some light on that next time we see her. Which reminds me, she'll be expecting us. Cangoar, would you like to come meet her?"

"Heck yeah. I've never met a dosara."

I glanced at Cangoar and gave Bannabard a bit of a grin. "Oh great, just great. Now you've done it. We'll never be rid of him! You owe me an elk, by the way."

"Don't worry your scaly brown head. I'll get you an elk. In the meantime, would you like what's left of this one?"

"Uh, no thanks, you go ahead."

My gaze turned to the eastern sky while I waited for Cangoar to finish. Somehow my thoughts turned to Mum. What would Urraca say if she found out I was a fugitive from the Drakebureau? It'd probably be something like, 'you dug your pit – you get to lie in it.'

16.   Farshen

Cangoar finished eating and the three of us took off – Bannabard on my back. We flew along the Farnheim River heading mostly west and a little south. The river grew wider and the landscape flatter, with bluffs and mesas on the left and right. Thick forest gave way to grasslands and an arid desert. At some point I realized what I had seen from a distance – what looked like the river growing abnormally wide – was actually the canyons of Farshen.

The sun had nearly reached the horizon while a meandering silver ribbon below reflected whatever light managed to reach the bottom. We dropped below the top of the canyon, which was wider than it was deep, and I guessed we were still eight or ten furlongs above the water. Dark shadows contrasted with intense reflections coming off the water.

I followed my tail-challenged friend as he swooped down to within less than half a furlong of the river. We landed on a ledge at the mouth of a cavern in a smooth gray and mostly horizontal formation some hundred-and-fifty feet above the canyon floor.

"Good choice," I said as Bannabard climbed down. The cave was close to water and was one of many in the formation. "It will be hard to find us here – should anyone come looking."

"Where are the trees?" Bannabard muttered.

I looked up at the top of the canyon. "This is a desert. Did you think we'd find trees? And we won't find any elk or bear either."

We bedded down for the night, but I was excited – too excited to sleep. The future looked dim unless we could figure out a way to expose Ilgregious and clear our names. And if we did, would we be able to convince the other leaders to put an end to what he was doing with hatchlings and blue apes?

Cangoar watched Bannabard drift off to sleep. "He'll be snoring, I'll wager."

I grinned a little. "Not as loud as you, I'm guessing."

"Yeah, right." Cangoar looked outside. "What happens now? Do we just hang out and wait for your friend Jendal, or put a plan together?"

My gaze followed his. "A plan? Really? What kind of plan?"

"I don't see why the two of us can't go hunt down that skinny little drambat and have him arrested."

I scrunched my nose. "That's a battle I don't think we can win."

"Why not? They're just drambats. I should have killed Ilgregious when I had the chance. If I had, we wouldn't be hiding out in a cave in a desert with nothing but a few catfish and scrawny lizards to eat."

I gave Cangoar as piercing a look as I could muster. "You'd have been arrested and thrown in the Viper Vault."

"It would've been self-defense. He was about to kill me! And don't forget — he killed Lutjen and Laudus."

"You know how the Drakebureau works," I said. "Drakes of a scale thrash tails together. Pinhammer and his toadies would never stand for an apprentice at the Viper Vault killing one of their leaders — even if it was self-defense."

"Maybe you're right, but Ilgregious doesn't even have scales!"

"Cangoar, could you tell me more about how you survived — when Lutjen and Laudus didn't?"

"Well, you know how tough we nickelnecks are," he said.

I smiled. "Yeah, right. Those malwracks were bigger and stronger than you."

"Bigger maybe, but who says they were stronger? I'm quicker, and I fought in the B.E.G."

I nodded at the stub of his tail. "How long until it grows back?"

"What's that?" Cangoar asked.

"Your *tail* of course."

Cangoar looked out into the dark canyon. "Oh, that. It'll grow back in a year or two. You'll see."

"That's not bad." I knew it would be at least two years. "You still haven't answered my question."

"What's that?"

I gave him a hard look. "It's fine if you don't want to talk about it, but I'd like to know how you survived when Ilgregious tried to kill you."

"Oh, yeah. Well, first I disabled him with a snort of stink breath. Then I gouged out his right eye and knocked him over with my tail, and then I got away when he fell to the ground. I should have put an end to that foul little lizard when I had the chance."

Cangoar swished the stub of his tail, grinned, then looked away.

"But you didn't, and that's not how you described it earlier."

Cangoar glanced at me, then peered into the night sky. "Well, actually, I uh... it's like I said before. I asked for help from the big drake in the sky, and I guess he heard me. When Ilgregious' eyes turned red and he tried to get inside my head – as near as I can figure – it backfired. The first time, when he took me hostage, those red eyes bored into my head and everything went black. It felt as if all hope had been sucked into a lava pit. But the second time it felt like the dark stuff went into *his* head instead of mine. That's when he fell over – and I took off."

I allowed a slight smile to cross my face.

Good thing I'm here, or we'd never get the story straight.

"You didn't really gouge out his eye, did you?"

"Well, I kinda made that up. But the point is, I think Melohim heard me. It felt like he helped me. Can you imagine? And now I feel like a gator running from a toad. What if he's killing more hatchlings as we speak? We should be hunting him down rather than hiding out in Farshen. Melohim would help us save the hatchlings, don't you think?"

My eyes narrowed and turned to the night sky. "Even if he exists, you can't assume Melohim will be there to save you every time you ask him. Why didn't he save those two malwracks?"

Or Pa for that matter.

I bobbed my head and flicked my tongue.

"I don't know about those two malwracks," replied Cangoar. "But I'm guessing Ilgregious will kill again if he gets the chance. And if Melohim helped me once, he will help me again. For the hatchlings, right? Don't you think he cares about the hatchlings?"

Melohim? I don't think so.

I looked past him into the dark canyon. "You can't save everyone. And where was Melohim when that baby arsnatcher got thrown in the pit?"

"You're right. I can't save everyone. But hatchlings and apes and who knows what else might be dying right now."

I turned to Bannabard, who was sleeping soundly. "Yeah, maybe they are, but I don't pretend to know whether Melohim even exists, let alone what he will or won't do if we run off and try to stop Ilgregious without Jendal. I think we should stick to the plan."

"He's just a drambat, right? And why wouldn't Melohim be with us on this?"

My gaze turned back to the night sky. "Just because you think a being from the Phoberon saved your sorry tail-challenged butt once doesn't mean it's real or that he'd do it again. And it doesn't mean that he's appointed you to save the world from Ilgregious and his minions. These things are best handled by the Drakebureau. That's why it's there."

"But what if I'm right? What if drakes are dying while we sit here and waste time hunting geckos in the desert? Let's go hunt down that slime-sucking slug-slurper."

I watched Bannabard's chest rise and fall. "Males," I muttered. "You can go hunt drambats if you like, but I'm going to wait for Jendal." Suddenly it felt good to defend Jendal's plan. "Perhaps she'll help us expose Ilgregious for what he is. Then we'll be able to let the Drakebureau handle it. She said she'd help us, and I believe her. More importantly, I believe in the Drakebureau."

"Suit yourself, Alfedora. You can hang around with a blue ape in the desert if you like, but I need to do something."

Cangoar started toward the canyon, then glanced back. "It was nice running into you, Alfedora. Best of luck to you. You and your little blue friend."

"Same to you. I hope you find what you're looking for."

Cangoar thrashed the stub of his tail back and forth. "I'm not looking for anything except Ilgregious and his toady little drambats."

"Oh, sorry. My mistake. Stay safe."

He headed out of the cave and stood on the ledge overlooking the river. He glanced back, then arched his back and flipped a wing. A full moon lit his silhouette and I watched until he disappeared behind the eastern wall of the canyon.

17. KARDOOL'S NEIGHBORHOOD

K rimeny's attention was focused on Cangoar as he talked about hunting down Ilgregious and his drambat hoard. She approached Jendal, her eyes darting left and right. "Did you hear that? He's abandoned you and your sorry little plan! *Exactly* what I was hoping for – now I'll get to *take* his tail-challenged little butt!"

"Whoa, calm down a bit," said Jendal with a sigh. "He may be heading down a separate path, but that doesn't give you the right to hand him over to Ilgregious and his minions."

Krimeny circled around and got up in Jendal's face. "Who's going to stop me? You?"

Jendal smiled slightly. "Yeah, if it came to that – for your sake I hope it doesn't."

Krimeny backed off and glared at Jendal. "For my sake? Yeah, right. But how about we make a deal?" She looked away, then said in a soft and soothing tone, "I'll back off Cangoar if you back off Ilgregious and his drambats."

Jendal's weakness is she actually cares about the slimy little stink-fests – in the realm of light energy and light matter!

"Why should I?" asked Jendal. "Ilgregious has broken every law in their society. And Melohim knows about it. All of it."

Krimeny let a muffled shriek escape and held her ears. "Don't use that name!" she demanded. "You know what it does to me."

Jendal glanced toward the Light. "You can't win, you know."

"Says who?"

"You might as well give it up and ask him to forgive you. Anything would be better than the path you're on. And for what? For pride? So others might be impressed with the strength of your resolve? Do you honestly think more dosara will join Korgarag's rebellion?"

She looked away, then glared at Jendal. "Shut up, Jendal! You know nothing!"

It pains me to even look at her. All bright and shiny. Don't they know how annoying they are?

Krimeny gazed into empty space. "The enemy talks about caring, trust, and respect, yet everything he created in this realm is an insult to who *we* are. Don't you see? They're as much an insult to you as they are to me. And does anyone know *why* he pretends to love those disgusting little vermin? Their scales are disgustingly slimy, and there's not one of them that doesn't stink to high heaven."

"They do have a certain aroma," answered Jendal. "Personally, I find it quite charming."

"You would. And yet the enemy limits our ability to interact with their world. He's a control freak – always has been. Keeping *us* from interfering in their silly, meaningless, worthless little lives. And for what? So they can eke out their useless, petty existence? It isn't fair. He's never been fair. But Korgarag understands. He's one of us – not like the Enemy. Korgarag agrees with those of us who want real choices about who we are, what we worship, and who we follow."

Jendal shook her head. "Melohim is not the enemy. I respect him above all because he alone has earned our respect. Not because I am forced to."

"Respect? You actually worship him, am I right?"

"But of course – he's earned that. Even you should know that."

Krimeny started to turn away, then got all up in Jendal's face – her eyes half shut because of the bright light. "Yeah, right. Earned it my butt. He never had to fight for power like we do. And why should *he* make all the rules? But dosara like you are too thick-headed to understand how he treats us – like stupid, weak, frail little children – subservient to his every whim." Her voice cracked a little. "But you don't believe that – do you, Jendal? You need to wake up and smell your delusions."

"Easy, easy. Your head's going to explode. Maybe you're right. Maybe I don't get it. But you do, don't you, Krimeny? Do you even remember what life was like before the Rebellion? You were once a great dosara, strong and free – stronger and freer than you are now. But look at yourself now. You're less than you were – you grow weaker every day and increasingly enslaved to your lust for power. Melohim's simply giving you the corruption you've chosen."

She got up in Jendal's face again and sneered, "That's my point – yet another example of how unfair he is." She gave Jendal an icy glare, but Jendal returned a blank expression as if she had no idea what they'd been talking about. Krimeny drifted off without bothering to look back. Obviously this dosara is beyond hope – too thick-headed to understand how enlightened arsnarms have become. She will never understand our movement. Her mind remains infected by silly notions of faith, hope, and love when there is really *nothing* but the will to power. Krimeny smiled and drifted away – feeling superior in every way to her adversary. Black empty space was so much nicer than Jendal's disturbingly bright countenance. One day she and Korgarag will become masters over all of it. One day they will defeat Melohim himself!

Cangoar reached Flargellion before daybreak after flying half the night. He looked down as he approached and saw what looked like Pinhammer and a few security drakes heading toward the Viper Vault. Their silhouettes were barely visible against the dark mountain, and he watched as they landed outside the Daor Gate. They'd be investigating the murders of Lutjen and Laudus no doubt.

The sun would be up soon and there'd be a bounty on his head if Ilgregious had anything to do with it. He barely skimmed the treetops as he banked toward Trool. It wasn't long before Lake Hornsniffler appeared after cresting a hill – along with a hazy first light. He landed, took refuge in the woods, and figured he'd hide during daylight.

He settled in behind some bushes next to a game trail as it began to rain. It would be a boring day, but he'd make the best of it. What if he found a drambat – any drambat? How much fun would it be to interrogate, especially if it resisted? But he thought better of going after one in daylight – what drambat wouldn't be suspicious of a nickelneck in Trool?

His eyes grew heavy as he watched some clouds go by, and by the time he woke dusk had crept over the region. An elk wandered down the game trail in the twilight, reminding him he had worked up an appetite. It was nice to find game so easily. He looked up as he ate and noticed a light in a cavern across the lake.

A faint but steady drumbeat reminded him of what Alfedora had described a few nights ago. Maybe Ilgregious is in there – maybe he's got some hatchlings. He followed a game trail around the lake and got close enough to peek inside, but it was just a family of drambats playing a game.

"Who goes there?" asked a somewhat squeaky voice behind him.

He froze for a second, then spun around and would have knocked the drambat over with his tail if he had one. "Oh, uh, hello. The name's... Slimfidget," he said, a lot less confidently than he would have liked. "I must have gotten lost. I was out training for the B.E.G. and ended up here. What is this place?"

"You are in the eastern part of Trool, near Lake Hornsniffler," said the drambat with a flick of her tongue. "Brangboor would be that way," she said, pointing northeast. "We don't see many nickelnecks around here."

"I guess not," he answered.

"You might want to be careful," said the drambat as she waved a paw. "Rumor has it that a nickelneck murdered some guards over at the Viper Vault and set some prisoners free. I think his name is Canbore or something. He's considered stoked and dangerous."

Cangoar glanced at the ground and scrunched his nose.

Really!? My name's become known already!?

"A twisted one, that is. As twisted as you'll ever see," continued the drambat.

Cangoar bobbed his head. "Yes, indeed who could do such a thing? It's too bad about those poor devils at the Viper Vault, but I hadn't heard there was a nickelneck involved. How terrible! Well thanks for filling me in on the news and the directions. I'll be off to Brangboor now. Hope they catch those guys – and best of luck to you and your family." He shuddered at the words. Best of luck to you and your family?

"Thanks. Same to you," said the drambat.

He took off toward Brangboor, heading north and east, knowing he wouldn't find his quarry in that direction. What about circling back and toasting the little buzzard? No, he might be seen or heard. Ilgregious' toadies would be on him like flies on bear scat. Instead he flew on under cover of darkness until Hornsniffler was out of sight and dropped into a meadow a few miles north and east of the lake.

The moonlight revealed a high meadow in some foothills overlooking a valley to the east. A flash of light at the north end of the valley caught his eye. It was unusual to find drambats this far east, but they were the only species which kept a fire in their lairs.

He looked up one side of the valley and down the other. The only lit cave in sight – it was above a creek in the valley and nestled in a hill on the west side. He guessed about a tenth of a furlong above the water. He glanced left, then right – not a soul. He crept closer, ducking behind big rocks, trees, and bushes. Soon he heard some singing or chanting from the cave and stopped to listen. Some of the words were, "Power, puke, and green blood too, we are your servants through the slough."

He flicked his tongue. Servants through the slough? That's a reach if ever there was one! He climbed up the hill a little, stretched his neck, and saw about fifteen or twenty drambats in a circle. A lone spewler stood in their midst – a good head taller than the others. Many of the drambats screeched and howled and bonked heads as the chant continued. A purple haze filled the room.

He peered through the fog but saw no sign of Ilgregious. The haze seemed to emanate from a point above the spewler's head and grew thicker as he watched. Soon it was too thick to make out the drambats on the other side.

The spewler looked up and said, "I am Kardool and am here to serve you, oh great and mighty Queen of all things Dark. May your kingdom know no bounds and may there be no end to your reign – your Magnificent Malfeasance!"

The haze grew thicker and made it difficult to see the spewler. Cangoar nearly lost his footing as a powerful voice responded to the spewler's words. It was like lightning and thunder, crackling and rumbling from the midst of the haze.

"Will you allow me to look inside your heart and mind? I must see if you are worthy of my gifts," the voice rumbled.

141

The spewler, the drambats, and even Cangoar trembled.

"As you wish, my Lord and Master, I…"

The spewler's words were cut short as part of the purple haze dove into his gaping mouth. The spewler's eyes grew wide as he fell over on his side.

"I see you grew up in a fairly normal home, as normal as could be hoped for," said the voice, a bit muffled now that it was coming from inside the spewler. "Ah, but I see a lovely little dark spot in your soul. Pa was never there for you, was he? I see he spent his time sleeping and leaving you and your siblings to your own devices. And where was Mum? She was out hunting gold, of course. And there you were – just a hatchling. Getting pummeled by your older brother every other day and twice on Tuesdays."

Cangoar scrunched his nose as the muffled voice continued.

"Yet you never mentioned it to Mum or Pa. Why was that? Oh, you didn't trust them to take care of you? You knew he would pummel you even worse if you did? This was very wise on your part. And because you were so wise at such a young age, I have a gift for you – a very special gift. For you – and you alone. I shall grant you the ability to wield dark energy and use its power to rearrange memories in the minds of your adversaries. You shall wield great power if you obey only me."

"Yes, your Malfeasance. I am at your service!" muttered the spewler.

Cangoar watched as the purple haze left the spewler's body. The spewler gasped for air, his chest heaving. He stumbled back to his feet and stood there, looking at the ground and panting.

Eventually he looked around at the others in the circle, gathered himself, and said, "I am Kardool. Let us give thanks to our great and mighty Queen! Queen of all things Dark!"

The drambats resumed their dirge. "Power, puke, and green blood too, we are your servants through the slough!"

They repeated the chant a few times, then began to disperse. But as the haze dissipated, the light from the cavern illuminated the silhouettes of five drambats heading his way.

18. AND BOB'S YOUR UNCLE

He had lingered too long. He turned and took off – hoping by some chance they wouldn't see him in the night sky.

"Hey, what's that?" asked a high-pitched drambat.

"That's a big one! Must be a nickelneck or a young malwrack, sure as my name's Frismipper," said another. "I'll bet he's been spying on us. After him, you toadies!"

"I'm not chasing no nickelneck! Who do you think I am?" whined the high-pitched voice.

"Snerl, don't be a twit! We can out-maneuver him – and it's five against one. He won't stand a chance! Now get moving before I spill yer guts out!"

Cangoar headed north and east toward Brangboor.

"He's faster than us. How we gonna catch *him?*" asked the high-pitched drambat.

"He can't fly forever!" yelled another. "He'll have to land sometime. And when he does, we'll be on him like slugs on slime."

Cangoar glanced back at the drambats in the moonlight. This really sucks. He could simply outrun them – but his cover was blown. If he turned on them now, there'd be a firefight which would be visible from a long distance. He looked ahead as he crested a hill. There. A spot where he'd have cover to engage his pursuers. He banked to his right and landed in a valley beside a river. He spun around as five drambats landed a few furlongs away.

The tallest one glared at Cangoar. "What were you doing in our valley, nickelneck?"

"I was training for the B.E.G. and got lost!" he shouted.

"Yeah, right! And flaming flamingos will be flying out my butt any second now!" yelled the tall drambat. "Trool has penalties for spies like you!"

"Nobody cares about drambat penalties and flaming flamingos won't be the only thing flying out your butt!" exclaimed Cangoar as he started toward them.

"Bu-bring it ah-on, na-nickelneck," stuttered the smallest one, trying to sound confident while glancing to his left, right and behind.

Cangoar licked his chops as the drambats started moving toward him. "Be careful what you wish for!" he exclaimed as his pace quickened.

He had nearly reached the drambats when he halted abruptly, puffed out his chest, and spewed a cloud of toxic fumes. The small drambat got caught and fell over in his tracks. The others broke off their advance and held their breath. The tall drambat dragged the small one out of the cloud by his tail, but before he got far Cangoar sent him sprawling with a swipe of his claws.

He followed with a fireball which engulfed the drambat and ignited the noxious fumes. The fumes blew up and sent the other drambats sprawling. He dispatched the small one with a swipe of his claws. The tall one spun to his right, attempting to douse flames on his tail and right wing. Cangoar finished him with another fireball and then glanced around.

Three left.

They were limping off toward the woods, injured and apparently unable to fly. But as he turned to give chase, ten more drambats landed in the meadow – led by the spewler from the ceremony.

Oh, crap!

Now it's going to be really tough to keep his cover.

"Hey Cangoar!" yelled the spewler. "You probably have no idea who I am, but I remember you – from the B.E.G."

Cangoar studied the spewler. "I know who you are. You're a member of the Drakebureau."

The three injured drambats scurried behind the others. Thirteen drambats and one spewler – shouldn't be a problem. Cangoar began moving toward them. "Kardool, isn't it? I wouldn't expect a spewler like you – a member of the Drakebureau – to be leading a hoard of drambats in such a dark ceremony!"

Kardool bobbed his head and chuckled. "Nobody cares what you expect," he sneered. "But we do care about you. How's your tail – Canbore? Does it wake you up in the middle of the night? Or does it simply make it more difficult to maneuver while you flit about, spying on spewlers and drambats?"

Cangoar scrunched his nose and picked up his pace. "I saw you bowing to that purple haze in the cave. What's up with that talking purple haze? You don't really think it'll give you power, do you?"

Kardool bobbed his head. "I didn't realize you were so interested in our affairs. Perhaps you'd like a demonstration of the Dark Queen's power – up close and personal!"

Kardool scratched his left arm until it bled – then his eyes glowed yellow. Not red like Ilgregious'. And before he could react, that same dark and heavy presence invaded his mind and took control of his thoughts – just like when Ilgregious did it. His limbs grew heavy, as if he were running in a tar pit. Dark thoughts bored into his brain. His legs stopped moving completely. He fell over in his tracks, unaware of his body – or the drambats sneering at him. There was nothing but a dark, heavy presence and the spewler's Voice inside his head.

"Oh, how lovely!" exclaimed the Voice. "You actually believe? Do you honestly believe family, friends, and the pursuit of treasure are what's important in life?!! Ah, but no need to worry. I'm here to help you douse those delusions! And I see you've served at the Viper Vault! How noble is that!? But no need to worry that bumpy brown head of yours – those efforts won't go un-rewarded. I have plans for you – a job which is much more important and rewarding than anything at the Viper Vault."

Cangoar grimaced as he tried to push the Voice out of his head. But it was no use. A sense of helplessness took over – as if his soul were shrinking.

"But wait. What's this?" continued the Voice. "Ilgregious killed those guards, invaded your mind, and even captured you. What a frightening experience that must have been! Ah, but never fear, I'll be able to make that all better – with just a word or two."

Cangoar rolled up in a near fetal position, his frame convulsing slightly.

"However did you escape?" asked the Voice. "Oh, I see. You believe *Melohim* helped you? I'm sorry, but you've been fooling yourself my dear

145

friend. Now everyone will see why Drakedom has no room for those who believe in fables about superior beings who don't exist. Fables about a being who is naught but a myth – a toothless toad's tale. Melohim only exists in the minds of the weak. Naught but a lie posed by superstitious drakes to control weak-minded beings like yourself. But I am your true friend – to set you free from such delusions."

Suddenly his mind cleared as he exhaled and tilted his head toward the Voice. He no longer felt threatened. No need to fight. What had he been thinking? "You are?" he asked expectantly.

The Voice softened and continued in a higher pitch. "Oh, but of course, my young nickelneck. I am your humble servant – to the bitter end! I want your mind to be clear as a cold winter sky. You will soon be certain – to know the truth that nothing exists beyond this realm. The Phoberon is a myth. We know nothing except what we can see, hear, smell, touch, and taste. This realm is all there is. This realm is all that is real – what our lives consist of."

Cangoar nodded obediently. "Yes. What can be seen and smelled and tasted – all there is and ever will be."

"There now, doesn't that feel better?"

"And Melohim doesn't exist," Cangoar parroted in a monotone voice, speaking to no one in particular – with a blank expression on his face. "Melohim is nothing but a myth. Naught but a toothless toad's tale."

"Yes. Yes, indeed. Nothing but a myth, a legend at best. A lie at worst. As is the Phoberon," said the Voice in a soft, soothing tone.

"Yes – the Phoberon – nothing but a myth."

"You have done well my dear friend," cooed the Voice. "A new world is opening up to you. And now I have something else to help you with."

"You do?"

"Yes. Yes, indeed. The *truth* would be difficult for anyone else, but I know *you* can handle it."

"How do you know?"

"Did you not just now embrace the *truth* – the reality that this realm is all there is?"

"Yes."

"And that Melohim and the Phoberon are nothing but myths – designed to control the weak-minded?"

"I did."

"Then you are no longer a weak-minded fool. Can you see that you are more than a tool and deserve to know the truth?"

"Yes. I can handle it, your Darkness."

"Very well. This will help you. Will you accept it, even if it is difficult?"

"Yes, I can accept it."

"I know you can, but *will* you accept it?"

"Yes, I will accept it."

"Ok, then. It was *you* who killed those guards and set the prisoners free that night at the Viper Vault. *You* are the one who should be punished. Will you embrace the truth – difficult as it may sound?"

Cangoar started to look away – but somehow the Voice which forbade him. He nodded. "Yes, I see it now. I killed those guards. I must be punished…"

"Yes. So very unfortunate – but anyone can see you simply couldn't help yourself. You did it because you are in love with the other nickelneck, the female."

Cangoar flicked his tongue twice. "Yes. I did it to save Alfedora. I must be… I think I'm… I *love* her."

"And you must love her very much to have risked *everything,*" continued the Voice in a soft and soothing tone. "And although it's a pity those guards had to die, maybe they deserved what they got."

A serious expression appeared on Cangoar's face. "Yes. Of course. They deserved to die!" Cangoar's legs thrashed a bit as he tried to stand up. "They were coming to get her. They would've killed her. Killed her until she was *dead!* I had to do it. I did it to save *her.*"

"Very good, my friend," intoned the Voice softly. "Yes, and if the others could see it the way you and I do, they'd recognize you for the hero you are. But they won't, will they?"

Cangoar scrunched his nose. "No. They'll never understand – not like you."

A vapid grin appeared on his face – the Voice had given him a new perspective on things – a new purpose even. And now there was little else inside his head except the Voice.

"You've done well, Cangoar. I'm quite proud of you," said the Voice with a pat on his shoulder. "It wasn't easy fighting two malwracks at once. But you did it, you won, and you saved Alfedora."

An image of himself fighting Lutjen and Laudus popped into his head.

"And how did you do it?" asked the Voice.

"Do what?"

"Defeat two malwracks at once."

"Oh, yeah. Well, Lutjen screeched, but of course that doesn't work on nickelnecks. And then I hit 'em both with some stink gas, and while they were stumbling around, I shot 'em with a couple of fireballs. Two shots – one to each malwrack's neck. That's all it took."

"Wow, how impressive is that? You truly are a great warrior, my gray-necked friend. I'm going to release you, and we'll fly back to Flargellion together. You will turn yourself in at the Viper Vault, and I'll do my best to convince them that yours was a crime of passion. I'm sure they'll go easy on you once they understand the intention of those guards. And you, my friend, will testify that you did it for her. Everything you did was for *her*. And when the Drakebureau understands that – once they understand the *real* truth, they might just give you an award for chivalry and courage. Taking on two full-grown malwracks is nothing to sneer at."

Cangoar was still lying on his side but bowed his head. His voice bordered on syrupy as he whimpered, "This is all so very kind of you, your Drakeness. I'm afraid I don't deserve this."

"No, you don't," said the Voice.

He exhaled suddenly and deeply as the Voice withdrew from his head. After a minute or two he struggled back to his feet and stared into the sky with a blank look on his face.

"Can we kill him now?" asked one of the drambats as he bobbed his head – along with a few others.

"No, you idiot!" exclaimed Kardool as he took a swipe at the drambat – which managed to stay just out of reach.

"I'm going to take him back to Flargellion where he'll testify about those guards at the Viper Vault. The rest of you can fly back to the cave and clean up whatever's left of the ceremony."

"Yes, your Drakeness," answered the drambat. "But we caught him spying on us – on you, your Drakeness! Let's kill him now and be done with it."

Kardool bobbed his head and glared at the drambat. "You're either particularly brave or singularly stupid. This nickelneck is the one who killed those guards at the Viper Vault – and justice must be served! Now run along before I burn the tails off the lot of you!"

Several drambats sneered and took a step toward Kardool. Cangoar's eyes narrowed as he scrunched his nose and lowered his big brown head. Perhaps he would roast the dissenters as an example for the others. He glanced at Kardool, who glanced back at him. Together they scrunched their noses at the drambats.

The spewler grinned and yelled, "Be gone, you silly little drambats, while you still have tails and wings and breath in your lungs!"

The drambats looked at Kardool, then at Cangoar, and scattered like flies.

Cangoar and Kardool took off for Flargellion after the others were gone. A spewler and a nickelneck traveling together would have been a fairly rare sight, but they arrived at Flargellion in the middle of the night. There was no one except a solitary guard who was on duty at the Viper Vault – a malwrack sleeping noisily in the guard hut.

Kardool gave the guard a nudge. "Hey you, wake up!" he snarled. The big malwrack didn't budge. "Wake up, you brute! I've got a prisoner."

Still no response. Cangoar nudged him a little harder, but the malwrack continued snoring. Cangoar nudged him even harder, but the malwrack snorted and rolled onto his right side and kicked wildly. Cangoar took the brunt of a kick from the malwrack's right-rear leg. A high-pitched, penetrating screech followed – and a split-second later everything went silent.

Cangoar picked himself up after the kick and shook his head. He glanced around and saw Kardool rolling on the ground and clutching his head with his paws. He shook his head again and felt his ear flaps release. "Your Drakeness! Are you okay?" he asked as Kardool writhed on the floor and clutched his head.

The malwrack struggled to his feet and yawned. He glanced down and muttered, "What's up with him?"

"Must have a headache," replied Cangoar. "My name's Cangoar. This is Kardool. And you are?"

"Oh, hey there. My name's Barl. Pleased to make your acquaintance. What brings a nickelneck and a spewler to the Viper Vault this time of night?"

"I ga-guess I'm here to ta-turn myself in," stuttered Cangoar. He looked away and shook his jowls. What did he just say? And why was he stuttering?

"Why, what have you done?" asked Barl with a raised brow and suddenly more alert than he had been. "I've never seen a dragon – let alone a nickelneck – turn itself in before. Are you sure you don't have a few loose gold nuggets inside that brown head?"

"Yeah, I guess so. I mean, err, yes. Yeah. I'm sure. I didn't come all the way from eastern Trool for nothing." Cangoar's voice trailed off as he spoke. He sounded less confident than he wanted and felt as if two parts of his brain were on the verge of arguing with one another.

Barl glanced around the guard hut and bobbed his head. "Well, this is highly unusual. You understand this is the Viper Vault and not a detention center for hatchlings. What is it you're turning yourself in for?"

Cangoar stared at the malwrack. "I think. I mean, I uh. I'm thinking... Well, those two guards were going to kill Alfedora that night. And I think I might have killed them to save her life. And I might have set her and that blue ape free." His voice ended on a high note – as if it were more of a question than a statement.

"You *think* you might have killed Lutjen and Laudus? You *think?*" The malwrack glared at Cangoar. "Either you did or you didn't. Which is it?"

Cangoar looked at the ground and shook his jowls again. "Sorry, my memory's a bit fuzzy. But yeah, as I recall, those guards were about to kill my friend Alfedora. But I saved her. Saved her from certain death, I did. I think. I did." He winced and looked at the ground for a second or two. "I'm thinking Alfedora and I are – well, you know. We're – how do I say it? I think we're in, I'm in..." He was about to say the l-word but somehow couldn't quite get it out of his mouth.

"You're in deep, deep dragon dung, is what you are," interrupted the malwrack. He turned and began digging through a pile of rusty irons. "You better be making this stuff up. Lutjen and Laudus were friends. Ah, here it is."

And with amazing dexterity for a malwrack his size, he slammed a shackle around Cangoar's snout and locked it in place.

Barl grinned, pulled the chain taught, and got up in his snout. "You're in *my* prison, now – you filthy nickelneck. Ain't nobody gonna break you out. Not tonight, not tomorrow, not never. You can bet your tail-challenged butt on that one!"

Kardool stumbled to his feet. "WHAT'S GOING ON?" he shouted. "OH GOOD. I SEE YOU'VE ARRESTED OUR PRISONER."

"No need to shout, your Drakeness," said Barl in a louder-than-normal voice. "I'm going to lock this one up. We'll see what Pinhammer and the rest of your Drakenesses want to do with him. He claims to be the one who murdered those guards a couple of days ago."

"YOU'VE GOT TO BE KIDDING ME? DID HE CONFESS THAT JUST NOW?" shouted Kardool. "I HAD NO IDEA HE WAS SO DANGEROUS! GOOD JOB GETTING A CONFESSION OUT OF HIM. I BROUGHT HIM HERE TO COOL OFF AFTER HE HAD A RUN-IN WITH SOME DRAMBATS. I GUESS I'M LUCKY HE DIDN'T KILL ME TOO!"

Cangoar knew it was a pack of lies – but looked at the ground and said nothing. Somehow his allegiance to this spewler had come to be more important than truth. He shoved any disloyal thoughts aside. Loyalty had suddenly become more important than truth.

"Yes indeed. You were lucky he didn't, your Drakeness," said Barl while smiling politely. "It's one thing for a guard or two to be murdered. But I couldn't bear the thought of losing a distinguished leader like yourself. I mean, like you, your Drakeness. Your Drakeness."

Barl attempted to bow to the spewler but was still a head taller than Kardool even with his head bowed and his right-front leg bent.

"WHY THANK YOU, YOU'VE BEEN MOST HELPFUL," shouted Kardool. "BUT IT'S QUITE LATE AND I REALLY MUST BE GOING. WHAT DID YOU SAY YOUR NAME WAS?"

"The name's Barl, your Drakeness. And if you'd remember me when they replace Lutjen as head drake around here, I'd be much obliged."

"NICE TO MEET YOU, KARL!" yelled Kardool as he headed toward the Daor Gate. "I'LL BE SURE TO PUT IN A WORD FOR YOU TOMORROW WHEN THE DRAKEBUREAU RECONVENES."

"Thank you, your Drakeness. That would be most kind, your Drakeness. Uh, the name is Barl, your Drakeness."

His voice was a bit too cheery, and Kardool had already vanished before he finished anyway. He flicked his tongue and led Cangoar to cell three-hundred and twenty-seven. He locked him up in the same manner Alfedora had been locked up by Lutjen a few nights earlier. He clamped shackles on his legs and ran a chain from each to an anchor in the floor. He finished with a chain from the snout shackle to a floor anchor.

The malwrack picked up the tail shackle and laughed. "Guess we won't need this one! Oh, and I have to ask – nickelhead. Why did you let yourself get dragged in here by that scrawny little spewler – even if he is a member of the Drakebureau?"

"The name's Cangoar, your Guardness. Kardool said it was my duty to turn myself in – my duty to society."

Really? My duty to society?

He looked away as the reality of where he was started to sink in. Now he was locked up – where he used to be a *guard*. On top of that he'd confessed to the murders of Lutjen and Laudus. Those guys had been his friends.

"Ha! Your duty to society?!" exclaimed Barl. "I think you've got weevils in your head. I'll bet you can't wait for me to do *my* duty for society!"

"Yeah, right," he muttered, not caring whether Barl heard or not.

Barl headed to the guard hut. "Stupid nickelneck," he snarled. "Maybe now I can get some sleep."

Paul Krueger

19. Canyon Living

While Cangoar was out chasing Ill-greega-butt, Bannabard and I hunted and fished and ate and slept and fished. Mostly we waited in the cave in Farshen, wondering what the others were up to and what would become of ourselves and Cangoar.

I gazed at Bannabard as he gnawed on a catfish. The shadows in the canyon had grown short – like my patience. "I'm so sick of fish and lizards I could just spew – like flaming stink gas!"

The ape kept gnawing. How rude was that?

"And on top of that, I think I've lost weight – probably more than you weigh, not that I needed to."

The ape still didn't respond.

I shook my jowls. "Where's Jendal, and what's she been up to? All this sitting around doing nothing – what a waste! Wasting time and wasting away. Makes me wish I'd gone with Cangoar."

A disembodied voice replied, "You'd have been corrupted like he was – possibly worse."

I glanced in the voice's direction as Bannabard jumped nearly a foot in the air. A translucent, black orb oscillated behind him.

"Would it kill you to warn us before you do that?" asked Bannabard as he spun around and faced the voice.

The floating orb transformed into a female blue ape, winked at me, and said, "Oh, right. Sorry about that."

I grinned slightly. "Good to see you, Jendal. We're beginning to wonder how much longer we'd be stuck here."

Jendal nodded. "It's good to see you too. Hopefully your time here hasn't been too unpleasant. Perhaps you are feeling a little useless out

153

here in the desert, but there are challenges before us. Challenges which ought to be of interest... especially to you, Alfedora."

"What challenges?"

"Cangoar is in trouble."

"I knew it!" I exclaimed with a bob of my head.

"What happened?" asked Bannabard.

Jendal glanced at Bannabard, then turned to me. "He's turned himself in for the murder of those guards. He's locked up in the Viper Vault, just like you were. I'm afraid he's confessed to killing those guards."

"Hold on a second!" I exclaimed as my eyes grew wide. "Why would he do that?"

"It's a sad tale, I'm afraid," said Jendal.

I glanced at the ground, then glared at Jendal. "Did Ilgregious invade his mind and unhinge it like before?"

"Yeah. His mind's been messed with, but it wasn't Ilgregious. This was someone else."

I shook my jowls. "Wait. What? So Cangoar actually believes he murdered those guards – and Ilgregious isn't the only one doing mind tricks?"

Jendal nodded.

I bobbed my head. "You're kidding. Now there's two?" I looked away, not really wanting an answer. My eyes narrowed. "Is this one doing conjuring ceremonies too?"

"Whether they do ceremonies or not doesn't matter as much as you might think," said Jendal in a matter-of-fact tone. "What matters is how we react. But there's something else – this one's a member of the Drakebureau too."

I glared at Jendal. "Great. Just great." I shook my jowls. "We're up against not one, but two members of the Drakebureau – one of which wants us dead!" I bobbed my head. Again. "And if that's not enough, Cangoar thinks he's guilty of murder! And you're worried about how *we* react?!"

"Yeah, I think you've got it."

Bannabard thumped his chest. "I say we go get Cangoar out of the Viper Vault!"

154

"Hang on," I said as I glared at Jendal. "What were *you* doing when Cangoar's mind was being messed with? When they convinced him he murdered those guards?"

"I wasn't allowed to interfere, if that's what you mean," said Jendal.

Her eyes seemed to penetrate my soul. I scrunched my nose and exposed my fangs. "You mean you – just let it happen?"

Jendal nodded. "I get it that you care about your friend and wish I would have intervened. To stop this evil dead in its tracks."

"Yeah, you got that right," I said with a bit of a sneer. "Why didn't you?"

"It would have been a violation of Kardool's free will."

"Wait. Wut?" I glared at her even harder. "Who's Kardool?"

"He's a spewler," said Jendal. "Represents spewlers on the Drakebureau."

I bobbed my head. "And he's allowed to corrupt Cangoar's mind because he's on the Drakebureau?"

"No, of course not," said Jendal in a matter-of-fact tone. "But he's been given free will – like any other drake or ape. It would be wrong for one of us to interfere with that – just like it would be wrong to interfere when someone here does something good."

"So you admit you have the power – you could have stopped it."

"That's not the point," said Jendal. "Melohim is the ultimate power, yet he limits himself in his interactions with his created beings. He gave us moral agency – and doesn't relinquish that even when some choose to misuse it. He respects our moral agency."

I bobbed my head and scrunched my nose. "Wut? So he respects Kardool more than Cangoar?"

"No," said Jendal. "He doesn't respect one person above another. And He certainly doesn't respect bad choices – choices which deny truth. Respect must be earned. But Melohim respects Kardool's freedom to choose as he will. And he doesn't take away a being's ability to make choices, even when they choose badly. Kardool has chosen a dark path which will corrupt everything he touches, including himself. He has given himself over to a lust for power – and to forces he doesn't understand."

"What about the one Ilgregious calls 'the Dark Queen'?" I asked. "She messed with Cangoar's mind – but you weren't allowed to stop her?"

"Not if it meant violating Kardool's free will," said Jendal. "He gave himself up – to let her channel her dark deeds."

"Just to be clear, you stood there and watched Kardool corrupt Cangoar's mind – because you didn't want to violate that slimy spewler's free will?"

"Yeah, that's right."

Bannabard thumped his chest. "It's up to us now. We're the ones who can make a difference."

I thrashed my tail. Twice. "I guess Bannabard's right. We can't just leave him there." I glared at Jendal. "Will you set Cangoar's head straight while we're on our way?"

"You want me to get inside his head and re-arrange his thoughts?" asked Jendal.

"Yeah, why not?" I asked. "I'll be your channel for good. If the Dark Queen can do it through Kardool, why not you – through me?"

"I'm not like her, just like you're not like Kardool."

I glared at her. "But you have powers – same as the Dark Queen, right? Why not use them to straighten things out inside his head?"

"She can't just invade his mind," said Bannabard as he turned to Jendal. "You can't, right?"

"No, I can't. We must respect his beliefs and choices."

"What about respecting his *life?*" I bellowed. "They're going to put him to death!"

"It will do no good to save his body if we do violence to his person," answered Jendal.

"How would fixing the lies in his head do violence to his person?" I asked. "Violence has already been done to his person. This is what he needs – whether he likes it or not."

"That's just it," said Jendal. "He must make that choice on his own. We cannot make it for him."

I bobbed my head. "You're making this a lot harder than it needs to be – all because you're worried about violating free will or something. The Dark Queen doesn't care about any of that. Why should we?"

"No she doesn't," answered Jendal. "But that is what makes us different, and that is why Cangoar needs your help. I will never use my power to invade another being's mind. You and Bannabard were there that night. He needs to hear the truth. Your side of the story can help him recover and make up his own mind."

"I'm game if you are," said Bannabard, looking up at me.

"I guess," I muttered. "For Cangoar." I glared at Jendal. "And in spite of her fixation on free will. Maybe there's something we can say or do to help him get his head on straight."

"I'm sure there is," said Jendal. "And you should know that he might not *want* your help. Whether Cangoar will embrace the truth or not remains to be seen."

"Cangoar's life is hanging by a newt's tail and you're treating it like it's a game," I said with a bit of a snarl. I bobbed my head and looked away. "What if Cangoar refuses to embrace the truth? What then? Do we let him sacrifice himself for a lie?"

"Yes, if that is his choice," answered Jendal. "Once we stop respecting the beliefs and choices of others, we become less than what we were meant to be. Relationships matter – but a relationship without truth isn't worth having."

"So we need to let Cangoar choose, even if he chooses badly..." My voice trailed off at the end. It was already decided what we would do. I looked out into the canyon and thought about how strange this all was. Here I was hanging out with two apes – and in Farshen of all places. "Well, I'm guessing it'll be a whale better than sitting around and wasting away like a dead deer in the desert sun. Do we have a plan, or are we going to figure out what to do when we get there?"

Jendal nodded. "The fact that Cangoar turned himself in and has chosen to be there complicates things. You are his only connection to what's real. Your mission is simply to remind him of what happened that night – from your perspective."

I glanced at the ground. "I'm guessing it's going to be like trying to convince a fat fiadhain that pigs can fly."

"Indeed, these are no small challenges before us," nodded Jendal. "But there is always hope. Yet hope can be a two-edged sword. Most of us hope for food, shelter, friends, family, fruitful lives, health, and security. And those are good things, but those hopes can drive us down very different paths."

"Gold. Don't forget gold," I interrupted.

"Oh yeah, we mustn't forget gold," said Jendal. "One path leads to self-concern and avarice where we trust only ourselves – where we choose safety instead of freedom and popularity instead of what's right. Another where we trust providence and the goodness of others, while embracing whatever blessings and challenges come our way."

Bannabard glanced around. "Don't you find that discouraging?"

Jendal's eyes twinkled. "At times – yes I do. But it's an opportunity to find out what we're made of. And while you two may have felt like you've been wasting time the last few days – our time is now short if we're going to help our friend. I'll meet you on the east side of Flargellion at dawn, in the woods outside the Daor Gate."

Late afternoon shadows invaded the canyon as Jendal disappeared. I took off heading east and a little north with Bannabard on my back – gladder than a badger to be out of there. If I never ate another carp or catfish that'd be fine with me. It felt good to be in the air again, and I immediately began scanning the ground for suitable game.

A short while later we crested the ridge of the canyon. The sun had snuck below the horizon behind us. In the twilight I spotted an area where the Farnheim River meandered through a broad flood plain in a meadow surrounded by thick forest. I dropped into a low glide a few feet above the water. I would be no good to Cangoar or anyone else if I wasted away from hunger.

My hunting instincts served me well. A small herd of bison were bedded down in some tall grass next to the river. Silently I banked left and attempted to land as quietly as possible behind eight of the slumbering beasts. But my exuberance got the better of me as I overshot the landing and impaled one with the claws on my right front foot.

The buffalo jerked, bellowed, and squealed. It roused the others and they all took off running. I veered sharply to my right and caught the injured one. Bannabard went sprawling over my left shoulder. I was getting ready to enjoy real food again – when Bannabard limped out of some nearby bushes.

"Where'd you get off to?" I asked. "Are you okay?"

Bannabard didn't answer. I stopped chewing long enough to look up at him. He stood there glaring at me.

"Well, you know. It's been a while since… since *real* food."

"I'm happy for you. But maybe next time you could warn me or let me off first?"

"Oh, right. How'd you hurt your leg?"

"I landed on a bison. It took off running and tried to throw me off. I managed to grab one of its horns with my left hand and a handful of hair with my right. But it bucked for all it was worth and threw me into that thicket of bushes over there."

I gave him a blank stare. "Sounds like fun to me."

Bannabard shook his head. "Yeah, a real kick."

"Urrrmmm," I rumbled. "This is so much better than fish. It's been a while since I've had anything like this. Would you like some?"

"Uh, I'm uh… I'm good thanks." Bannabard looked away. "Maybe I'll find some fish or tubers or something in the river over there. Let me know when you're ready to go."

Bannabard would let her eat by herself. He stretched out in some tall grass next to the river. The sound of crunching bones and rushing water persisted as he looked up at the stars and wondered what would become of his species even if they succeeded in exposing Ilgregious and his lackeys. It was great that there was a ruling body of dragons. But would they really care about treaty violations with blue apes?

His thoughts turned to Lais and their two sons. They had no way of knowing what he was doing or where he was. He wished he could tell them where he was and what he was up to. "Gorby's death won't be for naught if I can help it," he muttered as he rapped a fist on his chest.

20.   TREADING LIGHTLY

t was a clear night with a bright crescent moon as Bannabard and I arrived at Flargellion. I banked toward a grassy knoll among some trees behind the B.E.G. stands with the blue ape clinging to my neck. I touched down, then glanced to my right at a stand of trees.

"Would you mind terribly if I dismount first?"

I grinned slightly. "Oh please. You had fun riding that buffalo and you know it."

"Yeah, right," said Bannabard.

I let him off and we headed down a trail and into the forest. We hadn't gone far before we found a low area amidst some tall pine and fir trees – just off the trail to our right. "We'll hang out here until your friend Jendal shows up."

"Oh, so now she's *my* friend?"

"Well, you're the one who found her, not me. And besides, she always takes the form of a blue ape – an attractive ape, don't you think?"

Bannabard looked at the ground for a second. "I hadn't really noticed."

I scrunched my nose. "Yeah, right."

Bannabard thumped his chest. "I already have a mate. And how weird would that be? Attracted to someone – not just from another region or another part of the world, but from the Numinous?"

"She doesn't look like she's from the Phoberon – at least most of the time."

"Give it a rest, would you? I can't even imagine what her realm is like."

"Yeah, I can't either. But there's something about her I can't wrap my tongue around. Why do you think she does it?"

"Does what?"

"Comes to help us – to help you. Do you think spending time in our realm is dull and boring, or do you think she enjoys it?"

"I have no idea – maybe it's in her nature to help others."

"Ya think?" I asked. "What would it be like to be a dosara – would you even care about gold?"

"I don't imagine they care much about gold."

"Spending time here would be *really* weird, then. Why would you even come if you didn't care about gold? Yet there's something about Jendal that would attract anyone. Something about her transcends the power she wields. There must be a catch, don't you think?"

Bannabard looked up and smiled. "Catch? I don't think so. I get the feeling she's simply good. Maybe you should ask next time you see her."

I bobbed my head. "Maybe I'll do that. Or maybe not. Jendal's nice and all, but nobody's *that* nice. There must be something in it for her. A big pile of something. Maybe not gold, but something a dosara considers just as valuable."

"Yeah, maybe," said Bannabard. "If you say so."

I shook my jowls. "I think it's time we're done talking about Jendal. Bannabard, it's good to hear you have a mate. Any other family back in Seedred?"

Bannabard looked at the ground. "Yeah, I have three… err, uh, two sons in Ape Town."

"Oh how nice! To be honest when I first met you, I wouldn't have thunk it."

"Thunk what?" he asked in an annoyed tone.

"Thunk you had a family. I'll bet your mate is lovely, as blue apes go."

"Yeah, thanks. She certainly is. I love her *and* my sons." He looked away.

"I'm sorry about your little one."

Bannabard's eyes were moist as he turned and gave me a piercing look. He stood up, pounded his chest, howled, spun around twice, then charged and stopped abruptly, his face a couple of inches from mine. "Why?" he asked before looking away and snorting a couple of times.

I scrunched my nose. "Why what?" I felt gases building inside me. "You shouldn't charge like that – it can do things to a dragon."

Bannabard gave me a fierce look. "Drambats. Why kill a young ape?"

I turned to one side and belched a good five seconds, then waved the gases away with a paw. "Sorry. That's better. Hate to waste a fireball like that but didn't want to roast ya. Yeah, well. I'm guessing Ilgregious is evil – like, pure evil. You saw what they did to those malwracks. And that Dark Queen must be even worse. I saw her give him strange powers. Apparently as a reward for making sacrifices – like throwing hatchlings into lava pits."

Bannabard looked at the ground and turned away. He threw his head back, howled, and then pounded the ground with his fists.

"They burned Gorby!!"

"Yeah, I know. Let it out. Belch it out – like I did."

Bannabard hung his head. "No one should lose a son – not like that."

"I can't imagine," I said as I put a paw on his shoulder. Bannabard sat on the ground and stared vacantly at the morning sky. I was almost afraid to ask but figured it might help get his mind off his son. "Do you have any other family in Ape Town?"

Bannabard glanced up at me. "I used to, but my parents died in the Great Ape Wars. My brother was killed by some drambats three years ago."

"I'm sorry to hear that. You've lost a lot of family members."

"Yeah. You learn to take the days one at a time. But this thing with Jendal – it's helping."

"How's that?" I asked.

"It wasn't long ago I was convinced this realm is all there is. But then she showed up. Obviously from the Numinous. Maybe my son and my parents and brother crossed over into some altered state or something. It gives me hope. Like maybe they're still around. Maybe I'll get to see them again. The whole after-life thing. What do you think?"

"Oh my, yes!" I exclaimed. "I've always believed in an after-life." As if! But I wasn't going to dash his hopes of seeing his family again. I was reminded of Pa.

I'll never see him again.

My eyes narrowed – part of me wanted to say, 'Get real, suck it up, and get on with your life. What's done is done.' Instead, I said, "It's something to hang onto when we're in a dark place."

"You don't think it's a crutch – a sign of weakness?" he asked.

"What's that?"

"Belief in an after-life?"

I turned and gazed at the sunrise. "No – not at all."

How stupid is this? Talking to a blue ape about the after-life!

But I would be kind. He just lost his son. "Jendal does things not even dragons can do. I guess we have to believe her when she says she was sent by Melohim. But don't you find it difficult to believe in a being who never shows himself? This Melohim – who claims to be all-powerful, yet allows innocent hatchlings to get thrown into lava pits?"

"Like you said, Jendal can do things. And when she says Melohim sent her, I believe her," said Bannabard with a thump of his chest.

"I guess I would agree if I didn't have the Drakebureau to hold onto. That's what I believe in – not some being from another realm." I bobbed my head and stared at an orange and blue sky to the east.

Bannabard's eyes narrowed. "Drakebureau or not, there's no denying what she does and says."

"Maybe we'll just have to agree to disagree."

"Yeah, I suppose. But Jendal is simply too good of a person, or being, or thing, or whatever she is – to be pulling the wool over our eyes. But what about you? Do you have family?"

I flicked my tongue. "Well, Pa died from an infection, and Mum's been hanging out in her lair on the north end of Lake Luellian ever since."

"Sorry to hear about your pa. Were you close?"

I looked at the ground and thought about how to change the subject. "Yeah, we were close, but I was pretty young when he died. I have an older brother named Slithester. I haven't seen or heard from him in decades. Last I heard he'd found a lair somewhere near Smilf where he's settled in with a mate and is raising some young drakes of his own."

"It's good to hear you still have your mum. Do you see her much?"

"No, not a whole lot, but I was over there just the other day." I paused and glanced at the sky. "I guess she means well, like most mums. But truth is – we don't get on all that well."

"Sorry to hear that," he said. "But I'm afraid I don't know what that would be like. My parents died when I was young."

"That sounds tougher than a frozen fiadhain in February," I said as I studied a few orange and yellow clouds against an increasingly blue sky. I was done discussing family and didn't want to hear any more about his either. The truth was, Urraca made me feel powerless – as if I would remain a hatchling forever.

Bannabard smiled. "You got that right, but I got through it, and you know what they say…"

I gave him a slight grin. "No, what do they say?"

"What doesn't roast you makes you more fire-resistant."

"Really? That's what they say, eh?" I made sure my grin wasn't an entirely friendly one but thought better of taking it to another level. If I scared the crap out of him it would be fun but might he not be easy to find if he took off in the forest.

"Yeah, well, maybe it's a saying best kept among blue apes," he said with a slightly sheepish grin.

A disembodied voice interrupted. "Hey guys, what's up?" A black orb appeared and transformed into a blue ape.

I'd seen Jendal do it before, but it still creeped me out a bit.

"Cangoar is scheduled to testify at a hearing this afternoon, so we'll need to move quickly. He's embraced Kardool's lies and probably won't want to hear the truth. He'll be glad to see you – but until he's able to let go of the lies, he won't want our help."

I stood up, flicked my tongue, and gave Jendal a hard look. "Won't want our help? If he'd rather be locked up than talk with us, then what's the point of risking our necks?"

"Easy. I'm just saying it'll take some time for him to come around."

Bannabard looked at me, then at Jendal. "I know we should respect his choices, but who wouldn't want to get out of the Viper Vault?"

I bobbed my head. "Someone who isn't in his right mind."

"Exactly," said Jendal. "And even if he gets past Kardool's lies, he still might decide to stay and face the Drakebureau."

"No way!" I exclaimed as I glared at Jendal. I lowered my head until I was almost in Jendal's face. "I love the Drakebureau – but Ilgregious wants him dead."

Jendal didn't flinch. "Yeah, but Cangoar must make his own choice. Just like it's up to you whether you want to try to help him – or not."

I backed off a bit and gave Jendal a cold stare. "Fair enough – but if he decides to testify and doesn't tell the Drakebureau what they want to hear, Ilgregious and that other drake will have him executed."

Jendal glanced at Bannabard, then at me. "Yes, that could happen, but we must not stand in his way if that is the path he chooses."

"And what if he rejects the truth and decides to stay?" asked Bannabard.

"He will have chosen what he has chosen," said Jendal. "If he chooses to flee, we will help him – but if he decides to stay, we must support him whether he stands for the truth or rejects it altogether."

I gave Jendal a piercing look. "If he chooses to believe Kardool's lies, there's *nothing* we can do?"

"I'm afraid so," said Jendal.

Bannabard looked at me, then at Jendal. "You talk as if we can choose to believe whatever we want."

Jendal smiled and said, "The choices we make in life are rooted in things we believe and things we care about. Alfedora takes to the air because she believes her wings will carry her. You came and met me because you believe there is hope for Cangoar and because you care about him."

"Yeah, there's hope all right," I said with a bob of my head. "I just hope he'll pay attention when we tell him the truth."

"And with Melohim's help, he will," answered Jendal.

I flicked my tongue. "Where was Melohim when Ilgregious threw the little ones into that lava pit, or killed those guards?"

"Ilgregious thinks the only way he can find his way in life is through creating fear in others," said Jendal. "It's a bit ironic that his fear of never being loved is what drives him to violence – to create fear in others."

"And yet Melohim allows him to do it," said Bannabard.

Jendal nodded. "Melohim will not violate the free will of those who choose a dark path. But in the end they will be given what they have chosen. As will we all."

My eyes narrowed. "You gotta be pulling my wing!" I muttered. "Only the Drakebureau can put an end to this nonsense. Once the other leaders find out who Ilgregious really is and what he's done, they'll put an end to him and his toadies throwing hatchlings into lava pits."

I gazed across the meadow and up at the twin horns of Flargellion. 'Might doesn't always make right,' had been Urraca's words when I was young. Yeah, right. Everything I'd ever experienced had been just the opposite. It felt like might really did make right. The way Urraca treated me was proof of that. And now Cangoar's life was in the claws of Kardool and the Drakebureau. Yet here we were with Jendal – a powerful being from the Phoberon. Will she use her powers to save his life? Of course not! I was beginning to despise the free will thing. How can Melohim be good when he's created a universe in which only the bad guys can violate it?

21. Neither Fish, nor Flesh, nor Good Red Herring

I flicked my tongue. "You know they're going to kill him if he stays – no matter what he believes."

Bannabard and Jendal turned and faced the mountain with me. Jendal nodded. "Perhaps they will."

"Let's go find Cangoar and see if he'll talk to us," I said, scrunching my nose.

"As luck or providence would have it, I'm pretty sure he will – talk to you, that is," said Jendal.

"Why do you say that?" asked Bannabard.

"Cangoar thinks he's in love with Alfedora."

"Say WUT?" I asked as I scrunched my nose. "Where'd he get *that* idea?"

"It was something Kardool and the Dark Queen put in his head. They convinced him that he killed those guards because he was in love with you. But enough chit-chat, there will be a guard at the Daor Gate this time of day. There's another way in. Follow me."

I bobbed my head. "Hold on one dad-gum minute. If Cangoar thinks he's in love with me, then he'll do whatever it takes to get his tail-challenged butt out of there."

"With all due respect, I'm sure you hold a special place in his heart," said Jendal with a blank stare. "But he might be willing to sacrifice his feelings for you – for what he perceives to be a higher cause."

"Makes sense to me," said Bannabard.

"You *would* say that," I said.

"I'm afraid I have to agree with Bannabard," said Jendal. "I wouldn't want Cangoar to give up his principles for his passion, even when the object of his affection is as worthy a drake as yourself. And I don't think you would either, at least not in the long run."

I scrunched my nose. Jendal had a point – no one wants to be mated to a mouse.

Wait, what am I thinking?

I flicked my tongue. "I guess you're right. Forget I said anything."

We followed Jendal down a trail and were nearing a small lake when Jendal turned and faced me. "Okay. Stop right there. Alfedora, you get to go first."

I glanced around. There was nowhere to go except farther down the trail. "Go where?"

Jendal pointed at the ground below my feet. "Beneath us is an underground passage which leads to the Viper Vault. Stand still and get ready to land on your feet. I'm going to use dark energy to create a phase-shift in the ground beneath you – temporarily transforming it into dark matter. Trust me. You'll be fine – it's a fairly short drop. Just remember to bend your knees a little, land on your feet, keep your mouth closed, and don't extend your wings."

Bannabard nodded. "Relax, Alfedora. It'll be okay."

I took a step back and glared at Jendal. Something strange was about to happen and I didn't want any part of it. "No way. Ain't nobody messing with dark matter beneath *my feet*." My eyes narrowed. "What's the *matter*... with you?"

"Everything will be fine," said Jendal. "Remember, land on your feet, keep your mouth closed, and don't extend your wings. Are you ready?"

I glared at Bannabard, then at Jendal. "Ready for what?"

"We're going to go find Cangoar," said Bannabard.

"Oh, yeah. I'm good with *that*," I said with a little more enthusiasm than was called for.

"Here we go," said Jendal with a hint of a smile. "Alfedora, if you could take one step to your right. There. That's good. Now if you could look down and bend your knees slightly."

Jendal touched the ground beneath me with her right forefinger and suddenly I was falling. I looked up and tried to grab something – anything. My legs flailed as I fell – *into the ground*.

"Whooaa!" I yelled as the heads of my friends disappeared. I looked down but it was too late. The rocky floor of a cavern came at me fast. I was about to extend my wings when my rear feet hit the ground. My belly followed, then my neck, and then my chin – which hit the ground hard.

"Woohoo!" yelled Bannabard.

His yelp interrupted the ringing in my ears. I glanced to my left. He landed on his feet and stood there with a stupid grin on his face. "Alfedora – you okay?"

I was lying on my belly with my butt in the air and my front legs sprawled out in front of me. It took a moment for my head to clear and the ringing to stop. I struggled to my feet and glanced around. The cavern was dimly-lit. There was a light in front of us. "Huh? Oh deah, I gedd doe, bud I dink I bid by dongue."

Bannabard's eyes grew wide. "Don't talk. Your tongue – it doesn't look good. I'm not sure what to do with that."

The familiar translucent black orb appeared and hovered in front of me.

"Alfedora nearly bit her tongue off," said Bannabard.

"Deah, I dearly bid by dongue doff."

"Oh my," said the orb as it transformed into Jendal. "Don't talk. Whoa. Nickelnecks don't mess around when you bite something. Just a second – hold still."

She touched my tongue with her forefinger and said some words I didn't understand. A strange sensation passed through my tongue, my mouth, and even my head.

"There you go – good as new!" exclaimed Jendal as she turned aside and waved a hand in front of her face. "And you do have quite the uh… Uh, your breath has quite a malodorous aroma."

"Nice of you to say that. And hey – I can talk again. Thanks!"

"Yeah. Thanks a bunch!" exclaimed Bannabard.

Jendal started toward the light and glanced back at us. "The Great Hall is straight ahead. Let's go find Cangoar."

We followed her through a passageway and saw the light was coming from a large cavern up ahead. The entrance to the Viper Vault was visible on the opposite side. Torches on the walls lit up a pair of doors to our right – doors to the Great Hall.

Large letters had been etched in stone above the doors and were centered between two antlered elk skulls mounted to the wall. Their racks had seven points each, and the letters formed the words, "Goldgiefa fram Ligdraca" which was old Draconian and meant something like 'Gold-giver of the Fire-breathing Drakes'. I was surprised I remembered that – from ancient obelisks class I think.

Apparently the Drakebureau was in session because the doors were closed and a malwrack was stationed outside. Jendal took a deep breath and blew air at the guard. The guard sniffed the air and smiled, then turned in a circle, laid down, closed his eyes, and went to sleep.

Jendal whispered, "Follow me."

We crept across the floor of the cavern. The only sound was the guard snoring and my tail dragging on the ground.

"Alfedora, can you pick up your tail?" whispered Bannabard.

"Not while I'm walking. You'll have to carry it."

Bannabard gave me a hard look. "You're kidding."

"Nope. Can't pick it up – not when I'm walking."

Bannabard and I went ahead while Jendal released the guard. We crept to the guard hut. This guard was fast asleep too, even though it was mid-morning.

I glanced back but Jendal was nowhere to be seen. "Where'd she go now?" I whispered in an annoyed tone.

Bannabard crept into the guard hut and found the cell block listings. "Twittleburp. Cell two–thirteen: awaiting trial," he whispered. "Hey Alfedora, there's a drake in here named 'Twittleburp'."

I flicked my tongue and whispered, "That's nice. Don't know him."

"It's funny, right? Do you think it's a drambat?"

"If you say so. Focus. Can we focus on Cangoar?"

Males. It doesn't matter what species they are.

Bannabard continued in a whisper. "Coonbarq. Cell four–ninety–six: sentenced. Grimsnip. Cell four–hundred and two: terminated. Ah, here it is. Cangoar. Cell seven–twenty–seven: in process." He studied the facility map. "I know where he is. Follow me."

I followed him to the third aisle where we took a left. Cell seven-twenty-seven was near the end of the row. Cangoar's shackles and chains had him facing the door and through the bars I could see his eyes were closed. "Cangoar – wake up," I whispered.

Cangoar opened his eyes, then shook his jowls. "Hey Alfedora. Good to see you. Hey Bannabard. How'd you guys get here?"

"Good to see you too," I answered. "Jendal helped us. I guess the real question is, how'd *you* get here? They've got you locked up tighter than a stack of gold in a malwrack's lair."

Cangoar lowered his head a bit. "Uh, yeah. I guess... Actually I... I turned myself in."

I gave him a hard look. "What for?" I asked.

Cangoar flicked his tongue and closed his eyes. "I'd rather not talk about it."

"Jendal tells us you think you killed Lutjen and Laudus that night. Is that right?"

"Jendal – she's that arsnarm you were talking about, right?"

"Well yes... and no," answered Bannabard. "Jendal is from what you would call 'the Phoberon', but she's no arsnarm. She's a dosara. She sent us here to help you remember what happened that night."

"I know what happened."

My eyes narrowed. "You couldn't have killed Lutjen and Laudus."

Cangoar glared at me with an annoyed expression on his face. "What makes you say that? I killed them to set you two free. I'm here because I deserve to be..."

"Deserve what?" I asked.

"I deserve to be punished – for murder."

"Why would you commit murder and risk your life to set me free?" asked Bannabard. "You didn't even know me."

Cangoar glanced at me and looked at the ground. "Okay, so I did it for Alfedora. You were in the same cell."

"Yeah. I would've left Bannabard's butt tied up," I said.

"Okay, whatever," said Cangoar.

"Jendal was the one who set us free," said Bannabard. "She says your memory's been messed with."

I bobbed my head. "Yeah, she says Kardool's in league with Ilgregious and the Dark Queen. They're trying to frame you for killing

171

those guards. But we know it was Ilgregious who killed Lutjen and Laudus, not you. Kardool got inside your head and convinced you that you did it. He wants you to take the fall for his friend Ilgregious."

"Yeah, you're right. I killed those guards and Kardool is my friend – he's helping me," said Cangoar with a blank expression. "I deserve to be punished."

I bobbed my head. "You're not listening. Kardool is *not* your friend."

"Right. He's my friend, and I killed those guards."

"That's not what you told me," I said as I glared at him. "You said Ilgregious got inside your head and was about to kill you, but somehow you managed to escape."

Cangoar grinned, then looked me in the face. "Oh, Alfedora, my sweetheart, my serpentine, my little boll weevil."

I glared at him. "I'm nobody's weevil." I turned to Bannabard. "Did he just fat-shame me? What's a weevil, anyway?"

Bannabard shrugged.

Cangoar flashed a grin. "I'm so sorry, Alfedora! Obviously her mind's been clouded by her feelings – for me."

I gave him a disgusted look, but he didn't seem to notice.

"And I have to ask, my little boll weevil, why didn't Ilgregious kill *me?* Like, how's a skinny little drambat able to kill Lutjen and Laudus, but not me?"

My eyes narrowed. "Listen up, weevil brain. You told me Ilgregious kept you alive because he wanted you for a hostage."

"Hostage? Yeah, right. What makes you think Ilgregious was even there?"

"You told me he was. And later, when he was about to kill you, you asked for Melohim's help and he saved you when Ilgregious tried to invade your mind a second time."

Cangoar looked away. "I would never say that. Melohim is nothing but a myth – a toothless toad's tale."

I looked down for a second. "Do you remember telling me how Ilgregious' curse backfired? How he fell to the ground when you escaped?"

"Uh sorry, no. Really? When did I say *that?* Maybe you guys would like to come back tomorrow? I'll be testifying at the Drakebureau in a little while and need some time to get thoughts together."

Part of me felt sorry for his tail-challenged butt, but he needed a firm hand. I glared at him – the meanest glare I could manage. "No, we're not coming back tomorrow, and you didn't kill those guards."

"You're not coming back?" Cangoar dropped his head. "Yeah, you're right, I don't deserve that."

"Cangoar!" I exclaimed slightly above a whisper. "Look at me." I waited until his eyes met mine. "We're here to save your life, you toad-tongued, slug-slurping nickelneck. Let's go back to the beginning. This whole thing started while I was on my way to Flargellion and I saw Ilgregious and a gaggle of drambats calling out to the Dark Queen and throwing an arsnatcher – just a hatchling, mind you – into a lava pit. Do you remember that?"

"Oh wait, I do remember something like that." Cangoar looked at the ape, then back at me. "Poor little arsnatcher. No hatchling deserves to be thrown into a lava pit unless it's dead first."

Bannabard looked away, his eyes glistening. "No, certainly not…"

I put a paw on his shoulder. "Well, the next day the Drakebureau was in session, and Bannabard crashed the meeting and appeared in the middle of the Stone Ingot and told the leaders how drambats were killing off blue apes. Does that ring a gong?"

"Oh yeah, I remember. What a trick that was!"

"And he created such a ruckus that the leader cleared the room. And as I was leaving I heard Ilgregious deny what Bannabard said, and that's when I told them everything I saw the night before – at the lava pit."

Bannabard nodded. "Yeah, I was *really* grateful you did that. Did I ever thank you for that?"

I flicked my tongue. "Uh, no… Well, it was my word against Ilgregious' and then the leader of the Drakebureau had us arrested and thrown in here. Does you remember that?"

"Yeah, I guess so. Why else would they arrest you?"

"Exactly. And later that night Ilgregious showed up and wanted to kill us because I had seen him sacrifice that arsnatcher. But he had to get past Lutjen, Laudus, and *you* to get to us. So he killed the malwracks and took you hostage. He wanted to silence us before we could testify. We'd be dead by now if Jendal hadn't gotten us out of there."

Cangoar's eyes widened a bit. "Oh yeah, I remember that cell door! The bars all melted – like twenty malwracks blew it up with firebolts – all

173

at once! But you're wrong about Lutjen and Laudus. They were going to kill you – kill you until you were dead! Which is why I killed them first and got you out of there."

Bannabard pressed his face between the bars. "Parden me, but your side of the story doesn't hold water. Whoever got us out melted the bars on that door, and you couldn't have done that – not by yourself."

I nodded. "Yeah, you had a key. You'd just unlock it."

Cangoar flicked his tongue a few times. "Maybe you guys have a point." The vault went quiet. A minute or two seemed like an hour or two and then he bobbed his head – as much as the shackle allowed. "Maybe you're right. But killing Lutjen and Laudus – I can see it happening inside my head, clear as I see you two right now. How is it in my head if it isn't real?"

I scrunched my nose "Kardool's in league with the Dark Queen, just like Ilgregious. Jendal says he got inside your head and twisted your memories. Inside out, upside down, and backwards."

Cangoar tried to look away – but the snout shackle wouldn't allow it. "And then there's this. I remember fighting drambats in a meadow, but there weren't that many. How is it I didn't wipe them out? That part's a bit fuzzy except the part about fighting those malwracks. Hard to believe I won a fight against two malwracks in the guard hut, eh?! I guess you can do anything when you're fighting for... *true love*."

I gave him a hard look. "You may be good, but you're not *that* good. And here's another thing – you told me you should have killed Ilgregious when you had the chance. You said you were his prisoner. Why would you be his prisoner if you were the one who killed Lutjen and Laudus? Remember that shackle we helped get off your snout?"

Cangoar struggled against the chain, then put his head back down. "Yeah, I remember that. What you guys are saying – maybe it makes some sense. Kardool must be..." Cangoar's voice trailed off and the cell went quiet again. But then his eyes narrowed and he said, "Yeah, that's right. It really would make more sense if you had a crush on me and not the other way around."

I looked away. "Your life's dangling by a spider's thread and your worried about who's got a crush on who. Ain't nobody got a crush on nobody, ya big weevil-headed toady."

174

Cangoar flicked his tongue and scrunched his nose. "I'm not your toady – not yet anyway!" he exclaimed with a grin. "So you guys are saying Kardool got inside my head and convinced me that I killed those guards – all because he was protecting Ilgregious? That's just twisted."

I bobbed my head. "Yeah, twisted like a pile of whale gizzards."

"That's just nuts," said Cangoar. "How could anybody do that?"

Bannabard drew his face up to the bars of the cell door. "I don't know how he does it, but the Dark Queen helps him. They get inside a drake's head and re-arrange memories – kinda like what you said Ilgregious does."

Cangoar bobbed his head. "Yeah right. Who's the Dark Queen?"

"She's an arsnarm – a being from the Phoberon who wants us all dead," answered Bannabard. "The Dark Queen is wreaking havoc in our realm and using Ilgregious and Kardool to do it."

"That's just silly. The Phoberon is a myth," said Cangoar.

"Jendal isn't a myth," answered Bannabard. "Just ask Alfedora."

I scrunched my nose. "I used to think so, but she's no myth – that's for sure. Whether the Phoberon is real or not I couldn't say." I wasn't willing to admit *anything* about the Phoberon – not if it meant Melohim might be real.

"It's real alright," said Bannabard. "We call it the Numinous, but Jendal calls it the realm of dark matter and dark energy."

I bobbed my head. "Whatever. In any case the Dark Queen wants to twist things up like a big pile of whale gizzards. And if you let her, she'll convince you it's a good thing to throw hatchlings into a lava pit."

"Jendal was the one who melted the bars off the cell door and got us out before Ilgregious could kill us," continued Bannabard. "And she's the one who brought us here to talk to you today."

Cangoar flicked his tongue through the shackle. "Yeah, maybe that makes sense."

I looked him in the eye. "Bannabard's right. Jendal's here to help."

Cangoar closed his eyes for a second. Then he picked his head up and strained against the shackle. "Towering turds of an arsnatcher! You guys are messing with my mind! I'll be testifying before the Drakebureau in a few hours, and now I'm not sure *what* my story is."

My eyes flashed. "You don't have to testify if you don't want to. Jendal can get you out of here and give you time to get your head on straight."

Cangoar looked at the ground. "I'm not looking for help from you, or Jendal, or anyone else." He glared at us both. "I don't know what you guys are up to. I want to trust you, I really do. My head says 'yes', but my heart says 'no'."

I had no response – it felt like I'd said enough already. Maybe I'd be rubbing salt in a wound if I said any more. I interrupted the silence and said, "Perhaps we should leave you to your thoughts."

"Yeah, that would be best. Thanks for stopping by."

Cangoar watched Alfedora and Bannabard turn to leave. What they said about Ilgregious and Kardool and the melted steel bars was a lot to chew on. He knew they were here to help, but they turned everything inside his head into a muddled mess.

For some reason his friends headed down a corridor leading to aisle two. They disappeared around a corner and leaping lizard gizzards if Barl didn't come up aisle three just a few seconds later. He put his head down, closed his eyes, and pretended to be asleep.

Barl spoke in a low voice. "Cangoar. Wake up, you toad-eating freak!"

"Hey – my buddy's back! What's up, Barl?"

"I have a message for ya," growled the malwrack in a gravelly tone. You've been eating so many toads – you're starting to look like one!"

"I'll bet you say that to all your prisoners."

"No, that one's just for you, but that's not why I'm here. Your hearing with the Drakebureau has been delayed for a couple days, which means you'll be with us a little longer. Kreemdill will be almost as disappointed as I am that he won't be executing you today."

Cangoar flicked his tongue. "Hey Barl, thanks for the news. You're like a ray of sunshine – on a cold morning in January."

Cangoar watched Barl waddle back down the aisle without saying a word. What would his story be when it came time to testify? Could he trust his own thoughts?

Paul Krueger

22. Convictions and Choices

Cangoar snored noisily. "Cangoar, wake up!" I exclaimed – a bit louder than a whisper.

"Shhh, not so loud," whispered Bannabard, his face up in my grill.

"Shhh yourself," I said – still slightly above a whisper. "Cangoar, you awake?"

"Huh? What? I am now. What's all the whispering about?"

"Keep it down!" whispered Bannabard. "There's a guard in aisle one."

"Oh, right," whispered Cangoar. "Good to see you guys. What's up?"

I flicked my tongue. "We heard your hearing's been postponed and wanted to see how you're doing."

"How'd you hear about my hearing?"

"Jendal," answered Bannabard.

"Oh, right," whispered Cangoar. "She's that arsnarm – the one who knows everything,"

"Well, not everything," I said in a hushed voice. "How are you this morning?"

Cangoar gave me a hard look. "Some of what you guys said yesterday made sense – I just wish I could believe it."

"What don't you believe?" I asked, glancing down the aisle in both directions.

"You don't understand. I remember that steel door – I'll never forget the melted steel on the floor, but..."

"But what?" I interrupted.

"I see it in my head like I'm looking at you right now. I killed those guards and set you two free."

Bannabard glanced at me, then turned to Cangoar and whispered, "You know, there's a few things that don't quite add up about that."

"I know," whispered Cangoar. "What are they?"

"There's no way you could have melted those steel bars," said Bannabard.

"Yeah, I got that part." Cangoar put his head down. "What else?"

Bannabard glanced at me then turned to Cangoar. "Pardon me for saying this, but there's no way you could have killed two malwracks by yourself."

"Yeah, you wouldn't have a snowball's chance in a drambat's lair of pulling that off," I said. "You may have fought in the B.E.G., but you'd need your tail and then some to even think about taking on one malwrack, let alone two."

"Maybe I disabled them with stink gas, then hit 'em with two quick fireballs," said Cangoar as he struggled against the chains.

"Yeah maybe. But why mutilate their bodies?" I asked. "Those weren't nickelneck claw marks, and there weren't any burn marks either."

"You've got a point," whispered Cangoar. His eyes narrowed. "You guys are messin' with my head. Again."

"No, you toad-eatin' freak!" I exclaimed in an emphatic whisper. "Kardool's the one who messed with your head."

Cangoar tried to bob his head, but the chain held fast. "I know you guys are trying to help, but I don't know what to believe. And I don't know what my story will be when it's time to testify at the Drakebureau."

"Yeah, I imagine that would be more than a bit stressful," I suggested. "Thinking you killed two malwracks – guards you used to work with. But there's an alternative to testifying."

"What alternative?" whispered Cangoar.

"Jendal can get you out of here. Some time away – regain your bearings, clear your head, and get on your feet again."

"I'm already on my feet. Besides, you know how Flargellion operates. They don't take kindly to escapees. They'll send Kreemdill out to bring me back – dead or alive. But if what you say is true, it won't matter what I say."

"You're probably right," I whispered. "And I hear Kreemdill prefers to bring 'em back dead."

Cangoar turned to Bannabard. "She agrees with me, but how come I feel bad about it?"

"What you say may or may not matter to the leaders of the Drakebureau," whispered a fourth voice. "But it will matter to you. And it will matter to those who are close to you."

"Who said that?" whispered Cangoar as he glanced left, then right. His jaw dropped as a semi-transparent black orb appeared and transformed into Jendal. "This must be that arsnarm you guys were talking about."

"I'm no arsnarm. I am a dosara, and my name is Jendal – at your service. I've heard a lot about you and am pleased to make your acquaintance. It was noble of you to go after Ilgregious, even if a bit naive."

Cangoar gave her a blank stare. "How do you know I went after Ilgregious? Alfedora, did you tell her?"

"I didn't tell her," I answered. "She sees things."

"Oh, right," said Cangoar.

Jendal nodded. "I have my ways. But that was a brave thing you did."

I grinned and scrunched my nose. "Brave? Yeah, right. Stupid is more like it."

Cangoar gave me a hard look. "Sure. Go ahead, Alfedora. Yuk it up." He flicked his tongue towards Jendal and said, "How did you see me when I went after Ilgregious? I don't recall seeing you."

"I am from the realm of dark matter and dark energy. What you call 'the Phoberon'. I watched that conjuring ceremony and after – when you fought those drambats."

Cangoar's eyes narrowed. "The dosara and the Phoberon are nothing but toothless toady tales."

"And yet you are talking to a dosara now," said Jendal.

"Kardool is the leader of the spewlers," answered Cangoar. "He said the Phoberon is a myth."

"That's a lie – one of many he and the Dark Queen planted in your head."

Cangoar arched his neck and fought against the snout shackle. It looked as if the chain might break when he relaxed and slumped to the ground. "You're a dosara – and you spied on me?" he whispered.

"I guess you could look at it that way. Melohim has sent me here to help blue apes, and I watch what is relevant in your realm. I've seen dark forces arrayed against both communities – blue apes and dragons. I'm afraid the lies and murders won't stop with Lutjen and Laudus."

"What do you mean, they won't stop?"

"Ilgregious and Kardool love power above all other things," said Bannabard. "And they'll do anything to get it, including pinning those murders on Cangoar or one of us."

"Over my dead body," I said while bobbing my head. "Once Farl and the other leaders hear what that lying, conjuring, sleaze-a-saurus has been up to, Ilgregious will be the one that's locked up."

Cangoar gave Jendal a hard look. "You were there when I fought those drambats?"

"Yes, and you might not remember – when Kardool invaded your mind. It's a sad sight to see a sentient being's mind corrupted. Our memories are a big part of who we are."

I glared at Jendal. "Then why didn't you stop Kardool from messing with his mind?"

"I'm not allowed to interfere with this realm unless someone asks Melohim for help. Believe me, I wanted to, but my hands were tied."

"Your hands were *tied!?*" I exclaimed in a voice slightly above a whisper.

"Yes. Melohim never violates free will – and neither will I."

I bobbed my head and looked away. "So Cangoar is on the verge of losing his mind, not to mention his *life,* because you didn't want to violate *Kardool's* free will?"

"I think you're starting to get it," whispered Jendal.

"Really?" I whispered. "You can melt steel bars like butter and you got me into Flargellion by turning solid ground into thin air, but you couldn't stop Kardool from messing with Cangoar's mind?"

Jendal nodded. "Right. Like I said, a dosara can only intervene when someone asks Melohim for help. But nobody did."

"Say what?" I asked. "The Dark Queen can interfere, but you can't?"

Jendal's eyes narrowed. "Neither can she without Ilgregious and Kardool. They provide channels through which she can work her evil deeds. And she will chew them up and spit them out when she is done with them. But suppose I had intervened. Suppose I stopped Kardool and the Dark Queen from invading Cangoar's mind. I cannot save one being by violating another."

I bobbed my head. "In what universe would it be a bad thing for a dosara to stop a scrawny little spewler from messing with what's inside a nickelneck's head? Or, maybe, Phoberon forbid, stopping an even scrawnier drambat from murdering innocent hatchlings?"

"In every universe Melohim ever created," whispered Bannabard.

"You catch on quick," said Jendal. "If I use force to stop them from doing evil, I'd be doing to them what they did to Cangoar and that hatchling."

I bobbed my head. "How's that?" I whispered. "No one would die."

"I'd be imposing my will against theirs – by force. It would be violence."

"Yeah, what a violent thing to stop Ilgregious from burning a hatchling alive or that spewler from infecting another being's mind with lies." I scrunched my nose. "Let me get this straight. You can't intervene unless someone in our realm asks for help – from Melohim?"

"Yeah, that's right," whispered Jendal.

I looked away. "But not everyone believes in Melohim. Could this get any stupider?" I muttered – mostly to myself. "The Dark Queen can invade Cangoar's mind, but you're too nice to stop it?"

"Not too nice. I prefer to think of it is as respectful," said Jendal.

"If she did stop them, she would be on a similar path to theirs," suggested Bannabard.

"Yes, I would," whispered Jendal. "Most creatures fail to respect free will the way Melohim does. Violations of free will are violence – whether it is physical, mental, or emotional. The Dark Queen's subjects do her bidding because they think she is giving them real power. But her servants fail to see the corruption their lust for power creates – in their own lives and the lives of those around them. Or that she will consume them in the end. If the power hierarchy is all there is, those at the top will feed off those beneath them. She grants an illusion of power – temporary and dangerous."

I bobbed my head and thrashed my tail. "Yeah, right," I muttered. "The Drakebureau is no illusion." I peered at Jendal. "But why would the Dark Queen care what happens in this realm? Isn't the Phoberon a better place to be?"

Cangoar bobbed his head as much as the shackle allowed. "Yeah, what's up with that?"

"Korgarag and Krimeny are at war with Melohim. They are consumed with pride and want to prove he was wrong to create this realm and the beings that inhabit it," said Jendal. "They view every creature in this realm as an insult to who and what they are. And to be honest, there are times I wonder why Melohim allows evil from our realm to infect this one. But I have learned not to question when, why, or how he does what he does."

I turned to Jendal and whispered, "How could you not question *that?* If Melohim cared about the beings he created in this realm, why would he allow the Dark Queen to work evil against us? How can we respect a being who claims to be benevolent and all-powerful, yet allows hatchlings to be burned alive – at the hands of some scrawny little drambat?"

"You raise some good points," whispered Jendal. "When bad things happen to innocent beings, it should be upsetting to all. But if Ilgregious and Kardool are not able to choose evil, neither would they be able to choose good. And so it is for all beings."

"What good is Melohim, if he won't protect innocent hatchlings from the likes of Ill-greega-butt?"

"Melohim did not create amoral puppets. There is an oracle in the Obelisk which says, 'he has not given us a spirit of fear, but of power and of love and of a sound mind.' In a sense our choices shape us and make us what we are."

I bobbed my head and whispered, "I get the choices thing, but there are limits, right?" I looked at the two apes. "If Melohim is the ultimate power, yet allows beings from the Phoberon to give power to drakes like Ill-greega-butt for sacrificing hatchlings – what sort of Supreme Being is *that?* I say give Ill-greega-butt what he's chosen. Throw *him* in a lava pit."

"I wish – but then we'd have the Drakebureau on our butts," said Bannabard with a thump of his chest. He peered at` Jendal. "If Krimeny is allowed to invade minds and wreak havoc and even murder young apes and hatchlings, but you don't use your power to stop her, what can *we* do?"

"You may not be able to see your role, but that is part of the drama being played out," answered Jendal. "In view of recent successes by the

Dark Queen and her servants – how will we respond? Will we lose hope and give up, or will we stand against the lies, fear, and violence being propagated?"

"Yeah, right," I muttered. "You want *us* to take a stand? I'm nearly done with all this talk about Melohim and strange beings in the Phoberon." I bobbed my head and flicked my tongue. "You want us to take a stand against Ill-greega-butt and Kardrool, but you won't lift a paw to stop the Dark Queen?"

Jendal's eyes narrowed. "I will enforce Melohim's rules of engagement if the Dark Queen violates them – you can be sure of that. But if Ilgregious and Kardool – or any other drake – gives her a channel through which to work, they are moral agents and I will not violate their choices."

"Not even to save innocent hatchlings?" I asked.

"Your concern for hatchlings is a credit to you and we must do what we can to save hatchlings," said Jendal. "All the more reason we must work together to expose the evil that has invaded your realm – and trust the Drakebureau to exercise its authority."

I bobbed my head. "Ilgregious and Kardool *are* the Drakebureau."

"Yes, but so are Farl, Gailryder, Pinhammer, and others. We must trust the process – while hoping truth and justice prevail."

I peered at Jendal. "This would be much easier and faster – if you would simply use your powers to put an end to that stuff. How many hatchlings could be saved?"

Jendal's eyes grew fierce. "The end doesn't justify the means."

"But that's what you want the Drakebureau to do, isn't it?"

"Yes," said Jendal. "According to agreed-upon laws and customs – and to protect the society of Drakedom."

"Not to mention Blue-Apedom," said Bannabard.

"But what if the Drakebureau doesn't do what's right?" asked Cangoar.

I scrunched my nose. "We cannot control what the Drakebureau will or will not do."

"Yes," said Jendal. "We must focus on what we can control. Ilgregious, Kardool, Krimeny, and Korgarag believe they can control others through fear and coercion, and that leads them down an evil path. But Melohim created all beings to be free – only through his design can

184

we find integrity and truth in our interactions with others. But enough speculation about the nature of good and evil. Cangoar, do you believe you killed those two guards?"

Cangoar flicked his tongue. "No, I guess not – I can't get past the melted bars on the cell door and the mutilated bodies of the malwracks. I guess what Alfedora and Bannabard said about Kardool and his mind tricks is the only thing that makes sense."

Jendal's eyes narrowed. "A wise decision – and now you get to choose. You can stay here and testify, or you can come with us and save that for later – but the opportunity might not present itself again."

Cangoar looked at the ground. "What's the chance I'd testify later, if I leave now?"

Bannabard thumped his chest. "They'll hunt you down, but if they can't find you, I'm guessing Ilgregious and Kardool will find another scape-lizard to take your place."

Cangoar bobbed his head as much as the shackle allowed. "If I run, we're all still fugitives, and there's a good chance they'll find someone else to pin the murders on."

"Right!" I exclaimed, thrashing my tail back and forth. "And if you stay and testify, there's a good chance they'll kill you."

"Yes, but there's always hope," said Cangoar as he relaxed against the chains. "If I leave now, another drake will become their scape-lizard, the truth will be buried, and innocent drakes and blue apes will die. I couldn't live with that."

I bobbed my head and gave him a hard look. "You've decided to stay and testify." I looked away. "You might as well throw yourself in a lava pit!"

Jendal looked at me. "His fate is in Melohim's hands now. We must respect his choice and honor his courage."

"Easy for her to say," I muttered as I turned my back and headed away from Cangoar's cell. I found little solace in the notion that we were done talking about Melohim, arsnarms, dosara, and the Phoberon.

23. Cangoar's Choice

"**W**ait here while I check on the guards," whispered Jendal as we crept toward the guard hut.

Bannabard and I waited in a passageway – out of view around a corner. It had only been an hour or so, but the stale air made me feel as if we'd been in the Viper Vault for a week.

"All clear," whispered Jendal. "The guards are asleep. Follow me."

The three of us made our way to the forest, and once we were safely out of sight, I spun around and faced Jendal. "I can't believe you're letting Cangoar do this. You *know* his mind's not right!"

"You're upset," said Jendal. "But there's nothing we can do for him now. Cangoar trusts his fate to Melohim. I'm asking you to do the same."

I bobbed my head and scrunched my nose. "They're going to kill him – whether he testifies or not. What good is *that?*"

Jendal put a hand on my shoulder. "He's taking a stand for what he believes and the other leaders will hear the truth. And the last time he trusted Melohim it saved his life."

"Yeah, right. Where was Melohim when Kardool put those lies in his head?"

"I can't answer that. Perhaps you'd like to ask him yourself."

"You mean, like, talk to him?" I looked at the ground and shook my head. "That's not gonna happen."

Jendal's eyes flashed. "Why not? Cangoar did. Why not you?"

"Uh, no thanks." I turned and looked to the meadow. "I'm happy to take a stand against violence toward hatchlings. But I'm not about to trust a being who claims to be the benevolent creator yet allows hatchlings to be burned alive in lava pits."

Jendal glared at me and flared her nostrils. "Well okay – that's up to you, Alfedora. When Cangoar testifies, he's going to contradict Kardool's story. There's nothing more you two can do here. I must ask you to head back to Farshen while I monitor the situation here. I'll be in touch."

She disappeared before either of us could respond.

I scrunched my nose. "Farshen? Really?"

"I'm afraid so," said Bannabard.

"And now she's gone. She asks us to head back to Farshen and then just disappears." My eyes narrowed. "Why Farshen? Why can't we hang out in my lair?"

"That's one of the first places they'll look," suggested a disembodied voice.

"Wow. Really? You vanish, then you listen in on us?"

"Oh, sorry. I guess I'll have to work on that." A translucent black orb appeared between us. "I'm asking you to trust me – Ilgregious will be looking for you two."

Bannabard glanced at me. "Jendal's right."

The orb pulsed slightly. "I'll meet you in Farshen in a day or two and let you know what's going on. Trust me, I won't leave you hanging."

I flicked my tongue. "It'd be easier to trust myself."

Bannabard glanced at the orb and then gave me a hard look. "Our goal is to expose Ilgregious' dark deeds to the Drakebureau, right?"

I looked at the ground. "Yeah, I guess..."

"Let's trust Jendal, go to Farshen, and see how things play out."

I bobbed my head and glanced between Bannabard and the black orb. "Let me be clear. I'm doing this for Cangoar and the Drakebureau – not because I'm on some weird mission for Melohim or anything."

"See ya in Farshen," said the disembodied voice.

The orb disappeared. Bannabard climbed on my back, and we took off – heading west and a little south.

Cangoar snored while someone tried to wake him. It was Alfedora. They were just outside his lair overlooking the Salmonella River.

"Morning already?" he asked.

"No, it's afternoon. Time to wake up, sleeping beauty."

But then her voice changed – much deeper. And there was a nudge – more of a shove, really.

"Give me another minute… my little dung beetle," he muttered.

There was another shove, this time harder.

"I'm nobody's dung beetle!" growled the voice. "Get up now or you never will."

"Huh?" Cangoar opened his eyes halfway. Oh crap – it was Barl. Not Alfedora. "Come back tomorrow. I'll be awake then," he muttered.

Barl whacked him up the side of the head with a paw. "Come back tomorrow? Get moving – or there won't be a tomorrow."

Cangoar glanced around. Barl and another guard were unhooking his chains. The guard attempted to grab the stump of his tail, then grabbed a leg instead, apparently intending to drag him out by it.

Cangoar wrested his leg away from the guard, struggled to his feet, and snarled, "All right, all right. Where we going?"

"You're on your way to a hearing in the Great Hall," said Barl with a certain giddiness in his voice. "It seems Pinhammer wants to get to the bottom of who killed Lutjen and Laudus, and if it turns out to be you, we'll be turning you over to my friend Kreemdill here."

"Yeah, nickelneck. You'll be mine, all mine," said the other malwrack. "I promised the other guards your death would be slow and painful – as slow as I can make it."

Cangoar scrunched his nose. "Aren't you just a little bucket o' sunshine." He moved past the other guard and toward the cell door. "Thanks for the heads up. But don't hold your breath – I didn't kill anyone. I'm one of you guys, remember?"

"Yeah, we remember," said Barl. "That's what makes it even more disgusting. I can't believe I'm breathing the same air as you, you newt-farting, toad-sucking sorry sack of serpent gizzards." Barl yanked his snout shackle while the other guard kicked him toward the door.

"Thanks," muttered Cangoar at the guard behind.

They entered the Great Hall and found a spot near the front of the gallery. The Drakebureau was already in session.

"Silence!" shouted a nearly ancient spewler from the head of the Stone Ingot.

The spewler squeezed a fat fiadhain – and the hall went silent when it squealed. Cangoar licked his chops. It must be nice to have a fat fiadhain all chained up, but what a waste to use it for *that*.

"All right!" the spewler exclaimed. "We shall now hear the case of two drambats – Karnburp vs Tarlfarn."

Cangoar hadn't noticed the seven stalls to the right of the Stone Ingot. The drambats stood in the first two. He figured the stalls were designated for plaintiffs, defendants, and maybe witnesses. Bison skulls capped the front corners of each. They were big enough for a malwrack, and the drambats' heads barely cleared the walls. Cangoar grinned slightly. They looked like hatchlings in oversized play pens.

The spewler turned to one of the drambats. "Karnburp, I understand you live a bit east of Lake Hornsniffler and are accusing Tarlfarn of absconding with some silver coins you claim belong to you. Is that correct?"

"Yes, your Drakeness," answered the drambat.

"And you, Tarlfarn, are from the foothills north of Hornsniffler?"

"Yes, your Drakeness," answered the other drambat.

"Karnburp, please describe to those gathered here today and in your own words – what happened eleven nights ago."

The drambat flicked his tongue. "It was a full moon, and Tarlfarn found the silver coins I had stashed in some bushes near my lair. They belong to me, your Drakeness. Tarlfarn needs to hand them over – hand them over now," said the drambat in a pathetic, somewhat whiny voice.

"I didn't find them by your lair," answered Tarlfarn.

"Oh yeah? Why don't you prove it," whined the other drambat.

Tarlfarn scrunched his nose. "I can't, you twerp. How can I prove where I found them?"

The spewler cleared his throat. "Karnburp, please explain to the Drakebureau why you stashed your silver coins in some bushes, rather than your lair."

This is pathetic. Cangoar looked away. Just let them fight over it. It'd be less annoying – and a lot more entertaining.

"I was… out hunting, your Drakeness," said Karnburp in a bit of a whiny voice.

189

Tarlfarn glanced at the leader. "Well isn't that convenient..."

He was interrupted by drakes in the gallery who hooted, bonked heads, and chanted, "Roast the whiner, roast him now! Roast the whiner, roast him like a cow!"

"Silence!" interrupted the leader. He gave the fiadhain another squeeze, the boar squealed, and the hall went silent.

Cangoar and nearly every other drake in the gallery turned and stared. He licked his chops at the fat fiadhain which was glistening with sweat. The hall went dead quiet – nothing but the sound of the boar struggling against the chain.

A few stomachs gurgled before the spewler interrupted the silence. "Karnburp, I'm afraid if you can't prove that you stashed the silver coins where Tarlfarn found them, I have no choice but to dismiss the case."

"Why are we wasting time with a dispute over a few silver coins?" asked the malwrack who towered over the Ingot. "No self-respecting drake gives a newt's butt about silver."

"Pardon me, your Drakeness, but I do," said the whiny drambat with a bit of a tremor in his voice.

"Well, can you prove where you stashed the coins?" asked the leader as he drummed a claw on the Ingot.

"No, I guess not," said the drambat.

"Whew, glad that's over!" exclaimed the malwrack. "Now maybe we can get to some *real* business."

"Hold on. I haven't dismissed the case yet," groused the leader as he reached toward the fiadhain without squeezing it.

"Well, what are you waiting for?" asked the malwrack.

"I'm waiting for you to shut your deep-fried squid hole," answered the leader.

The malwrack grinned. And why not? He's a malwrack – the only one on the council.

The leader looked up and glared at the malwrack. "Are you quite finished, Gailryder?"

"Yes. I believe I am, your Drakeness. Thanks for asking."

"Thank goodness," said the leader with a bit of a sneer. "Are there any questions or further discussion from Karnburp vs. Tarlfarn?"

"No, your Drakeness," said Tarlfarn.

"None," said the other drambat.

"Caaase… dismissed!" exclaimed the leader. "You are free to go."

Cangoar scrunched his nose. The spewler had dismissed the case a little more triumphantly than was warranted for such a minor dispute.

"And now for the next order of business. The Drakebureau calls the nickelneck Cangoar to the witness stand concerning the murder of Lutjen and Laudus at the Viper Vault. Cangoar, you may take the stand when you are ready."

Barl led Cangoar to the first stand.

"Cangoar, do you know who I am?" asked the leader.

"The leader of the Drakebureau?"

"Yes, that is correct. My name is Pinhammer, but you may address me as 'Your Drakeness'. Cangoar, do you swear, upon the Obelisk of Hornath, that the testimony you are about to give is the truth, the whole truth, and nothing but the truth, so help you, Melohim? If so, please raise the big claw on your right paw and say, 'Yes, your Drakeness, I do so swear – so help me, Melohim.'"

Cangoar took a deep breath, closed his eyes, and asked for help from Melohim before proceeding.

"I do so swear – so help me, Melohim," he said, parroting the words while wondering if he'd be able to keep his story straight.

Pinhammer glared and flicked his tongue at him. "You didn't say, 'Yes, your Drakeness' and you didn't raise the big claw on your right paw!"

Crap – now the spewler's ticked off.

"Cangoar, do you know how many witnesses I have sworn in over the last three months?"

"Uh, twelve?"

"Forty-seven. And do you know how many of those forty-seven failed to raise the big claw on their right paw?"

"Uh, none?" he stammered as he glanced at the other drakes gathered around the Stone Ingot. They appeared more amused than ticked off. He glared at Kardool who sported a larger grin than the others.

"Correct. None. Until you, that is." Pinhammer glanced around the table with a self-satisfied grimace. "Let's try this again, shall we? Do you swear upon the Obelisk of Hornath, that the testimony you are about to give is the truth, the whole truth, and nothing but the truth, so help you,

Melohim? If so, please raise the big claw on your right paw and say, 'Yes, your Drakeness, I do so swear – so help me, Melohim.'"

Cangoar raised the big claw on his right paw slowly and stared at it for a moment before turning to Pinhammer. "Yes, your Drakeness. I do so swear – so help me, Melohim."

Various drakes in the gallery snickered.

"Very well," said Pinhammer in a lower tone and with a certain gravity in his voice. "Loturgious and Quinpin, you may begin questioning the witness. Remember, no one is on trial yet. We are simply gathering facts so we can piece together the events which took place the night of the murders."

"Indeed, we are," began Loturgious. "My dear Cangoar, would you be so kind as to describe to the esteemed leaders of the Drakebureau, using your own words, and to the best of your ability, what happened that night?"

Kardool was next to Ilgregious at the Ingot and leaned in close to the drambat. "Of course he's going to confess!" he whispered emphatically. "Have you lost faith already?"

Ilgregious nodded slightly and answered in a whisper, "No, of course not – but he better! We don't want this to drag on for weeks and weeks. Pin-ham-butt-brain and the others will try to unearth every shred of evidence from here to Gellion and back."

Kardool scrunched his nose. Ilgregious' lack of confidence in the Dark Queen's power was disturbing at best. Does the drambat deserve her gifts? Certainly not as much as he did! "I'm confident it won't come to that," he whispered.

Ilgregious leaned in even closer. "If it does, I'm guessing Gailryder and the guards will grow impatient."

Kardool nearly fell over from the drambat's foul breath. He looked up, inhaled deeply, then turned back. "Yeah, and if they do, we might be able to get them to question Pinhammer's leadership."

"Indeed," snarled Ilgregious.

Pinhammer glared at the drambat and the spewler. "Ilgregious and Kardool! Is there something you'd care to share with the rest of us?"

Cangoar gave Ilgregious an icy stare.

I should have toasted him when I had the chance.

"No, uh... No thank you, your Drakeness," answered Kardool.

"Then let us proceed – shall we? This matter deserves our undivided attention!" exclaimed Pinhammer, looking around at the others. "Two guards are dead!"

"Yes, your Drakeness," replied Kardool and Ilgregious almost in unison.

Pinhammer cleared his throat. "Loturgious, would you be so kind as to repeat the question?"

"Cangoar, would you please describe to the esteemed members of the Drakebureau, and in your own words, what happened that night – the night Lutjen and Laudus were brutally murdered?"

The snartch spoke with confidence. Cangoar tried not to stare at the nickelneck leader. Farl was his name. Surely he'd be sympathetic to his story – assuming he could keep it straight. He began slowly and deliberately. "The night started as a normal shift in the guard hut at the Viper Vault."

He glanced at Ilgregious and Kardool. What he was about to say would paint a bull elk's eye on his chest.

"Lutjen, Laudus, and I were on duty for the night shift. Laudus was in charge, as was normally the case. Earlier that day, a nickelneck named Alfedora and a blue ape had been brought in. They were locked up – pending an investigation about a disturbance here in the Great Hall. Lutjen and I went to the cell block and checked on the prisoners, and as we returned, we heard Laudus arguing with Ilgregious about something. It sounded like Ilgregious wanted him to turn Alfedora and the blue ape over to him and his band of drambats. There were about thirteen drambats with Ilgregious – more or less."

"He lies!" shouted Ilgregious furiously. "I was NEVER at the Viper Vault! He's trying to cover his tail-challenged butt! He wants to frame someone else for those murders!"

"Here, here," said the other drambat leader.

"Quiet!" shouted Gailryder in a voice that shook the cavern. "I want to hear what the nickelneck has to say."

"Indeed," said Pinhammer in a deep-throated voice while glaring at the malwrack. "Let Cangoar finish his testimony. Everyone will get their chance – in due time."

Kardool and Ilgregious began whispering again, this time more fervently.

"Ilgregious, do you or do you not have something to say?" asked Pinhammer.

"Yes, your Drakeness. Please excuse the distraction, your Drakeness, but earlier today something important came up which directly involves this case. Kardool and I would like to request an immediate recess."

Gailryder glared at the drambat. "I'll bet you would," he sneered. "Let's hear what Cangoar has to say first, and then you can have your recess."

"Silence!" shouted Pinhammer, reaching for the fiadhain, but not giving it a squeeze. "Thanks for your input Gailryder, but I'll decide whether we go to recess – or not." He cleared his throat before continuing, "Now, what was it you need a recess for?"

Ilgregious glanced at Kardool, then at Pinhammer. "Thank you, your Drakeness. Earlier today, it came to our attention that new evidence has surfaced which has a direct bearing on this case. However, due to the temporal nature of the evidence, it is important that we adjourn immediately. We hope to retrieve this evidence before it is lost – possibly forever." The drambat's eyes widened as his voice slowed and trailed off at the end.

Gailryder glared at the drambat and leaned in close. "Temporal nature of the evidence?"

Ilgregious was unfazed by Gailryder's derision, as if he expected it or even welcomed it. "Yes. Yes, temporal indeed."

"And if we don't retrieve it right away, we may not get another chance," added Kardool.

Pinhammer looked down, paused for a second or two, and then continued without looking up. "Recess granted! But make it snappy. We'll adjourn for four hours. If that doesn't give you time to gather your evidence, we'll continue without it."

"Yes, your Drakeness," said Kardool.

Pinhammer gave Kardool and Ilgregious an icy stare. "Be back in four hours. Don't make us continue the proceedings without you. Barl and Kreemdill, please take the prisoner back to his cell."

24. Discordant Diversions

Kardool and Ilgregious nearly flew to the Morinair Gate – beating everyone else out of Flargellion. Kardool glanced up rather than look at Ilgregious. The twin peaks were lit by a late afternoon sun.

"I thought you said you had Cangoar under control," snarled the drambat. "I should have known you'd mess this up."

"Don't try to make this about me," sneered Kardool as he glared at Ilgregious. "He was completely convinced he killed those guards when I left him at the Vault the night before last. Someone got to him – and convinced him otherwise."

"I'll bet it was that female nickelneck and that insolent blue ape," said Ilgregious.

Kardool flicked his tongue. "What is it with those two? Why aren't they both dead?"

"I had them, but somehow they escaped," said Ilgregious with a sneer.

"And now it seems we're stuck in a bit of a tar pit." There was some satisfaction in Kardool's voice. "Or should I say you rather than us?" He was looking forward to a time when he wouldn't have to work with this clumsy little drambat.

"You forget who is with us," said Ilgregious as he spat on the ground.

Gross – drambat spit. A disgusting shade of a purple-green which nearly hit his left front paw. "Hey, watch that. And no, I didn't forget," said Kardool with an edge in his tone. "The Dark Queen is likely watching us now. She needs to know we can handle this irritating little situation gracefully."

"Exactly," said Ilgregious as he got up in Kardool's snout. "We need something dramatic – something to divert the Drakebureau's attention away from Cangoar." The drambat scrunched his nose and grinned, exposing a broken fang among needle-like and crooked teeth.

Kardool bobbed his head. "Now we're talking!" He glanced around – making sure they were alone. "Yes, a distraction. Something as bad or worse in the minds of the Drakebureau than the death of those guards. What are you thinking?"

Ilgregious looked up with a grin and a glint in his eye. "What if we kidnap... the Leader?"

Kardool flicked his tongue. "Yes. Yes, indeed. Let's grab him now – while he's on the way to his lair."

Ilgregious thrashed his tail back and forth. "And then we'll take him somewhere – somewhere hidden. And if he resists, we'll sacrifice his butt."

Kardool bobbed his head. "No doubt our beloved Queen will want to mess with his mind!" he exclaimed, but with a little more enthusiasm than intended. Needles ran up and down his spine at the thought of getting inside another drake's head – especially one as important as the Leader. It didn't matter that Pinhammer was a spewler like himself. He was naive enough to actually believe in the Drakebureau! As if all six species should have a voice in running things. Pin was a fool and lacked his vision – only a spewler was smart enough to rule things properly. Pinhammer would never know what it means to wield the power of the Dark Queen, nor the exquisite elegance of a few well-placed lies. Even a snartch could see how lies were often necessary – what with the likes of Gailryder and Farl lurking about.

Ilgregious thrashed his tail back and forth. "Do you think they'll work this time?"

"What's that?"

"Your mind tricks."

"Certainly!" exclaimed Kardool as he wrapped the drambat up the side of the head. "But they're not *my* mind tricks. They're the Dark Queen's! We must never doubt her powers. You should have seen what we... uh, she, did to Cangoar. He was completely convinced he was in love with the female – that he killed those guards to save her. It was a beautiful thing."

Ilgregious flicked a fly off his snout with his tongue. "Yeah, and we saw how that turned out, didn't we?"

Kardool glared at him. "Someone got to the nickelneck – you know that."

They took off and headed toward Trool – just long enough to avoid suspicion – and then made a wide circle and headed back west. Like everyone else on the Drakebureau, they knew Pinhammer's lair was in the foothills west of Flargellion.

They intercepted the spewler in flight and motioned for him to land. The three of them touched down in the flood plain of a stream about half-way between Flargellion and the foothills.

"Have you found the evidence? Do you have it?" asked Pinhammer expectantly.

"Regretfully no, your Drakeness," said Kardool.

Ilgregious pointed to his left front leg – they had yet to decide which of them would invade the spewler's mind. Kardool's eyes narrowed as he glared at Ilgregious and pointed to his own leg.

"Can you give us a second, your Drakeness?" Kardool asked. "We have something we need to discuss – in private."

They turned their backs to Pinhammer. Ilgregious got up in Kardool's snout and whispered, "Let me do it. You had your shot with Cangoar."

Kardool's eyes flashed as he raised above the drambat. "We need him alive!" he whispered emphatically.

"What for?" whispered the drambat.

Kardool took a half step toward Ilgregious, their noses inches apart. "We can't risk *that* until we consolidate our base."

Ilgregious bobbed his head. "Okay. We'll do it your way for now," he whispered. "But promise me – in the end he's mine."

Kardool nodded, spun back, and faced Pinhammer. "As I was saying, we don't have the evidence yet, but that isn't important right now." He scratched his left front leg until it bled.

"What are you doing?" asked Pinhammer.

Kardool looked up and mouthed the words, "Thank you" as he felt a surge of dark energy. It was all he could do to focus the power on Pinhammer's left ear.

"Not important? What do you mean it's not important? There's nothing more imp–" Pinhammer's voice drifted off.

In his mind's eye, Kardool rode a wave of dark energy and entered the spewler's auditory canal, twisting and turning along neural pathways inside the Leader's brain – searching and hunting for episodic memories which could be manipulated and twisted to their advantage. What a privilege! To wield the Dark Queen's power inside the head of the Leader of the Drakebureau!

A sense of reverence overtook him. The Dark Queen had given him the power to manipulate, twist, and rearrange neural pathways. He could create false narratives at will. Narratives which would enable them to get their claws on the power they needed to accomplish Her Darkness's purposes. "Everything's going to be all right," said Kardool in a monotonic, soothing, and high-pitched voice, as if he were talking to a hatchling. "Pinhammer, your Drakeness. We are here now. Ilgregious and I are here to keep you safe."

Pinhammer lost control of his extremities, fell over on his right side, and grinned. "You are?" he asked tenderly, softly, expectantly.

"Yes. We're here for you," answered Kardool. "Close your eyes and focus on my words. We're here to save you from a most dreadful fate. And you know what?"

"No, what?" asked the Leader as he closed his eyes.

"I have something to tell you," said Kardool – slowly and deliberately. "You do?"

A sly grin emerged on Kardool's face. This was more exhilarating than when he'd gotten into Cangoar's head. The leader of the Drakebureau was responding like a pre-pubescent hatchling on the way to its first flight lesson. "Yes, it's something important – something unexpected," he answered softly. His facility with words combined with the Queen's dark energy – this was a whole new art form, one that he alone was able to wield. Ilgregious could terrify, but only *he* could create false realities in their minds.

"Oh goody, I like surprises. Is it a surprise?" asked Pinhammer.

"It was a surprise to us, but I don't think it'll be a surprise to you." A memory appeared of Pinhammer being bullied by a malwrack when he was just a little older than a hatchling. "I see you've long suspected Gailryder and Farl – this is very wise of you."

"It is?" he asked in a syrupy voice.

"Yes, very wise indeed. Ilgregious and I have learned that they are plotting to kill you and take over the Drakebureau. Everyone knows they've had it in for spewlers and drambats. I'm afraid they've been taken captive by a lust for power."

"Yes, I've known that for quite some time," answered Pinhammer in a soft tone. "They want to take control – everyone knows that."

"Of course they do," continued Kardool. "I'm afraid only you and a few other leaders are standing in the way of their plans for drakeocide."

"Drakeocide? Oh my goodness, no! They wouldn't dare!"

"Indeed they would, your Drakeness," said Kardool. "You heard Gailryder railing against drambats just a while ago. We're little more than roaches in their view."

"Yes. Intolerant xenophobic haters if ever I've seen one."

"I hate to say this – but we've been informed of their plan to confiscate all gold from the weaker species."

Pinhammer's expression turned fierce. "I've long suspected that Gailryder and Farl of… of treachery. We must have them arrested at once! We'll find a couple of not-so-cozy cells in the Viper Vault – just for them!"

Kardool's grin widened slightly. "Yes, your Drakeness, that would seem to be the course a strong leader such as yourself would take. But we have discovered there are guards at the Viper Vault who are in on the plot. You know how malwracks stick together."

"A conspiracy?" asked Pinhammer, his eyes growing wide.

"Yes, I'm afraid so. It's been going on for quite some time."

Pinhammer scrunched his nose. "How did you find out about this?"

Kardool licked his chops and looked away, and as he did Pinhammer tried to get up.

Whoa, big guy, not so fast.

He refocused on Pinhammer's left ear and exhaled as the spewler's body relaxed again.

"An excellent question, your Drakeness. The arsnatcher Brakken has infiltrated their ranks."

"Well, I must say. You've certainly done your homework."

Kardool paused and exhaled again. "Thank you, your Drakeness. But I'm afraid we've just begun to scratch the surface. We have no idea how many have joined the conspiracy – but we suspect Farl may have recruited the nickelneck gaggles."

Kardool felt the words reverberate inside Pinhammer's head. The Dark Queen's power was creating false realities in the Leader's mind. It wouldn't be long before they were embedded in his heart also.

"The nickelnecks?!" asked Pinhammer.

"Yes. Nickelneck gaggles. And so, for your well-being and the well-being of drakes everywhere – we feel it best if you were to go into hiding while we expose this treachery and bring order back to the Drakebureau. We simply couldn't bear to lose you, your Drakeness."

"Hiding? I don't think so. Wait. Wut? What's wrong with my legs?"

Pinhammer struggled to get up. It was all Kardool could do to keep a grin from emerging as Pinhammer's body failed to respond.

"Oh, don't worry about your legs," he said in a matter-of-fact tone. "Your legs will be back in short order, but there's something else you should know. Ilgregious and I aren't the only ones who couldn't bear to lose you to those dreadful malwracks or nickelnecks."

Pinhammer quit struggling and a goofy smile appeared on his face. "You're not?"

"No, your Drakeness. There are many others depending on you – drambats, spewlers, snartches, and arsnatchers. And that is why you must go into hiding until we can sort this thing out."

"Yes. I must go into hiding – for all drakes everywhere." Pinhammer relaxed. "We're quite fortunate to have you two on our team."

Kardool kept another grin hidden as he released his hold on Pinhammer's mind.

A little while later Pinhammer shook his head and struggled to his feet. "What happened? How did I get down there?"

Kardool leaned in and steadied him. "It must have been quite a shock to your system when we told you what the malwracks and nickelnecks are up to."

"Oh my goodness, yes – quite embarrassing I'm afraid." Pinhammer looked at Kardool. "A real shock to think that there's an insurrection afoot, but I'm okay now. And yes, we must find a suitable hiding place – I wouldn't want to disappoint my comrades."

Kardool flicked his tongue. "Certainly. And I must say it's a privilege and an honor to serve you, your Drakeness. But where shall we hide you?" He looked away as if engrossed in deep thought.

"Wait," said Ilgregious as he glanced at Kardool before turning to Pinhammer. "I know a perfect cave near Lake Hornsniffler. My clan of drambats is there. They'll keep you hidden and safe until Kardool and I can expose the traitors and bring them to justice."

"Yes. That might work," said Pinhammer. "Of course, it has never been in my veins to run from a conflict. But I suppose, given the circumstances..." He flicked his tongue. "I suppose this would be the prudent thing to do. Given the circumstances, of course."

"Yes, a difficult but wise choice indeed, your Drakeness," suggested Kardool. "And they may be hunting for you even now. I believe it would be best to wait until sunset and fly to Trool under cover of darkness, your Drakeness."

"Yes, indeed," said Ilgregious as he glanced at Kardool. "We would do well to wait in the woods until nightfall."

The sun was getting low as Pinhammer and Ilgregious followed Kardool into the woods and waited for darkness. "I should like to return to Flargellion so that when the Drakebureau reconvenes I can tell them you've taken ill, your Drakeness. If the insurgents suspect you've gone into hiding, they might come looking for you."

"Yes. I think that would be wise," said Pinhammer.

"An excellent idea," said Ilgregious with a flick of his tongue.

Kardool bobbed his head. "It's settled then. I'll meet up with you at Lake Hornsniffler later tonight. I bid you a fond farewell and trust you know we'll be working hard to expose this seditious plan. I assure you, your Drakeness, we'll get to the bottom of this insurgency – one way or another."

"I look forward to your report," said Pinhammer.

Kardool headed back to the meadow and took off toward Flargellion. A slight grin appeared as he flipped a wing and took off. Manipulating Pinhammer's thoughts had been easier than taking newt gizzards from a hatchling.

Gailryder wrapped his claws on the Stone Ingot. The Drakebureau had reconvened at the appointed time, but Ilgregious, Kardool, and even Pinhammer – were missing.

Farl bobbed his head. "I'm as surprised as a bear in a malwrack's lair that they're not back yet," said Farl in a sarcastic tone.

Most of the others around the table snorted or chortled with the exception of the drambat Qualmsneed and the spewler Quinpin.

"Yeah, but why isn't Pinhammer here?" asked Brakken the arsnatcher. "He's never late."

The hall went nearly silent. Gailryder scrunched his nose. Nothing but the sound of a few claws tapping on the Ingot, a few rumblings from the bellies of those who hadn't eaten in a while, and an occasional snort. He interrupted the silence – "Any ideas on what Ilgregious might be up to? Is anyone surprised he isn't here with the new evidence he was so excited about?"

"I'm sure he and Kardool are doing their best," offered Qualmsneed.

"Yeah, I'll bet they are," said Brakken and the snartch Gothamar almost simultaneously.

Quinpin flicked her tongue. "Even if they *are* gathering evidence, where's Pinhammer? Why isn't *he* here?"

"That's a very good question, my young spewler," said Gailryder. "Something's rotten in Lairmark and I'll venture to say it isn't my grandma's squid-and-sardine goulash."

The hall had gone quiet when Kardool walked in. "Hello, everyone," said the spewler – speaking slowly and deliberately. He gazed at the drakes around the Ingot. "I suppose you're all wondering where Pinhammer and Ilgregious are."

Quinpin's eyes lit up. "Indeed, we are. Where's Pinhammer?"

Kardool glanced at Gailryder, then at the others. "It's unfortunate, but the evidence we were looking for is not available just now. And when Ilgregious and I saw Pinhammer on his way here, we told him we didn't have it. Pinhammer answered that he isn't feeling well and headed back to his lair. He suggested I relay the news that he wouldn't be here and adjourn the meeting."

"How sick is he?" asked Quinpin.

"He said he wasn't feeling too good. Looked a little pink around the nose and ears – usual stuff. But we expect he'll be good as new in a day or two."

Farl bobbed his head and flicked his tongue. "Do you know if he intends to reconvene the hearing concerning Lutjen and Laudus?"

Kardool looked up at the nickelneck with a vacant expression. "Yes. He said we'll reconvene when we have the evidence, or when he's feeling better – whichever comes first. He'll notify us so we'll have time to get our schedules in order. In the meantime, Ilgregious and I will work on securing our evidence, which has a direct bearing on this important case. Pinhammer will want us all here – and with no distractions when we reconvene."

Gailryder flicked his tongue. "Yeah, I'm sure he will. I guess it's settled then. If there are no other questions, meeting adjourned."

There were murmurs and whispers as the leaders made their way out of the great hall and headed toward the Morinair Gate.

Gailryder and Farl were the last to leave. Once the others were out of earshot the malwrack leaned over and whispered, "One of us needs to go check on Pin and make sure nothing weird is going on."

"Right," whispered Farl. "I'll go."

"That's weird," muttered Kardool. Farl and Gailryder were usually the first ones out. He hung out in the meadow outside the Morinair gate and pretended to be stretching a stiff wing. When the malwrack and nickelneck finally emerged, he watched as they took off into the early evening sky. Farl headed toward Brangboor and Gailryder toward Smilf.

Kardool exhaled, glanced around, and took off toward Trool. It was obvious they suspected something, but it didn't really matter. Nickelnecks and even malwracks were no match for the Dark Queen's power.

26. A Meeting of the Minds

It was late and the last rays of the sun felt good on his back. Farl had flown far enough towards Brangboor that he was free to circle west without being seen. He descended to the treetops and banked left, completing a near one-eighty. Flargellion's twin peaks were just visible to his right, and Pinhammer's lair wasn't too far west on his current trajectory.

He landed next to a meandering stream and headed up a path. The path ascended through a dense pine forest and ended at a boulder in the side of the hill. "Pinhammer, you in here?" he shouted.

No answer. He worked the boulder free, shoved it to the left, and poked his head in. He shouted again, "Pinhammer, you in here?"

Still no answer. The opening was tight for a nickelneck, but he squeezed through. Gailryder had been right as a fat fiadhain – Pinhammer was nowhere to be found. There were no signs of a struggle – Pinhammer's huge stash of gold was neatly stacked in a corner. Farl squeezed back out, glanced back at the stacks of gold, rolled the stone in place, and took off for Gailryder's lair in Smilf.

Kardool reached Lake Hornsniffler just as the sun disappeared behind the western hills. He poked his head inside Ilgregious' lair. "How's Pinhammer?"

"Pinhammer? He's fine... for the moment." Ilgregious grinned slightly. "My guys are taking good care of him – a few stones to your left."

"Good to hear," said Kardool. "Let's keep him safe until we convince the others to grant us the power to rule in his stead."

Ilgregious scrunched his nose. "He's expendable! Let's do it now – we could blame Gailryder and Farl. I'd be happy to organize a ceremony – the Red Lair is just a flip of the wing over that hill. I'm sensing the Dark Queen wants to feel the fear pulsing through his veins as much as I do!"

Kardool flicked his tongue. ""Hang on, my scale-challenged friend. The Dark Queen wants to wield power in this realm – we mustn't let an opportunity to seize control of the Drakebureau slip through our claws. The others might grow suspicious should Pinhammer disappear completely. Once our plan is complete and our grip on power is secure – he'll be all yours."

Ilgregious bobbed his head vigorously. "You lost control of Cangoar – and now you want to risk letting Pinhammer continue as Leader?"

Kardool ignored the drambat's angry tenor. "Someone – probably that female nickelneck – must have gotten to Cangoar," he replied in an even tone. "If you and your minions had done your job, that never would have happened."

"We don't know that," said Ilgregious with a snarl. "Besides, how could she have gotten into the Viper Vault?"

"It doesn't matter. What matters is convincing the other leaders that Farl and Gailryder are planning a coup. If we can create division among the leaders – it might give us the opportunity we seek."

Ilgregious flicked his tongue. "A division? Yesss," he hissed. "But I have one request."

"What's that?"

A somewhat twisted grin emerged as Ilgregious bobbed his head and thrashed his tail back and forth. "I want to take Pinhammer to the Red Lair – and offer him up to her Darkness."

Kardool looked away. They had already agreed on that – this drambat needed to get his head on straight. "Yes. Great," deadpanned Kardool. "You needn't worry. I have no long-term interest in that bloviating buffoon. Once we have control of the Drakebureau, you can do as you wish."

The drambat's grin grew wider. "Yesss," he hissed. "And the next step in taking control of the Drakebureau will be…"

Kardool interrupted, "Will be to convince the others that Gailryder and Farl have kidnapped Pinhammer and are planning a coup. We'll remind them how malwracks and nickelnecks despise members of the smaller species – and how they'll be after you, me, and Qualmsneed next."

Ilgregious bobbed his head. "Yesss," he hissed. "Drambats, spewlers, and snartches – we'll all be in danger. Along with anyone who supports Pinhammer!"

"Exactly. No one wants a civil war. And if we play our cards right…"

This time it was Ilgregious who interrupted. "We'll be able to convince the Drakebureau to enact emergency measures to put an end to their evil insurrection."

Kardool thrashed his tail back and forth. "Yes. We must do whatever it takes to save Drakedom from being torn apart by their bigotry and lust for power." He looked away and flicked his tongue. "Emergency measures, indeed. You and Qualmsneed must get word to the other leaders that there'll be an emergency meeting – at midnight, tonight. At some obscure, unexpected place – perhaps Grindenmar Crossing, on the way to Smilf."

"Yesss," hissed Ilgregious. "Grindenmar works. It's not too far, and everyone knows where it isss."

Kardool scrunched his nose.

Why is this drambat hissing like a snake?

"While you're notifying the others, I'll pay a little visit to our guest of honor and make sure he's comfortable in his new digs. I don't need to remind you to make sure Gailryder and Farl aren't invited."

"Soundssss good," hissed Ilgregious. "I'm off to Qualmsneed's."

Kardool watched as Ilgregious flipped a wing and took off, then headed to Pinhammer's 'hideout'. He had to crouch a little to poke his head inside. The opening was drambat-sized, but the lair was larger than expected. Pinhammer was snoring, and there were three drambat guards posted just inside the entrance, two of which were also snoring.

The snoring was consistent – interrupted by an occasional snort. The smallest snored faster than the others and sputtered along in a high-pitched whine – almost a whistle. Kardool stopped and listened for a moment. The pitch and timing of the other two varied yet maintained a unified rhythm. Pinhammer's was the slowest and deepest and formed a bass line for a sort of melody. The drambat who was awake was tapping his foot but stopped and came to attention when he noticed Kardool.

"Trimlung, is it?"

"Yes, your Drakeness. How may I assist you?"

"I need you to wake our guest. After that you may make yourself and these two sleeping beauties scarce for a while. We have some business to discuss."

"Wha – what kind of business?" asked the drambat.

"Silence!" snarled Kardool. "What I discuss with Pinhammer is no concern of yours. Or your sleepy little comrades."

"Yes your Drakeness," answered the drambat as he nodded and bopped his two companions on the head. "Wake up, you fools – Kardool is here!"

Kardool waited until the drambats left before rousing Pinhammer and making sure he was in a 'good place'. He reminded him of the rebellion, and once he was satisfied Pinhammer was on board with the narrative concerning Gailryder and Farl, he started to head out.

"I trust you'll let me know how the meeting goes," said Pinhammer.

Kardool looked out into the night sky – he shouldn't have mentioned the meeting. "Yes, your Drakeness, you'll have my report first thing in the morning."

Kardool stepped outside and called the three drambats back to their posts. He was confident Pinhammer's mind was in the hands of the Dark Queen – there'd be no mistakes this time.

"Make sure no one but me goes in or out of here, do you understand?" Kardool lowered his head slowly until his nose was inches from the lead guard's. "If you mess this up, you'll find I'm not as forgiving as my charm and refined speech might suggest."

"Yes, your Drakeness," said the guard. He turned to the others and said, "Guys. Listen up – we're rotating the watch. Two on, one off – twenty-four seven. No one gets in or out without Kardool's permission…"

The guard's voice trailed off as Kardool took to the air, heading south and east. After a few hours, he saw a light on the ground. It was the edge of malwrack country, but that was no malwrack's lair – no malwrack keeps a fire. It was just outside an entrance to a lair and though it wasn't a clear night, the clouds were high enough that it could be seen from a good distance. He landed outside the cave and glanced around. A few hills guarded either side of the Furlong River. Grindenmar Crossing was just downstream.

Ilgregious, Qualmsneed the drambat, Quinpin the spewler, and Brakken the arsnatcher had arrived ahead of him. The cave was small and Kardool waited outside as the others climbed over and around one another trying to make room for Gothamar the snartch who had yet to arrive. The mouth of the cave was wide, but not very tall, and the back end of it was narrow.

Eventually Qualmsneed, the smallest among them, wedged himself in the narrow end, furthest from the entrance. Kardool found a spot between Qualmsneed and Ilgregious, while Brakken, being the largest, situated himself in the entrance with his tail and rear legs outside. Gothamar showed up and Brakken backed out so she could get in.

Ilgregious cleared his throat once they were all situated. "My fellow drakes, you're probably wondering why Kardool and I have called this meeting. My apologies for the short notice and the tight quarters, but for the safety of our beloved Pinhammer, it was necessary to hold this meeting in secret."

"Where are Pinhammer, Gailryder, and Farl?" asked Brakken as he glanced at the others. "I should think they'd be here."

Ilgregious gave Brakken a vacant stare. "Indeed, my silver-scaled friend, how right you are. Gailryder, Farl, and especially Pinhammer are the reason we've called this meeting in secret. I'm afraid Pinhammer has gone missing, and it has come to the attention of certain members of this body that Gailryder and Farl have hatched a plot – a nefarious plot I'm afraid. They are plotting to do away with our beloved leader and seize control of the Drakebureau."

"Oh my goodness, and gag me with a gargoyle," said Qualmsneed excitedly. "That is a nefarious plot! Is this the evidence you two were after? If so, we must act quickly to stem the stench of sedition and the rip-tide of rebellion!"

Ilgregious flicked his tongue. "Yes, and thank you, Qualmsneed. Indeed, that was the evidence we were after. Obviously we couldn't speak of it earlier."

Kardool kept a grin from emerging – Qualmsneed's reaction was better than he could have hoped.

"Gailryder's had it in for Pinhammer for decades," added Quinpin, her eyes flashing in the dimly lit cavern.

"Yes. Yes, indeed," sneered Qualmsneed.

"Beyond belief," grumbled Gothamar as she bobbed her head in a circular motion.

"The nerve of those beasts!" exclaimed Brakken with a flick of his tongue. "They should be exiled to Farshen, or maybe worse."

"Yes. Exiled to Farshen!" shouted Quinpin.

"No need to shout," said Kardool. "But I appreciate your enthusiasm. Let us act quickly to save Drakedom from a truly terrible turn. We must do whatever it takes to squelch this threat to our beloved Drakebureau. But this is not just a threat to our beloved leader. This is a threat to all drakes everywhere!" Kardool looked at the floor – working to keep a smirk from appearing. He and Ilgregious would leverage these delusions of their own importance – delusions which would be quickly squashed once they were in control.

"Well spoken!" shouted Qualmsneed enthusiastically.

Quinpin snorted.

Brakken's eyes grew wide as he glanced around with bulging cheeks, then let go of a fireball which hit the ceiling. Remnants of burning goo dripped from the ceiling and a bit of it landed on Gothamar's tail.

"Ooh – get it off!" she exclaimed.

Qualmsneed brushed the flaming goo onto the floor.

"Ooh, thank you so much," said Gothamar.

"No worries," said the drambat.

"Easy," said Kardool. "Let's save that for later, shall we?"

Brakken scrunched his nose. "Sorry. I got excited."

"Where do we begin?" Qualmsneed asked while looking around at the others. "What's our first step towards squashing this heinous rebellion and protecting the integrity of our beloved Drakebureau?"

"We need to find Pinhammer," said Brakken. "We need to make sure he's safe."

"Agreed!" exclaimed Quinpin.

"He could be anywhere between Farshen and Nuellian," said Gothamar.

"We'll need help," said Brakken. "The six of us can't possibly cover enough ground in a timely manner. How much time do you think we have before Farl and Gailryder make their move?"

"I'm afraid no one knows except them," said Kardool in a soft, high-pitched tone, his words trailing off at the end.

Qualmsneed glanced around at the others. "What if they've already…"

"Already what?" asked Brakken.

Qualmsneed bobbed his head. "You know – done away with him?"

"Then they'll be brought to justice and face the consequences for their treachery!" exclaimed Gothamar. "Either way we'll need to organize a search party."

Brakken flicked his tongue. "Pinhammer is the only one who has the authority to mobilize the gaggles."

Gothamar glanced at the others. "Since Pinhammer is not here, perhaps one of us could be granted temporary authority to act in his stead. I move that we nominate two candidates and put it to a vote."

Kardool flicked his tongue and glanced at the ground – they actually think this was their idea.

"I second that," said Quinpin. "I nominate Kardool."

Ilgregious gave the female spewler a hard look. Oh, sure. She nominates *him*. As if spewlers hadn't held the reigns long enough. Ah, but no worries, the Dark Queen had chosen him long before she chose Kardool. He grinned slightly.

How many sacrifices has Kardool made to Her Darkness?

"I nominate Gothamar," said Brakken. "She's sincere and studious – for a snartch, that is. And she's been with us as long as anyone can remember."

"Thank you, Brakken," said Ilgregious. "And now that we have our candidates – are we ready to vote?"

"I'm quite ready," said Qualmsneed.

"Sure," said Quinpin and Brakken almost simultaneously.

Ilgregious bobbed his head. "All those in favor of Gothamar as interim head of the Drakebureau while Pinhammer is away, raise your right front paw!"

Gothamar and Qualmsneed raised theirs.

"We have two votes for Gothamar. All those in favor of Kardool for interim head of the Drakebureau, raise your left front paw!"

Brakken, Quinpin, Ilgregious, and Kardool raised their paws.

Ilgregious thrashed his tail back and forth. "We have a majority. Kardool has been elected interim head of the Drakebureau! You have the cavern, your Drakeness."

Kardool flicked his tongue and licked his chops. "Thank you Ilgregious – and thank you all. I assure you – once the rebellion has been squashed and Pinhammer has been restored to his rightful place as leader of the Drakebureau, I shall step aside immediately and resume my role as humble servant – as representing spewlers on the Drakebureau. That being said, I agree with Brakken and Quinpin! Our first order of business is to form a search and rescue mission for our beloved leader. I would think the drambat reserve gaggles should be sufficient."

Gothamar glanced around, then gave Kardool a piercing stare. "What about the snartch or arsnatcher gaggles? Surely you're going to include other species in the hunt for Pinhammer."

Kardool gave her a blank stare. "No. I have more important things in mind for the other gaggles."

"What kind of things?" asked Brakken.

"We will send the others out to find Gailryder and Farl. The insurgents must be arrested, brought back to the Viper Vault, and put on trial for conspiracy and sedition."

"I'm afraid that's easier said than done," groused Gothamar. "They won't give up without a fight, and I'd rather not take on a malwrack or a nickelneck – not with ten gaggles."

"Don't forget the others," said Kardool confidently.

Ilgregious grinned slightly and glanced at Kardool, then back at the female snartch.

Gothamar bobbed her head and flicked her tongue. "Do you honestly believe the malwrack and nickelneck gaggles will participate in a hunt for Gailryder and Farl?"

"Why not?" answered Kardool flatly. "The traitors must be dealt with before a civil war breaks out. Nickelneck and malwrack gaggles are sworn to protect the Drakebureau like everyone else."

Ilgregious bobbed his head. Asking malwrack and nickelneck gaggles to hunt down their own leaders – he was getting newt bumps at the thought.

"Yeah, I guess you're right," offered the snartch.

Brakken bobbed his head and looked away. "Good luck with that one."

Kardool gave the arsnatcher a hard look and flicked his tongue. "Brakken, you with us?"

"I don't want to be fighting no malwracks or nickelnecks," answered the arsnatcher. "Especially Gailryder or Farl."

"Right," said Kardool. "I don't want any of you or your charges fighting *them*. Anyone who finds them must not be a hero. Send word, stay hidden, and wait for help."

"Help from where?" asked Brakken.

Kardool glanced around at the others. "From the malwrack or nickelneck gaggles."

Gothamar gave Kardool a hard look. "Your plan is completely dependent on recruiting the malwracks and nickelnecks," she said with a bit of a sneer.

"Yes, it is," answered Kardool. "But Ilgregious and I have friends in high places. You needn't worry – we have word that the malwracks and nickelnecks will join us."

Ilgregious flicked his tongue and fought to keep a grin from emerging. He and Kardool have a friend in high places, all right.

Brakken glanced at the others. "Well, if you're sure the malwracks are with us – I guess I'm good."

"Me too," added Gothamar. "We must do whatever it takes to save Pinhammer and put an end to this treachery."

Kardool glanced at the others. "If there are no objections, Ilgregious and Qualmsneed will direct the drambats in a search for Pinhammer, while Quinpin, Brakken, and Gothamar mobilize the spewler, arsnatcher, and snartch gaggles. I'll mobilize the malwrack and nickelneck gaggles, and together we'll search for Gailryder and Farl. But remember – whoever finds Gailryder or Farl must not be a hero. Send word and wait for reinforcements. We want neither casualties nor an escalation of hostilities."

Brakken bobbed his head. "Yes, your Drakeness, we must avoid an escalation at all costs."

"Indeed," said Gothamar with a flick of her tongue.

"It's settled then," said Kardool as he glanced around the cavern. "Meeting adjourned! In the morning we'll mobilize the gaggles and begin the search for our beloved Pinhammer and those two traitors."

Brakken backed out of the entrance and Ilgregious, Kardool, and the others followed. Ilgregious and Kardool watched as the others took off. They seemed to be in good spirits as each headed toward his or her assignment.

Kardool turned to Ilgregious. "Okay, we're good now. Pinhammer is yours to do with as you like."

"Yesss," he hissed as he watched Kardool take off. He flicked his tongue and licked his chops. "The Dark Queen will be quite pleased," he mused. "Quite pleased, indeed."

26. It Begins

Ilgregious flew to Trool and gathered the drambats for a summoning ceremony in the Red Lair. "Tonight will be a night to remember. Prepare the lair for a very special guest. I'll be back shortly."

"Yes, your Drakeness," answered Flithy – lanky but not quite as tall as Ilgregious.

It was a short flight to the cavern where Pinhammer was being held. The guard at the entrance tried to greet him. "Good evening, your Drakeness. The prisoner is…"

He shoved the guard aside and went in. He found the spewler snoring and jostled him a bit. "Wake up and come with me, your Drakeness. We must move you to a safer lair," he said. He had to be polite about it, but soon that would end.

"Huh? What?" Pinhammer waved a paw and fell back asleep.

Ilgregious flicked his tongue. "Pardon me, your Drakeness, but we must move you to a safer place. Gailryder and Farl were seen heading this way. We believe they are looking for you, your Drakeness."

"Gailryder and Farl are looking for you…" muttered Pinhammer, his words interrupted by a snore.

"Wake up, you snorting, slug-slurping, serpent!" snarled Ilgregious.

Pinhammer picked up his head and scrunched his nose, exposing his fangs, yet his eyes remained closed.

Ilgregious took a step back. The spewler's fangs were twice the size of his – and he had only one.

Pinhammer's right eye opened. "Oh, yes. Yes, indeed. Time to wake up." He snorted, shook his jowls, and said, "Oh, why hello Ilgregious. What were you saying?"

Ilgregious took another step back and wiped the base of his neck. Yuuuck – spewler slobber. He was about to scratch his right front leg, but instead glared at the spewler. "We've received word that Gailryder and Farl are looking for you. We must move you to a safer place, your Drakeness."

Pinhammer's eyes widened. "You don't say. They're coming to Trool?"

Ilgregious looked away for a second. "There were reports last night of a sighting west of Flargellion. We don't think they'll come here, but just in case we would like to move you to a more secluded lair – one where you'll be sure to remain hidden."

"Oh my," the spewler said. "Were they alone, or were there others?"

"We think they were alone, but we've posted lookouts and are taking every precaution. The other lair is well hidden and will keep you safe. No one will find you there. Never. Not ever." Ilgregious' voice trailed off. He looked away as a slight grin emerged.

"Oh good. Sounds like a plan. How'd that meeting go last night? Do we have a plan for dealing with the traitors?"

"Yes, your Drakeness. I'll tell you all about it once we get you to a safer place," he whispered. "But we must go quietly. Their spies could be anywhere." He flicked his tongue, hoping he wouldn't have to discuss the plan, or anything else for that matter.

"Oh, my goodness, yes," said Pinhammer in a voice which was almost a whisper. "Mum's the word."

"Great, let's get you out of here."

They took off for the Red Lair which was just a minute or two away. An orange glow radiated from the lair's entrance and was visible from the air. Two drambats welcomed them as they landed.

"This is an unusual choice," said Pinhammer in a disapproving tone. "Easily seen from the air – I thought you said it was hidden."

"How right you are," said Ilgregious in a hushed but urgent tone. He turned to the drambat in charge of preparations and bobbed his head. "What were you thinking, you slug-slurping slime sucker?" He slapped him up the side of the head with a paw. "You weren't supposed to roll the stone away until *after* we arrived."

"Oh yes. My apologies, your Drakeness," said the drambat.

"Well don't just stand there, get moving! Once we're inside, roll that stone back in place!"

They went inside and as Pinhammer watched the stone being rolled back, Ilgregious scratched his left front leg a few times. His leg started to bleed, his eyes glowed red, and he focused on Pinhammer's right ear. He felt the Dark Queen's power surging within.

Giddy with a sense of power, he rode a wave of dark energy as it worked its way inside the spewler's auditory canal. It twisted and turned along neural pathways, searching and hunting for episodic memories which could be used against him.

A variety of memories presented themselves. They were like story boards – images from the spewler's life. One was a memory with Pinhammer's friends and his mum on his twelfth birthday. Yuk. Way too cheery. And what's worse, they were playing *glour.*

Ilgregious nearly looked away but didn't. It could interrupt the connection – he reminded himself to focus. Ah, there's one. The spewler was just a few years older than a hatchling and was being taunted by a bully – a malwrack no less. He felt dark energy reinforcing the memory by replaying itself over and over again. The spewler's body went limp and he fell over on his side.

They were only slightly older than hatchlings, but the malwrack was three or four times his size. It made fun of his diminutive tail and stomped on it as he chased him around a meadow not far from Mt. Flargellion. The spewler was too young to fly and scurried away as fast as his short little legs could take him. Pinhammer's body went rigid, and his legs began flailing wildly as he lay there on his side.

It was delicious to watch what was going on inside the spewler's head. How the malwrack's long legs were faster, and every time it caught him it would step on his tail and pin him down for a few seconds. Then it would drop a loogie on his head and laugh before releasing him for another chase.

"What's the matter? Malwrack got your tail?" asked the malwrack, jumping on it with all his weight. Parts of it turned purple. The spewler remained focused on his injured tail and inability to escape. Eventually he gave up. His legs quit flailing, and in his mind the malwrack was jumping up and down on his tail continuously, pulverizing it into a purple-and-red ribbon. No one but Ilgregious and the Dark Queen could see how the Leader of the Drakebureau had become helpless as a hatchling.

Ilgregious bobbed his head. His red eyes flashed around the cavern. "Bind him with chains and let the ceremony begin!" he shouted.

Three drambats chained up the spewler. Ilgregious released his hold on the spewler's mind as they dragged him over to the lava pit. Fifteen drambats formed a half circle and chanted to the tune of an ancient dirge. "Power, puke, and green blood too, we are your servants through the slough!"

Ilgregious grinned and waved his skinny front legs as if directing the chorus. Pinhammer writhed on the ground and struggled to get free from the chains. His eyes grew big as a few drambats screeched, others howled, and some shot flames in the air. A purple luminescent haze filled the cave.

"Ooh, we are frightened, aren't we?" said Ilgregious with a twisted grin. "And well you should be. But you needn't worry. Pin-ham-butt-brain – it will all be over sooner than you think. And the Drakebureau won't have to listen to your insufferable bloviating... ever again!"

Ilgregious glanced around at the others. Their faces reflecting orange light as the lava pulsed and gurgled, its light dancing on the walls and ceiling.

The drambats chanted a new phrase, "Toss him, burn him, roast him on a spit. Toss him, burn him, fry him in the pit!"

The cavern fell silent after eight or ten repetitions. The only sounds were the churning lava and Pinhammer's chains rattling around as he struggled to free himself.

"There's nothing quite like the sound of a prisoner's struggle just before they become one with their molten grave!" exclaimed Ilgregious with a twisted smirk. Two drambats bonked heads and another shot flames in the air. He lifted his front legs and yelled, "For the sake of drambats everywhere and for our beloved Dark Queen – do it! Do it now! Toss him in!"

It was anything but a toss. Four drambats struggled to roll the spewler – nearly twice their size – into the pit. The spewler's eyes grew even bigger as he strained against the chains, squirmed, and thrashed his tail.

One of the drambats took a shot from Pinhammer's tail and fell into the pit. One of his wings was immured by molten magma – he screeched but was unable to escape. The screech – along with his life – was snuffed out a second or two later. The other drambats looked at one another, then roared and howled.

Eventually the remaining three managed to roll the chained-up spewler rolled into the pit, where he burst into flames as molten magma engulfed his body. The chains turned orange and melted. His scaly exterior lasted longer than the chains but only prolonged the inevitable. The spewler screeched and writhed for a few seconds and then fell silent.

Pinhammer's final screech was swallowed by a burning, bubbling abyss as he inhaled a noxious mixture of sulfurous gases. For a moment he felt his inward parts being cooked from the outside as glowing orange lava ate away the chains and made its way through his scales. The pain vanished as he left his body and watched the last of it disappear, mercifully followed by what was left of his burning head.

His first inclination was to flap his wings as he floated above the pit and studied the others below. He soon realized he could float without them and only a slight move of either wing changed his position. He hovered wherever he pleased and with little or no effort.

The last remnant of his tail dissolved and disappeared in the glowering pit. An other-worldly peace and calm took over his heart and mind and drove away any feelings of remorse at the loss of his body or of his life in that realm.

He tried hurling a fireball at Ilgregious, but there was nothing. Then he floated lower and took a swipe with his claws at one of the drambats who had rolled him into the pit. Still nothing. He had crossed over into the Phoberon and could no longer interact with their realm. There was nothing to do but watch and listen as Ilgregious and the others carried on with their ceremony.

An unseen presence made the plates along his spine stand on edge. He glanced left and was startled by a dark, hooded figure within a few tail lengths. Strange that he hadn't noticed it before. He backed away as he studied it.

It was somewhat like a pale gray ape which had lost nearly all its fur, except it was much bigger – nearly twice his size and with wrinkled, pasty-gray skin. It was draped in a black cloak and had a chin almost as pointy as its nose. Its attention was fixed on Ilgregious while it expelled something purple from its mouth. It appeared to be working hard to generate the purple haze and seemed to absorb any light in its vicinity.

The hooded figured extended its right hand toward Ilgregious, and it came as no surprise when the drambat began floating about the room without using his wings. He commanded the other drambats to bow to the Dark Queen and to himself, whereupon they ceased their chanting and bowed low, uttering something about how great Ilgregious was.

The hooded figure looked away and scowled, which caused Pinhammer to wonder why she had an interest in the silly little drambats at all. It was now obvious this was the Dark Queen – one who wielded a power far greater than anything in their realm. Powerful – and hopefully as altruistic as he had been when he had been leader of the Drakebureau. He liked to think of himself as being concerned about those less fortunate than himself – perhaps to a fault.

She appeared to be expending a lot of energy, and from this new perspective – there was a sense that she was somehow debasing herself. But none of it mattered much. Not to him – not anymore. The Dark Queen's business was no concern of his – he was no longer an agent in that realm, nor did he want to be. He was content to observe and had feelings of ambivalence, even apathy, to what was going on below. The old struggles in the other realm seemed petty and insignificant to him now. He lingered over the proceedings for a few moments, then floated up through the roof of the cave. Somewhere in this realm, he sensed a power which exceeded anything the Drakebureau could ever hope to wield. Exceeding the power of the Dark Queen herself.

He floated higher and realized he could move great distances with very little effort – a few flicks of his tail or wings. He had read the Obelisk as a young spewler, but what little he remembered about the Phoberon! What wonders would he see as he ascended above the earth's atmosphere? The sun, which had been hiding behind the earth's shadow, presented itself from this new perspective. He stared directly at it without hurting his eyes, and beyond it there appeared to be an ocean of living, animated beings which grew more concentrated near a luminescence which exceeded that of the sun – yet was much more distant.

It pulled on something inside him as if his very soul required something from it, but he couldn't put a claw on what. He guessed that it was the seat of Power but sensed that somehow it transcended even that. And as he moved towards the Light, he passed by the sun but felt no heat or radiation from it. The distant Light had a quality as if it had substance – as if it were necessary for his existence in this realm or any other.

So this is what crossing over is like. It doesn't end in the realm he had lived in all his life. Perhaps more attention should have been paid to what was written in the Obelisk about such things. But that would have been politically and socially unacceptable. When one is in a position of authority, it is best not to dwell on things such as the Phoberon or thoughts of an afterlife. The Obelisk had been denounced as mythology by scholars – and for good reason. An effective leader must remain focused on the harsh realities of one's own realm.

"Even if I were able to go back and talk to those fools, I wouldn't tell them what it's like on this side," he muttered to himself.

It was far better to remain blind to such things, and to focus on making the realm they inhabited a better place. After all – he alone truly understood the intricacies of what it took to keep six different dragon species focused, motivated, and under control. Perhaps he should have torn down the Obelisk when he had the chance.

And as he pondered these things, an uncomfortable sensation, accompanied by a desire to turn away from the Light, swept over him. No, the Obelisk ought to remain, but only as a symbol which must never be taken seriously and never actually read. And on he went, debating whether he should have torn it down, and whether he would go to the Light – or not.

Ilgregious watched Pinhammer disappear beneath the lava's surface as the drambats chanted, "Double trouble, slimy and green, give us your power, oh mighty Dark Queen!" Some screeched, some snorted, and others shot fireballs at the ceiling. Ilgregious completed a full circle around the cave, then touched down gently where he started.

The chanting stopped – except for a single rotund drambat which continued with his eyes closed. He quit when the drambat next to him nudged him hard enough to nearly nock him over. Ilgregious looked up and saw a dark figure in the midst of the haze, and the others must have seen it too, because the room fell silent. The figure raised its arms and stood head and shoulders above all others.

"You have done well, my servants," the Dark Queen said in a voice that crackled and thundered and shook the Red Lair.

The drambats bowed low, all except Ilgregious who stood and stared with an enraptured look on his face.

"You too, my servant," warned the Dark Queen. "You must bow to me like the others. Bow to me now!" she exclaimed in a voice like thunder.

"Forgive me, your maleficence," he said as he bowed low. "I was carried away by your magnificence." But as he bowed, his eyes remained riveted on Her Darkness as orange light from the pit danced around yet shed no light on her countenance. Her features were defined by varying degrees of shadow – except for red pupils which glowed and appeared to hover in empty eye sockets.

"We have a great opportunity before us, now that those who would hinder our progress are no longer in power," said the Dark Queen. The cavern shook as she continued, "Together we shall fight for fairness and equality for all species. Let the weak be made strong, and the mighty be laid low!"

One by one the drambats stood and snorted and shot flames in the air. And as they jumped about and bonked heads and carried on about what great things they were going to do, Ilgregious watched Her Darkness disappear into the haze.

"Whoa, I forgot how taxing it is to make an appearance in that realm," muttered Krimeny to herself. She felt weak – as if she were a putrid little drambat herself, and was *not* looking forward to drinking from that rancid river again. Livenmoore. A rancid but necessary evil to gain access to their realm. Only the Enemy could think up such a thing. And why would He name it that? It should be called Pukenmoore. But no need to dwell on *that* – it's been a good day. Pinhammer is gone, and those revolting little winged reptiles have control of the Drakebureau.

"Korgarag will be quite pleased."

"Quite pleased, indeed," said Jendal.

Krimeny spun around and raised a threatening hand but then relented. She drew back and held her breath. How was it fair that Jendal – a pedantic follower of the mundane, should be stronger and brighter than *her*?

She looked away, inhaled deeply, then glared at Jendal with a sly grin. "It won't be long before they'll be killing one another, stealing each other's stuff, and turning their world into the hell-hole it really is. And then we'll see how much satisfaction Melohim gets from that realm and those rancid little beasts. A realm of light energy and light matter! Whoever heard of such nonsense?"

Jendal smiled. "Melohim chose to create that realm and the beings which live there. Do you think he needed *your* permission to do it?"

Krimeny looked away. "Why not? If he really cared about us – he'd focus his attention on our realm, not theirs."

"Why are these creatures and their realm so abhorrent to you?"

Krimeny's eyes flashed. "Join us! Then you will understand what an abomination it was that he created those rank little odor-fests and that stupid little realm they inhabit."

"Thanks, but no thanks," said Jendal. "I find those creatures charming."

"Really?" asked Krimeny. "They're gross – an insult to anything normal. What was the enemy thinking?"

"I wouldn't pretend to know Melohim's thoughts."

"More dosara will join our cause once they see how fragile their world is – and the useless struggles of beings in that realm. One day we'll make it clear just how stupid it is to serve the one who cares more about those smelly, weak little beings than about real *power*. He'll wish he'd never created that realm, nor the beings that inhabit it. There'll be no end to their suffering and misery – all because he protects free will – theirs and ours. And I... uh... wait. No, Korgarag... will be feared and revered above all others, including Melohim himself."

They watched Pinhammer sputter and stop and start, as he alternated between moving towards and away from – the Light.

"You really believe that – don't you?" asked Jendal.

"And why not? We've seen quite a few dosara join our side, despite the obstinance and interference of beings like yourself."

Jendal nodded and smiled slightly. "Yes, indeed. We are bothersome, aren't we? But you look like you could use some rest. Were your interactions with their realm a drain on you?"

"No, but you are! You have no idea what a challenge it is to drink from Livenmoore. It should be called 'Liven-less'. Maybe you think it is refreshing – in fact he deceives you while you wallow in your ignorance. Perhaps one day you will learn how bitter it truly is and how it eats away at your insides."

Krimeny scowled as she sped away from Jendal and Pinhammer. Her excitement grew as she thought about telling Korgarag the good news of Pinhammer's death. He'll be pleased. Her scowl morphed into a grin – he'll be very pleased indeed.

27. NEW OPPORTUNITIES

A firebolt whistled past Cangoar's left ear. "Where's the ref?" he muttered to himself. That shot was high, way too high – he ought to get a red rat for that one! Here comes another. Ha! Missed me! Now if he could just...

"Cangoar, wake up. You're dreaming," said a voice in a firm whisper. Someone nudged him. He didn't respond. But the voice persisted. "It's time. We've got to get you out of here."

A frown replaced the grin on his face. "Leave me alone. Can't you see I'm about to win my match?"

"Sorry to interrupt," said the female voice. There was another nudge. "Cangoar, wake up. We need to get you out of this place."

"Huh? Get who out of where?" he asked, his eyes mostly shut. "Is the Drakebureau in session? Am I late for my hearing?"

"No, it's me – Jendal. There isn't going to be a hearing. The Drakebureau's been compromised. We've got to get you out of here."

"No hearing?" He opened his eyes and stretched as far as the shackles allowed. "Oh. Jendal, it's you. Why are you here?"

"Shhh! Keep your voice down. We don't want the guards to hear. Pinhammer is dead. Ilgregious and Kardool have taken over the Drakebureau. There will be no hearing, or if there is, it will be a farce. Your life will be forfeit if you stay. I'm here to get you out. Will you come with me?"

Cangoar shook his jowls. "Yeah, sure," he muttered. "Wait. What about the hearing?"

"There isn't going to be one – will you come?"

225

"I guess – if there's not going to be a hearing. Wait. Did you say Pinhammer is dead?"

"Yeah. Pinhammer's gone – Kardool and Ilgregious have control of the Drakebureau."

Cangoar glanced out through the cell door, then back at Jendal. "Whoa. Monstrous mounds of malwrack manure. What happens now?"

"It's too early to tell," whispered Jendal. "Our challenges seem to be multiplying."

Cangoar nodded. "Okay, let's go. Where to?"

"To Alfedora and Bannabard – in Farshen."

She touched the shackle on his snout. It fell to the ground.

"Whoa, thanks," he whispered. "Alfedora said you could do things – but actually seeing it – is amazing." She went around and touched the shackles on his legs. Each sprung open and fell to the ground. He shook his jowls and shook the chain off his right rear leg. "Thanks," he said again.

"You're welcome," she whispered. "Keep it down – we don't want the guards after us. Follow me."

She touched the lock and the door of the vault opened – by itself. They headed down the corridor and peeked around a corner. Two guards tossed coins against a wall in the hall outside the guard hut. Jendal blew at them through cupped hands. They slumped over and promptly fell asleep.

Cangoar flicked his tongue. They made their way past the guards, past the Obelisk, and out through the Daor Gate. In the moonlight he saw they were headed to the woods across the meadow. He followed the blue ape – dosara – whatever she was – into a stand of trees. "Jendal, hang on a second." He looked her in the eye. "Thanks. I... how can I repay you?"

"No worries. Just help Alfedora and Bannabard expose Ilgregious and Kardool. But let's talk about that later. Right now, we've got to keep moving. Once daylight comes, there'll be gaggles hunting for Pinhammer, Gailryder, Farl, and Alfedora. They'll be hunting for you too once they find your cell empty."

He flicked his tongue. "Why would they hunt for Pinhammer? I thought you said he was dead."

"I did, but only Ilgregious and Kardool know that. It's part of a ruse to convince the others that Gailryder and Farl are behind Pinhammer's disappearance."

He bobbed his head. "But where are Farl and Gailryder? Why aren't they setting things straight?"

"They don't know what Ilgregious and Kardool are up to – not yet anyway. I'll meet you in Farshen in a few hours and we can talk then. Be careful and fly low – especially once the sun comes up."

"No worries. I'll see you there." Cangoar took off into the night sky, headed west, crossed the divide, and followed the Farnheim River for a few hours. The sun snuck up behind him about the time he reached the canyons in Farshen. He scanned the sky to his left, right, above, and behind. No sign of other drakes anywhere.

The sun felt good on his back – there was always a chill passing over the divide at night. He felt the chill again as he dove beneath the top of the canyon and into the shadows. He flew low, just above the Farnheim and found the cave they used last time. He peered inside, but no luck. Alfedora and her blue ape friend weren't there.

A high-pitched sound – possibly a screech – from a cave just across the canyon caught his attention. It was muffled and distant and sounded as if it came from deep inside. He was sure it was a malwrack screech, but it would be weird for a malwrack to be in Farshen – they prefer coastal climates. Did they come here – hunting for Alfedora?

There it was again – across the way, and a little to his right. What if she's in trouble? With a jump and a glide, he landed at the entrance and crouched low. He glanced at the orange and magenta walls of the canyon behind him – now lit by the morning sun. Not good. It would be easy to see his silhouette against such a bright backdrop. He slithered inside as low as he possibly could and plastered himself against the wall to his right. He peered into the darkness.

There it was again – another distant screech of a malwrack. Plates on his spine stood up. And then he heard it a third time, but this time he realized it was close – too close to be a malwrack. He exhaled and grinned.

"Hey, Alfedora, wake up! It's me – Cangoar!" He glanced around. "Bannabard, you in here?"

His eyes were adjusting to the dim light and saw remnants of a fire. A few bones from fish and other small creatures were scattered about. "Alfedora, wake up! You'll have to catch up on your beauty sleep later. We've got important things to do."

"Huh? What things?" asked Bannabard. "Cangoar, is that you?"

"Yeah, it's me."

"Where did you come from?" asked the blue ape.

"Jendal got me out of the vault and sent me to find you guys. She's on her way with some important news." He made his way further inside the cavern. It was dusty – not a stalactite or stalagmite in sight. "Farshen. What a desert!"

"Yeah, tell me about it," said Bannabard. "What kind of news? Hopefully it'll mean we're out of here."

"There's stuff going on with the Drakebureau," Cangoar said. "Jendal will explain when she gets here."

And as he spoke a black orb appeared in their midst.

"What's up, Jendal?" asked Bannabard. "We thought maybe you forgot about us."

"Forgot? How could I forget you guys?" she asked as she transformed into her blue ape persona. "I think you're the one who's forgotten – you guys are the reason I'm here."

"We're not the only reason, though, right?" asked Bannabard.

"Uh, yeah, pretty much. Believe me, I've got better things to do than hang out in this realm – and if it weren't for you guys, I'd be gone. I'd be long gone. I'd be gone like yesterday's wind. I'd be gone like Alfedora's last meal. I'd be gone like…"

"Okay, we get it," interrupted Cangoar.

"But I didn't forget you guys. Some things came up that needed tending to. I hope you enjoyed your little holiday."

"Holiday? You call being stuck in this God-forsaken place a holiday?" protested Bannabard. "The river water's red with mud, there's naught but cactus, lizards, and catfish to eat, and apart from an occasional colorful sunrise or sunset…"

"Sorry about all that – but you seem to have managed," said Jendal, looking at the bones scattered about. "I'm afraid I have some bad news. Alfedora, you awake?"

"Wut… awake? Who… awake? Yeah, I'm awake." Alfedora raised her head momentarily, then fell back asleep with a snort.

"Alfedora!" exclaimed Bannabard with a smile. "Wake up, you fire-breathing enemy of all living things! Cangoar and Jendal are here."

~

"I… I'm not the enemy of all living things," I replied with a yawn. "But I could be. Did someone say Cangoar?"

"Yes, he did," answered Cangoar. "Hey Alfedora, how's it flapping?"

"Bannabard!" I exclaimed. "Why didn't you tell me Cangoar was here?"

"I did."

"Oh hey, Cangoar!" A dark silhouette was nearly black against the backdrop of the canyon wall. I nearly knocked Bannabard over as I went and slapped him up the side of his head.

Cangoar's eyes narrowed. "Good to see you too," he muttered. "What was that for?"

"You had me scared to death. I didn't think you'd leave that place in once piece. Glad to see you finally listened – what brought you to your senses?"

"It wasn't you – I can tell you that!" he said with a grin. "Jendal has some news concerning Flargellion."

My gaze bounced between the two apes – hoping we'd get out of this desert once and for all. "Jendal, it's great to see you – what news?"

"Good to see you too, and yes, I have some news – it's not great."

"Are you going to tell us?" I asked.

"Ilgregious and Kardool have killed Pinhammer and have taken control of the Drakebureau."

I nearly screeched. "Those toad-sucking rat turds have taken over the Drakebureau?"

"I'm afraid so," said Jendal.

I bobbed my head. "How is that possible?" I stared at Jendal. The cavern went silent as the others stared back at me. I shook my jowls and narrowed my eyes. "They killed Pinhammer!? I can't believe they killed the leader of the Drakebureau! Those monsters! Did they gut him like they did those malwracks?"

"No," said Jendal. "Things will get worse now that they have control. But as a wise dosara once said, 'An opportunity arises with every new challenge.' I'm afraid we have more than a few 'opportunities' before us."

"Opportunities?" I asked. "You call this an 'opportunity'?"

"Yes. And you should know that Kardool and Ilgregious have convinced the other leaders that Gailryder and Farl are plotting to take over the Drakebureau and are behind Pinhammer's disappearance."

"Someone needs to find Farl and Gailryder," suggested Cangoar. "Tell them what's going on and set the record straight."

Bannabard nodded. "No doubt Ilgregious and Kardool will have convinced the others how dangerous they are."

"Yeah, and then they'll try to get the nickelneck or malwrack gaggles to have Gailryder and Farl arrested," said Cangoar.

"I think we should hunt down Ilgregious!" I exclaimed, bobbing my head. "He's the one sacrificing hatchlings! Gailryder and Farl can take care of themselves."

"Maybe not," said Cangoar.

I glared at him. "You don't think so?"

Cangoar's eyes grew wide. "First they get inside your head – and when they do – you can actually *feel* it. Then everything goes dark, your blood runs cold, and before you know what's happening, they're putting stuff inside your head. And you don't know what's true and what isn't. It still feels like I killed those guards. But I guess I didn't. Right?"

"You see?" I snarled. "This is why we should hunt down Ilgregious first!"

"I don't think we can risk that," said Bannabard. "What if Kardool recruits the nickelnecks or the malwracks while we're hunting down Ilgregious?"

"Bannabard's right," said Cangoar. "We need to find Farl or Gailryder first."

"Maybe you guys are right," I said, flicking my tongue and giving Cangoar a hard look. "I don't have to like it, though." I glanced at Cangoar, then at the ground and headed out to the ledge overlooking the river. My gaze reached the river at the bottom of the canyon. I was disgusted that Jendal wouldn't use her powers to fix this. And why not?

She's just as powerful as the Dark Queen, right? But she won't. It's not fair – hatchlings will die and the Drakebureau will cease to function. Part of me wanted to take off and hunt down Ill-greega-butt myself.

Cangoar poked his head outside. "Alfedora – you okay?"

"Yeah, I'm fine. I was just thinking. It doesn't seem right that this is so hard. Why does it feel like it's us against the world? A world of lies?"

"It kinda is, I guess."

I bobbed my head. "It feels like we're isolated."

"Yeah – pretty cool, huh?" said Cangoar with a stupid grin.

I gave Cangoar a cold stare as Bannabard and Jendal emerged.

"Hey guys, everything all right?" asked Bannabard.

I glanced at Bannabard. "Yeah, we're okay," I said – with less conviction than I would have liked. I turned to Cangoar and exclaimed, "This is exciting, we have a mission!"

Cangoar's grin widened. "Yeah – a mission!"

I bobbed my head. "Hopefully Gailryder and Farl will help us expose these lies before they gain more traction. I'm guessing it won't be long before the sky is full of gaggles who think they're on a mission to save Drakedom by hunting down Farl, Gailryder, and us three."

"I'm afraid it will be dangerous and a bit lonely," added Jendal. "Only you three understand who will be on the real mission to save Drakedom."

"Gotta love the silvery in that!" I exclaimed.

"I think she means 'irony' – and what about blue apes?" asked Bannabard. "Do we have a role in this?"

I glared at Bannabard. "I said what I meant and meant what I said. Don't be putting words in my mouth! No self-respecting nickelneck gives a newt's tail about iron."

Bannabard looked away. "No need to get your tail in a twist – 'silvery' it is."

"Thank you," I said. "Silver maybe, but not iron. And of course blue apes have a stake in this. If Ilgregious gets his way, he'll wipe out the lot of you."

Cangoar bobbed his head. "It looks kinda grim, but maybe we have an opportunity to save Drakedom *and* Blue Apedom."

"Apedom. Is that a word?" I asked. "Everybody knows what Drakedom is. I just don't think *Apedom* is a word."

"Really?" asked Cangoar. "Evil, nasty, scrawny little drakes have taken control of the Drakebureau and you're worried about spelling?"

"It's not a word. Just sayin'."

"Yeah right, and 'silvery' is a noun," muttered Bannabard. "So, what happens if Gailryder and Farl don't believe us?"

"I think they'll believe us," said Cangoar. "Not even a drambat could make up this stuff. Besides, we all know how Gailryder feels about Ilgregious."

I flicked my tongue. "I have no idea how Farl and Gailryder feel about anything."

"Oh, sorry. I forget you guys never hung out with malwracks at the Viper Vault. So, any ideas on where we should start? I happen to know Gailryder's lair is in Smilf and Farl's is in Nuellian."

I thrashed my tail. "How about we start with Smilf?"

"Yeah, Smilf is closer," said Cangoar. "If Gailryder is there, we might be able to mobilize the malwrack gaggles and put an end to this coup d'état."

"I've never been to Smilf!" I exclaimed. "I hear the ocean is amazing this time of year! Wait. What's a coup d'état? Is that something malwracks eat? Like giant snails or something?"

"No," said Bannabard. "It's when someone tries to take over the government."

"Oh – I thought it was a delicacy. Like deep-fried squid." I bent my left front leg and Bannabard climbed up. "This is exciting! We're on a mission!" And it didn't hurt that Cangoar was with us. I'd follow his tail-challenged butt anywhere.

"I'll meet you three in Smilf," said Jendal as we took off heading a little south and mostly east. "Be stealthy! And don't go into Gailryder's lair without me."

"What'd she say?" yelled Bannabard.

"I think she said, 'stay healthy and don't eat Gailryder's fare without me'," I yelled. "Wow, I guess she must be hungry. I didn't think dosara ate food in this realm."

"Me either," said Bannabard.

28. A Malwrack's Descent

"I'll bet acorns to a stater Ilgregious is behind Pinhammer's disappearance," muttered Gailryder while munching on whale gizzards. His lair was in some bluffs overlooking the ocean to the east, and the morning sun shone in directly this time of year – welcome heat for an old malwrack. They were up early even though he and Farl had been up late discussing Pinhammer's disappearance and what to do about it.

"But even with a dozen drambats, those overgrown vultures would have been hard-pressed to overpower Pin," said Farl.

Gailryder looked out over the ocean. "Yeah. It doesn't add up."

"And there were no signs of a struggle. But if it was Ilgregious, what do you suppose his game is?"

"I have no clue, but I'll bet it isn't glour. He can kiss his gold goodbye if he's done anything to Pinhammer."

"And his leathery butt," added Farl. "Do you think he kidnapped him?"

"Nah. That wouldn't be possible – even with ten drambat gaggles. Besides, the only reason for kidnapping Pinhammer would be for gold, or if he were planning some sort of insurrection."

"Yeah," said Farl with a flick of his tongue. "There's been no demand for a ransom."

Gailryder scrunched his nose. "Just a guess – but we're just guessing. It's time we mobilize the gaggles – and get some cold hard facts."

"Can we do that without the Drakebureau?"

"It'll be fine as long as we report our findings when we're done."

"Cool. Let's flip a wing."

They took off heading south and west toward Soilerama's lair, which was just a couple hills away.

"No one's here," said Farl as they landed and peered inside a south-facing cavern. "Empty as a cracked dragon egg."

There were gold coins scattered about. "That's weird. He usually keeps a neat stash – neater than mine," said Gailryder.

"He doesn't use much bedding, does he?" asked Farl.

Gailryder popped his head outside. "It's outside the cave and down the hill."

"Maybe he left in a hurry."

There was a trail of skid marks in the dirt. "Or was dragged out."

"Who could have dragged a full-grown malwrack out of his lair?" asked Farl.

Gailryder glanced at Farl, then spun around at the sound of a screech. It was too loud and too severe to be hatchlings at play. "That sounded like it came from Slimgiblets' lair." He peered across the valley.

They took off, crested the hill on the other side of the valley, and were greeted by two malwracks standing outside a cave. They were looking up at the sky – as if guarding something. Farl barely managed to dodge a firebolt from the bigger one.

"That was no warning shot!" exclaimed Gailryder. "Soilerama, what are you doing? It's us – you overgrown iguana!"

The malwrack glared at him defiantly. "Gailryder! You and Farl are under arrest for the kidnapping of Pinhammer. Come quietly, or we'll knock you out of the air!"

"You're kidding. Who sold you that viper vomit? If you believe that, I've got a lair in Farshen to sell – ten gold coins."

"We don't want a fight," shouted Soilerama. "But we'll do whatever it takes to protect Drakedom from an insurrection."

"Insurrection? The only insurrection I'm aware of is you and whoever fed you these lies."

Gailryder swooped in, dodged a firebolt from Soilerama, and knocked the other malwrack off his hill-side perch with a whack of his tail. It was Pearmonger – another gaggle leader. The malwrack tumbled into a gully on the left side of Slimgiblets' lair.

"We've got them, your Drakeness!" shouted Soilerama, as he turned and took a shot at Farl.

"Soilerama, who are you talking to?!" shouted Gailryder. "Is Pinhammer in there?"

"None of your business!" shouted Soilerama.

Gailryder circled behind while Farl took a run at Soilerama, dodged a firebolt, and enveloped the malwrack in a cloud of greenish-brown fumes. Gailryder came in fast, but the fumes were thick, and it was tough to make out his target. He was nearly on top of the cloud when Soilerama stuck his head out and launched a firebolt.

He had no time to react – the firebolt clipped his left wing and sent him careening into the gully toward Pearmonger. Pearmonger was waiting and screeched into Gailryder's right ear as they collided in a heap at the bottom of the gully. Gailryder's his eyes grew big before everything faded to black.

~

"Hope no one gets seriously hurt before Gailryder wakes up and we can straighten this out," muttered Farl to himself. His buddy was out cold. He climbed higher, looked back, and launched a fireball at Soilerama. The malwrack avoided it easily from that distance. He circled like a vulture, keeping an eye on Gailryder while watching for firebolts.

A spewler emerged from the cave with a third malwrack trailing behind. The malwrack was huge – larger than Gailryder and with a vacant expression on his face.

Hang on. Kardool? What's he doing here?

He circled and watched as Kardool scrambled toward Gailryder who was sprawled out in the gully. The third malwrack followed Kardool around like an overgrown fiadhain on a leash.

"Hold him down!" scolded Kardool as Gailryder began to stir.

The huge malwrack put a paw on Gailryder's neck which made him struggle even more.

"Don't suffocate him!" shouted Kardool. "We don't want our prize damaged!"

"Uh, sorry," muttered the malwrack.

While Farl circled and watched, Kardool clawed his left forearm until it bled. And if that wasn't weird enough – the spewler's eyes began to glow yellow. He'd never seen a spewler do *that* before. He launched a fireball that nearly hit Kardool in the tail.

"Will someone please shoot down that nickelneck!?" shouted Kardool.

"We're trying!" exclaimed Soilerama. "He's too far away to get a hit on him."

"Well go chase him off or something!"

"No malwrack can keep up with an airborne nickelneck," complained Pearmonger. "And screeches don't affect them."

"Well go get two or three buddies and get after him!"

Soilerama and Pearmonger took to the air as Farl took another shot at Kardool which just missed taking off his right-rear leg. That was close — almost got him. He tucked his wings and went into a steep dive heading straight at the malwracks. They split up and everything went silent for a moment as Pearmonger let out a screech.

"You lame-brained lizard!" exclaimed Soilerama, just loud enough that Farl could make out his words. "All that did was hurt *my* ears. When he gets close, put him in a crossfire!"

"Right!" exclaimed Pearmonger.

With the others engaged in a dogfight, Kardool scratched his left front leg until it bled. He focused his gaze on Gailryder's right ear. "Oh, how precious! You think you're the *real* leader of the Drakebureau!?"

He grinned slightly as dark energy coursed through his eyes — he could feel it boring into the malwrack's big black head. A euphoric appreciation for the Dark Queen's power gripped him — but with a sense that it could turn on him in an instant. "I see. You believe you and your nickelneck friend are the real protectors of Drakedom?" he asked with bit of a sneer. "And you're the last line of defense if evil should ever gain a foothold? As if good and evil actually exist! But no worries my dear friend. The Dark Queen and I are here to set you free from your delusions."

He nearly lost focus as he reveled in the power he would wield over this malwrack. Her power was in his claws — Her Darkness had given it to *him*. "In time, you will come to understand, like I have, that right and wrong are nothing more than feelings. Feelings which can be ignored. Power is really all there is. Only fools think it better to be loved than to be feared. Malwracks may be bigger and stronger than other species, but they lack the vision and will to wield Power in its purest form. Soon there will be a new reality – a reality in which all drakes everywhere will slink, slither, and shake their jowls at the mere mention of my name. And it all starts with giving you – the great Gailryder – a reality makeover."

Out of the corner of his eye he caught sight of something in the air. The nickelneck was coming in fast. He ducked as a fireball narrowly missed taking off his head. There was a warm – no, a hot sensation. He glanced back – the bony plates on his back were singed and glowing slightly.

He cowered behind Gailryder's hulking frame and popped his head up just enough to see Soilerama on Farl's tail – both heading straight for him. The malwrack fired a shot, but it missed the nickelneck and nearly hit Gailryder in the leg.

"Watch that!" shouted Kardool. "You idiots, it's two against one! Why are you letting him get so close!?"

"You'll have to do better than that if you're going to bring *me* down," shouted Farl.

The nickelneck banked sharply to the right and circled behind Pearmonger. He shot a fireball up the malwrack's back side which busted a wing and sent him crashing into the hillside just below Gailryder.

Kardool bobbed his head.

Farl was circling back when Slimgiblets, still holding Gailryder down, lit him up with a firebolt which sent him crashing into a couple of pine trees just above and to the right of where Pearmonger landed. Soilerama was on the nickelneck in an instant.

The nickelneck's tail was severed and his left wing broken as Soilerama put a paw on his neck and held him fast.

Farl struggled but was no match for the malwrack. "Why are you guys… fighting us?"

"Farl!" shouted Gailryder, struggling while Slimgiblets pinned him down at the base of his neck.

"I'm glad that's finally over," said Kardool dryly as he turned to Soilerama. "Hold onto the nickelneck until I tell you otherwise!" he yelled.

Gailryder felt the spewler's yellow gaze penetrate his right ear again. It felt warm and sharp – like a heated claw boring into his head.

"Perhaps now we can get back to the business at hand," muttered Kardool. "Where were we? Oh yes. We were about to create a new reality for our prize – the leader of the malwracks!"

Gailryder craned his neck and looked at the malwrack who was holding him down. "Slimgiblets. Why are you helping…"

His voice trailed off as a dark Presence overtook his thoughts and tried to set itself up as the One – the One and Only Thing inside his head. He closed his eyes tightly. It seemed impossible to resist.

"What have you done with Pinhammer?" interrupted Soilerama.

"I haven't done anything. With Pinhammer." It was hard to speak, hard to focus on anything but the dark Presence – the Menace. "Why don't you… ask Kardool," he grunted. "He'd know better than I what happened to Pin…"

"Silence!" shouted Kardool. "The malwrack lies, everyone knows that. He's trying to throw us for a loop – he wants to take control of the Drakebureau!"

Gailryder pushed back against the Menace inside his head and for a moment was able to focus on what was going on around him. "Let me up, Slim, and I'll get this spewler to tell us what's really going on." It was all he could do to get the words out. Slimgiblets didn't budge.

"Quiet!" said Soilerama. "We know all about it. How you and Farl threw Pinhammer into a lava pit inside mount Agorg and are plotting to seize control of the Drakebureau."

It was a struggle, but Gailryder opened his eyes for a moment. "What! Are you crazy?!" he exclaimed. "Who told you that? Kardool – what lies have you been spreading!? You don't believe this spewler's lies, do you – Slim?" He struggled – if he could get free for just a second he would make that spewler tell the truth – or squash him like a bug.

"It wasn't something Kardool said," replied Soilerama. "I saw you do it! I was there – three nights ago."

Gailryder winced and closed his eyes. The Menace was hungry, or angry, or both. "You've lost your mind," grunted Gailryder. "I haven't been anywhere near Agorg in years." He tried to ignore the Menace – tried to focus on happy thoughts, hoping to drive it out of his mind. Do. Not. Let it. Take control.

"Silence!" shouted Kardool.

Gailryder's eyes shut hard as the Voice crowded everything out of his mind and set itself up as the One Thing, the Only Thing. It took over – dark and sharp and unyielding. He felt its strength and perceived that its goal was to twist or turn or flip his memories upside down and inside out. Everything inside him focused on expelling this invasion, this violation of his being. But the Voice was strong – too strong even for him. All he could manage was a scrunch of his nose.

"Ah, there it is. You sent Farl to check on Pinhammer – to see if he was safe!" exclaimed Kardool.

How is Kardool able to see what the Menace is doing inside my head?

His mind was stronger than the spewler's, but the other was stronger than either of them. Kardool was there, but this Menace – this Voice inside his head – was like a force of nature. Maybe a force beyond nature.

"You never knew this, but Farl was the one who killed Pinhammer and reported him missing," said Kardool in a tone as smooth as snakeskin. "Your best friend at the Drakebureau betrayed us all and treated you like a sack of deep-fried leeches."

"He did?" asked Gailryder – no longer cognizant of who was speaking or where the words were coming from.

"Yes, and there's another," said the Voice. "Long have you suspected the drambats of plotting an insurrection, but now you can see that it was Farl and the nickelnecks who are, and always have been, the real enemies of freedom and peace in Drakedom."

"Farl and the nickelnecks are the enemy," mumbled Gailryder. He embraced this 'Truth' as his own. How could he have been so blind? "Farl!" he exclaimed.

"Yes, it has been Farl all along," said the Voice inside his head. Suddenly he became aware of Kardool. How could he have doubted him? Had not this spewler been his friend all along?

"You have done well, my big friend," said Kardool in a soft, soothing tone. "Let the truth soak in. And then you will lead the malwrack gaggles in allegiance to me and me alone. Only my leadership can save Drakedom from being torn apart by the nickelneck insurrection. And you, my friend, will have a prominent role to play in heading off this crisis."

"Together, we can wipe out the rebels," said Gailryder monotonically. "This cancer of nickelneck ambition must be eradicated! Only then will we restore peace and unity to Drakedom."

"Very good," said Kardool. "And what else?"

"All must unite in support of you, your Drakeness."

"Yes," said Kardool. "Anyone who opposes me is an enemy of our Great Society. Everyone must support the Great Society of Drakes – or be eliminated."

"Those who refuse to support your Drakeness will be eliminated," parroted Gailryder.

"Yes, yes. Well spoken! Your contributions will not go un-rewarded," said Kardool enthusiastically. "And you can begin by dealing with one who has witnessed our little discussion and felt bold enough to interrupt our discourse. Perhaps this fool fails to have a full appreciation for *the Cause*."

Kardool gave Soilerama a cold stare. "Release Gailryder. He has some business to tend to. There is one among us who thinks himself worthy of leadership. Perhaps he thinks himself more worthy than I."

Gailryder shook his jowls as he got to his feet. His thoughts were fuzzy, jumbled, confused. Perhaps he'd bonked his head during the struggle? He flicked his tongue and gazed at Soilerama. The fool had dared to question the Leader's authority. He bobbed his head and let loose a firebolt which tore through the malwrack's neck. Soilerama's body fell to the ground in a heap.

Gailryder's eyes met Pearmonger's as he scrambled out of the gulley, dragging a busted-up leg. Pearmonger looked at Soilerama's body, glared at Gailryder and hurled a firebolt straight at his head. Gailryder ducked and hurled himself at Pearmonger. The ensuing exchange of claws and teeth ended quickly as the hobbled malwrack was no match for Gailryder's quickness and strength.

Kardool chuckled. "Well done, well done, my friend. And now you must deal with the real traitor. The first step of many toward ending this insurrection. The insurrection of the nickelnecks."

Gailryder hesitated. He gazed at Farl lying unconscious – unable to defend himself. He scrunched his nose as his friend labored to breathe.

"Finish him off!" shouted Kardool. "Do it now. Do it for Drakedom!"

Gailryder's eyes narrowed as he glanced at Kardool and then at Farl and then back at Kardool. Had Farl been his friend? The nickelneck must have deceived him – just as he intended to deceive everyone else. "This nickelneck's a liar and a murderer. I do this for Drakedom." He turned toward the nickelneck, inhaled, and launched a firebolt – an accurate shot which severed the nickelneck's gray neck instantly.

Kardool bobbed his head and swished his tail back and forth. "Together we will deal with the greedy power mongers among us! Those who oppose fairness and equity in Drakedom!"

"Yes, your Drakeness," said Gailryder with a blank stare.

Kardool gazed at the malwrack carcasses. "How unfortunate that Farl was able to kill Soilerama and Pearmonger before you defeated him. Nickelnecks are more dangerous than we thought. We must hunt down all remaining rebels and squash the rebellion before more lives are lost!"

"Yes, your Drakeness," said Gailryder and Slimgiblets almost in unison.

Gailryder knew it was a lie. Was it a sense of self-preservation, or his new-found allegiance to the Leader which kept him silent? It didn't really matter. He would say and do whatever – anything to protect the Leader and whatever narratives he might wish to convey. It was every drake's duty to support the Leader – for the future of Drakedom. "Unfortunate indeed," said Gailryder evenly.

"Come, my friends," said Kardool in a gentle, even soothing, tone. "We must organize the malwrack gaggles! They must hear of the nickelneck rebellion and of Soilerama's and Pearmonger's demise at the hand of Farl."

"Yes, your Drakeness," said Gailryder as they took off to find the gaggle leaders.

28.   An Armadillo Trail

Kardool watched as the malwrack leaders organized their gaggles and prepared to head to Brangboor.

"We'll follow you, your Drakeness," said Gailryder as he turned and faced Kardool.

But it would be an unnecessary risk to put himself in harm's way. "Oh, I don't think I'll be needed," said Kardool. "I'm pretty sure the nickelnecks will join us once they see your strength. But if they refuse, you know what to do."

"Yes, your Drakeness," said Gailryder. "And what would that be?"

Kardool gave the malwrack a fierce look. "Wipe them out. Every last one."

"As you wish, your Drakeness."

Gailryder didn't look him in the eye – Kardool would simply have to trust the Dark Queen's power to keep the brute obedient to the lies inside his head. "I'm going to leave you in charge while I head back to Trool. Meet me there – once the negotiations with the nickelnecks are complete."

"Yes, your Drakeness."

Kardool took off toward Trool, and an hour or two later found Ilgregious busy organizing the drambat gaggles.

Ilgregious bobbed his head. "Flithy, do you have your gaggles ready?"

"Yes, your Drakeness."

"Good. And are Scibbarren, Turvey and the others ready as well?"

"Yes, your Drakeness."

"Eggssellent," hissed the drambat leader. "The blues apes will have seen their last sunset before this day is done!"

"Are you planning an attack on the blue apes?" asked Kardool.

"Yes, and it will be glorious! We're off to the Great Seedred Forest – to put an end to the tyranny of blue apes – once and for all."

"Very well," replied Kardool. Blue ape tyranny was a fabrication of course. There had never been any such thing. As far as he knew there hadn't been an attack by blue apes since the Great Ape Wars. But he would humor the skinny, scaled-challenged drambat – at least for now. "Together, we'll lead drambats and spewlers in a glorious campaign! It'll be the first time in history when drambat and spewler gaggles fight together – united in bringing justice to Seedred!" There was a modicum of enthusiasm in his voice, but it made no sense that Ilgregious would do this now – not when they were still consolidating their power at the Drakebureau.

"NO!" shouted Ilgregious. "You will lead nothing! The drambats and spewlers have rallied to *my* plan and *my* leadership. No one shall deprive them of the privilege of following *me* into battle!"

Kardool looked away and flicked his tongue. Does this drambat really think an attack on the blue apes makes even a lick of sense right now? A polite grin appeared on his face. "As you wish, your Drakeness."

Ilgregious looked at Kardool with a blank stare. The spewler was quite a bit younger than himself but his demeanor reminded him of his uncle Loadstifle when he was just a hatchling. His older sister had been little more than a hatchling herself when she was ambushed by a band of apes while hunting in Seedred. And when she failed to return that night, he took it hard – really hard. He wailed and thrashed about until finally his uncle took him on a search for her. Unfortunately, they found what they were looking for. There wasn't much left except her head, parts of her wings, and her tail.

"Blue apes!" exclaimed Loadstifle as they studied the carnage. "That's why young dragons aren't allowed to hunt in the woods by themselves. Take a long look at what they did to her and let that be a lesson to you. Blue apes are not to be trusted, nor to be trifled with. The only good ape is a dead ape."

Ilgregious never forgot those words nor what happened that day, but he was just a hatchling and didn't learn until decades later that the rogue apes had been caught, tried for inciting a disturbance against dragons, and found guilty. In the meantime, his anger and hatred for apes became involuntary, almost like breathing. It didn't matter that those apes had paid for the crime with their lives. And now, finally, he would seize the opportunity to wipe out all apes – in one single, glorious raid.

"I'll tag along with the spewlers," replied Kardool. "It will be a grand day for Drakedom when we put an end to these destructive conflicts which have caused so much grief over the years." He wasn't about to be out done when it came to putting a spin on things. Yet this attack was clearly an armadillo trail – and a dangerous one at that. None of the other leaders shared Ilgregious' hatred for blue apes – a species whose numbers had dwindled to near extinction. Yet somehow the Dark Queen empowers this fool. Maybe he was her first option on the Drakebureau? But now she had him. What if he didn't have to share power with this skinny little slime-slurping slug-sucker? Surely Her Darkness sees how much more effective his leadership could be. "What a shame that would be," he muttered under his breath.

"A shame what would be?" asked Ilgregious.

"Oh. Sorry. I was thinking out loud. What a shame it would be if even a single drake were lost while we're vaporizing those little blue vermin."

"A shame indeed," replied Ilgregious. "But it's time for us to head to Seedred and make whatever sacrifices are necessary for the well-being of Drakedom and the world at large."

Kardool didn't really care, and apparently Ilgregious didn't either – if a few of their compatriots perished along the way. He gazed at the ground.

"What if we postponed your operation until after we've consolidated our control of the Drakebureau?"

"No!" exclaimed Ilgregious. "We have suffered long enough at the hands of blue apes!"

"But don't you want to know what happened to Farl and Gailryder?"

"No!" exclaimed Ilgregious. "Uh, what – Farl and Gailryder?"

"Yes, Farl and Gailryder. I have some very good news. Her Darkness must be pleased – quite pleased."

Ilgregious scrunched his nose. "What news?"

"Gailryder has been turned – his allegiance is with us now. He has killed Farl and is leading the malwrack gaggles on an attack in Nuellian."

Ilgregious glanced away. "That is good news. How was Gailryder was turned?"

"The Dark Queen, of course," said Kardool with a bit of a sneer. "Her Dark Power flowed through me like a river – Gailryder was helpless as a hatchling. He believes Farl killed Pinhammer and was leading the nickelnecks in a rebellion. He is doing our bidding now."

"That is good newsss indeed," hissed Ilgregious. "And now Pinhammer is gone and the malwracks are on their way to Nuellian?"

"Yes," answered Kardool.

"Egggscellent!" exclaimed Ilgregious. "Then we are free to go ahead with an attack on Ape Town!"

It was dark in the outer parts of the Phoberon as Jendal approached Krimeny. "Does it worry you that Kardool is looking to rule without Ilgregious?" Jendal asked.

"No, not in the least," replied Krimeny. "Good for him, I say. It's about time, don't you think?"

Jendal looked off in the distance, toward the Light. "I don't know about that, but if they start fighting among themselves, aren't you concerned that their little coup d'état might fail?"

"Yeah, right. Let them duke it out I say. In the end I'm rooting for Gailryder. He keeps his thirst for power hidden, but once the nickelnecks have been wiped out, there'll be no one to oppose him. I look forward to the day he comes to me and asks for the power I've given to Ilgregious and Kardool. Imagine the two of us ruling Drakedom – with an iron fist! None would dare oppose us."

Jendal shook her head and looked away. Nothing like counting your drakes before they're hatched. "What makes you think you can trust Gailryder? What if one day he were to wake up and shake off your lies like Cangoar did?"

"Nonsense! Have you even been paying attention? Dark energy has created an alternate reality in his mind, and it's been nothing short of magnificent! He's killed three of his friends and turned against the nickelnecks. And why? Naught for a *lie*. And the lie in his soul is corrupting him as we speak. He's mine now. There'll be no turning back – not for him. As for Cangoar, Alfedora, and that blue ape? I'm sure it won't be long before they meet the same fate as Farl and Pinhammer."

"If that happens – and I don't think it will – but if it does, there won't be much of a fight left. What will you do then?"

"There will always be more drakes to corrupt, more hatchlings to sacrifice, more power-struggles to enflame."

Jendal looked away. "I fear your little power trip will be the undoing of Drakedom *and* the blue apes."

"And that is your weakness," snarled the arsnarm derisively. "Why would a great dosara like you care about these pathetic little vermin? Let them wipe each other off the face of the planet I say! Let them prove what a mistake it was to create that putrid realm and its weak little creatures."

Jendal shook her head and smiled gently. "What if our roles were reversed? What if you were the one facing extinction and the loss of your loved ones?"

"That's the beauty of it," sneered the arsnarm. "I'm not!"

Jendal looked away. "You don't get it, do you?"

"Get what?" asked Krimeny.

"It isn't just about us versus them, or me versus you."

"Okay, then what's it about?"

"That maybe Melohim cares about all beings – and in all realms."

"Why Jendal, what a lovely sentiment! Don't you get tired of caring for others just because *he* does? Where's the freedom in that? When are you going to grow up and be true to who *you* are and what *you* want?"

Jendal glared at Krimeny, then looked away. "That's just it. I *am* being true to who I am and what I want. I am being true to how Melohim made me – it's a lot simpler that way."

"Yeah, right," snarled Krimeny. "You expect me to believe that? I don't know what's worse – saying it or actually believing it. I say, Melohim, schmellohim!"

"You really believe that stuff about your rebellion and your supposed grievances against beings in their realm. You think you're enlightened and free, yet you're becoming enslaved by your own lust for power. Once Korgarag's done with you, he'll use you up and discard you too."

"Ha!" said Krimeny with a bit of forced enthusiasm. "We'll see who uses up who in the end."

Jendal didn't answer as Krimeny flitted off toward a region in their realm which overlooked Lake Luellian.

30.   In SMILF

Bannabard clung to my neck as I followed Cangoar over Grindenmar Crossing – a confluence of two rivers in a small canyon with caves on either side. We were flying just above the treetops, and I had wondered if we knew where we were going. It would have been easy to fly in a circle and not know it without landmarks and an occasional reference point on the horizon. But Cangoar had done well. Grindenmar was just north and a little west of Smilf – a region known for its gold and precious metals and inhabited mostly by malwracks. We crested a hill. On the other side of the valley I spotted the bloody remains of a nickelneck and two malwracks on the ground. "Down there!" I shouted.

"Whoa, what's going on?" shouted Cangoar as he went into a dive.

I followed and landed next to the remains of a nickelneck. I bowed as Bannabard dismounted and stared at another body on the other side of Cangoar. "More bodies," I said as I scrunched my nose. "There's been too many – since Ill-greega-butt sacrificed that hatchling. I wonder who that used to be."

"Green gizzards of a thousand lizards, I think that's Farl!" exclaimed Cangoar. "Or what's left of him. I remember him at the Stone Ingot when the Drakebureau was in session. And the other two were Soilerama and Pearmonger. They worked at the Viper Vault, same as me – and they were gaggle leaders."

"I can't believe how big he is," I exclaimed, amazed at the size of Soilerama's body and at the same time disgusted by the carnage.

"Yeah. Whoever took him out must have been a real hell-raiser," said Bannabard. "I wouldn't want to run into him on a battlefield."

"It's possible you already have," said a disembodied voice.

I nearly jumped out of my scales as a black orb appeared between Cangoar and I. "Would you mind warning us?" I stammered with a hack and a cough. "Before. You. Do. That. You nearly. Scared. The fumes. Out of me."

"Oh, yeah. Sorry about that," said Jendal as she transformed into a blue ape. She winked at Bannabard.

"She enjoys that – too much, I think," I said.

Jendal's eyes narrowed. "This is the work of Gailryder."

"Gailryder? Really?" asked Cangoar as he bobbed his head. "We were counting on him and Farl to expose the truth. What the newt's butt is going on?"

"Gailryder has turned," said Jendal in a somber tone. "He fought against it, but his mind has been corrupted by Kardool and the Dark Queen." She paused and looked at Cangoar. "You know better than any of us what that's like. His mind is bent. He's in Kardool's service now – little more than a tool."

"A very powerful, very dangerous tool," said Cangoar. "And yeah, I do know what that's like. But I'm over it now. I mean… I'm pretty sure I didn't kill those two guards. I think. Probably not."

"Of course, you didn't," I said with a snort.

Cangoar glanced at me, then at Jendal. "Gailryder and Farl were thick – thick as thieves," he said with a vacant look. "I can't believe this."

Jendal nodded. "Kardool and the Dark Queen have convinced him Farl killed Pinhammer and was plotting to seize control of the Drakebureau."

"That's a lie!" exclaimed Cangoar. "Farl's no murderer! And he hated serving on the Drakebureau! Every drake from here to Gellion knew that."

I thrashed my tail and scrunched my nose. "Let me get this straight. Gailryder killed Farl because of some stupid lie?" I studied Farl's decapitated body, then looked away. "How can this be happening? Drakedom was supposed to be better than this. Now there are three members of the Drakebureau who can't be trusted and two good ones who are dead."

"Farl's gone and Gailryder's been turned," said Bannabard. "Without them we don't have a snowball's chance in a lava pit."

"This is just wrong," said Cangoar with a sneer. "Stupid wrong. If they can corrupt Gailryder, well, there ought to be an oracle against such things. We don't stand a chance against malwracks, even if we recruited every nickelneck, arsnatcher, and snartch under the sun."

"What nickelneck would believe us now anyway?" asked Bannabard. "It'll be our word against theirs."

I bobbed my head and thrashed my tail. "It would be easy to give in and just give up. But I've seen my family fall apart – I'm not about to stand by and watch that happen to the Drakebureau. We all need to get a grip!" I exclaimed.

"Easier said than done," snarled Cangoar.

I glared at him. "There's no use screeching over spilt squid. I'm not putting up with this nonsense about Ilgregious and Kardool taking over the Drakebureau! It's just a drambat and a spewler we're talking about."

Cangoar thrashed the stump of his tail. "But – Gailryder and the malwracks."

"Yeah – so what? I stood there and watched when Ilgregious threw that hatchling into a lava pit – there was no time to react," I said, my eyes narrowing. "But if I knew what was gonna happen, that arsnatcher might be alive today. Well now we know what these slime-slurping slug-suckers are up to. And I'm *not* gonna sit by and watch another hatchling – arsnatcher, snartch, or whatever, get burned alive because Ill-greega-butt and his minions are having delusions of grandeur!"

Cangoar's eyes narrowed. "You know what? Alfedora's right," he said with a bob of his head. "Right as a fat fiadhain! We've got to fight these creeps or die trying. Maybe Melohim will be with us and maybe he won't, but either way we've got to fight! For the society of drakes – for Drakedom – for every drake in Gaia."

Bannabard nodded, his gaze bouncing from Cangoar to me to Jendal. "Yeah! And for Apedom!" He pounded his chest with one fist, tossed dirt in the air with the other, then knuckled up and spun around twice. "For Gorby, my parents, my friends, and even Farl!" he howled. "Count me in!"

I bobbed my head. "Who knew? Apes are kinda fun when they get excited."

Cangoar snorted, then bobbed his head. "Now all we need is a plan. Anybody got one?"

I flicked my tongue and glanced around at the others. "I have an uncle who organizes nickelneck gaggles. Maybe we could talk to him."

"You think he'd listen?" asked Cangoar.

"Eam's a cantankerous old drake, but when I was young, I was his favorite niece – until I tied his tail to a stalagmite and ran off with a gold stater."

"I say we go for it," said Cangoar. "I'll bring some gold – as a peace offering."

"That couldn't hurt – he loves gold, that's for sure."

"Alfedora, you and Bannabard follow me. We'll grab some gold at my lair, and then head to your uncle's."

"I'll meet you at her uncle's," said Jendal.

I thrashed my tail back and forth. I couldn't help but admire how excited Bannabard was. And now he'll be fighting for his family. Urraca kicked me out of my family. And why? Because I distracted Rotbald during a match? It was the Drakebureau that sponsored those Games, not me. Damn, I missed Pa. I flicked my tongue and scrunched my nose.

The carcasses were already beginning to stink, and I was glad to leave that place as Bannabard climbed up and we took off for Brangboor. We arrived at Cangoar's lair a few hours later – when the sun was low. The entrance was lit by the late sun and overlooked the Salmonella River.

"Your lair isn't too far from mine," I said, a little more cheerfully than intended. "Quite a bit messier too! Are you sure they didn't...?"

"Didn't what?" he asked.

"You know... ransack the place?"

"Very funny. Perhaps you should stay and tidy up a bit while Bannabard and I go visit your uncle."

I grinned slightly. "Thanks, but no thanks. I wouldn't know where to begin."

"I'm sure you wouldn't."

"C'mon, you two," said Bannabard. "We need to keep moving."

"Yeah, let's get moving," I said with a bob of my head. "My uncle's lair is at the north end of Lake Luellian."

"I'll follow you," said Cangoar.

Bannabard climbed up and we took off, flying low – just above the trees and just off the eastern shore of Luellian. Cangoar was right behind as we landed in a meadow next to a river. Jendal was waiting for us. I bowed and Bannabard climbed down.

"Hey Jendal," said Bannabard.

"Glad you guys could make it," said Jendal.

"What did you say your uncle's name was?" asked Bannabard.

"His name is Eam, and I'm afraid he won't be too fond of blue apes. No offense, Bannabard."

"None taken. That name sounds familiar – was he in the war?"

"Yeah, he was a commander. He told us war stories when I was a hatchling. I think he lost a brother and an uncle when a band of apes ambushed them in the middle of the night. I think he said it happened near the Galtan River."

"Yeah, I might have been there," said Bannabard. "A gaggle of nickelnecks were flying low next to a cliff, and a few of us managed to jump on their backs and break their wing bones. We were able to down a few, but most of my buddies didn't survive."

"Sorry to hear that," I said. "They used to tell us stories about how unpredictable apes are – the most dangerous of adversaries."

"And so we were," said Bannabard. "We were fighting for friends and family – just like your uncle."

I flicked my tongue. "It's easy to forget that when you only hear one side of the story."

"Yeah. There's been no love lost between our species, that's for sure. Which makes me think it might be best if Jendal and I stay out of sight."

"We don't have time for that," said Jendal. "Eam needs to know what we're up against and that you and your friends will be standing with us."

"We're with you, but our numbers are limited."

Jendal nodded. "What's important is your determination to take a stand, not the size of your foot."

"Thanks," said Bannabard. "Gailryder saved my life at Flargellion. It really sucks that he's been turned."

"Ok, let's do this," I said as I poked my head inside Eam's lair. "Hey, uncle Eam! It's me, Alfedora! Uncle, you in here?"

"Hang on – just a minute!" answered a muffled voice.

I took a step back.

"Oh, hey Alfedora! How've you been?" asked Eam.

"All right, I guess."

"It's good to hear your voice! How's my favorite niece? It's been way too long I'm afraid."

"Good to hear you too," I said with a flick of my tongue.

"I'd heard you've been getting along in spite of that little tiff between you and your mum. She's always been kinda hard for me to figure out."

"Yeah, thanks. Me too." I was a little embarrassed to be talking about Mum in front of the others. "I'm here with a few friends – we have a question for you – something's come up."

"Sure – anything for my favorite niece and her friends. What's up?" Eam stepped out of the cave and glanced at the others, then glared at Bannabard and Jendal. "What in the name of Flargellion are you doing with those two!?" he snarled. "I know there's a truce, but what makes you think it's okay to hang out with a couple of grapes!?"

A few of his scales were frayed and gray around the edges, but there was a glint in his eye which reminded me of Pa. "Ah, yes. let me introduce these guys," I said, trying to maintain a calm tone. "Uncle Eam, this is Cangoar. He lives south of the lake and lost his tail to a malwrack in the B.E.G. And this is Bannabard. He's a blue ape, not a grape, and he's from the Great Seedred Forest. And this is his friend, Jendal. She's from… a different region altogether."

"Pleased to meet you," said Cangoar. "I've heard a lot about you from my ape friends."

"You have, have you? Well, it couldn't have been anything good – not from them!"

I glanced at Cangoar, then at Uncle, and then back at Cangoar. Maybe this wasn't such a good idea.

Cangoar flicked his tongue twice. "Not good, unless you mean the part about how you led the nickelnecks in quite a few successful campaigns during the Great Ape Wars. And… here's some gold as a token of our appreciation for your work in the war."

"Thanks! I'll take that," groused Eam as he snatched a leather bag out of Cangoar's paw. "You have a silvery tongue – for someone who hangs out with grapes, that is."

My eyes narrowed. "Uncle, there's something we need to talk about – something important."

Eam glanced at me, then turned his gaze back to the bag. "Well, all right. Follow me. It wouldn't be prudent to stand around out in the open with a bag of gold. And certainly not with a couple of grapes. No telling who might be watching."

The four of us followed him inside and watched as he dumped the coins out and started sifting through the pile. I was surprised he didn't make Bannabard and Jendal wait outside. Maybe he was distracted?

"Any staters? I'm particularly fond of staters. So you grapes were in the war, eh?" he asked without looking up.

"Really? Grapes?" I muttered.

"I was," replied Bannabard in a matter-of-fact tone. "We feared your species most. You and your kin were the toughest of all, including the malwracks. Our heaviest losses were when we fought nickelnecks."

"We all had losses," replied Eam. "There are those who talk about the war as if those were the glory years. They were anything but *that*."

"Nevertheless, difficult times provide opportunities for effective leaders to step forward – you were certainly one who did," added Jendal.

"I did what was necessary. To take care of our own," answered Eam. "You speak as if you were there."

"I wasn't involved directly, but I had a certain vantage point. I was able to see some of the battles and have heard quite a few stories."

Eam looked up from the pile of gold coins. "Then perhaps you'll know that I lost a brother and an uncle in that war. Which is why I don't abide my niece hanging out with the likes of you two."

31.   UNCLE KNOWS BEST

I glanced a bit nervously between Eam, Bannabard, and Jendal.

"We're no longer your enemy," asserted Bannabard. "We live under the Treaty of Flargenmoore – at least that's what we agreed to. And Alfedora and Cangoar don't feel resentment toward us, nor we toward them."

"Ah, yes, the Treaty," snarled Eam. "If you're going to hide behind *that*, you should at least obey it. As for these two, they are young and foolish. If they saw what I saw, they'd know better. Your kind are ruthless killers, not to be trusted. Certainly not befriended."

"Yeah, ruthless when defending family and friends," said Jendal. "Would you have done any less?" She paused for a moment. "*Did* you do any less?"

"Why are *you* even talking?" asked Eam. "Shouldn't Bananalard be the one talking, since he was actually there?"

I looked outside. Sure. Way to go, Uncle. Dodge the question and assert your sense of moral superiority.

"Yeah, I probably should," said Bannabard. "But Jendal has a unique perspective on things. By the way, it's 'Bannabard', not 'Bananalard'. We're here because we need your help, but it isn't only apes who need your help. Alfedora and Cangoar need your help too. In fact, all drakes everywhere… need your help."

"All drakes everywhere? Help for what? Alfedora, what's this grape talking about?"

I looked away and flicked my tongue. Nice. If he weren't my uncle… I started to head outside, then turned back and glared at him. "We're here because Ilgregious and Kardool have taken over the Drakebureau. They've done away with Pinhammer and Farl. They've got everyone convinced that Farl killed Pinhammer so he could take over the Drakebureau."

"That's just crazy!" snapped Eam. "Everyone knows Farl has no ambitions to lead the Drakebureau. He's been trying to pawn off his stall at the Stone Ingot for decades. I've turned him down five times myself. Why would anyone think that of Farl? Of all the drakes in Gaia, he'd the last one…"

"Listen to me!" I interrupted. "They want everyone to believe that by killing Farl they were saving the Drakebureau from a coup d'état."

"Wait a second. Did you say they killed *Farl*?" Eam pushed aside the gold coins and glared at me. "Is that what you said?"

I stood still and stared. There was fire in his eyes.

"I'm afraid he's gone, sir," said Cangoar in a steady, even tone. "We saw his body on a hill side in Smilf just a couple of hours ago, along with the malwracks Pearmonger and Soilerama."

Eam bobbed his head, then looked at the ground. "I never had much use for the Drakebureau and Flargellion and all that stuff. But Farl, well, he and I go back a ways. He was the best commander a nickelneck gaggle ever had." His eyes narrowed as he flicked his tongue. "You grapes are lying!" he snarled. "Alfedora, these grapes are feeding you conspiracy theories!"

"Why would they do that?" I asked.

He bobbed his head and scrunched his nose. "Maybe they want revenge."

I wouldn't have believed it if I hadn't seen Uncle's chest expand with my own eyes. "Uncle, no!" I shouted, but it was too late. I watched in horror as he launched a fireball at Bannabard and Jendal who were standing near the entrance. Jendal spun around instantly and turned her back to shield Bannabard. It was weird how emotionless it was. There was no shriek, just the splat of a mass of flaming goo which covered Jendal's backside nearly completely.

Her body glistened in the flaming goo and lasted long enough to disperse the heat and the fire. And when it was over, Bannabard stood motionless behind an oscillating black orb. The orb floated toward Eam and hovered there. Eam's eyes grew big, while his gaze bounced between the orb and Bannabard – and back again.

"Don't do that again – *ever*," bellowed the orb.

Her voice shook the lair, and everything went silent in my head. I had never been in an earthquake but figured this must be what it was like. A stalactite broke off and hit Eam on the head. "Nice," I muttered with a slight grin.

"Ouch!" he complained as a paw went to his head. "We don't get many earthquakes around here." He looked at the ceiling.

"That was no earthquake – that was me," said Jendal as she transformed back into a blue ape.

"Oh. You. Why are *you* still here? I was hoping I got rid of you."

"Nope, and unless you want more, I suggest you listen to your niece."

I started to bob my head but thought better of it. "Uncle, there's something you should know about Jendal."

"Why are these grapes still here?" he grumbled.

"Uncle Eam, look at me!" I scrunched my nose. "Jendal looks like a blue ape, but… How can I describe her?"

"There's more to her than what you see," said Cangoar.

"Yeah, right," grunted Eam. "And I may look like a nickelneck, but really I'm a fire-breathing overgrown fiadhain with wings, fangs, and scales."

I bobbed my head, glanced outside, then glared at Eam. "She's a dosara from the Phoberon – more powerful than any ape or drake in this realm. She's here to help the blue apes – and us too – if we'll let her." I looked at the ground in disbelief. I'd just spoken about the Phoberon – as if it were real.

"You're kidding, right?" asked Eam.

I scrunched my nose. "I wouldn't kid about something like this."

Eam glared back at me. "You've always been my favorite niece, but maybe you've got a few newts runnin' loose in that pretty little head of yours." His eyes narrowed as he turned to Jendal. "If you're so powerful, why not just wipe out all the bad guys and be done with it?"

"If I wiped out all the bad guys, there'd be none of you left," said Jendal with a grin. "And even though there are times I'd like to, Melohim doesn't work that way – and neither do I. We never violate free will."

"Melohim-shmellohim," said Eam. "Alfedora, you don't believe this nonsense, do you?"

I looked away.

"Your uncle is a bit 'belief-challenged', like many others of his generation," said Jendal in a matter-of-fact tone. "Perhaps another demonstration? What about another earthquake? Oh, I know. Maybe he'd be impressed if I made those gold coins disappear."

Eam flicked his tongue. "Perhaps nonsense is too strong a word."

"Very good," said Jendal. "See, he really *can* be a nice nickelneck. Alfedora, you may continue."

I scrunched my nose. "Like I was saying, Jendal wants to help us expose those who are bent on taking over the Drakebureau. Their plan is to divide and conquer – we believe Ilgregious and Kardool are organizing the malwrack gaggles as we speak."

Eam glared at me. "Did you say Ilgregious and Kardool are behind all this? Alfedora, do you really expect me to believe that scrawny drambat and geeky little spewler are behind the deaths of Farl and Pinhammer? That's stretching your neck a little thin – don't you think?"

"I know it's hard to believe, but yeah, that's what happened. Ilgregious and Kardool have certain powers. They get inside a drake's head somehow. It happened to Cangoar, and now they've done it to Gailryder. He's been turned."

"Ilgregious and Kardool?" stammered Eam. "Those two turned Gailryder? He and Ilgregious get along like snakes and fiadhains."

"Yeah – they have powers, almost like our friend Jendal. Ilgregious and his toadies killed two malwrack guards at the Viper Vault a few days ago. And before that I saw him sacrifice a hatchling during some weird ceremony near Lake Hornsniffler."

Bannabard looked down, then went outside.

I waited until he was clear. "That skinny little drambat has powers from someone he calls 'the Dark Queen'. After the sacrifice he floated around the lair without using his wings and demanded the other drambats bow down to him! It was creepier than a hundred centipedes crawling over a stash of gold. And Kardool has powers too – he can bend a dragon's thoughts however he wants. Jendal says Kardool and that Dark Queen messed with Gailryder's head – and got him to kill Farl."

"Nonsense!" shouted Eam as he bobbed his head and scrunched his nose. "Gailryder and Farl were thick as a pair of chameleons in a flower garden."

Cangoar bobbed his head. "Don't underestimate their power to twist what's inside a dragon's head. Kardool and the Dark Queen got inside my head and convinced me that I killed those guards at the Viper Vault. It was weird – I didn't know what was real. I even went to the Viper Vault and turned myself in. I was even ready to testify – testify against myself! I would still be locked up or dead if Alfedora and Bannabard hadn't helped me get my head on straight."

"Oh, yeah. I remember hearing about those guards. Quite the scandal, that was! Everyone was talking about it. But how did a tail-challenged nickelneck like you kill two malwracks?"

"If you please, your Drakeness, I didn't kill Lutjen and Laudus – I just thought I did."

"Now that's just stupid. How can you *think* you killed a couple of malwracks? Either you did or didn't."

I peered at Eam. "No, uncle, you're not listening. Like he said, Kardool and the Dark Queen got inside Cangoar's head and convinced him he was the murderer. But really it was Ilgregious and his drambats who did it."

"Now that's just crazy!" snorted Eam. "What have you guys been eating? You know better than to eat those red mushrooms with the white spots."

"We haven't been eating mushrooms," I said.

"Well, everyone knows a scrawny little drambat like Ilgregious couldn't take down a malwrack – not with fifty of his buddies."

I looked away and exhaled. "None of it makes sense until you understand that Ilgregious and Kardool got inside their heads using the Dark Queen's power."

Cangoar shook his jowls. "Yeah, once that happens, there's nothing you can do to defend yourself."

Eam scrunched his nose. "They mess with what's in your head? Really?"

"Yeah," answered Cangoar. "And it happened to me. Twice."

Eam bobbed his head. "How in the name of Flargellion did Ilgregious learn to do that? Even a drambat ought to know better than to go around mucking with what's inside a drake's head. Someday I'll teach that drambat some manners!"

"I'm sure you will, Uncle," I said.

"Jendal says there are twisted beings from the Phoberon," said Cangoar. "They help them do these things. It's nasty."

"Now we're getting somewhere," replied Eam, bobbing his head. "You both have newts on the loose – which is why you're hanging out with grapes. Seriously? You want me to believe beings from the Phoberon are helping Ilgregious and Kardool take over the Drakebureau?"

"I think he's starting to get it," said Jendal.

Eam bobbed his head and glared at Jendal. "Okay, I get it – you can do things. Things I can't explain – not yet anyway. But let's just say the Phoberon really does exist. Why would Melohim let evil beings do stuff in our realm, and why would they bother with the weakest species – if they're so great and powerful?"

"They used to be dosara like me," said Jendal. "But they have corrupted themselves and wish to corrupt others. They hate Melohim and all that he has created – especially beings in this realm. But they can only work here through those who give them an opportunity."

Eam looked at the floor, flicked his tongue, then glared at Jendal. "Well, if the Big Guy really cares about us, why doesn't he put a stop to such things?"

Jendal nodded. "It is by His design – all sentient beings are free moral agents, including all species of dragons, apes, the dosara, and even arsnarms. It should be no surprise there are some who misuse that freedom – some who choose badly."

I bobbed my head, glanced at Eam, then glared at Jendal. "Do you expect us to believe an innocent hatchling, and Farl, and Pinhammer, and those two guards – they all died because Melohim wants those sleazy, slime-slurping, slug-suckers to be free-moral agents?!"

Jendal's eyes flashed. "Yeah, I know. It isn't easy – especially when innocent beings suffer. But there is no real love without free will. Some choose to love others and the source of life itself, while others choose to love power and the ability it gives them to impose their will on other beings. Some will do anything to get it, but eventually they become addicted – corrupted and enslaved by their love for it. In the end, their lust for power consumes them."

I scrunched my nose. "So why doesn't Melohim, if he exists, give Ilgregious what he chooses? If he chooses death for others, how about giving him *that*?"

"Indeed," said Bannabard as he poked his head inside the lair.

"And what about Farl?" asked Eam. "He didn't want to die. He didn't choose *that*. Did Melohim give him what he chose? Is that what you call it?"

"In a sense, yes," said Jendal. "He chose to give his life fighting for what he believed and for those he cared about."

Eam stared at the floor, then shook his jowls. "So it's true. He's really gone – no joke?"

"I'm afraid so," answered Cangoar.

I looked at the others, then outside. "Hell yeah, it's a joke," I muttered. "*If* he's even real, Melohim should have been there to protect those little ones. He should've been there to take care of Pa and me – and Farl and those guards at the Viper Vault."

"You never asked him," said Jendal.

I bobbed my head. "Maybe it's easy for you and Bannabard and even Cangoar to believe Melohim is good. That he even exists. You don't know what it's like to lose your Pa, get kicked out of your lair by your own Mum, and watch a bunch of drambats throw a helpless hatchling into a lava pit."

"You are right, I don't," said Jendal. "But Melohim understands – there's a part of him that has experienced more pain than you can imagine – a part of him that transcends all suffering – in both our realms."

I glared at Jendal. "What good does that do? The Drakebureau is the only good we have that's real. And we'll be able to trust it again someday – once we expose Ilgregious and Kardool for the lying monsters they are."

32.   THE GRAND KAHUNAS

E am bobbed his head and snarled, "Farl's gone, dammit! Hard to believe. You couldn't replace him with ten nickelnecks – ten malwracks even."

"Believe it," said Cangoar. "We saw his body in Smilf."

Bannabard thumped his chest. "Okay! So where do we go from here?"

"I need to find out if the gaggle leaders will join the resistance," muttered Eam.

I bobbed my head. "What resistance?"

"We are the resistance. Along with anyone who wants to join us."

"And what if no one does?" I asked.

"That's possible – maybe even likely, but we'll do what we can even if we have to go it alone. Either way I'll regret it forever if I don't give my buddies a chance to join us."

"What buddies?" asked Cangoar.

I'd heard the stories. "His buddies from the war."

"They might turn against us once they find out the malwracks are fighting for the Drakebureau," suggested Cangoar.

"It's a risk we'll have to take," said Eam. "But if what you guys said is true, Gailryder might be organizing the malwrack gaggles as we speak."

"Will there be a fight?" asked Cangoar.

Eam flicked his tongue. "It depends."

Cangoar flicked his tongue. "Depends on what?"

"Depends on whether Gailryder comes to Brangboor and if he does, who he brings and how reasonable he is."

"He wasn't all that reasonable when we signed the treaty," said Bannabard.

"Yeah, and now he thinks we're the enemies of Drakedom," I said.

Eam bobbed his head. "Yeah. I'm guessing if they come, it won't be for whale gizzards and ale." Eam's voice dropped off and his gaze turned to the ground. "Gailryder and I fought together… in the war." He glanced at Cangoar and I. "We need to prepare for the worst. Like yesterday. Alfedora and Cangoar, you guys with me?"

"Yeah, I'm in," said Cangoar.

"Me too," I said.

"Great. Alfedora and Cangoar come with me. You two grapes can stay here," he said, looking at Bannabard and Jendal. "And don't mess with my gold, or I'll feed you to a malwrack."

"Blue apes have a stake in this too," I protested.

"What stake?" asked Eam.

"Ilgregious and the drambats have been picking them off, a few at a time, since the end of the war," I said.

"Fine, they can fight when the drambats come. What's a couple of blue apes against malwracks?" asked Eam.

"It won't be just two," replied Bannabard. "There's a few hundred of us."

"We really don't have time for this. But I guess there's no stopping you two." Eam didn't wait for an answer. "Well, let's get moving. Bannabard, you can ride with Alfedora, and your friend…"

"I'll meet you there," interrupted Jendal.

"It's sixty furlongs from here. Quite a hike for an ape."

"Don't worry, she gets around," I said.

"Well then, let's get moving," said Eam.

We flipped a wing and headed south – flying just above the trees along the eastern shore of Lake Luellian.

"Fripel and Riler will be with us, even if the others aren't," yelled Eam.

I was flying next to him with Bannabard on my back. "Who?" I yelled.

"Fripel and Riler. They're my buddies! Crusty old farts who'll never let you down."

Cangoar and I followed as Eam flew just above the Salmonella River before ascending a near-vertical wall. Bannabard's grip tightened as we headed nearly straight up. We flew up the right side of a towering waterfall known as Smurgum Falls and which fed the Salmonella River. About three furlongs above the river we crested a cliff and leveled off over a flat land mass, known as Beetdred Mesa.

A pair of creeks were lit by the full moon and twisted through wooded flatlands before they coalesced and dove off the mesa behind us. I followed Cangoar and Eam along the one on the right until we landed at the base of another near-vertical wall. It was mostly granite and appeared to extend the width of the plateau.

We had flown too low to see the top of Findred Mesa, but I had flown over it a few decades ago. Beetdred and Findred were conjoined and formed a pair of nearly circular, mostly tree-covered mesas from which various creeks found their way to the surrounding plains. The vertical wall was the eastern edge of Findred Mesa and was about two and a half furlongs taller than Beetdred.

I bowed my left front leg and Bannabard climbed down next to a waterfall which fed the creek we had followed.

Eam poked his head through the cascading water and yelled, "Riler, you in here?"

"Go away, nobody's home!" exclaimed a gravelly voice which sounded like it was far away.

"Riler, it's me, Eam. Come out and show your scales, you old bag of leather!"

"Who's calling me an old bag of leather? Eam, is that you?"

"Yeah, it's me you brown-bellied slug-sucker!"

"Rich, real rich! Especially coming from an old emerald-pooper like you," said the gravelly voice. "What's up, my friend? And why are you poking your ugly gray snout through my waterfall in the middle of the night? Need my society – you poor, lonely buzzard?"

"Yeah, right. Is Fripel around? I have something you guys need to hear."

"Must be serious, if the great Eam wants to talk to *both* of us. Hold on – I think he's in the next cavern. Fripel, you awake?"

Apparently, there was more than one cavern behind the waterfall.

"What now?" asked a higher-pitched voice. "I was about to doze off after counting my gold."

"Counting your gold?" asked the gravelly voice. "You haven't found any gold in decades. Let me guess. Two thousand, four hundred and thirteen staters, four hundred and ninety-three aurei, and one hundred and seven solidi."

"And don't forget the seventy-eight drachmas."

A dark, gray-and-brown shape approached the other two behind the waterfall.

"You guys got a minute?" asked Eam. "I have some news. Important news."

"Ooh, important news!" exclaimed the gravelly voice. "Are you going to just stand there or are you going to spit it out?"

"Careful what you ask for," warned the higher-pitched voice. "We don't want him to start spewing stuff, do we?"

"Very funny," answered Eam. "I'm here with my niece and a few of her friends. Are you going to invite us in, or would you rather come out and meet the crew?"

"Come in, come in, of course," said the gravelly voice. "You, your niece, and her friends are most welcome. What can we do you for?"

Eam ducked inside. "We're here because Farl and Pinhammer have been killed and my niece's friends are saying it's part of a plot to overthrow the Drakebureau."

"No way!" exclaimed the gravelly voice. "Farl's gone?"

"Damn shame, that is!" exclaimed the higher-pitched voice, "Farl was the greatest nickelneck I ever had privilege to fight with."

"Yeah, he'll be missed. But there'll be time to remember him later. Right now, we've got to try to stop the Drakebureau from falling into the wrong hands."

"Well, bring your niece and her friends inside and let's talk about it," said the gravelly voice. "I can't believe it. Farl's gone." There was a slight tremor in his voice.

"Pull yourself together, nickelneck," said the higher-pitched voice.

"You didn't know Farl like I did," muttered the gravelly one.

"Let's introduce you guys," said Eam as he poked his head out and motioned for us to come in.

I followed Eam in and was surprised how big the lair was – big enough for all of us and more. Cangoar, Bannabard, and then Jendal appeared through the wall of water.

"Guys, I want you to meet my buddies, Riler and Fripel," said Eam. "We fought together in the war."

"Whoa, wait a second," said Fripel, the one with the higher-pitched voice. "How is it that the great Eam lets his niece run around with a couple of grapes?"

"Well the female, she uh, well... She's hard to dismiss. Apparently, she saved Cangoar's life once."

"Well, just because your niece has taken a liking to blue apes doesn't mean we have to," said Riler, the one with the gravelly voice. "What's it to us if she saved an ape once?"

"No, Cangoar is a nickelneck," said Eam.

"You want us to believe a blue ape saved the life of a nickelneck?" asked Fripel in an annoyed tone. "Hey Riler, I think Eam's got a few newts runnin' loose inside that fat head of his."

"Very funny," said Eam. "Farl's dead and you guys are cutting up."

Riler flicked his tongue. "Yeah Fripel, ease up, would ya? What I'd like to know is, what's a blue ape got to do with Farl and Pinhammer?"

"The female isn't really a blue ape," answered Eam. "She claims to be a dosara. Says she was sent here to help the apes."

"A dosara? What's that?" asked Riler.

"Says she's from the Phoberon," answered Eam. "A being with powers."

"No kidding! Well let's at least hear them out," said Riler enthusiastically. "We can roast 'em later if we don't like their story."

"You can try, but it probably won't work."

"What do you mean, it won't work?" Fripel asked.

"I tried, and, well... it didn't work."

Riler's glance bounced from Fripel to Eam. "You tried to smoke 'em, and it didn't work? Your igniter failed?"

"No, my igniter didn't fail. The female, the dosara or whatever she is, shielded the other one. And then she hit me on the head with a stalactite."

"You let a grape hit you with a stalactite?" asked Fripel. "You have gone soft, haven't you?"

"No, I didn't just *let* her," answered Eam. "She did it with her voice somehow. I think she used her powers."

"She didn't!" exclaimed Riler. "This I gotta see. Imagine being able to throw stalactites around with just your voice!"

"Riler's always had a thing for the Phoberon," said Fripel. "I think his mom dropped him on his head when she was teaching him to fly."

Eam glanced at Fripel, then turned to us. "Guys, this is my niece Alfedora and her friends – Cangoar, Bannabard, and Jendal."

"Alfedora and Cangoar, it's nice to meet you. I'm Fripel. Sorry about your tail, mate," said the tall, rather skinny nickelneck with a bit of a smirk. "Did it happen in the games, or somewhere else?"

"Enough chit-chat!" interrupted Riler who had thick, heavy legs, big paws, and a patch over one eye. "I'm Riler! Which one claims to be a dosara?"

"That would be me," answered Jendal.

"He said you hit him on the head with a stalactite using only your voice. Is that true?"

"Yeah, you could say that," answered Jendal. "But that's not important right now. Alfedora, would you please explain what's going on for these two?"

I flicked my tongue. "We're here because drakes and apes are dying and the Drakebureau is in trouble."

Jendal nodded. "There are challenges before us, the likes of which haven't been seen since before any of you were born."

"What do you mean since before we were born?" asked Fripel. "Riler and I – we're older than any ape that's ever swung from a vine. Certainly older than you."

"She's not really a blue ape," said Cangoar.

"We're here because we need your help," I said, bobbing my head. "We need help if we're going to take a stand against the forces of Ilgregious and Kardool."

"Forces of Ilgregious and Kardool?" Fripel bobbed his head and scrunched his nose. "Those two? A geeky little drambat and a prissy little spewler? I'd like to know what forces they command!"

"Well, Gailryder and the malwracks for starters," said Cangoar.

"Gail? You've got to be ripping my tail," exclaimed Riler with a stern look. He looked at Cangoar's stub. "Oh. Sorry."

267

"Forget it."

Fripel glared at Eam. "Let me get this straight. You come in the middle of the night with two grapes and two young nickelnecks, to recruit us to fight against Gailryder and the malwracks?"

Cangoar bobbed his head. "Hey, I turned ninety-seven last year."

"Like I said, two young nickelnecks," said Fripel.

"Here's the thing," said Eam. "That slimy little spewler has convinced Gailryder and the other leaders that he and Ilgregious are defending the Drakebureau from a rebellion."

"What kind of rebellion?" asked Fripel.

I scrunched my nose. "That Farl and us nickelnecks – are plotting to take over the Drakebureau. That's why they killed Farl – in Gailryder's mind we're the enemies of Drakedom." I looked at the ground. There had been a bit more excitement in my voice than I intended.

Eam bobbed his head. "I'm guessing the malwracks are already on their way – and when they get here it won't be for a platter of whale gizzards – or even deep-fried squid."

33.   To Fight, Flee, or Join the Powers that Be

I stared at Uncle for a second. "You think they're on their way now?"

"If Gailryder really believes Farl was trying to take Flargellion, then yeah," said Eam, his eyes narrowing. "I'm guessing the first thing he'll want is to find out how many nickelnecks are loyal to Farl."

"That would make sense," said Fripel. "And if he believes there's a rebellion, he'll want to recruit us to help squash it."

"And what if we don't want to be recruited?" I asked while thrashing my tail.

Fripel gave me a hard look. "If we don't join up..."

"They'll wipe us out," interrupted Eam.

"Exactly," said Cangoar.

"Nobody's going to win against the malwracks," suggested Riler. "If you can't smoke 'em, eat smoked whale gizzards with 'em! That's what Pa always said. I say let 'em recruit us. Anything's better than a fight with Gailryder and the malwracks."

"You don't know what you're saying," I said. "You'll regret the day you joined Ilgregious and Kardool."

"She's not kidding," said Cangoar. "There's no joining those guys without giving up who you are and everything you believe."

"What are you talking about? We fought side by side with Gailryder in the war," snarled Riler. "If we can't trust him – who can we trust?"

"That's just it," said Cangoar. "Gailryder isn't in his right mind. He killed Farl because of the lies Kardool put in his head."

"Why would Farl believe a spewler?" asked Riler. "And what lies?"

Cangoar bobbed his head. "That Farl killed Pinhammer while attempting to seize control of the Drakebureau. He believed it because Kardool put it into his head using the Dark Queen's power."

"Kardool did it to Cangoar, and now he's done it to Gailryder," I said as I scrunched my nose and narrowed my eyes, then turned to Riler. "Farl, Pinhammer, four malwracks, and who knows how many hatchlings are dead because of a few *lies*. It's absurd – I know."

"And if Gailryder turned on Farl, he'll turn on us too – in the blink of a newt's eye," said Eam.

"Hang on," said Fripel. "Why did Farl kill Pinhammer?"

"No," I said. "It was Ilgregious who killed Pinhammer. But Kardool and Ilgregious want everyone to think Farl did it."

"Eam, I think your niece has a few newts running loose," said Fripel. "Does it run in the family? There's not a drambat alive that could kill old Pinhammer – especially that skinny little scale-challenged rodent, Ilgregious! Old Pin would've squashed him with one toe I'd wager."

"That scale-challenged rodent killed two guards at the Viper Vault," said Cangoar with a grim look. "Malwracks. And don't be going on about Alfedora like that, or I'll..."

"You'll what?" asked Fripel in a derisive tone. "Take a swing at me with your tail?"

"Hey, Alfedora's got an admirer," said Riler with a grin.

"Easy guys," said Eam. "He's just a kid."

Fripel gave Cangoar a hard look. "Okay Cangoar. Please, do tell. Exactly how does a toady little drambat like Ilgregious kill two malwracks *and* the head of the Drakebureau?"

Cangoar flicked his tongue and glared at Fripel. "He has some weird power from someone he calls the Dark Queen. His eyes turn red and he gets inside your head, your thoughts go black, your legs go numb, and you fall over – helpless as a hatchling. And then his toady little friends get to work. They rip. You. Up."

"Hold on," objected Fripel. "What's this stuff about a Dark Queen? Sounds like farty-snartch tales to me!"

270

"No, it's true," I said. "The Dark Queen is a fallen dosara – an arsnarm. She hates everything and everybody. She's using Ilgregious and Kardool to try to destroy everything that's good in the world. She even hates deep-fried squid!"

"Jendal is the Dark Queen?" asked Riler.

"No," I answered. "Jendal is nothing like the Dark Queen."

Fripel slapped Riler up the side of his head with a big brown paw. "Pay attention, you flea-flicking toad-sucker."

"I've never flicked a flea in my life," said Riler with a flick of his tongue.

"And the Dark Queen was once a dosara – like Jendal," I said as I glanced at Riler, then Fripel. "But now she's bent – full of dark thoughts, lies, corruption – stuff like that."

Cangoar's eyes narrowed. "And there are some – like Ilgregious and Kardool – who are willing to do whatever it takes to tap into the Dark Queen's power."

I bobbed my head and flicked my tongue. "Yeah, she gives power to drakes who practice the most disgusting stuff! Like throwing *innocent hatchlings* into lava pits. And that's why we've got to do whatever it takes to save the Drakebureau."

"Well, why don't we do what they're doing?" asked Riler. "Let's sacrifice a drambat or two. Then Jendal can give us her power – nobody'll miss a few drambats. Jendal, can you make me firebolt-proof?"

I glanced at him sideways. "You're joking, right?"

He kinda has a point. Jendal won't do just anything, but the Dark Queen uses her powers to do whatever Ill-greega-butt and Kardrool help her get away with.

"Of course I am," said Riler. "But how cool would it be to be *firebolt-proof?* I'd be the malwrack's screech at the next B.E.G.!"

Fripel glared at him. "You really are joking, right?"

"Oh yeah. Right. Joking. Of course." Riler stared at Jendal and licked his chops. "What can we do? Is there anything we can do to get just a little bit of your power?"

"No," said Jendal coolly. "My powers cannot be bought or sold. Just remember one thing. Ask Melohim for help when you need it. Who knows? If you've been a good little drake, he just might answer. And if you're lucky – he might send me."

"Yeah, right," said Riler with a bit of a snarl. "Well, if Jendal won't give us her powers, why don't we hold a session for the Dark Queen?"

I glared at him as hard as I could and glanced around at the others. They wore expressions of disbelief.

"C'mon guys. You know I'm joking, right?" he said, glancing around.

Jendal gave him a blank stare. "Others have gone down that path. And they'll survive for a while and maybe even have some success in their quest for power. But the Dark Queen will corrupt their hearts and minds – eventually she will use them up, abandon them, and leave them with nothing. They'll be consumed by their own lust for power."

"What about those who go down a path that's not so dark?" asked Bannabard.

"There are consequences for the choices we make, for good or for ill," answered Jendal. "Everyone's life, including the Dark Queen's, are a witness to Melohim's goodness. In the Phoberon, Melohim is giving the Dark Queen the corruption she has chosen. And one day it will be a ludicrous thing to behold the vanity of a wraith-like figure too weak to stand against her own shadow yet wanting others to worship her the way she worships herself."

I bobbed my head. "So Melohim allows the Dark Queen to give Ilgregious and Kardool the power to wreak havoc in this realm because he loves everyone and protects their ability to make choices?"

"Yeah, you could put it like that," answered Jendal.

"Hold the toad," exclaimed Riler. "You're saying you won't give us power like the Dark Queen has given Ilgregious and Kardool?"

Fripel bobbed his head. "I can't believe you even said that! We're talking as if Melohim and this Dark Queen are as real as that waterfall!"

Jendal gave him a blank look. "In the Phoberon, no one questions whether they are real or not. It would be like questioning whether that waterfall, this cave, or the sky itself are real. The arsnarms – as powerful as the Dark Queen might seem in this realm – they look at Melohim and tremble."

"Who knows what is real and what isn't?" asked Eam. "What we do know is Farl is dead and we're either going to have to fight, flee, or join the powers that be."

I scrunched my nose. "And a statesman shall you be."

"Yeah, right," muttered Fripel. He looked away and shook his head. "But I refuse to speculate about what my ears cannot hear, or my eyes cannot see."

Riler turned to Jendal. "Any chance we'll get to see you hit Fripel on the head with a stalactite using nothing but your voice?"

"Nope. Not gonna happen. One must not seek power for its own sake – one must seek to align one's life with Melohim's kingdom and his good nature. There are those who will do whatever it takes to get power, but that isn't a life I want to live."

"Me either!" I exclaimed a little more boisterously than I intended. I glanced around, then bobbed my head and said, "The only power worth having comes from the love of friends and family!"

Cangoar bobbed his head.

Bannabard thumped his chest.

I scrunched my nose. Love of family. Yeah, right. I couldn't believe I just said that.

34. Clouds on the Horizon

"**W**ell said, Alfedora!" exclaimed Uncle Eam as he turned to Fripel and Riler. "Guys, what do you think – do we sit on our tails and wait around for the malwracks, or round up the gaggles and prepare to meet them with a show of strength?"

Fripel bobbed his head. "Things could get really ugly really quick if we go snout to snout with Gailryder and the malwracks. Do we really believe he turned against Farl?"

Cangoar thrashed his tail. "We saw Farl's body in Smilf. Only a firebolt from a malwrack could have done that."

"In that case we need to show our resolve," said Fripel. "I'm not one to shoot the first fireball, but we mustn't allow ourselves to be intimidated – not even by Gailryder. Count me in. I say round 'em up."

Riler glanced around at the others before turning to Jendal. "I was going to hold out for that stalactite trick, but I guess that's not happening."

"No, it's not," she answered.

"I hate to admit it, but Fripel's right," continued Riler. "If Gailryder shows up in force, we need to be prepared. We need to show the malwracks that the truth about Farl and Pinhammer's deaths – and this so-called insurrection are worth fighting for. Part of me wonders what it would be like to go tooth, wing, and claw against a malwrack. I can't say I'm looking forward to going up against firebolts, but I'll gnaw on a hundred green geckos if my fangs, claws, fire, and wings are not at your service. Let's go round up the boys, eh Fripel? We wouldn't want our gaggle leaders to be caught playing pitch-a-grote when the malwracks get here."

Fripel flicked his tongue. "Yeah, right," he said with a smirk. "Eam, you and the others wait here. We'll go round up the gaggles."

"Okay," said Eam. "I'll meet you at the north end of the lake in three hours."

Uncle Eam and I followed Fripel and Riler as they ducked under the waterfall and headed out. The sun had been up a while, and we watched as they took off heading north and east – flying just above the treetops in the afternoon sun. They folded their wings in a dive and disappeared below the mesa's tree-covered cliff. I turned to go back inside when something on the southern horizon caught my eye. It looked like a distant cloud but something wasn't quite right. I stared as it grew slightly bigger – moving in the wrong direction. "Oh, crap!" I muttered. "Hey Uncle, do you see that? That's no cloud!"

Eam bobbed his head. "Alfedora, you're right! I'll bet toad legs to a stater that's Gailryder and his gaggles."

Both of us studied it as it moved north – the other clouds were moving east.

"Holy fart smellers, there's a bunch of them," said Eam. "I was hoping they wouldn't be here for another day or two."

Eam followed as I ducked back under the waterfall. My eyes narrowed as I turned to Cangoar, Bannabard, and Jendal. "The malwracks are coming!" I exclaimed – a little louder than necessary.

"No way!" exclaimed Cangoar.

"Way!" I answered.

Eam bobbed his head. "They'll be here in less than an hour. I need to catch up with Fripel and Riler and let them know. Cangoar and Alfedora, hang here with your ape friends. I'm not sure when we'll be back. Lay low and stay out of sight."

"I'd rather go with you," I protested.

"Thanks, Alfedora. I'm sure you'd be an excellent fighter, but you've never been trained to fight in a nickelneck gaggle."

"It's fine," said Cangoar. "Alfedora, you and I will meet the malwracks before they reach Lake Luellian. We'll create a distraction – maybe we can buy your uncle and his buddies some time while they get the gaggles mobilized."

I bobbed my head. "Yeah, we'll distract them and buy you some time."

"You won't stand a chance by yourselves against those malwracks," said Eam.

"We're faster than them, right?" I asked.

"Yeah, but I don't want my favorite niece dodging firebolts."

"We'll be fine, Uncle."

"No closer than two furlongs. Promise?"

"Promise. Two furlongs."

The four of us followed Eam outside and watched him take off.

My gaze turned to the shifting shadow as it approached from the south. It hovered in the distance and grew bigger as I watched. "Do you see that?"

"Yeah, I see it," said Cangoar.

I bobbed my head. Again. "There's a bunch of them."

"I'll be with you," said Jendal. "Engage their leader if you can."

"Will do," I said. I scrunched my nose – it was good having Jendal on our side, but I remained skeptical – where was she when that hatchling was sacrificed? I shook my jowls. "Bannabard – you can hang out here, or is there something you would like to do?"

"I have some friends who live near that tree over there," he said, pointing to a large old elm which hung over the edge of the mesa. "See if you can lead a few malwracks under its branches and we'll launch an attack from the tree."

"Would you like a lift?" I asked.

"Yeah, that'd be great."

Jendal disappeared as Bannabard faced the tree and howled longer and louder than I thought possible. He climbed on my back and Cangoar and I took off heading for the elm which was just to the right of the crest of Smurgum Falls.

We flew low across the mesa, and Cangoar circled while I landed near the huge old elm and let Bannabard down. I took off and watched as about two dozen apes emerged from the forest and met him at the base of the tree. They greeted one another with fist, elbow, and forehead bumps. They followed Bannabard up the tree – like a giant fuzzy blue caterpillar.

Cangoar shouted, "Let's head for the leader!" as I flew up to meet him.

"Right! But what then?" I asked. The 'cloud' of malwracks was close enough to recognize distinct gaggles. They looked to be a few dozen furlongs south and east of Beetdred and were headed north.

"Looks like they're headed for Eam's lair!" he shouted. "Once they're due east of the mesa, we'll engage and see how many we can draw this way."

I could feel my heart pounding. Spiny plates stood up along my spine. "Are we going to attack?" I shouted.

"Hell, yeah we're going to attack!" yelled Cangoar. "Hit them as hard as you can. Aim for the joint where the wing attaches to the body. Maybe we can knock one or two out of the sky. The main thing is lead them this way once they come after us."

Yeah. Once they come after us.

We headed southeast – on a collision course with the leader. It wasn't long before they were close – close enough that I could see the green in their eyes. I launched a fireball. It was a fairly good shot as far as I could tell, but from that distance the leader dodged it easily and returned a firebolt. It missed us way left.

"That wasn't even close!" I yelled.

Cangoar followed with another shot. It missed the leader but hit another drake which fell out of formation and shook its head wildly. It appeared to be having a hard time seeing, but I took my eyes off it when I noticed the lead malwrack veer to his left and head straight for Cangoar and I.

"After them!" shouted the leader.

I glanced back. The whole malwrack squadron was in pursuit.

"Alfedora, head for the elm. I'll be right behind you!"

My pace quickened. We banked right and headed for the base of the huge tree which barely clung to the edge of the cliff. Cangoar took the turn wider than I did and fired a couple of volleys. One hit the lead malwrack in the right rear foot and another hit a malwrack in the tail.

"Wow. I can't believe they're all chasing us!" shouted Cangoar.

"Yeah, isn't that wonderful!" I exclaimed as I dodged a firebolt.

I had never been shot at by malwracks. The reality of it started to sink in. No rules, no aiming at nothing but tail, and no such thing as sportsmanship. They would like nothing better than to sever our heads with a firebolt. And we them. The B.E.G. seemed as tame as a game of pitch-a-grote.

Fripel and Riler arrived at the lair of one of the gaggle leaders. "Slugsneer! I need you to round up as many leaders as you can and meet us back here," commanded Fripel.

"Really?" asked the nickelneck. "I was just finishing a round of pitch-a-grote with my cousin."

"Pitch-a-grote, indeed," muttered Fripel. "I'm sure you two were bombing it, but Eam wants the gaggles assembled. And he wants it yesterday!"

"All right already," answered Slugsneer. "Yesterday, my butt. What now – another drill?"

Not wishing to alarm his fighters, Fripel didn't give them the details. They weren't even sure the malwracks were coming. He watched Slugsneer take off and noticed Eam approach from the south. He gave Eam a hard look. "What's going on?"

"We've got two dozen malwrack gaggles heading up from the south. They'll be here shortly, and I'm guessing they aren't bringing Slynkberry ales. This could get ugly quicker than the flick of a frog's tongue."

"Two dozen?" Riler asked. "Malwrack gaggles?"

Eam glanced at Fripel and then at Riler. "Yeah. They brought a load. You don't send every gaggle you've got unless you're expecting a fight."

Cangoar was close behind as we approached the elm tree. The malwracks weren't far behind him, and their huge wings moved faster than I would have expected.

"Get as close to the trunk as you can!" shouted Cangoar. "We want to give Bannabard and his buddies a good shot at these guys."

"You got it!" I yelled.

The huge old elm stood majestically on the edge of the cliff next to Smurgum Falls. My right wing came within inches of its lower branches. I recognized Bannabard's voice as I passed underneath.

"Not the nickelnecks!" he shouted. "The malwracks! Attack the malwracks! And don't forget to plug your ears!"

I looked back as Cangoar passed under the tree – with the malwracks close behind. I dodged a firebolt as more than a dozen apes launched themselves at various malwracks. I launched a fireball – maybe it would keep the malwracks focused on us – anything to help Bannabard.

Bannabard watched as Otger leapt onto a young malwrack who was just behind the leader and then launched himself at an older malwrack who followed the young one. He landed squarely on its back and grabbed the base of the malwrack's left wing. He glanced back and watched Haldor leap at another malwrack. But the malwrack saw him coming and rolled to its right in mid-air. "Haldor!" he shouted as his friend missed and began flailing in a free fall.

Bannabard's malwrack did a barrel roll and he lost sight of Haldor. His legs dangled as he held on to the base of its wing. The malwrack lunged at him with gaping jaws – stretching its neck as far back as it could. Teeth like swords snapped at his legs. He hiked a foot up on the wing, and it gave up trying to reach him with its teeth.

The malwrack righted itself and Bannabard firmed up his grip on the base of its wing. "For Haldor!" he shouted from his knees, as he attempted to break the bone at the base of the wing with his arms. But it was as thick as his arm. It didn't budge, let alone break.

He worked to get a better grip, planted his feet at the base of the wing, and tried again. "For Haldor!" he yelled as he wrenched the base of its wing with all the strength his legs and arms could muster. It barely bent. He gathered himself for another attempt when the malwrack twisted back and launched a firebolt. He ducked as the firebolt severed it's left wing a few inches above his hands.

The malwrack screeched as it went into a spiral. It was all he could do to hold onto the stump while they tumbled through the air. He closed his eyes hard as the world spun. He thought of Lais and his sons. An image of Gorby being carried off by a drambat shoved its way into his mind.

This would not be the end. Not for him or his family. He opened his eyes, set his feet on the stump, and leapt at the malwrack's neck. He managed to grab it with his left arm and nearly slipped off but managed to wrap his other hand around it. He clung tight and exhaled. The Great Ape Wars taught them there was no better place to be on a falling dragon than its neck.

The noise of fast-moving water at the base of the falls came up and met them. He gulped as much air as his lungs could hold. A loud smack was snuffed out by rushing turbulence as the malwrack smashed into the river. He let go of the malwrack's neck as the river rushed in to fill the void above the malwrack's body. He tumbled and rolled before being sucked toward the surface.

The turbulence vanished quickly. His mind's eye was still spinning as he went from spiraling and falling through the air to floating weightless in the current. He righted himself and shoved off from what must have been the malwrack's left shoulder and kicked toward the surface.

He surfaced and gasped for air as he began kicking furiously for shore. If the beast got its bearings, it would be five times faster in the water. He emerged from the river and crouched low while he watched the surface and backed away from the water's edge as quietly as possible.

The dragon's head broke the surface about half a furlong away. His heart skipped a beat – but then he saw it was facing downriver. He backed away quietly – eyes glued to the back of the beast's head. His right hand landed on a boulder – he dove behind it and breathed.

The malwrack headed to the opposite shore and dragged itself out of the river. Blood oozed from the stump where its right wing had been. It glanced around before collapsing at the water's edge. Bannabard turned and bounded into a nearby stand of trees – thankful he had taken down a malwrack and lived to thump his chest about it.

Cangoar and I were able to out-distance the malwracks, but not without considerable effort. My chest muscles burned. I had never flown so hard for so long – while glancing back for firebolts.

Cangoar veered right. "Alfedora! Incoming!" he shouted.

A firebolt whizzed beneath me and singed my left-rear paw.

"Follow me!" shouted Cangoar as he banked left, went into a dive, and headed toward Smurgum Falls.

"Oh good – now we get a break," I muttered to myself. I shook my paw and went into a dive while glancing back. "Hey Cangoar, there's only two now!" I shouted. The other malwracks had banked right and were back on course toward Luellian.

"Suh-weet! Do you think we have Jendal to thank for that!?"

"Thank Jendal? Yeah, right – I think it was our flying!"

Cangoar leveled off and headed toward the west side of the mesa. We began an arduous and steady climb around the north side of Beetdred toward the top of Findred Mesa. My chest muscles burned worse than before as I glanced back at the two malwracks on our tail. By the time we leveled off the other malwrack squadrons were nearly out of sight. We put some distance between the two on our tails and went into another dive. The two malwracks followed as we dove along the western wall of Findred.

I glanced ahead – it was about three or four furlongs to the rocks below. My head was on a swivel as I glanced back every few seconds. I dodged a couple firebolts and caught up with Cangoar. We dove nearly straight down – parallel to and about half a furlong to the left of the only waterfall on the west side of the mesa.

"Alfedora! Get ready to put on the brakes – but watch for firebolts!" he shouted.

"Ya think?" I muttered to myself. I was right behind as Cangoar banked left and angled toward the falls – headed between the water and the rock wall behind it.

It was tight enough that I had to twist sideways to get through – one wing pointed at the ground while the other pointed at the sky. Likely too tight for malwracks.

Our wings were extended, but we were moving fast when we exploded from behind the falls. Instinctively I folded my wings as my eyes grew big – the malwracks had anticipated our exit point and bore down on us.

Krimeny approached Jendal as they watched the dogfight from the Phoberon. "Why don't you just wipe out those malwracks?" she quipped. "You could put an end to this conflict in an instant. But no, you'd rather play your little games – creating illusions while you convince yourself that you're helping those weak, putrid, disgusting little pets of yours."

"Why Krimeny, you talk as if you really care," said Jendal in an overly sympathetic tone. "I am genuinely touched."

"Does that mean you'll do it?"

"You know I can't wipe out the malwracks – just like you can't wipe out the nickelnecks."

"Get real, Jendal. You sent an illusion to get the whole lot of them chasing after just two nickelnecks. Melohim allows you to deceive the malwracks, but won't allow you to destroy them?"

"I shouldn't have to tell you this, but you know as well as I do that he gives them what they choose – no more, no less. And they have chosen to follow Kardool's lies. I am simply giving them a few more delusions on top of the lies they have already embraced. You, of all beings, should know what that's like."

"Ha! The pot calling the kettle black! Come on Jendal, you know you want to do it! But your delusions about love and free will keep you from acknowledging the fact that this realm and the pathetic little creatures who inhabit it are an affront to *our* strength and *our* power."

"I would cease to be a servant of truth and freedom if I did what you suggest."

"You call that freedom?" asked Krimeny sarcastically. "And what is truth, for that matter? Only fools believe such things. In the end there is only power – and one day the dark prince will wield all of it."

"You know as well as I that Korgarag grows weaker," said Jendal dryly. "He put his faith in a lie and deludes himself with false hopes of power and glory. If you dared to consider the truth with an open mind, you would see the madness behind it. Melohim simply gives him what he chooses – and Korgarag grows weaker. He reaps the corruption he has sown."

Krimeny's eyes flashed red. "Melohim has never played fair – and now he's allowing you to interfere with our plans and antagonize us while you're at it! We'll see who reaps what." She grimaced as she turned and flitted away.

36. DrakeDom Caving

I was on Cangoar's tail as we emerged from behind the falls and veered up and away from the mesa. The malwracks had anticipated our trajectory and came at us fast. I twisted left, narrowly dodging two firebolts as the malwracks streaked by. The turbulence which followed sucked us into their path. We got our wings under us, flipped into a dive, and took up the chase. Cangoar's maneuver had worked – the malwracks missed and we were on their tails.

The trailing malwrack had a cleft in its tail – I dubbed it 'Clefty'. Maybe it wasn't a good idea to name a malwrack you're trying to shoot out of the sky, but the name stuck in my head. Cangoar fired a shot which lit up Clefty's tail but failed to slow him down.

I missed a shot at the other malwrack and was lining up a second when the beast spread its massive wings, nearly came to a halt, spun around in mid-air, and swiped at me with its claws. I twisted away. Its claws missed, but its tail didn't – pounding me in the ribs and knocking the wind out of me.

Clefty circled back and came up behind me. I tumbled through the air – struggling to catch my breath. The malwrack drew closer. I managed to flip my wings and get back into a dive. I dodged a firebolt and heard the sizzle as it buzzed my left ear.

That. Was. Close.

The malwrack launched another firebolt. I extended my wings and banked hard to the right. Clefty sailed by with Cangoar hot on his tail, and I flipped into another dive right behind. I took a shot which just missed Clefty's right wing, then followed as Clefty and Cangoar banked left, went into a climb, and headed up toward the other malwrack.

284

"Alfedora, it's time for a Noxious Nellie!" shouted Cangoar.

"Heck yeah!" I shouted.

The three of us flew nearly straight up, while the other malwrack tucked its wings and headed straight for us. Clefty banked left, circled behind, and launched a firebolt. I dodged it while Cangoar dodged one from above. We pulled hard, leaving Clefty in our turbulence – heading up as the other malwrack bore down on us. My chest muscles burned as Cangoar and I dodged firebolts from above and below.

"Get ready!" I shouted. "On the count of two!"

We slowed our ascent as the malwracks each shot a firebolt. "One, and two!" we shouted in unison. We each spewed a plume of toxic fumes and veered sharply away from one another and from the converging firebolts. The firebolts ignited the fumes, and the malwracks flew into the middle of a toxic inferno.

The descending malwrack's speed carried him through with only minor burns, but Clefty was not so fortunate. The screech was cut short as everything went silent in my head. Its left wing was lit as it twisted in a descending spiral. It reached for its neck with a paw and flailed furiously with the other wing.

"Yurnasal!" shouted the other malwrack as it glanced at its buddy and then launched a firebolt which I easily dodged.

I dove after the other malwrack. We both hurtled past the spiraling Clefty. Cangoar joined me and we lit it up before it could make another move. The malwrack took one in each wing, one in the tail, and dropped like a rock.

Cangoar and I leveled off, gathered ourselves and watched the demise of the malwracks on the rocks at the base of the mesa. I took a deep breath. It felt good to glide and ride the wind without glancing back for firebolts.

"Great job, Alfedora!" shouted Cangoar.

"Thanks, you weren't so bad yourself!"

We flew parallel to one another, then banked right and headed back to Riler's lair. We descended to the base of the cascading water, touched down, and scrambled under the waterfall into Fripel's cavern.

"That was awesome!" exclaimed Cangoar as he raised his right-front paw and held it up in the air.

I scrunched my nose. "I can't believe it! We just defeated two malwracks!"

"C'mon. High three. Don't leave me hanging."

I didn't know what he wanted, so I spat at it.

"Yuk. What are you doing?" he snarled, wiping off his paw on a stalagmite.

"Wow. That. Was. Amazing," I exclaimed, still catching my breath. "Sorry, I have no idea what a high tree is. I'm supposed to water it – right?"

"High three, not high tree. And no, you don't water it, you slap it with your paw – it's what we do at the Viper Vault."

"Oh, right. Like I was supposed to know *that*."

"Yeah, well, stick with me and you'll learn lots of things," he said with a slight smirk. "And yes, that was amazing! Nothing like a fire fight with a couple malwracks to get your gizzard going sideways."

I shook my jowls and thought about Eam and the others. Were they able to get the gaggles mobilized? I headed back to the waterfall and poked my head through the rushing water. I immediately pulled back. "Cangoar!" I exclaimed. "Come look."

We poked our heads through the wall of rushing water.

"Holy newt mange!" he snarled.

The sun had slipped below the horizon and the sky to the east was lit with orange and grey and lavender clouds. We bobbed our heads in unison and watched in silence as distant malwrack screeches could be heard from the skies over Lake Luellian. Blooms of what looked like yellow and orange stars appeared and disappeared against purple and orange clouds in the distance. It would have been beautiful – if it didn't mean my uncle and his friends were fighting for their lives.

The negotiations hadn't lasted long. A little more than an hour earlier Eam led Fripel, Riler, and the other gaggle leaders to a large meadow on the eastern side of Lake Luellian. "Fripel, you take half the gaggle leaders to the north end of the meadow and remain hidden in the forest."

"Will do," said Fripel.

"Riler, you take the other half to the caves on the northwest end of the lake and remain there until I give the signal."

"Will do. What's the signal?" asked Riler.

"I will shoot a fireball toward the Salmonella River if the negotiations fail – I want all gaggles in the air. In that case we'll be in for a fight. If I shoot a fireball toward the north end of the lake, the negotiations will have been successful and your gaggles can stand down."

"Let's hope you're successful," said Fripel.

"Indeed," said Riler.

Eam and a few other leaders took to the air as soon as the malwracks crossed the southern shore of Lake Luellian. "Gailryder!" shouted Eam as he approached the malwracks from the north. "What brings you and your friends to our cozy little community?"

"We're here on Drakebureau business!" shouted Gailryder. "We've flown a far furlong and would like a break. Let's land and we'll tell you and your boys all about it – once we're on the ground."

Eam and the others banked left and came to a heading parallel to the malwrack leader and his gaggles, about a furlong west of the formation. "I'd rather talk in the air," he yelled. There was no way he was giving up the one advantage he had – speed, maneuverability, and fresh wings. "What Drakebureau business?"

"Farl has killed Pinhammer and tried to seize control of the Drakebureau!" shouted Gailryder.

Gailryder sounded so convincing that Eam had to remind himself it was a lie. "That's a lie from Kardool and Ilgregious! It's a ruse to get you and your gaggles to do their bidding."

"That's where you're wrong!" shouted Gailryder. "And my guess is Farl…" The malwrack's voice wavered slightly. "My guess is Farl wasn't alone in his plot to murder Pinhammer and take control of the Drakebureau."

"You don't sound very confident about that!" shouted Eam.

"Do you deny your involvement in the plot!?"

Eam bobbed his head. "Gail, you know that's crazy! Farl was the only nickelneck we could get to even think about serving on the Drakebureau. He found the proceedings boring, the gallery annoying, and he hated spending time away from Brangboor. We had to twist his tail to get him to do it. He had no interest in taking over the Drakebureau, and neither do we. You were his friend – surely you knew that!"

"All I know is Pinhammer is dead!" shouted Gailryder.

The malwrack's huge fangs were visible – even from a furlong and a half away. "And what about Farl? Where is he now?"

"He was foolish enough to attack Kardool – I'm afraid your friend is gone."

"He was your friend too!" exclaimed Eam as he felt gases building inside his chest. "You're in league with Kardool! Did you kill Farl?!"

"Farl killed Pinhammer. He had it coming – and you will too if you're part of his conspiracy!"

"The only conspiracy I'm part of is the one to stop Kardool and Ilgregious from taking over the Drakebureau." Eam scrunched his nose and exposed his fangs. It was hard to believe that the great Gailryder had been blinded by the lies of that scrawny little spewler. "Open your eyes, Gailryder! Maybe you'll see what they're doing to you!"

"They haven't done anything except help me understand who my friends are," bellowed Gailryder. He paused before snarling, "And who they aren't!" he exclaimed before launching a firebolt at Eam.

Eam had never known Gailryder to act on pure emotion, but he was far enough away that the firebolt was easily dodged. He watched it fall – along with any hope for a peaceful resolution – as he banked away from the malwracks. He shot a fireball toward the Salmonella River, signaling his charges on the ground. Three dozen gaggles of six or seven nickelnecks each flipped wings and took off. They sorted themselves into three squadrons and fell behind Eam, Fripel, and Riler. "Follow me!" he shouted to his squadron leaders. "And watch for firebolts!"

"It's on!" shouted Fripel.

"Like slime on a frog's butt!" shouted Riler.

"After them!" shouted Gailryder.

Eam's squadron banked south, Fripel led his squadron north, and Riler continued west. No one knew what to expect – nickelnecks had never fought malwracks before. His squadron leaders would use their speed and maneuverability to split up the malwrack hoard. "Remember, don't engage until you have them outnumbered!" he shouted.

"Grinsnipe, get after the ones headed south!" shouted Gailryder to one of his squadron leaders. Five malwrack gaggles banked a full turn and went after Eam's squadron. Gailryder led a squadron west in pursuit of Riler, while a third squadron continued north and went after Fripel and his squadron of twelve gaggles.

Eam glanced back. There were about thirty malwracks in pursuit, and a few firebolts flew by. The first four were easily dodged, but one firebolt severed the trailing nickelneck's tail. The nickelneck squealed like a fat fiadhain stuck on a nickelneck's claw. He shook his jowls. "Fly hard and focus!" he shouted as another firebolt hit its mark and the squealing nickelneck became the first casualty. "Pick up the pace! Fly hard and watch for firebolts!" he shouted. They continued south for a while then banked west. The malwracks began to fall behind, and he slowed the pace a bit.

To the north Riler's squadron was on a parallel course with his own, then banked left and flew hard to the south while gaining altitude. Eam stayed his course until Riler banked west and lined up behind Eam's malwracks. Eam slowed a bit – setting Riler's squadron up for an attack.

"They've slowed down!" shouted the malwrack leader. "Get after them!"

The malwracks behind Riler's squadron screeched a warning, but it was too late. The maneuver had worked. Riler and his nickelnecks went into a dive and came in fast and hard. Eam picked up the pace and led his squadron in an ascending turn.

Riler and his drakes hit the middle of the malwrack squadron hard with fireballs, noxious fumes, and flailing claws. Four or five malwracks lost a wing and spiraled toward the rocks below. A few more lost both wings and dropped like rocks – their heads, legs, and tails flailing as they fell.

Eam's squadron finished the turn and launched a second wave. Malwracks bobbed their heads – too disoriented to shoot back. The fumes seemed to affect their vision or their ability to focus. In any case they were easy targets and five more met their demise. "For Brangboor!" shouted Eam as he banked to his right and prepared to make another pass.

But as he did, a young malwrack screeched and began shooting back. One firebolt took out a drake he knew well – second cousin to Alfedora on her father's side. Another fatally wounded a drake from the foothills northwest of Luellian.

"Attack, you idiots!" shouted another young malwrack.

The young malwrack took out a third member of the squadron using his claws and let out another screech as he did. The sound of the screech seemed to energize the others. Eam and his squadron came in hard and fast as the melee grew fiercer and more chaotic.

Claws and fireballs and firebolts flew in every direction as a more disorganized flurry of fighting broke out. Eam was helping two brothers he'd known since they were hatchlings finish off a malwrack when a chorus of screeches from the north pierced the air. Gailryder and his five gaggles had caught up to the fight.

"Light 'em up!" shouted the malwrack commander.

A firebolt severed the right wing of one of the brothers as he spewed noxious fumes. The second brother dodged one firebolt only to have his neck severed by another. Eam and Riler and their squadrons fought furiously, but nickelnecks began falling – like the water over Smurgum Falls.

36. Greased Firebolts

I hadn't realized how parched I was until Cangoar and I drank from the bottom of the waterfall just outside Riler's lair. It felt as if I could sense the cool water seep into every crevice of my body. I thrashed my tail back and forth – even that felt rejuvenated. I glanced at Cangoar's stub. Too bad – but he'd have a new one in a couple years. "You'll get your tail back soon, right?" I muttered – I wasn't going to mention my burgeoning fear.

There was no answer as we took to the air and headed north and a little east, toward flashes of orange and yellow light which appeared and disappeared against increasingly dark clouds in the distance. A distant malwrack screech sent shivers up and down my spine. The plates along my back stood up and fought the wind – as if protesting where we were headed.

Everything went silent as we drew closer and the malwrack screeches engaged the flaps in my inner ears. The screeches must either be from habit, or reactions to being hit by fireballs. "They know screeches don't affect us, right?" I grimaced as a nickelneck tumbled toward the ground in a spiral – one of its wings tore off. "How wrong is that?" I muttered.

A malwrack spiraled as his wing burned and flailed. I glanced at my right wing and wondered what that must feel like, then watched as the malwrack managed to splash down in Luellian. The nickelneck hadn't been so lucky.

The stink of noxious fumes grew stronger as we drew closer to the melee. Cangoar banked right and headed toward a malwrack who was circling back for a run. "Alfedora! Let's get that one!" he shouted.

It was time to mix it up, but this was way more chaotic than our previous dogfight. I tried not to think about what it might feel like to have a wing shot off – by a firebolt. But the thought was already in my head. I accelerated and drew up next to Cangoar as gases and a small mass of fat coalesced inside my chest. My senses were lit. I became aware of every sight, smell, sound – even the feeling of the wind on my face and paws. This was primal. This was kill-or-be-killed.

Cangoar and I let go of fireballs almost in unison. Mine tore through the malwrack's left wing but didn't hit anything structural, while his severed its tail.

"This isn't the B.E.G.!" I yelled, then scrunched my nose. It was a weak attempt at humor, and all it did was accentuate the fears in my heart and mind.

"Very funny!" shouted Cangoar. "Stay focused. It's on us now!"

The malwrack screeched, banked left, glanced back at the stump where its tail had been, and headed straight at us. My eyes grew wide as a firebolt headed straight for my head. I thrust my head down. The firebolt took off the tip of my tail after barely missing my head.

It felt like a scorpion sting – but it would hurt a lot more if it had been more than just the tip. I glanced up – the malwrack was still coming at us. Cangoar launched a fireball. I fired and banked left as a firebolt buzzed under my right wing.

That was close, and this malwrack's good. It got off two shots almost as quickly as we did together. I was ready to launch another when the malwrack lost a wing from one of Cangoar's shots. I watched it tumble for a second, then banked back toward the melee.

"Nice shot!" I yelled.

"Look out!" he shouted.

I ducked as a firebolt lit up the plates along my spine.

That nearly took my head off.

"Thanks!" I yelled.

Cangoar bobbed his head. "You bet! You okay?"

"Yeah, just a little hot."

"Yes, you are!" he shouted.

I grinned slightly, but before I knew it, another malwrack was after us.

"Malwrack coming at ya!" I yelled as I thrust my head down, folded my wings, and went into a dive. I veered left to dodge a firebolt, and the malwrack followed – but Cangoar didn't. Now it was just me and the malwrack. Tree-covered hills south and west of the lake came up to meet me.

The ground approached quickly. I twisted right to avoid a firebolt, as the malwrack spread its wings and pulled out of its dive. I waited a moment, then flared my wings. My chest muscles strained against the momentum and the turbulence from the malwrack. It was all I could do to avoid a few trees at the top of a hill. My eyes narrowed as I pulled up right behind my target. Two quick shots and its right wing was busted up. I glanced back and saw a trail of smoke spiraling into a stand of trees.

I had beaten a malwrack. Rotbald, and maybe even Urraca, would be proud. "Urraca? Yeah, right," I muttered. I went into an ascending turn and headed back to the fray. A firebolt buzzed my left wing. It would've hit me had I not banked right. Another firebolt smashed into the ground, at an angle – like rain in a windstorm. I looked up and saw a nickelneck being chased by another malwrack.

"Alfedora, heads up!" shouted Cangoar.

"Oh sure," I muttered to myself. "Like you couldn't have yelled a little sooner?!" I craned my neck. The malwrack pulled out of its dive, but Cangoar didn't.

"Alfedora!" yelled Cangoar.

"Pull up!" I yelled.

His wings were extended, but without his tail the maneuver wasn't as precise or quick as it needed to be. I twisted right and barely avoided a collision with Cangoar, but as I did a firebolt tore a hole in my left wing. It was a clean cut that didn't hit any bones – about the size of a dragon egg. The wing was functional, but it burned as air pressed through. It was painful – *really* painful. I eased into a glide.

"Sorry!" yelled Cangoar. "How's your wing?"

"It hurts like hell!" I said as I glanced at Cangoar then looked ahead. The malwrack had pulled out of its dive and was in front of us.

"After him!" yelled Cangoar.

"Really? What about my wing?" But there had been no structural damage and it went numb before he had time to answer. I winged up and yelled, "Yeah! Let's get him!" I flew furiously to catch up. Cangoar might have a stub for a tail, but that nickelneck could fly – and fast.

The malwrack twisted right to avoid a fireball from Cangoar.

"Do that again!" I shouted.

"Do what?"

"Launch a fireball – same spot."

Cangoar did, and I launched another fireball just to the right of his. The malwrack veered to avoid Cangoar's, then was lit up by mine.

"Great shot, Alfedora!" exclaimed Cangoar.

"Thanks! You set it up!" I shouted. The malwrack's right wing was busted up, and I was still admiring our work when a firebolt buzzed my right wing. I glanced back. There was no letting up – another malwrack was in a dive and headed right for us.

"Malwrack on our six!" I shouted. The other malwrack was in a dive and pushing hard.

"Cangoar!" I shouted. "Firebolt!"

He glanced at me as a firebolt ripped through his right wing. I nearly screeched, but when he didn't go into a spiral and banked left I saw that the wound was like mine – a hole but no structural damage.

I dodged another firebolt with a twist to my right as the malwrack came out of its dive just above me. It was moving faster than I, and the pressure from its wings forced me lower – not a good feeling. I had to move up to avoid a few trees when it ripped a few scales off my back with one of its claws.

I missed the trees, but that *really* hurt. My wings froze in a glide. I glanced back – maybe two or three scales had been ripped off. I shook my head, winged up, and took off after the beast. I pulled hard and barely missed the treetops at the crest of the next hill.

I shot a fireball which hit the malwrack's right, rear foot. I gained altitude, took aim, and just as it veered left to avoid a shot from Cangoar, I fired another shot that hit the base of its right wing. We watched it spiral and crash into the side of a hill.

"Nice shot!" shouted Cangoar.

"Thanks."

"How's your back?"

"It hurts!"

The dogfight had taken us a few furlongs west of the main battle.

"You're bleeding. You should head back to Riler's lair!" he shouted.

With each flap of my wings there was a prickly feeling up and down my spine. I looked back. The wound was about halfway to my tail and two scales were missing. It was oozing, but from what I could tell it wasn't bleeding so bad that I couldn't continue.

"No way!" I shouted. "As long as there's a fight, I'll be in it." I banked right and headed toward the battle.

"You sure?"

"Yeah. I'm sure."

We gained altitude and headed toward the melee and were still a furlong or two out when it happened. I recognized Eam as he twisted in mid-air, dodged a firebolt, then looped back around in the tightest turn I'd ever seen by a drake his size. "Holy fart smellers, that old drake can fly!" I said. Eam closed on a malwrack while another came at him from the side. "Eam look out!" I yelled, but it was too late. The firebolt tore through his neck – his body went limp and fell from the sky. I screeched.

Fripel was behind Eam when it happened. He bobbed his head and screeched three times in quick succession. A few other nickelnecks yelled, "Scatter!" and "Retreat!" Eam was gone and apparently Fripel had seen enough – better to live and fight another day.

The malwracks had won the battle, but I wasn't ready to go into hiding – I felt cheated. I screeched as long as my lungs had breath.

"This way, Alfedora!" shouted Cangoar as he motioned west and a little north. "Alfedora!" he shouted.

I stayed my course, pretending I hadn't heard and wanting to pick off one or two more malwracks.

"Alfedora!" he screeched.

I continued ignoring him until he flew up next to me and nearly caused a mid-air collision. "Go with the others and save yourself," I shouted. "I'm going to avenge my Uncle Eam!"

"Alfedora, look at me!" he exclaimed. "Now is not the time. I'm sorry about your uncle! But getting yourself killed won't do anyone any good."

"He was the last family I had left."

"What about your mum?"

"Yeah, right. Do you see her anywhere?"

"Okay, but what about us – Bannabard, Jendal, and… me? We're your family now."

"Jendal's not real. And she certainly isn't my family."

"She may not be a real blue ape, but she's real all right. I'd still be rotting in that cell if it weren't for her. And she really cares."

I scrunched my nose. "She did nothing to help that hatchling before Ill-greega-butt threw it in the lava pit. And where was she when Kardrool invaded your mind? Or Gailryder's for that matter?"

"I don't have an answer for that, Alfedora. Maybe you're right, maybe Jendal's right – maybe you're both right. But getting yourself killed isn't going to help us expose Ill-greega-butt and Kardrool. We need you – now more than ever. This time we fly away. Fly away and live to fight another day."

I glared at Cangoar. "Maybe you're right. Eam's dead because of some lie going on in Gailryder's head. Will the truth ever be known?"

"I don't know," said Cangoar. "But I'm willing to fight for it. And I know you are too."

Silently, Cangoar and I banked left. A firebolt singed my tail. I looked back as the malwrack headed back toward its gaggle. A dull ache replaced the adrenaline that had lit my senses.

Fripel flew up alongside us. "Head for Gellion or Farshen. We'll find refuge there and re-group later. Sorry about your uncle, Alfedora," he said before veering back toward his squadron.

I had heard about Gellion – that it was the land of snartches and arsnatchers. I'd never been there, but it had to be better than Farshen. I glanced back and saw we were clear of malwracks. A few gave chase to some of the other nickelnecks, but most were rallying around their leader in what appeared to be some kind of victory formation.

Victory. Yeah, right. They may have won the battle, but were Gailryder and his gaggles anything more than tools? They would do Kardool's bidding, unaware that Gailryder's mind had been corrupted – and by a spewler no less! How many hatchlings would Ilgregious sacrifice? How many minds would Kardool corrupt? Maybe Urraca had been wrong – maybe might does make right.

Jendal headed east and a little south, where she found an ape climbing a vine on the eastern edge of Beetdred Mesa. "Hey Bannabard, what's up?"

He flinched and nearly lost his grip on the vine, then replied in an annoyed tone, "Not me! Not yet anyway! You seem to get some sort of sick satisfaction out of sneaking up on me, don't you?"

"Of course not. Okay. Maybe. Maybe just a little. Can I help you?" It was always a kick watching him react to unexpected voices from unseen sources.

"Uh, no thanks. I'm doing just fine, thank you very much."

"There's something you need to know – something important."

Bannabard shook his head and looked around. "Where *are* you?"

"I'm right here, but I don't want to transform right now."

"Why not?"

"Because there isn't much time. Ilgregious is launching an attack as we speak. Ape Town needs your help."

Bannabard stared at the mostly transparent black orb as it floated to his right. His eyes grew wide. "He's attacking Ape Town?"

"Yes."

"Lais! Hotch! Reebus!" he exclaimed. He slipped down the vine a foot or two, then caught himself. "We need to organize our fighters!"

He reached up for the next part of the vine, but by the time he did, it wasn't there. Instead of dangling off a cliff, he found himself on the ground in a forest and nearly fell over. His weight was on the outside of his right foot – in an awkward position as if he were still climbing the vine. His arms flailed overhead, his left foot in the air, yet somehow managed to avoid turning his right ankle.

"Keep going, you're almost there," said Jendal with a bit of a grin as she appeared in front of him.

"Very funny," he answered. "Where am I?"

"You're in Seedred Forest. Ilgregious, Kardool, and their minions are on their way as we speak. They'll be here in a few hours. You and your friends need to prepare for battle if you hope to save Ape Town. Ilgregious intends to wipe your species off the map."

Bannabard stared at the ground and thought of his friends and neighbors. More than a few, himself included, would be pumped to take

297

a few shots at some drambats. But what about the Elderarn? His gaze hardened. They would want to discuss how to respond in a committee – hesitant to do anything that might lead to a war with the Drakebureau. Would there be time for that? The apes had a right, no, a duty, to defend themselves against an invasion. And he would make that happen with or without the Elderarn. "Ilgregious and Kardool – an invasion? Really? They would be in violation of the treaty of Flargenmoore!" he exclaimed. "But if they do, we'll have to fight. It'll be on like slugs on snartches!"

"They'll be coming from the southwest."

"Yeah, from Trool. Is there anything you can do for us?"

"I'll be here to help, but I can't fight a war for you."

"I understand." She disappeared before he could thank her. "Dad-gummit! She shows up when you don't expect her and takes off when you want her to stick around."

"Hey, Bannabard!" exclaimed Otger. "How's it going?"

It was good to see a familiar face. "How did you get here?"

"I... can't really say," replied Otger with a puzzled look. "Just a second ago I was crossing the Salmonella River, and now I'm *here*."

"Hey guys," said Haldor. "Where did you come from?"

"We were going to ask you the same thing," said Otger. "Bannabard, do you know how this is happening?"

"Never mind," said Bannabard. "I'll explain later." Jendal was clearly up to her tricks. "Haldor! Otger! It's great to see you guys!"

"Hey, Bannabard! Hey Otger!" said Yellpeeler from behind Haldor.

"Hey, guys, what's up?" said Wingalorn.

More familiar faces. "This is getting good," said Bannabard. "Hey Yellpeeler and Wingalorn! It's great to see you! We don't have much time – I need you all to listen up. The drambats are planning an attack on Ape Town – as we speak."

"The drambats? They wouldn't dare!" exclaimed Vineriler, who appeared alongside Wingalorn seemingly out of nowhere. "That would be a violation of the treaty. The Drakebureau wouldn't allow that, would they?"

"Vineriler! It's great to see you!" exclaimed Bannabard. He looked up, thankful he and Wingalorn had survived. "Yeah, it's a violation, but there's been changes at the Drakebureau – it seems those in charge no longer care about treaties. We're on our own now – we can no longer depend on the Drakebureau. I'm afraid we have no choice but to fight for our loved ones, for Ape Town, and for the survival of our species."

"Are you sure about that?" asked Vineriler.

"Yeah, I'm sure. Ilgregious killed Pinhammer – he and Kardool are taking over."

"What about the Elderarn?" asked Otger. "We don't dare launch an attack without their approval."

It was no surprise he'd bring that up. "There's no time for that. I have word the drambat gaggles will be here in a few hours. We either round up the apes and fight or sit by and watch the drambats wipe out our friends and families. They're on their way now – to wipe Ape Town off the map."

Otger thumped his chest. "Bannabard, you better be right about this."

"Ilgregious and his gaggles are on their way as we speak, sir."

"It won't hurt to organize our forces," said Vineriler. "It's not like we're going to Smilf and attacking them."

"We have a right to defend ourselves," said Haldor.

Yellpeeler pounded his chest. "Boo-ya, baby! It's time for pay-backs! Who's looking forward to downing a few overgrown turkeys!?"

Haldor and the others hooted, threw leaves and branches in the air, and beat their chests. Bannabard howled, beat his chest, ran sideways back and forth, then spun around and smashed a hollow log with his fists.

"Yeah!" shouted Yellpeeler as he spun on his heel with a wide grin.

Bannabard pounded his chest once more. "We need to get the females and little ones to safety. Two of you need to go and get word to take cover and find safety – away from Ape Town."

"We'll go," said Wingalorn and Haldor in unison.

"Great!" exclaimed Bannabard. "Meet us at the western edge of Seedred where the Galtan River enters the forest when you get back. I need two more to round up as many fighters as you can, and whoever's left can help me scope out ambush sites along the river."

"I'll go," said Otger.

Yellpeeler nodded. "I'm in!"

"Great. You know where to meet us." Bannabard followed as the others scaled trees and grabbed vines. They swung off toward Ape Town, while Bannabard and Vineriler headed upriver. He followed

Vineriler and it wasn't long before they reached the western edge of Seedred and landed on a large hickory tree on top of a cliff overlooking the river. "Whoa, check out the view!"

To the west were miles of grass-covered rolling hills dissected by an occasional river or stream. Big old elm, oak, and hickory trees were scattered in meadows and along the banks of rivers. Lake Boughregard was about six furlongs to the northwest – an oxbow which had once been part of the Galtan, and like the river, its shore was mostly lined with trees.

The drambats would come in low to avoid being seen and were likely to follow the Galtan – the most direct route to Ape Town which provided cover. They would pass over the southern edge of Boughregard and pick up the river where it enters the forest. Bannabard was visualizing ambush sites when Wingalorn and Haldor swung up beside him.

"The females and young ones are moving to safe locations in the woods, your Apeness," said Wingalorn.

"Good to hear," replied Bannabard. "But don't call me 'your Apeness'. That sounds too much like anus."

"Yes, your Apeness," said Wingalorn and Haldor in unison.

He looked away with a slight smile. He knew that was coming. It had been a long time since he had overseen anything and would have considered that a weak request himself. Never let them see you sweat. "Thank you, your Smart-Apenesses," he answered.

Before they could respond, Otger and Yellpeeler returned with fighters swinging behind them as far as he could see. "Well done, boys!" he exclaimed.

"Yeah, well done!" exclaimed Wingalorn and Haldor. "His Apeness is quite pleased!"

Bannabard turned to Wingalorn and Haldor with a stern look. "Say it again and I'll tie you both to a tree and let the drambats have you."

"Yes, your Apeness," answered Wingalorn and Haldor.

Bannabard shook his head and looked away. "Don't just hang there, go report to Otger. Maybe he'll know what to do with you."

"Yes, your Apeness."

"Slingers and jumpers reporting for duty, sir," said Yellpeeler.

"Great job!" answered Bannabard. "How many?"

"Nearly three hundred."

Bannabard thumped his chest. "Booyah! I'd like twenty slingers and fifteen jumpers in the trees along the southern shore of Boughregard. That'll be the first wave. We'll station the rest on either side in the trees overlooking the river from here to Lunkswiller's."

"Will do, sir," said Yellpeeler.

Otger pounded his chest. "We stationed about fifty apes between Lunkswiller's Crossing and Ape Town – as a last line of defense."

"Great!" exclaimed Bannabard. "Let's hope they won't be needed."

"Indeed," said Otger.

"Yellpeeler!" shouted Bannabard. "Set the rest of your lines from here downriver to Lunkswiller's!" The river flowed through a canyon with cliffs on either side. Treetops were a good two hundred feet above the water in some areas and Bannabard figured the drambats would be flying low to avoid being seen.

"Roger that!" answered Yellpeeler.

Jumpers took positions in the trees while slingers found cover behind bushes, rocks, and tree-trunks along the edge of the canyon. Each slinger carried a dozen or so rounded stones – heavy enough to break the hollow bones in a drambat's wing.

In the other direction, the last of the apes made it to Boughregard and scampered up trees along its southern shore. Bannabard felt their excitement as they made preparations at the lake and along the river. He thumped his chest as a salute to their courage. He wondered what might happen after the battle. Would Flargellion retaliate? Ape Town would be hard-pressed to survive an attack by one of the larger species. He thumped his chest and shoved those thoughts aside.

The goal – their *only* goal – was for Ape Town and his species to survive the day. He looked up, grateful for help from Jendal. A few days ago he wasn't sure the Numinous was real. But now there was no denying it. He looked to the western horizon – where he expected to get his first glimpse of the invaders and thumped his chest once more. They would take a stand for their families, for one another, and for their species.

37. Duck Down Drambats

I looked up and screeched as Cangoar and I headed west in the night sky – just above the treetops. Eam. Was. Gone. All because Gailryder believed Kardool's lies. How stupid is that? And how many others will die – because a drambat and a spewler have turned to power-mongering with the help of lies from some stupid arsnarm, or dosara, or whatever the Dark Queen called herself.

"How are you guys?" asked a familiar voice.

"Jendal!" I exclaimed. "Thank goodness you're here. The battle's over, the malwracks won."

"Yeah, I know. Sorry about your uncle," said Jendal as she transformed into a blue ape – but with wings.

"Thanks. He was the only real family I had left." I tried not to stare at Jendal's wings as she flew alongside us. "Get a grip on yourself," I muttered to myself as I glanced at Jendal for just a moment. "When did you grow wings?" I asked. Could anything be weirder than a flying ape?

"Bannabard's in trouble," said Jendal, ignoring my question.

This was beyond weird. "Don't you *know* that a blue ape should *not* have wings!?" I exclaimed.

"Yeah, when did you grow wings?" asked Cangoar.

"Oh, sorry," said Jendal. "Trying to fit in is all."

"What do you mean, Bannabard's in trouble?" I asked. "Nickelnecks are the ones in trouble."

"Drambats and spewlers are on their way to Ape Town. Ilgregious intends to wipe blue apes off the map."

"Ilgregious!" exclaimed Cangoar. "He hates the apes."

"Yes, he does," said Jendal. "And Kardool is with him."

302

"That spewler gives me the willies," said Cangoar. "You sure he's with them?"

"Yeah, I'm sure."

Cangoar's eyes narrowed. "The blue apes can defend themselves – they're just drambats and spewlers. We're headed to Gellion. We need to organize the resistance – with the other nickelnecks."

I glared at him. "Cangoar!" I exclaimed. "I can't believe you don't want to help Bannabard! Ill-greega-butt and Kardrool will wipe them out if we don't do something!"

"It's Kardool, not Kardrool," said Cangoar. "I'm sure Bannabard and the blue apes will be fine. We have to go help Fripel and Riler organize the resistance."

"Suit yourself – I'll meet you in Gellion," I said. "I'm going to go help Bannabard. And I promise I won't tell anyone you're afraid – of drambats or spewlers."

"I'm not afraid."

"What then?"

"That spewler – he's worse than Ill-greega-butt. Gives me the willies!"

"Sometimes it's best to face your fears," said Jendal.

Cangoar bobbed his head. "Who said I had fears to face?"

"I did," answered Jendal. "I've seen what you've been through the last few weeks. You're right to fear the Dark Queen and her servants. And you were right when you asked Melohim for protection from Ilgregious."

"You've been watching me?" asked Cangoar sternly. "What gives you the right?"

"I was sent here to help. But I can't help unless I know what's going on."

"I thought that thing with Ilgregious was just a coincidence. You think Melohim actually heard me?"

Jendal nodded. "Ilgregious took down two malwracks at the Viper Vault. You didn't think you were stronger than them, did you?"

"I guess not," said Cangoar, a bit sheepishly.

"No, he didn't!" I exclaimed with maybe a little more excitement than intended.

"Gee thanks, Alfedora!"

I ignored the look he gave me, smirked, and said, "I was just agreeing with you. Don't get your tail all tied in a knot. Oh wait – you don't have a tail."

"Very funny," he muttered. "You don't know what it's like when your mind gets messed with and everything turned upside down…"

"What do you think?" interrupted Jendal. "Do you want to help Bannabard, or not?"

I gave Cangoar a hard look.

He looked away. "I guess…"

"Oh good! Let's go!" I exclaimed before he finished his thought.

Cangoar glared at me. "As I was about to say – it wouldn't be right to leave Bannabard hanging."

"Great. Do you know where Ape Town is?" asked Jendal.

"Yeah," said Cangoar.

"Good. I'll meet you there."

Cangoar and I banked right and headed northwest. I looked right, then left, but Jendal was gone. "She doesn't waste any time, does she?"

"I guess not," said Cangoar.

Slingcrank peered through oak leaves and branches at the first drambats as they crossed the western shore of Lake Boughregard. The invaders were here – just like Bannabard said. He was the leader of blue apes stationed along the southern shore and had instructions to wait until most of the line had passed. Timing was critical – if he gave the attack order too soon, the drakes who followed would engage and make a quick end of them all, not to mention ruining the element of surprise for Bannabard and the others downriver. The goal was a modest one – attack the end of the line and take out five or ten drambats.

The trees along the southern shore of the oxbow lake were on a hill overlooking the outer edge of what used to be a bend in the river. It gave jumpers and slingers enough elevation to reach any drakes which ventured in close. He waited silently as drambat after drambat flew by.

"Shhh!" whispered Slingcrank to the young ape next to him. "I know those are spewlers, but if we keep our heads on straight, they'll go down just like a drambat. And remember, we're to engage no more than a dozen."

They hadn't expected spewlers, but a whole line of them followed the drambats. In any case, the line of drakes was within a stone's throw and were flying conveniently low, just like they hoped. The sun was nearly up and there was enough light that he thought he saw the end of the formation. "Once we see the last of the drakes start to cross, I'll give the order," he whispered.

The lead spewler veered away from the trees and banked left. Coincidence, or did it hear him whispering? "Did you see that?" whispered his young friend.

"Yeah," said Slingcrank as the spewler circled back. "I'm afraid I have no choice," he whispered. "If that spewler warns the others before we launch, we will have failed our mission. Drambats down!" he yelled.

Jumpers jumped, slingers slang, stones flew, and drakes screeched. Soon there were three spewlers in the water while four others had apes on their backs.

"The trees, there are apes in the trees!" shouted the lead spewler. "Burn them! Burn them all!"

The slingers and remaining jumpers fled as fireballs lit up the trees. Slingcrank's young friend let a stone fly before scampering down. More than a few were caught on the ground. He watched as they leapt into the lake like animated blue torches.

Fireballs lit up the sky — nearly as bright as the burning branches below. Slingcrank leapt at the lake. A spewler appeared out of the dark sky, instantly bright — its brown and blue head illuminated by burning branches. He crashed into its left wing and grabbed its left rear leg.

The spewler veered left, righted itself, and then veered sharply right — narrowly missing a large tree. Claws tore at his right leg as he struggled to climb onto the spewler's back. With a lunge he reached the base of the spewler's left wing with his right hand. The spewler tried to shake him loose but he pulled himself onto its back. His other hand found the slender base of the wing. There was a crack and a screech as the drake and blue ape tumbled through the air. They crashed into the water and thrashed about as Slingcrank grabbed the spewler's neck. Three other apes piled on. The struggle didn't last long before the spewler's body went limp. He gave it a shove and watched as it floated away face down in the water.

Kardool had promised the spewlers would fight alongside drambats – but this changes everything. The apes had obviously known they were coming – no doubt there would be more ambushes ahead. How had they known – and would he warn Ilgregious? "I think not," he muttered to himself. If Ilgregious wants to lead this little incursion, he certainly wasn't going to spoil his fun.

"Your Drakeness, sir," said one of his gaggle leaders.

"Yes," replied Kardool in a somewhat annoyed tone.

"Would you like me to warn the drambats?"

"Oh, I think they already know!" exclaimed Kardool.

"How would they know if we didn't?"

"Apparently the great Ilgregious hasn't told us everything…"

"Do we know that, your Drakeness?" she asked.

"Well aren't you the brave one!" exclaimed Kardool in a derisive tone. "You might be a gaggle leader, but have you forgotten your place? Sticking your nose into matters which don't concern you? Any half-wit would understand that perhaps Ilgregious doesn't want spewlers interfering with his little raid on the blue apes."

"Yes, your Drakeness."

"You didn't think a member of the Drakebureau could be out-maneuvered by a bunch of blue baboons, did you?"

"No, your Drakeness."

"Very well then," said Kardool with a sneer. "Ilgregious shall have what he wants. And clearly what he wants is an opportunity for his band of drambats to prove themselves by executing this cleanup exercise by themselves. We would surely steal the limelight if we participated."

"Yes, your Drakeness," muttered the gaggle leader.

Kardool flicked his tongue. "It won't do to send my gaggles home without some sense of accomplishment," he muttered. Perhaps they would head to Nuellian, maybe check on Gailryder. But if the nickelnecks refused to join forces with Gailryder, there would be a fight. No, it would be best if they avoided any entanglements with nickelnecks – he would simply wait for Gailryder's report. "Send word to the other leaders – there's been a change of plans. I'm afraid a fight has broken out in Smilf, and we've been asked to help defuse the situation."

He scrunched his nose. Better for his gaggles to see two dead malwracks and a dead nickelneck in Smilf than to be caught in a firestorm in Nuellian. Really – it's the *narrative* that's important. How nickelnecks attacked malwracks. Actual carcasses would go a long way in convincing any skeptics just how dangerous the nickelneck rebellion really is. Kardool smirked, bobbed his head, and banked right.

A line of drambats approached from the east – as Jendal predicted. Bannabard studied the lead drambat – it was skinny and a bit longer than most. Hard to say, but it looked like one he remembered from the Stone Ingot. He watched the line, wrapping his knuckles on the tree as the drambats drew closer.

Blue apes had taken positions on both sides of the river from the western edge of Seedred down to Ape Town. He would give the order to attack once the last of the drambats reached his position. The plan was for apes to stay hidden and attack the line of drambats from behind – starting at the western edge of the forest and progressing toward the head of the line. The wave would move faster than the drambats could fly and catch the lead drambat – hopefully before it arrived at Lunkswiller's Crossing. If they maintained an element of surprise while attacking the line of drambats from behind, they might have a chance.

Apes downriver of Lunkswiller's would be the last line of defense and would attack on sight. The Crossing was about fifteen furlongs upriver from Ape Town and about thirty-two furlongs downriver from his position. Eventually their cover would be blown, and drambats would break ranks and light up apes and trees and anything else in their way.

"Well hang me upside down if that crooked snout and broken fang didn't belong to Ilgregious!" he muttered. "They must not be expecting any resistance." He looked away and closed his eyes. If he gave the order now they might be able to get Ilgregious – but he'd be giving up the element of surprise for the apes downriver. Thoughts of Gorby and the role Ilgregious might have played in his death crept into his head. This decision must be based on cold, hard logic – it can't be about *that*.

He slammed the heel of his fist on the tree trunk and opened his eyes as he considered his options. To hell with the plan – this wasn't about Gorby. He wouldn't let an opportunity to take out the lead drambat pass by.

"Drambats down!" he shouted.

Wingalorn and Haldor were studying the line of drambats from a tree just a few feet above Bannabard as the lead drambat approached. They were surprised to hear the attack order given so soon.

"Drambats down? Already?" muttered Wingalorn as he launched himself at the leader. "I've got the leader!" he exclaimed.

"I'm on the second one!" exclaimed Haldor. But the drambat saw him coming and twisted in the air. Haldor sailed by. He flattened his body as best he could – using his arms and legs to veer left. He narrowly avoided a large rock near the riverbank before splashing into the Galtan.

"Apes!" yelled the lead drambat an instant before Wingalorn crashed onto the base of its left wing and latched onto it.

The drambat twisted left in an attempt to throw Wingalorn off just as a stone from a slinger tore through the bones halfway up his right wing. The drambat shrieked as they went into a spiral but had the tenacity to reach back and snap his jaws, narrowly missing Wingalorn's right arm.

Wingalorn took a slinger's stone to his left hind quarters. His leg went numb, but he didn't lose his grip. He wrenched his hands and arms, snapping the bone at the base of the drake's left wing. The drambat shrieked again as they tumbled through the air while Wingalorn clung to the stub of a broken wing.

He hiked his feet on the drambat's back to shove off, but as he did the drake arched his back and craned his neck. He clamped his jaws on Wingalorn's left arm. Searing pain tore through his arm and shoulder, and then the drambat tossed him.

Wingalorn managed to flip his feet under just before he crashed into the nearly vertical wall of the canyon. His legs absorbed the impact and he vaulted toward the river. Thankfully the water was deep. He pulled for the surface and glanced around. His arm was throbbing and bleeding – but he had taken down a drambat and survived.

Haldor was downstream a little and the drambat was downstream of him. The current was swift as they floated through a narrow part of the canyon with sheer walls on either side. If it had been just the one drambat they would have caught up and put an end to him, but three others surrounded the wounded one – who was about a furlong and a half downriver.

The pain in Wingalorn's arm was sharp and nearly distracted him from the roar of some big water approaching. It was a bit of a struggle to keep his head above water while minimizing the use of his wounded arm. His eyes danced from one bank to the other, scanning for a landing.

"Wingalorn, how's your bender?" whispered Haldor.

"It'll be all right. Just a gash – nothing broken." He didn't want to say it, but it felt like the gash had already begun festering from the drambat's germ-infused saliva. They rounded a bend and a landing appeared to their left just above a long chute of steep, big-water rapids.

"Can you swim?" asked Haldor.

"Yeah, I'm good," said Wingalorn.

They pushed for shore but ducked low as the wounded drambat and his friends crawled out ahead of them. Lying motionless in the water, the two apes drifted by with just their noses exposed. They were past the drambats before resuming their push for shore. It was the last landing above the rapids, but it stretched downriver about half a furlong.

"Scibbarren, I want you to make sure there are no deserters," said one drambat, its voice carrying loud and clear over the water.

"Yes, your Drakeness," muttered the other.

"Well what are you waiting for?" snarled the first drambat. "Turvey, you go with Scibbarren. Leave Flithy here with me."

Two drambats took off with a grunt as Wingalorn and Haldor found cover behind a boulder next to the riverbank. They watched the other two drambats slip behind some bushes next to the wall of the canyon.

Wingalorn was debating whether they should attack when one of the drambats said, "Steady, while I set the bone."

309

"I don't want you to set any bones!" shouted the other. "Just stop the bleeding."

"If we don't set the bone, you may never fly again."

"You might need wings to fly, but I don't," sneered the other in a condescending tone.

"Yes, your Drakeness."

Wingalorn nearly jumped as a loud splash occurred just upriver from their position. It was a blue ape on the back of a drambat. The ape leapt at the drake's head just as it was about to launch a fireball and locked his arms around its snout.

A small amount of fiery goo dribbled out of the drake's mouth and onto the blue ape's arm. But the ape held on, holding its jaws shut while the drambat's eyes grew wide. Smoke and a little more flaming goo dribbled from its nose and from the gaps between its teeth.

A few seconds passed before the drambat's eyes went dark and a bit of smoke eked out of its ears. Its body went limp. The ape let go and watched as the carcass floated away and disappeared in the rapids.

"Did you see that?" whispered one drambat to another.

"Yesss," hissed the other. "Go get that monster! Burn him alive or better yet, cripple him and bring him to me!"

"Yes, your Drakeness," answered the drambat with a bit of trepidation in his voice.

Wingalorn and Haldor watched as the drambat emerged from the bushes.

"Let's jump him," whispered Haldor.

"Not yet," whispered Wingalorn.

The drambat slithered toward the river and just as he was about to slip into the water Wingalorn shouted, "Drambats down!"

He was loud about it, hoping the third ape would hear. The drambat spun to his right. Wingalorn and Haldor knuckled up and jumped him before he could get off a fireball. Wingalorn grabbed his tail while Haldor grabbed his neck.

The drambat arched left and snapped his jaws at Wingalorn, but Wingalorn grabbed his left rear leg with one arm and his left front leg with the other and pulled the legs together.

The drake fell over as the third ape splashed ashore. Haldor locked his arms around the drambat's snout and together they dragged it into the river, forced its head under water, and held it there. Eventually the drambat's body went limp. Haldor let go, and they watched it float away in the current.

$\backsim$

"Wingalorn, Haldor! It's great to see you guys," said Bannabard as he dunked his arm in the water.

"Hey, Bannabard!" exclaimed Wingalorn. "It's good to see you too. How's your arm?"

"It's fine – just a bit of singed fur."

"That was amazing!" exclaimed Haldor. "Nice job holding that drambat's jaws shut – just as he was about to…"

"Burn me alive?" interrupted Bannabard. "I'm just happy to have survived. Sorry you had to see that. You two all right?"

"Yeah, we're fine," said Wingalorn.

"Are you kidding?" asked Haldor. "Sorry we had to see that? My grandkids will hear about that one!"

"High praise indeed," said Bannabard.

Wingalorn pointed and whispered, "There's one in the bushes."

"Yeah, this one came out of the bushes too," said Haldor in a hushed tone. "It said something about setting a bone I think."

Wingalorn nodded. "The one in the bushes has two broken wings."

Bannabard circled behind the bushes to his right while Wingalorn headed straight at it from the riverbank.

"I wonder if there's a drambat in here?" asked Wingalorn loudly. "We'll get the scum-sucking toad-monger if he's in here!" He hit the ground as a fireball whistled a few inches over his head.

A pair of shadows crossed the riverbank and Bannabard looked up as two drambats glided their way. "Incoming!" he exclaimed in a voice slightly above a whisper.

Wingalorn and Haldor slid into the water and hid behind a boulder while Bannabard ducked low in the bushes.

"What will we tell him?" asked a drambat in a bit of a whiny tone as he landed on the riverbank.

"You can leave the talking to me," replied the other in a hushed voice. "But if you must know, we're going to tell him the drambats have nearly reached Ape Town, and everything is according to plan."

"How do we know that?" whined the drambat.

"We don't, you idiot!" exclaimed the other in a hushed voice. "And shhh!!! Put a damper on it before he hears us." The drambat headed into the bushes while the whiny one waited on the riverbank.

Bannabard barely heard a third drambat whisper, "Blue apes."

"Yeah, we're getting after them," answered the other drambat. "Why are you whispering and where's Flithy?"

"Shhh... you numbskull!" exclaimed the third drambat in an urgent whisper. "Flithy's dead, and there are blue apes in the river. Now go and get those apes!"

The drambat emerged from the bushes as the whiny drambat scratched the leathery skin on his belly.

"How's Ilgregious and Flithy?" asked the whiny one.

"Shhh, you lard butt. Flithy's dead and Ilgregious says there's blue a-a..."

His eyes grew wide as Bannabard leapt out of the bushes and onto the whiny drambat's back. Wingalorn and Haldor lunged at the other drambat's head from behind.

Bannabard locked his arms around the whiny drambat's snout when a voice behind him said, "Don't even think about it, ape!"

The voice was accompanied by the sound of wings beating the air. Six drambats surrounded them on the riverbank. Wingalorn let go of his quarry and Haldor went tumbling as the drambat flung him off. One locked jaws on Wingalorn's arm while another pinned Haldor to the ground.

"Let them go, or I'll break his neck," exclaimed Bannabard as the whiny drambat shut his eyes.

A tall drambat to Bannabard's right grinned and bobbed his head. "Go ahead, we don't care. He's just a whiny little slime bucket. Either way we'll roast you *and* your friends."

Another thrashed her tail. "Yeah, we'll roast you — and your friends!"

"Scibbarren, leave them to me," snarled a tall, skinny drambat as he emerged from the bushes.

"Yes, your Drakeness," she answered as they made way for their leader to join them.

Bannabard's eyes narrowed. "Ilgregious!" he exclaimed. "Looks like your wings have seen better days."

"Bannabard is it? We've been after you for quite some time – Kardool and I. How is it you've managed to elude us?"

"You killed Pinhammer, didn't you?"

Ilgregious bobbed his head and chuckled. "Why would a blue ape care about a sniveling old spewler like him, even if he was the head of the Drakebureau?" He glanced at the others and said, "Don't kill them just yet. I have something special for these three. As for Pinhammer, yeah, he met his demise in the Red Lair."

The drambats howled and shot flames in the air and bobbed their heads.

"But why would you care about Pinhammer? He threw you in the Viper Vault with a nasty stink-spewing nickelneck. But where is that traitorous, fume-infested friend of yours? Has she abandoned you? What a pity! But you were nothing more than a pet to her, were you?"

"She's a friend – more noble than you'll ever be."

"Ah yes. As if nobility were a thing. But soon it won't matter. Nothing will matter. You won't be able to care about anyone or anything."

Bannabard lunged at Ilgregious and locked his arms around the drambat's snout.

"Let my friends go, or I'll break your leader's neck!" he shouted.

"Get this ape off me!" exclaimed Ilgregious.

Bannabard wrenched Ilgregious' head around as three drambats piled on Haldor and another on Wingalorn. A sharp pain pierced his right arm as crooked, pointy teeth clamped down. His arm went numb. He let go of Ilgregious and pounded the drambat's nose with his left fist. The drambat's jaws remained locked, and he pounded it again. It was like pounding a set of knives into his own arm.

Wingalorn punched his drambat in the neck and it let go of his arm, but there were three others on him before he could make another move.

"Kill them!" muttered Ilgregious in a muffled voice.

"Wingalorn!" yelled Bannabard. He was about to deliver a blow to the drambat's neck when it tossed him at the wall of the canyon. Time slowed as he watched the granite wall approach. His left arm didn't quite make it up to protect his head before it thudded against the rock wall of the canyon. He slumped to the ground as a long shadow darted across the riverbank. It was the last thing he saw before everything went black.

I glanced down as a few drambats shot flames in the air before I recognized Bannabard, Ilgregious, and a few other drambats on the riverbank. "Down there!" I shouted.

Cangoar followed as we swooped in.

"Bannabard!" I shouted while launching a fireball which took out three drambats who were on top of what remained of one of Bannabard's friends.

"Nickelnecks!" shouted a drambat.

The others looked up and scrambled behind Ilgregious. One of them dragged Bannabard with it.

We landed on the riverbank as Ilgregious wrapped his tail around Bannabard's neck. Cangoar and I towered over the drambats and bared our teeth. I lowered my head until I was nearly nose-to-nose with the nasty little toad-fest. "Ill-greega-butt! Isn't an unprovoked attack on Ape Town beneath a leader of the Drakebureau?"

"What would a young nickelneck from Brangboor know about such things?" he snarled.

"I know more than you think, Ill-greega-butt. Let go of my friend!" I scrunched my nose exposing fangs nearly as tall as the drambat's head, but Ilgregious didn't back down.

The other drambats cowered behind him. "Back off, nickelneck, or I'll squeeze the life out of your pet!"

Cangoar took a step back as the drambat scratched his right front leg.

My eyes narrowed. "Let go of Bannabard, or it'll be the last thing you do!" I glanced at Cangoar as he eased back a bit farther.

"How dare you interfere with Drakebureau business!" exclaimed Ilgregious.

I thrashed my tail and nearly retched at the stench of his breath. "Since when is killing blue apes the business of the Drakebureau? I've seen you and your toadies. Conjuring for the Dark Queen – murdering innocent drakes and apes! Once the Drakebureau finds out what you've been up to…"

"They won't and you'll be dead!" he snarled. Ilgregious' leg was bleeding as he looked up at the sky. "Oh great and powerful Queen of all things Dark, grant thy power to thy servant. Grant me power to do thy bidding in this realm once more."

I held my ground. Cangoar took another step back as Ilgregious' eyes glowed red like no drake's I'd ever seen. Red eyes reached out like a pair of snakes – I felt them grab my left ear. A dark presence got inside my head. It felt like as if it was boring a hole in my brain. I tried to resist, but all I could see in my mind's eye was Rotbald staring up at me as the malwrack shot off his tail. Urraca tossed me out of our lair. I closed my eyes, bobbed my head, and thrashed my tail.

Holy tails of toothless toads! His eyes did that same thing at Robald's match! I forced my eyes open and peered at Ilgregious. "You! You were the one who distracted Pa! You and your glowing red eyes!" This was no longer just about us three. It was also about Rotbald and however many other hatchlings he'd sacrificed over the decades. "Jendal, we need your help," I muttered. It was a struggle to get the words out. I flicked my tongue. "Melohim, are you there?"

"Silence!" exclaimed Ilgregious. "Do not mention that name!"

"Does Melohim scare you?" I asked.

"Nonsense! He is nothing but a myth!"

I sensed the dark presence grow agitated and beat back the dark menace in my mind and shook my jowls. Now it was just my will against this skinny little drambat's. I let go a blast of noxious fumes.

"Good! Yesss," a disembodied voice hissed. "Feel my dark energy! Let hatred and anger take over and let dark energy course through your being!"

It was a higher-pitched voice than Jendal's, but it echoed up and down the canyon and caused the ground to shake – just like Jendal's back in Fripel's cave. I thrashed my tail. Ilgregious clutched his neck and coughed. His eyes went gray again.

"Yes. Give yourself to the power of my darkness, and together we will do great and mighty things!" rumbled the Voice. "Kill the drambat and take his place as a leader on the Drakebureau!"

I shook my jowls. This is what I desired – perhaps more than anything. But Jendal's words haunted me. Ilgregious and Kardool don't understand how the Dark Queen will use them up and destroy them in the end. I bobbed my head. Jendal hadn't been willing to use her power like the Dark Queen. Was she weak? Or maybe she just didn't care. Her Darkness wasn't afraid. But she was betraying Ill-greega-butt right before my eyes – just as Jendal said. And anyone could see why. This sniveling little scale-challenged toad sucker deserved to be betrayed. I was a strong young nickelneck. She wants to give me power – and I would use it to restore the Drakebureau. To set things straight. With Jendal it felt like we were fighting with our mouths tied shut.

"Yes!!" whispered the Voice. "You cannot rely on Jendal – but I will never let you down. Together we will right these wrongs and restore the Drakebureau to its former glory!"

I bobbed my head as Jendal's words about Her Darkness echoed in my head. In the end she would use us up. Mum had betrayed me – I knew what that felt like. I bowed and looked at the ground. "Melohim, if you're real, help me in my confusion. Help me do what's right."

"Stop!" screeched the Voice as it began to fade. "Stop!" it said as it faded.

"That's right!" exclaimed Jendal. "I'm with you Alfedora – you can do this!"

I'd almost bought the Dark Queen's lies. "I'll never join you!" I shouted. "And I'll never sacrifice a hatchling, not for you or anybody – your Dark Dankness!"

Ilgregious looked up at me and his eyes grew big. "Where is my Dark…"

"Queen?" I interrupted. "Look at me, you slime-sucking sleaze-a-saurus. It's just us now."

"Stay back, or your pet ape is dead!" snarled the drambat.

I flicked my tongue and hesitated. Should I care that this pathetic little toad-monger happens to be a leader of the Drakebureau?

Bannabard's mouth opened slightly as the drambat's tail tightened around his neck. His eyes began to glow red again. I felt dark energy gnawing at my brain as an image of Urraca forcing me out of our lair reappeared in my mind's eye.

I had shoved that image out of my mind before, and I could do it again. I chomped down on three quarters of the drambat's body, glowing eyes and all. The drambat writhed in my jaws as I moved my head back and forth gently while clamping down ever harder until its tail relaxed and released its grip on Bannabard.

I tossed the drambat in the air, and snap! A final shriek was cut short by the sound of crunching bones. It was nasty. Leathery skin and bones – and they taste even worse than they smell! I flipped the carcass in the air once more, snapped my jaws on it again for good measure, then turned and spit a limp, gray-and-crimson pulp out in the river.

I bobbed my head, turned to the other drambats and snarled, "Who's next?" They shrieked and scattered like flies. Cangoar took off after them, leaving me alone on the riverbank with Bannabard.

I coughed and spit until there was nothing left. I turned to my friend who was lying on the sand but wasn't moving. I nudged him gently with my snout.

"Bannabard… Are you okay?"

38.   OF DRAKES, APES, and ARSHARMS

I n the other realm Jendal gave Krimeny a puzzled look. "Are you disappointed Alfedora didn't join you?"

"No. She's nothing but a fool. She could have been powerful, and I would have given her great and mighty gifts," said Krimeny with a sneer. "Her compassion for the hatchlings will be her downfall."

"And what about Ilgregious?" asked Jendal.

"He was weak. I grow bored of drambats," replied Krimeny. "He let his emotions get the best of him and deserved what he got. Attacking the blue apes was short-sighted and foolish. There were more important things to be tending to. He should have known that. Besides, who needs a scrawny little drambat when I have Kardool, Gailryder, and the malwrack gaggles?"

Jendal looked away. "You're putting a lot of faith in Gailryder's allegiance. What if he turns?"

"That's where you're wrong, Jendal. I have no faith in his allegiance to me or Kardool or anyone else. Allegiance? Loyalty? As if!" she snarled. "He keeps his desire for power hidden, but it's there. It lurks in his soul like a malwrack hunting gold. I don't trust anything but *that*, and I will use it to control him – and many others like him. How is it you fail to see the beauty and simplicity in the singular quest – the quest for power? It has always been better to be feared than to be loved. Love is fleeting – uncertain, while fear is the one constant which overcomes all other virtues. But you are blind to that, aren't you? You have no idea how exhilarating it is to be free from the old anchors which blind us – things like loyalty, faith, and honor. Join us and get free of your fetters. Think of it, Jendal. You could be like us – free from the antiquated moral system which holds you back. Free even… from the tyranny of hope."

Jendal gave her a hard look. "I'm good, thanks. And yes, we are indeed blind. But isn't it true that Korgarag's desire for power has blinded him as well? That you and the other arsnarms *hope* you can win your rebellion against Melohim? Do not lie to yourself. You are not free from hope – the tyranny of hope – as you describe it."

"Yeah right," answered Krimeny in a condescending tone. "It has been eons since Korgarag and I entertained hope. We have no time for wasteful indulgences – we spit at hope!"

Jendal gazed at the light which overpowered the sun in the other realm. It was white with a tinge of blue and invoked a sense of reverence. Melohim had given her this mission – this one thing to do in this time and in this place. It was an odd thing to think that he trusted her with these challenges facing the realm of dragons and blue apes but was thankful for the opportunity. It made her love him even more. She turned back to Krimeny. Her gray, wrinkled skin had a tinge of red to it. "Your focus and dedication are admirable, but how do you stay motivated? What keeps you going – if not hope?"

Krimeny shook her head and glared back. "We are motivated by a will to power. There is nothing else – but I wouldn't expect you to understand *that*. Perhaps one day you will set aside your delusions and embrace extreme pragmatism, singularly focused on the struggle for power at any given moment. There is no time for idling away over distractions like hope and honor, right and wrong, or concerns for the well-being of others. Those things are for weak and delusional souls like yourself! It is why we will win in the end."

"Your words betray you," answered Jendal. "You hold onto hope – hope that you will win."

"We hold onto no such thing. There is no hope – not for Korgarag, me, nor any of the arsnarms. There is nothing but the next step, the next twist, the next manipulation, which will empower us and move our cause forward. Even you can see the progress we've made these last few days. We, the walking dead, are at war with the One who never fights fair. The One who gives those putrid little beasties something to care about – each other and some dribble about a life worth living. But our focus is singular. We will use every means possible to put an end to this charade of weak, ghastly little creatures who delude themselves with notions of family and freedom. As if! How can they be happy while they struggle to simply survive – eking out their useless existences in that loathsome little realm he has wrought?"

Jendal smiled and nodded. "You may not be willing to admit it, but your hope is for victory and the power you would wield if you won. And you trust in extreme pragmatism to get you there."

"Hope and trust indeed! Those things are for fools like you and your delusional friends," snarled Krimeny, her eyes glowing red and her head wagging, almost bobbing like a dragon in the other realm.

Jendal gave her a cold stare. "You deny faith and hope, yet they are what fuel your misguided passions. And you love no one other than the power you seek."

"You dosara are the misguided ones," scowled Krimeny. "Could you be any more narrow-minded!?"

She flitted off in the direction of Brangboor in the other realm and looked back as she drifted away. "Perhaps someday you'll let go of your delusions and acquaint yourself with reality."

Jendal watched her grow small as the distance between them increased. She smiled at the irony in Krimeny and Korgarag's mission. "Delusions? Delusions, indeed," she muttered.

"He'll be all right," said a familiar, disembodied voice.

I glanced to my left at the black orb. "Jendal! Thank goodness!" I gagged slightly, then studied the river. "Yechh. I didn't know drambats, or anything else for that matter – could taste so bad!" I spat, took a drink, and spat again.

"Good. Get it out," said the voice. "Better?"

"Yes. Better, thanks. Did you see what happened?"

Jendal transformed into her usual form – and without the wings. "Of course I did. You asked for Melohim's help – I was there and saw the whole thing."

Paul Krueger

"Was it wrong to kill Ilgregious?"

"No. You saved Bannabard's life, and likely your own – not to mention Cangoar and the remaining blue apes. Ilgregious chose a path of death and destruction and that's what he was given."

I scrunched my nose. "It felt weird, really weird – like it was too easy."

"Maybe that's because defending yourself and those you care about was the right thing to do."

"Yeah, I suppose so. But he was a member of the Drakebureau. I can't get that out of my head."

"Member of the Drakebureau or not, he was going to kill you and your friends."

"Yeah, I guess that's right." I flicked my tongue and said, "Thanks, Jendal."

"You bet. Ilgregious is in Melohim's hands now. But Ape Town is still in danger, and Cangoar could use your help. I'll stay with Bannabard if you'll lend Cangoar a wing and a fireball or two."

"I'm on it," I said.

I glanced around, arched my back, and took off. Trees burned along cliffs overhanging both sides of the river. Drambats had been burning everything in sight. I winged up, headed downriver, and spotted Cangoar on his way to Ape Town. I flew hard to catch up. We were nearly at Ape Town when we spotted a few drambats launching fireballs at huts.

"Down there!" shouted Cangoar.

I folded my wings and followed him into a dive. I took out two with one fireball and another with noxious fumes while Cangoar shot down three and knocked another out of the sky with his claws.

"Nickelnecks! Run for it!" shouted the lead drambat as we circled back for a second pass.

The drambats fled south. Weird that they didn't head toward Trool or try to warn the others.

"Ape Town's safe!" I shouted.

We headed upriver where drambats were still lighting up trees along both sides of the river.

"How's Bannabard?" Cangoar shouted.

"Jendal's with him. She says he'll be fine!"

321

"Oh good," said Cangoar. "You'd be lost without your little blue monster."

"Don't call him that," I yelled. "And yeah, I probably would. What's it to you?"

"Nothing. Sorry. I was just trying to lighten things up a little."

"Well, you failed." I was too worried to joke about him like that. Okay, maybe it was kinda funny.

"You can't blame a drake for trying," he replied as we came up on some drambats who were still shooting fireballs at apes in the trees.

"Who says I can't?" I asked as we went into a dive.

"Down there. Let's hit those guys hard!" he exclaimed.

We swept in on six drambats and lit them up, then swerved right and lit up three more. We glided side-by-side and watched as the other drambats fled like bats out of an erupting volcano.

"Great job, Alfedora!" shouted Cangoar.

"Thanks! You, too! I'm going to go see how Bannabard's doing." I banked left and headed upstream.

"I'm coming too."

"Do you miss your little blue monster?" I asked.

"Don't call him that. And what's it to you if I do?" he shouted.

Bannabard must've heard our wings. He sat up and looked around as we landed on the riverbank. "Hey Alfedora. Hey Cangoar! Where are the drambats?"

"The ones that are left are headed back to Trool," I answered. "Ape Town's safe, and it's good to see you awake."

"Thanks," said Bannabard. "Ilgregious, too?"

"He's gone," said Cangoar. "He won't be coming back – you can thank Alfedora for that."

"Wow – how did that happen?" He stared at the blood on my back. "Wait. Your back – are you all right?"

"Oh yeah, that. I ran into some malwrack claws – lost a couple scales I'm afraid. As far as Ilgregious goes, let's just say he tastes worse than he smells."

"You *ate* him?"

"No, of course not. Well, the thought did cross my mind. But no, he was going to kill you, me, and Cangoar – so I crunched him." I shook my jowls and spat in the river. Yuk. I lowered my head, rinsed my mouth, and spat again. "And then I spat his carcass in the river."

"It's good to see you awake and moving," said Cangoar. "That was a nasty rumble you got caught in."

Bannabard thumped his chest with a fist but was a little weak about it. "Yeah, I guess it was. I'm just glad Ilgregious is gone and Ape Town is safe. Thanks, guys." He stared at the bodies of his friends.

"Your friends – I'm so sorry," I said.

Bannabard looked down, closed his eyes, then looked up and howled.

I put a paw on his shoulder. "I'm sorry – if we'd have been here sooner."

"No, it's not your fault. Ilgregious and his drambats did this, not you. Wingalorn and Haldor – they were the best. I'm gonna miss those guys."

"I'll bet," I said.

Bannabard rose to his feet.

"Do you feel strong enough to fly?" I asked.

"Never was strong enough to fly. But I'm strong enough to hang on while you do. Where we going?"

"You tell us," said Cangoar.

"There's a meadow north of Ape Town where apes used to gather after a fight."

"Let's go see if anyone's there," answered Cangoar as Bannabard climbed on my back.

The sky was clear as we took off to the south, banked left, and landed in the middle of a long meadow surrounded by oak, elm, and willow trees. A stream ran along the west side and by the light of a full moon I saw a few apes gathered at the end of the meadow.

I bent my left front leg and let Bannabard down, then ducked as a stone whizzed by my head. Cangoar moved between me and the apes, his teeth bared with a menacing look.

"Don't shoot!" shouted Bannabard as he held up his hands. "They're friends."

"Bannabard!" shouted one of the apes. "Great to see you! – but what are you doing with a pair of nickelnecks!?"

"Otger! Great to see you," shouted Bannabard as he started toward them. "These nickelnecks are my friends – we've been through a lot together. Yellpeeler. Vineriler. Glad you made it!"

"Glad to see you too," shouted one of the apes.

Cangoar and I followed as Bannabard and the apes greet one another. They bumped the heel of their fists, crossed and bumped their forearms, then spun around and bumped their elbows over their heads. They finished by thumping their chests once with each fist.

"Why don't they just bonk heads?" I muttered.

"How are Haldor and the others?" asked Otger.

"Sorry, but Haldor and Wingalorn didn't make it," said Bannabard. "They died fighting Ilgregious and a few of his toadies." Bannabard thumped his chest. "The good news is Ilgregious is dead. And this is Alfedora and Cangoar. We can thank her for putting an end to Ilgregious – and we should thank them both for chasing off the last of the drambats."

"You're pulling my arm!" exclaimed Otger. "Since when do nickelnecks give a rat's butt about blue apes?"

I flicked my tongue in the blue ape's direction. "Since well, I guess since Bannabard and I got locked up in the Viper Vault together."

"Pleased to meet you," said Otger. "And thanks for your help. I never thought I'd say this to a couple of nickelnecks, but as a representative of the community of apes, you have our sincere thanks."

"Thanks, indeed," said two others with a bow.

"You're most welcome," answered Cangoar.

Otger nodded and turned to Bannabard. "Our victory today would not have happened without your efforts, Bannabard. I'm going to recommend you for a commendation."

"Thanks," said Bannabard. "High praise indeed. We should be proud of how everyone fought today. Please join me in a moment of silence for our fallen comrades who gave the ultimate sacrifice today."

The four apes closed their eyes, bowed their heads, and thumped their chests three times in unison. I bowed my head and nearly tried to thump my chest but didn't.

"Any news on your son?" asked Otger.

"I'm afraid he didn't make it," answered Bannabard.

"I'm so sorry," said Otger.

The three apes looked at Bannabard, closed their eyes, bowed their heads, and thumped their chests once more.

324

"Thanks," answered Bannabard with moist eyes. "Do we dare hope the drambat attacks will slow down now that Ilgregious is gone?"

"I certainly hope so," I said as my thoughts turned to Flargellion. "But even so, Drakedom is in trouble if we don't figure out a way to stop Kardool and the malwracks."

I glanced around at the others, then bobbed my head. "Please join me as I bob my head for my uncle Eam and the fallen nickelnecks who died fighting the malwracks."

Cangoar and I looked around at the apes, closed our eyes, screeched, and bobbed our heads four times. I opened my eyes. The blue apes stared back with blank expressions.

"You fought the malwracks – and came here to help us?" asked Otger.

"Yes," I answered. "Gailryder has sworn loyalty to Kardool. They have taken control of the Drakebureau."

"Who is Kardool?" asked one of the apes.

"Kardool is…" My voice trailed off as I looked away and noticed a band of apes dragging a drambat out of the forest – barely visible in the moonlight. "I'm afraid Kardool has replaced Pinhammer as leader of the Drakebureau."

The others turned to see what I was looking at. The prisoner's feet, snout, and wings were bound by vines. It was being drug along on its side. The lead ape's jaw dropped when he saw Cangoar and I.

"Hey guys. Drop the vine and be ready – on my signal," he said in a low but firm voice. "One, two…"

"Fergal. Great to see ya!" yelled Otger across the meadow, turning his back on me. "No need to worry about these nickelnecks! They're friends!"

The apes made their way across the meadow and approached cautiously while dragging their prisoner behind. Bannabard bounded up to greet one of the apes. "Hey, Fergal, it's great to see you. How's Lais?"

"She's recovering – doing well."

Bannabard wrapped a fist on his chest. "Thanks for stitching her up. Any infection?"

"She's doing fine. There's been no sign of infection."

"Thank goodness! And the boys?"

"They're fine. Lais and her friends have been taking good care of them."

Bannabard thumped his chest again. "I can't thank you enough."

"No worries. Glad I could help."

"Glad you guys made it – I see you've caught a live one," said Otger. "What are you planning for him?"

"We uh, we… caught this one fleeing the battle," said Fergal as his eyes danced from Cangoar and I to the apes and back again. "Nickelnecks – really?" asked Fergal with a nod toward us.

"Yeah, these are my friends," said Bannabard. "Fergal. Guys. I'd like you to meet Alfedora and Cangoar. They defeated Ilgregious and helped us fight off the drambats."

"I can't tell if you're joking or making fun of me," said Fergal. "Why would a nickelneck give a toad's tongue about a blue ape's butt?"

"These nickelnecks and I have been through a lot together," said Bannabard. "They know what the drambats have been up to, and I expect we'll need each other moving forward."

I thrashed my tail back and forth. "Bannabard, I'm really glad to hear your family's okay."

"Thanks, Alfedora."

Fergal eyed me suspiciously. "I don't get it. What do nickelnecks have to do with drambats?"

"More than you might think," I said with a hint of a snarl. "What do you plan on doing with your prisoner?"

"Let's roast him over a fire and serve him up to the troops," said one of the apes.

"You can do what you like with him once we find out what he knows," said Otger.

"He's nothing but a spineless deserter," said Fergal. "He was heading away from the battle when we shot him down. We're guessing he must know something the others don't. What's your name, drambat?"

The drambat's eyes darted between Fergal and Cangoar and I, but there was no response.

"Perhaps I could help with the interrogation," suggested Cangoar.

The drambat pointed to the vine on his snout.

"That'd be great," said Fergal. "All right boys – take the vine off his snout. Let's see what he has to say for himself."

Cangoar moved in close as they removed the vine and lowered his head until his snout was a few inches from the drambat's.

The drambat glanced at Cangoar, then at me.

"What's your name, and why were you running away from the battle?" asked Fergal.

The drambat looked at the ground and said, "My name is Odelynd. I saw you nickelnecks attack the drambats and figured the Drakebureau sent you to put an end to our little tiff."

"Tiff? You call that a tiff?" I asked. "You were trying to exterminate my friends! But it didn't take long for you to abandon your comrades, did it?"

"Yeah, well, I was never really down with this attack on Ape Town," answered the drambat. "And we weren't going to last long against nickelnecks. But there are only two of you – where are the others?"

"There are no others," I answered.

"I could have sworn there were at least half a dozen," said the drambat.

"Clearly this one has more brains than heart," said Cangoar. "Let's smoke him now and be done with it."

"Uh, before you smoke me, could I ask a question?"

"You just did," said Otger.

"Hold on a second," I said, wondering if all drambats were like Ill-greega-butt and his toady little friends. "Let's hear what he has to say."

The drambat sighed. "I'm guessing the Drakebureau didn't really send you guys since there's only two of you. Which makes me wonder why you're helping blue apes."

"He's got that right," said Cangoar with a bit of a chuckle.

I flicked my tongue. "Let's just say we're no friends of Ilgregious and are a little less than sympathetic to what he's been doing to apes over the years."

"Good. There's his question," said one of the apes. "Can we smoke him now?"

"Hold on. No need to be hasty," answered the drambat. "I'm not the only one who's less than enamored with Ilgregious. There's actually quite a few of us."

"What are you saying?" asked Bannabard.

"I'm saying there's a number of us that would be willing to expose his, uh, shall we say, darker side? Maybe get him deposed."

"Too late for that," said Bannabard. "He's dead."

"We're wasting time," interjected Cangoar. "We should smoke him now or let him go and toast him as he flees."

"Easy, big guy," said Jendal.

"Where'd *she* come from?" asked the tallest ape.

"My name is Jendal – I'm a friend of Bannabard's. I think we should listen to the drambat's story."

"Hey Jendal, great to see you!" exclaimed Bannabard. "Thanks for all you've done for us. Guys, I'd like you to meet my friend Jendal. She let us know the drambats were planning an attack and helped us organize our defenses."

"How is it that I've never seen you before?" asked Otger.

"She's from another region," said Bannabard.

"I had no idea there were apes outside of Seedred! Nevertheless, we are in your debt," said Otger. "The Elderarn shall honor you as well."

"High praise indeed," said Jendal.

Bannabard nodded. "Let us take a moment to recognize Jendal, Alfedora, Cangoar, Wingalorn, and Haldor. Thanks to them, Ilgregious will no longer be tormenting blue apes."

The apes closed their eyes, bowed their heads, and thumped their chests with clenched fists. The sound of it echoed off the hills on the east side of the meadow.

"What about this drambat?" I asked.

"Well it can't hurt to listen," said Otger. "Let's hear him out."

"I, uh… first of all, I never bought into Ilgregious' ill-natured tripe," stammered the drambat. "I quit attending his ceremonies after the first one nearly fishified my gizzard. Couldn't eat for days."

I bobbed my head and scrunched my nose. It was weird to identify with a drambat – but I knew exactly how he felt.

"And this attack on the blue apes just seemed stupid to me," he continued. "When I saw you nickelnecks, I figured you were sent by the Drakebureau to put an end to the fighting. Our unit fled south – partly because we are outcasts and because it seemed best to make ourselves scarce until this conflict with the blue apes could be sorted by Flargellion."

"Make yourselves scarce?" groused Fergal. "You deserted your fellow drambats – not to mention any family members who may have been there."

"Oh, I don't have any family," answered the drambat. "My parents didn't survive the war. I was raised by my great aunt on my father's side. She passed on a while back."

"What about friends?" asked Otger. "You must have a few of those."

"Yeah, we stuck together – at least until these guys shot me down."

"Maybe it's a good thing you didn't fit in with those swag-bellied, conniving wart-mongers," I suggested.

"Don't encourage him," interrupted Fergal. "Next thing you know he'll be telling us how he fought on the side of blue apes during the war."

"Oh, I'm afraid the war was before my time," said the drambat.

"And now that Ilgregious is gone, what are your plans?" I asked.

"I don't know. I haven't really given it much thought," he answered. "I'll probably head back to Trool, try to set the bones in my wing, and see how the others are reacting to the situation. It will take me a while on foot I'm afraid."

"My guess is you're not alone in your concerns about Ilgregious and his power-mongering," suggested Jendal.

"What power-mongering?" asked the drambat.

"It would make sense that he didn't share his plans to take over the Drakebureau with just anybody," I said.

"Really?" asked the drambat. "He was going to overthrow the bureau? I'm not surprised – now that I think about it."

"Good thing we got him, then," said Otger.

I bobbed my head. "Except we didn't get his partner. He's taken Pinhammer's place – and has recruited the malwracks."

"You can't be serious," said the drambat. "There'll be no stopping *them*."

"Maybe not," said Cangoar. "We fought them last night – the malwracks, that is."

"You're kidding – the malwracks?" asked Fergal. "How'd *that* go?"

"It was a heck of a battle," said Cangoar. "Until we lost our leader, that is."

I bobbed my head and thrashed my tail, nearly knocking over one of the apes. "We lost a lot of drakes, and the nickelnecks have gone into hiding. In fact, we should probably get out of this meadow. It's not safe for nickelnecks to be out in the open. But it isn't just nickelnecks – all of Drakedom is in trouble if we don't figure out a way to stop Kardool and his toadies."

"Kardool's in league with the Dark Queen, same as Ilgregious was," said Bannabard.

"Who's Kardool?" asked the drambat.

"He's the leader of the spewlers – serves on the Drakebureau," I said.

"Well who's the Dark Queen?" the drambat asked.

"You know," I answered. "She's the one who Ilgregious did those conjuring ceremonies for."

"Oh, yeah. That was some creepy stuff right there," said the drambat. "I'd stay as far away from that as possible."

My eyes narrowed. "Then you've been to the conjuring ceremonies?"

"Oh yeah, I've seen 'em. Up close and personal – but never again if I can help it."

Cangoar bobbed his head and his eyes narrowed. "Kardool does conjuring ceremonies too," he said. "And anyone who refuses to serve Kardool and his minions, will become fugitives like us."

"Better that than a tool from Trool," said the drambat.

"No doubts there," I said with a bob of my head. I looked at the ground. My faith in the Drakebureau was beginning to slip. I had killed one of its leaders and had no hope for reconciliation as long as Kardool was in power. Kinda like there was no hope with Urraca. Ever since I could remember I had hoped to be a good and faithful servant of Drakedom and the Drakebureau. But that dream was gone – like that toady little drambat. I spat on the ground. "And if Kardool and his malwrack toadies ever caught up with us, they would lock us up – or worse. He would want us all dead," I continued. "But there's hope – our society consists of friends, family, and neighbors. It transcends the fair few who comprise the ruling body of dragons."

"Alfedora, be careful what you say," warned Otger.

"Indeed," said Cangoar. "Those who resist will be hunted, and there's no telling what Flargellion will become under the claw of Kardool and the malwracks."

The drambat flicked his tongue. "I tend to agree with Alfedora. Imagine that! A nickelneck! But like I said, I've been an outcast my whole life."

"Good to hear you're not all like Ill-greega-butt. He's a smart little drambat," I said with a slight nod to Cangoar.

Cangoar scrunched his nose. "Yeah, right. Alfedora, we should head to Gellion before the sun rises."

Jendal turned to me. "Alfedora, can you drop Bannabard off at Ape Town?"

My eyes lit up. "You bet I can. It's time Lais and his sons found out what he's been up to."

Bannabard thumped his chest. "Well okay!" he exclaimed. "Twist my arm!"

"And maybe Cangoar can carry one or two more back to Ape Town?" asked Jendal.

"Sure thing – glad to," said Cangoar.

"We'll swing back for the others if you'd like," I said.

"That'd be great," said Fergal.

Bannabard climbed on my back while Vineriler and Otger climbed on Cangoar. I swished my tail back and forth – excited about Bannabard rejoining his family.

"Works for me," said Cangoar. "Alfedora – don't forget to fly low."

"Yeah, but I doubt the malwracks will be looking for nickelnecks in Seedred Forest."

I took off with Bannabard and landed in a meadow just east of Ape Town.

"Say hi to Lais for me," I said as I let him down on a bent knee.

"Will do," answered Bannabard. "Hey Alfedora. Thanks. Thanks for everything! You too, Cangoar!"

"You bet, Bannabard. Glad I could help."

Bannabard watched Alfedora and Cangoar take off and thought about all they'd been through and then of Lais and their boys. He turned toward Ape Town, knuckled up, and bounded up the path. A few huts had taken damage and apes were tossing dirt and water on the fires.

"Hey Bannabard!" exclaimed one, then another.

"Hey guys," he said as he bounded past. He smiled when he reached his hut. Thankfully it hadn't been hit. He went in and found Lais. The boys were asleep.

"Hey hon'," he whispered. "Thank Melohim – you're safe!"

"Bannabard!" said Lais. "Thank goodness you're back."

We landed back in the meadow where two apes were waiting. "You guys ready?" I asked.

"Yeah, I'm Yellpeeler," said the smaller one. "And this is Fergal."

"Pleased to meet you," I said.

"What was it like?" asked Fergal.

"What was what like?"

"Crunching Ilgregious."

I looked away. "It was nasty. Just. Flippin'. Nasty."

"Yeah, but did it feel good to rid the world of that monster?" he asked.

"Yeah, it felt good all right, but I'd never killed a drake with my teeth before."

"Never?" asked Fergal.

"No, and especially not a member of the Drakebureau. Cangoar and I shot down a few malwracks a while ago – after they invaded Brangboor. And we shot down a few drambats who were attacking Ape Town, but other than that, I never harmed another dragon. Except there was that time when I was just a hatchling and I screeched, and Pa lost his match and…" My voice trailed off and I gave the apes a blank stare. Mum. "Sorry, but I gotta go – Mum could be in trouble."

"But what about Gellion?" yelled Cangoar.

I flipped a wing and took off toward Brangboor. A stiff wind out of the north didn't help, and the sun was nearly up by the time I landed in the meadow next to Urraca's lair.

"Mum," I called. "Wake up! It's me, Alfedora."

No response.

"Mum!" I called again. "You in here?"

Still no response. I rolled the stone away.

"Mum!" I yelled again, but the lair was empty. If the malwracks got her, there'd be hell to pay. But there was no sign of a struggle and Urraca's gold coins were stacked neatly in the usual corner. I rolled the stone back and turned toward the meadow.

"Urraca!" I muttered to myself. "She would have told me to get lost even if she had been here." I bobbed my head and was about to take off when the sun's first light streamed into the meadow through a gap in the hills behind me. A single beam lit up a tree in the middle of the clearing. Most of the tree's blackened bark had sloughed away, exposing the light-gray wood underneath.

The weathered wood seemed to glow. It was bright against a backdrop of dark-green trees. A few slabs of exposed sandstone in front of it formed what looked like knuckles, a thumb, and a forefinger. It was like an ape's hand, except tan with a narrow, light-gray forefinger pointing at the sky. It appeared to hover in the clearing – I stood motionless and stared. It reminded me of Jendal and the Phoberon. I watched the narrow beam disappear in the diffuse light of a new morning as the sun rose higher. And as the fist and forefinger faded into the surrounding landscape, I recognized the tree that had formed the spindly finger. It was the tree I had blown up after my fight with Urraca.

It all seemed unreal – the world was a different place than it had been. My family and the Drakebureau had taken turns for the worse. Eam was gone and I had no idea where Mum was – or if she was still alive. But the demise of my family hadn't really been my fault – as I once believed. Ilgregious was the one who distracted Rotbald, not me. Urraca had been wrong to blame me for Pa's death. Perhaps someday I would tell her about it. And how I had helped the blue apes. As if she'd care about that!

I licked my chops and held my head high. I had defended my friends, myself, and even Uncle Eam while it lasted. So what if Ilgregious had been a leader of the Drakebureau? A strange thought entered my mind. I would no longer venerate members of the Drakebureau without questioning their motives. I looked up, thankful that hatchlings and blue apes had been given a reprieve from Ilgregious and his drambats, and that I had played a part in that.

Maybe Urraca and I could agree on one thing — that might doesn't always make right. Jendal made me mad at times but lived as if she truly believed that. And even though drakes like Kardool wielded power, that didn't make them intrinsically good or morally superior to 'common' drakes like me. I flicked my tongue. It seemed strange that of all the drakes in Drakedom, I had been given the size, strength, teeth, and opportunity to set things straight between Ill-greega-butt and his victims. But that was one time when might really did make right. I glanced around and spat on the ground one more time.

About the Author

Paul G. Krueger is a writer drawing on disparate fields of study – geophysics and theology. *Alfedora and the Drakebureau* is the first book in a series and an allegorical exposition of the "principalities and powers" described in Ephesians 6. It was begun as a reaction to some young friends who were not allowed to read important books such as *the Chronicles of Narnia, Harry Potter,* or *Lord of the Rings.* These absurd restrictions came from a religious leader who taught that any book or movie which portrayed magic in a positive light was evil. They were told they would literally go to hell if they so much as read one of those books or watched the movies.

These wonderful works use magic to represent the spiritual realm and illustrate struggles between good and evil – rather than attempts to glorify the dark arts. This book is my first attempt to write what I hoped would be an entertaining and constructive series which uses dark matter and dark energy to represent another realm (or parallel universe if you prefer).

I'm happy to report that narrow-minded religious leaders will not be able to find a flick, flit, flutter, or even a hint of magic in this book. From my vantage point I find it shameful that a religious leader would deny young people an opportunity to discover these great authors and others like them – under weight of eternal damnation no less. It seems to me this Orwellian-like prohibition has more to do with controlling and manipulating their parishioners than promoting a Christian message. A message which, in my opinion, places an emphasis on free-moral agency. Heaven forbid my young friends should learn to think for themselves!

Contrasting those who use fear and coercion to manipulate others with those who treat others how they would like to be treated should be an obvious theme in this book. If it's not, I have failed in that endeavor. In any case, might doesn't always make right, especially if you're a wolf in sheep's clothing. Or a snake in the grass. Or whatever metaphor you prefer for those who try to manipulate and control others through fear and coercion.